# WHERE HAVE ALL THE GO-GO'S GONE?

## Richard Baran

Where Have All The Go-Go's Gone Series Book 1

TotalRecall Publications, Inc.
1103 Middlecreek
Friendswood, Texas  77546
281-992-3131     281-482-5390 Fax
www.totalrecallpress.com





ISBN:  978-1-59095-240-5
UPC:  6-43977-42405-1
Library of Congress Control Number:  2014944451

Printed in the United States of America with simultaneous printings in Australia, Canada, and United Kingdom.

FIRST EDITION
1   2   3   4   5   6   7   8   9   10

To my parents:  Chester and Arlette Baran and their extended families, my wonderful aunts and uncles.  Each of them had their own unique way to teach respect,  family values and a belief in God. Now they are gone, but never forgotten.  The stories are too priceless for that to happen.

# Author Richard Baran

holds a doctorate and two masters' degrees besides his bachelor's in business. A Navy veteran, he taught and coached for forty years at the secondary school and collegiate levels. His first novel, *The Jacket* was published in 2013 by Total Recall Publishers. Other publishing credits include a coaching text, *Coaching Football's Polypotent Offense*, a short story, *That Ain't No Walleye* and several dozen articles in professional business, education and coaching journals. Richard and his grammar school sweetheart, Carol Ann, have twenty grandchildren and they divide their year between Franklin Park, Illinois; Phoenix, Arizona and Minocqua, Wisconsin.

Visit www.richardbaran.com for more information.

# Acknowledgments

To my agent, Jeff Lovell: His impersonation of Max Bialystock still hasn't improved. He comes in a distant second, possibly third, to Jack "Duke" Mongan and Denny Toll. However, he is an incredibly creative writer and mentor. He can also stuff down more thin crust pizza at Chuck Romano's Restaurant in Rosemont, Illinois than the other three of us combined.

To my quasi critics, proof readers and assistant editors: Carol Fredrickson, Lisa Puck and Bucky Baran: Thanks for the comments and suggestions and, lest I never forget, Carol for your ever stinging remark of, "Blah, blah, blah," when shredding my most creative pieces of prose.

To Mark Puck: He, the computer guru, continues to provide me, the technological incompetent, with computer and web support.

To my first paying customer and autograph seeker, Bill Horn and his in depth comments about my first novel, *The Jacket*. Much appreciated.

To Harry Newman: Photographer extraordinaire, critic and super human being.

I hereby acknowledge the endless line of those who asked the two dumbest questions any writer dreads hearing: (1), "Am I in it?" and (2), "Do I get a free copy?" I love saying, "No!"

# <u>List of Characters</u>

**General Glen Forest Pepperwall:** Self-proclaimed Revolutionary War hero. He is a corrupt, conniving, lecherous coward and founder of Glen Forest on the Watercourse who fled the Battle of Savannah with his pregnant, half breed girlfriend, Arvia. She later kills him while he is making love to another woman. A long line of his ancestors have kept alive the myth of his Revolutionary War heroics.

**Berthold "Bo" Pepperwall:** Dreamer and intellectual. He carries an antique Zippo cigarette lighter as a good luck charm. Bo was teased and picked on by his childhood playmates and carries the nickname, Bo the Schmoe. He is slight of build with straight, black oily hair and a pencil thin mustache that sits at a horrific angle across his lip. His appearance gives "Bag Ladies" and aging B porn stars a bad name. He is perceived by others to be a loser, misfit and social outcast enhancing his nickname. Only his older sister, Arvia Pepperwall Bell knows he is a member of Mensa and received his doctorate at sixteen.

**Arvia Pepperwall Bell:** Last female descendant of the Pepperwall name. She is a dark skinned intriguing beauty of Native American and African American blood, her black hair always worn in a single braid down her back. She abhors foul language of any kind, including slang, and has tolerated her husband's infidelities until her toleration turned to her wishing he were dead

**Benoni "Ben" Bell:** Intelligent, handsome, preppy son of Arvia Pepperwall Bell and Mayor Quintin Bell. His dream is to be bass player in a rock band. He is the boyfriend of the high school librarian's daughter, Matilda and he hates his father.

**Quintin Bell:** Another in a long line of Glen Forest on the Watercourse lecherous, conniving, corrupt mayors and the only one not of Pepperwall blood. His political fund raising parties are exhibitions of debauchery that would make Emperors Nero and Caligula salivate.

**John Brown:** Attorney, former college football star and best friend, on the outside, of Quintin Bell. Inside, he despises Bell and wants to see him dead. He lusts over Arvia Bell, Quintin's wife.

**Matilda Newton:** Seventeen year old girlfriend of Ben Bell and the daughter of Amanda Newton, the high school's librarian. Her secret dream is to be an actress. Bo Pepperwall hires her under false pretenses to her mother and father to be Tinker Bell, the star attraction in his La Tinkerbelle's a Go-Go entertainment.

**Amanda Newton:** High school's librarian who dreams of being the school's principal. She is the ex-wife of Sam Geronimo Germono who she hates more than sin. Next on her hate list are Quintin Bell and John Brown who, along with Alice Nell Puffin, the pastor's wife, tried to make her part of their debauchery. She mistrusts almost all males except Benoni Bell, and she is overly protective of her daughter.

**Sam Geronimo Germono:** Ex-husband of the high school's librarian, Amanda Newton and father of Matilda. He left his wife for a man, a mistake that ended in tragedy. Down on his luck and a street person, he is a former saloon owner hired by Bo Pepperwall to run the beverage service at La Tinkerbelle's.

## Supporting Cast

## (Qirky Characters Who Put Fun in Dysfunctional)

There's a brainy spinster secretary who constantly entertains sexual fantasies about her boss; a morally loose blond bombshell and kinky wife of the local pastor.  The pastor loves gin'n tonics, saving souls and his wife—in that order.  They are joined by a Police Chief who never met a Scotch he didn't like and his wife who thinks she can sing like Barbra Streisand (she doesn't) and believes she resembles the late movie star, Jayne Mansfield.  She definitely doesn't.  A matronly owner of a coffee house who is a drinking buddy of the mayor's secretary, two bickering gays who manage La Tinkerbelle's a Go-Go's boutique, a social worker turned Belly Dancer dressed as a pirate and an Octogenarian rock band and a hog calling champion vocalist are more quirky characters.  Finally, there's a junk man who can get whatever he wants for a customer; illegal alien valet parkers dressed as pirates, the loyal head grounds keeper of the town's country club and a cantankerous judge who despises lawyers more than he does most criminals.

## So:  Where have all the flowers gone?

## Pete Seeger knew and so did the Cossacks.

# About The Book

Bo Pepperwall's intelligence dwarfed Mensa's parameters. He was perceived as strange thereby resulting in his being ridiculed by many, shunned by most and being called, Bo the Schmoe by all. Then he faced a dilemma. He had to choose between money (which he never had) and morals (which he also lacked). Should he weasel a part of his recently widowed sister's inheritance for a business venture or should he turn in the killer of her husband, his despicable brother-in-law? He chooses both. Bo opens La Tinkerbelle's a Go-Go, a 1960's retro discotheque in an abandoned factory building in a Chicago slum using a theme from the legend of Peter Pan. Surrounding himself with bizarre employees (each having a unique vision of reality) who put fun into dysfunctional, his dream nearly goes bust. Then a Chicago gossip columnist prints a story that has customers lined up and Bo collides with his dilemma. The collision buries him in money and public adulation. Success, however, can't cover his moral guilt in the surprise ending to Book 1 of this screwball murder mystery farce that is more farce than mystery.

# Chapter 1

## <u>General Glen Forest Pepperwall</u>

## (Chief Scarecrow)

Shake's Mortuary stood on one side of the picturesque turn-of-the-century town square of Glen Forest on the Watercourse; the other three sides made up of antique shops, quaint boutiques, Huss's Germania Inn and Mildred's Ennui Latte Emporium.  In the center of the square stood a bronzed monument honoring the town's founder, General Glen Forest Pepperwall.

The mortuary resembled more of an old fashioned ice cream parlor on the outside, which it had been until the ending of World War II.  The name, Shake's, was one third of the original name: Malts, Shakes, Moron Sundae's.  A giant double glass door had replaced the battered, scarred revolving one used over the years by kids to see how many of them they could jam into the four quartered panels.  The doors had Shake's in gold script letters on one panel and Mortuary on the other and separated two big picture windows that had a frontal view of the monument to General Pepperwall.  The General sat astride his reared back charger, his saber brandished, pointing at the small apartment above the mortuary rented by Amanda Newton the high school's buxom and Phi Beta Kappa divorced librarian and her teenage daughter, Matilda.

A crisscross walkway of flag-stone pavers joined a circular path around the monument. Mourners coming and going had no choice but to see the bigger than life size statue of General Pepperwall as they entered or exited Shake's. According to folk lore, all of it initiated by the General himself, his heroic feats during the Battle of Savannah were legendary; tales of his patriotic bravery lived on thanks to a generation of his bastard children, and their bastard children and their bastard children after that.

Throughout his conniving life, General Glen Forest Pepperwall never missed an opportunity to reinforce and embellish his self-proclaimed Revolutionary War hero status. "I spilled my very insides fighting alongside the Polish patriot, Count Casimer Pulaski," he had said to everyone who listened or pretended to pay attention to the braggart. "Count Cas was a brave man and my dearest friend."

History showed that Pulaski took a fatal bullet while volunteering to help America fight for independence. That same history did not specify that General Pepperwall's spilled insides were the result of his shitting in his pants as he fled from the Battle of Savannah. Historical archives made no mention of a frightened, conscripted sixteen year old slick-sleeve private, stale and fresh fecal and urine stains coating his military trousers, beating a hasty retreat from harm's way on his trusty steed. Eraser smudges across pages of history books obliterated the mention that the scared soldier wore epaulettes stripped from a dead enemy general and that the trusty stead was a sway back plow horse taken at sword point from two astonished, wide-eyed Negro farm hands that chose to pinch their noses shut instead of fighting for their horse. They didn't mind the loss of the pathetic nag, since the escaping private left them their plow and, eventually, pure air to breathe.

History also stayed mum to another important fact. Riding behind General Glen Forest Pepperwall on the same plow horse, one hand locked for dear life on the General's torn collar, the other pinching her nose shut, rode a beautiful half-breed, pregnant slave girl, Arvia.

The General's account of his spilled insides omitted the mention of retreat while inserting such heroics as being surrounded and outnumbered by wild-eyed enemies foaming at the mouth. He placed an emphasis on brandishing his own saber, slashing to bloody ribbons as many crazed mercenaries his blade could contact as he fought his way single handedly to and for freedom. His saber never stopped causing devastation to the enemy until he had galloped north out the back door of Georgia.

The General galloped north continuing to brandish his saber yelling, "Charge!" The only enemy he saw–indeed the only ones who heard his command–were a half dozen or so startled Negro women picking cotton. Their bewildered looks stayed locked on to him and his saddle mate until the duo plodded out of sight. Each of the women gave a sigh, released their nostrils and returned to picking cotton.

The plow horse finally stopped plodding, coming to a rest in Kaskaskia where his four wobbly knees welcomed the ground. He closed his exhausted eyes, let out a sigh of thanks and died. A year earlier, George Rogers Clark had captured the Illinois town from the British. A dozen years later, and roughly one hundred and twenty years after Louis Joliet and Father Marquette preceded him to Lake Michigan, the self-proclaimed general planted his roots with Arvia on a homestead plot near Lake Michigan he named Glen Forest. Joining them were their three bastard children, two cute girls, both having two different color eyes, one brown and one blue and a boy acting like a girl, his eyes fixed looking left.

The area where the General settled was Indian Territory. Like Chicago, with its translated Indian name meaning *Smelly Onions*, his homestead also had an Indian name. Because of its pungent aroma, swarming mosquito population and clinging humidity, even in the dead of winter, the General's homestead was known as, *Bastard's Manure Swamp*.  With noticeable alacrity the General changed the name on his land deed to Glen Forest.

Before the ink dried with the new name, the General began wheeling and dealing with the local Indians, a disreputable collaboration of Algonquin, Potawatomi, Miami and Hochunks. They had refused to let the white settlers from the east run them off their land.  The General quickly made a deal with them to expand his land holdings.  He swung his extended right arm from left to right and back again, boasting, "I'll give you my three children in payment for all of this," he said, to a delegation of four Indians led by their spokesman, Chief Scarecrow.  "And three more to be named later," the General added.

Scarecrow's title, like that of Glen Forest Pepperwall's, was self-proclaimed.  None of his tribal members, or those from other tribes, questioned his authenticity.  His pungent body aroma literally scared crows.  His scarred face and headdress also frightened most weary settlers into continuing on with their westward movement. Scarecrow's pock-marked face came as the result of too many encounters with the white man's fire water and not, as the settlers claimed, with his being a fierce warrior, somewhat like the General.  Scarecrow got drunk on a daily basis and, in the course of staggering back to his teepee, encountered too many trees with his face.

Scarecrow spoke broken English.  "Me also want all future baby makers," he replied to the General, his demands for all female children of child bearing age catching the savvy General off guard.

"Three," said the General, a gleam in his shifty, black eyes, holding up the exact number of fingers in front of Scarecrow. "The fruit of my loins will give you more children than this here swamp sprouts mosquitoes in the spring." Numbers were bandied back and forth, eyes continuing to shift, until the two charlatans, visions blurred and eyes crossing from sipping too much of the General's homemade firewater, reached an agreement. Scarecrow and his people didn't care about property ownership. To them, whatever they saw, wherever they set up their teepees belonged to them. As Scarecrow said to his people after the deal, "The paleface General is dumber than a grassy plain filled with Buffalo chips."

However, as with most of the deals, pacts and agreements made during his life, as well as cheating at cards and cheating on Arvia, the General forfeited on one of his payments. He substituted his son who acted like a girl. The son, Berthold, fell in love with Scarecrow's son, Weird Warrior. The two of them rode off on a single horse under cover of darkness one night heading south and west in search of a warmer climate and a more accepting community. To save face and his scalp, the General proposed a creative financing deal to Scarecrow and his people whereby he sold to them, at half price, an intoxicated, obese opera singer who had missed the last stage coach out of town. His deal also included a promise that the opera singer, whom he had called Trashetta, was more fertile than his two daughters and three, as of yet unborn children, their feminine genders guaranteed by the tribe's Medicine Man. "With that baby manufacturing machine you stole from me, and when those three infants reach womanhood," he boasted to Scarecrow, "you'll increase your tribal numbers tenfold."

Exaggerations were not new to General Glen Forest Pepperwall who often referred to himself as the Slashing Rapier. His boasting came to an end with his untimely death during the year 1818 when Illinois became the twenty first state in the union. The cause of his death was a shotgun blast to, where else, his posterior.

Arvia, upon discovering the General too many times in

lascivious acts with other women who used their charms in hope of a seeking a step or two up on the social rungs of the settlement, unloaded both barrels of a shot gun into her common law husband's bare backside while he made passionate promises to a local bar maid that included: "Climb my pleasure ladder, you sultry wench, and, at the top, I promise you a life of leisure." That was the General's favorite promise, one he never kept and the last one he ever made.

Arvia was found innocent of any wrong doing by an all-male jury consisting of those who had their spouses, mistresses and other favorite bar maids violated by the braggart General. She harbored no regrets about dispatching her common law husband into the hereafter and celebrated the General's untimely demise by appointing herself mayor of Glen Forest. Still proud of her marksmanship and her status as a single woman, she changed the name of the community her late philandering husband founded. Adding *On the Watercourse* to its name, she hoped, would have *Glen* and *Forest* be interpreted as one of nature's majestic wonders, not one of its blunders.

Arvia died exactly ninety days after attaining the age of ninety. During her life she solidified her friendships with the Indians who had stayed in the area, many of them respecting her trigger finger. It took some time, but she managed to locate her children, except Berthold, that had been used as collateral and quietly positioned all of them in a number of key governmental positions. In public, the children praised the late General Glen Forest Pepperwall, and said not a word as to the cause of his demise, his questionable deals, usurious practices, cowardice and their legal lineage. Their heirs were also quietly funneled into various municipal positions. They also praised the late General because it was the thing to do even though they had no idea what he looked like or who he was. As one male descendant said, "He was some old fart who had the same last name I do." Several generations later, by unanimous vote, the heirs transformed the legend of General Glen Forest Pepperwall, Revolutionary War hero and founder of the community bearing his name, into a bronze statue. He would live on forever in the middle of the town's new main square.

A plaque honoring the General, affixed to the base of the monument, made no mention of a private's soiled uniform britches or fleeing from battle. Only Arvia had known and she stayed haunted by the memory of the General's stench and lack of intestinal fortitude until her death.

Over the years, the novelty of the statue faded and most of the General's heirs had passed on, gone to jail or fled the state, most with embezzled funds. For many in the community they had hoped that the statue, its patina now covered with decades of bird droppings, would also pass on to a junk yard. Students from the high school, however, loved the statue. Graduation class after graduation class made it their senior prank to paint the private parts of the General's charger. Each year the classes would use a different color scheme. One year, the bicentennial year, the seniors showed their patriotism by painting the General's horse red, white and blue. The class valedictorian, Pamela Pepperwall O'Keefe, gave credit to the school's Art Department for the exhibition of patriotic art. The Art Department faculty, however, sported only crimson colored faces knowing that several artists from the senior class inscribed a message on the charger's private parts: *Patriotic Pecker*. A very creative graduating class managed to incorporate four colors into their prank. The view from the rear, two orbs under the horse's tail barely visible during the day, glowed with a florescent yellow at night. The pranksters were complimented as providing a provocative, but Picasso touch. Colors came and went as did the graduating seniors but the General stayed.

A long line of relatives, corrupt scoundrels and assorted connivers had followed Arvia into the mayor's office after her death. The most corrupt, a consummate conniver and swindler, was the current mayor, a womanizing power broker, Quintin Bell.  He had no Pepperwall blood, but what flowed through his veins was more rancid than all of those who preceded him in office.  Quintin Bell was the husband of Arvia Pepperwall, successor of the first mayor.

# Chapter 2

## Quintin Bell

### (Wanda Mensch and Margaret Farnsworth Pepperwall Jones)

Quintin Bell relished his role as mayor of Glen Forest on the Watercourse, the prestigious suburban village nestled along Chicago's North Shore. He wanted others to view him not as a political king maker but as the king himself, the kingfish, a mammoth pillar of the community, a towering combination of Gothic and Corinthian.

He knew why he coveted this regard: "Power," he said to his best friend and attorney, John "Scats" Brown, in the security of the attorney's downtown Chicago office on Michigan Avenue overlooking the Monroe Street Harbor. "And power, Scats, is spelled M-O-N-E-Y." Twin raised brandy snifters displayed the counter-clockwise swirls of blue agave tequila before the swirls seared the throats of the two friends. "And money, Amigo, comes from the greed of others," he continued, enjoying another satisfying swirl. "We, my learned barrister, have power because we know the Golden Rule of acquiring same," he said, his nostrils resting on the rim of the opulent crystal snorting the tequila's aroma. "Screw thine other, Scats, before he or she screws you."

His almost perfect Hollywood-leading-man lips replaced his

nose on the rim of the snifter for a moment.  Then the glass drifted to his lap resting in his cradled hands.  His manicured nails were unable to conceal several crooked fingers, mementoes of his days as a college All-American football player and several brawls in bars.  He inhaled the aroma of the tequila, closed his eyes, a look of pleasure on his face bordering on orgasmic and said:  "Says so in the Bible, Amigo.  Do unto others before they go ca-ca on your head."

As mayor of Glen Forest on the Watercourse, Quintin Bell was never shy about reminding the "thines" of what they should render unto Caesar.  "Scats, those greedy pathetic bastards who knock on my door lookin' for a juicy municipal contract aren't foolin' this guy," he said, as he watched the attorney refill their snifters.  "If they want Quintin Bell's John Hancock on a contract with my village, then they best lubricate my throat with a case of Mexico's finest," he said, holding up the crooked index finger of his right hand, "and maybe the finest from the United Kingdom and France," he continued without missing a sniff.  "Don't forget Spain, Italy and even Australia and South America."  His middle finger paired up with the first in a suggestive dance.  "Second, I expect them to cross my palm with silver, preferably the non jingling kind. You know several nice packets of dead presidents' pictures." He paused again.  "Of course, several ingots would make a unique offering to yours truly."  A third finger joined the dance. "And they'd better have a delectable bon-bon delivering the documents."  He paused, a slight upturn at the corners of his mouth, the subtle smile attracting many a fly to the spider and said, "I'm not known as the Candyman for nothin', Scats."  He smiled.  "I don't expect a fair damsel to deliver an envelope filled with goodies without my appreciation being shown."  His smile broadened.  "Goodies exchanged for goodies.  Isn't that how the quote goes, Scats?  Like an eye for an eye."  He winked at his friend.  "Like a tit for a tat."

Before the next work week started to skid down the back side of hump day, Mayor Quintin Bell's first index finger was recorded. A cardboard case with *Product of Mexico* stenciled across the four sides found its way to the gate house of his private residence. Products from Ireland, Scotland, France and other global alcohol producing countries also graced the gate house. Bulging business envelopes marked, *Personal* and wrapped with enough packing tape to seal the Titanic's gashed hull mysteriously turned up in the center drawer of his antique Oriental writing desk in the den of his mansion. The desk was a gift from an appreciative Japanese emissary. No one was ever seen entering or leaving the den.

Hump Day's downward time table produced a delivery paved by a sultry delivery lady, a chocolate cherry bon-bon. At precisely two o'clock, the delivery lady stopped at the Glen Forest on the Watercourse Country Club's Pro Shop counter and said: "I have an urgent delivery for Mr. Candy."

"Through the frosted glass door there," said the polite clerk and the club's teaching pro, "Yips" McDermott from behind the glass counter filled with boxes of golf balls, gloves and tees, all marked with the GFCC logo, a rapier underlining the letters. Yip's salivated. He could taste the bon-bon. His smiling envious eyes indicated the direction to the private steam room, his hands showing a continuous case of the tremors that would forever keep him out of PGA tournaments. "Make a right and a right and you'll be right there," he said, amused at his own direction giving.

The centerfold candidate left the carpeted Pro Shop, an exaggerated sway from her hips inches from colliding with golf bags and displayed clubs lining the aisles. The click of her stiletto heels echoed off the polished marble floor once she exited through the frosted glass door with her delivery heading for Mayor Bell's private locker room. Exquisite polished nails, usually a gloss candy apple red, accentuated the business envelope containing the signed legal documents and a sample of assorted goodies. The intrigued, but nervous courier handed the envelope over to his Honor the Mayor. A seductive tongue teased its way across an upper lip before dropping down for a slow return, her full lips sporting a sensuous gloss red coating. Seductive eyes stated: "Hi, my name is Eve. Do you have what it takes to be Adam?"

Quintin Bell put Adam to shame as more than one Eve discovered. "Thank you," he would always say in a polite voice to the current Garden of Eden messenger. He would be wearing only a Turkish towel around his waist, his feet in a pair of black Adidas shower shoes. His practice-makes-perfect smiling eyes savored the predictable telltale cracks developing in Eve's seductive smile. "Care to join me for a steam?" he would ask, giving a nod of his head toward the cedar door behind him, his towel now lying at his feet, the steamy glass peep hole leering at her.

Later, after a coed steam and shower, the bon-bon departed the Mayor's private locker room. She resembled a five pound box of chocolate cherries with creamy centers that had spent an afternoon in Bastard's Manure Swamp melting under a sultry August sun. Precisely a half hour later, Mayor Quintin Bell returned to his office. His ritual never changed. He gave his customary, cordial business type nod to his loyal secretary, Wanda saying: "Isn't it a beautiful afternoon, Miss Mensch?"

Seeing her boss, her heart skipping several beats, she would answer back, barely able to breathe: "It certainly is, Your Honor." Her anemic eyelashes with no signs of make-up would attempt a flutter, the attempt producing more of a watery blink as if she had been peeling an onion. Quintin Bell never noticed as he disappeared behind his office door. His nod had Wanda fidgeting with her slightly grey streaked bun and inserting a number two, yellow pencil into it with a series of jabs while her thighs quivered. In a moment she would send off the Mayor's stock reply pertaining to another new contract: "Much obliged," written on a plain, white note card, no identifying words printed anywhere, the only identification coming from the perspiration from Wanda's palms. The inside of Wanda's thighs cramped when she wrote the mayor's alias. Her shaking hand spelled out, "Candyman" while she knew one more Thine had been screwed, and disappointed she wasn't the Thine.

The majority of the Glen Forest on the Watercourse residents only heard rumors about a Candyman; but rumors were talk and talk was cheap. Wanda did not deal in cheap. Nothing cheap was ever taken seriously in Glen Forest on the Watercourse. Wanda herself had manufactured an occasional rumor or two after one too many glasses of her ninety two year old father's homemade dandelion wine, her father rumored to once having been a chef for the gangster, Al Capone. Wanda's rumors, "Devilish jocular barbs" she called them, drifted out under the closed doors of her apartment. The rumors helped her break up the tedious accolades she mass-produced for her boss. She vowed to protect his image to the death, the vow coming after she had received a dozen long stem roses along with a smile from "Hizzoner" on her first Secretary's Day. The vow also spawned a secret fantasy of Wanda's. She dreamed of being swept away in the arms of her knight in shining armor, The Candyman, galloping off into an Avalon sunset, a damsel ready to give her all like so many other damsels with limpid eyes gracing the covers of paperback books adjacent to supermarket check-out counters. A Christmas card with a generous bonus followed. A box of imported Swiss chocolates arrived on Valentine's Day accompanied by a red heart shaped card stating: "Will Thine Be My Valentine?"

Any negative comment about her boss was met with Wanda's special efficiency. Before the rumor monger realized, Wanda had published a series of press releases that both damned and embarrassed the culprit who dared to besmirch the good name of Quintin Bell.

Wanda's arsenal of press releases stood at attention, the ranks labeled from A to Z, waiting for her command to fire. The "A" in her category, obviously, stood for "adulterous conduct", while the "Z" had the rumor spreader waking up in either the Lincoln Park or Brookfield Zoo's primate houses, naked. Those who caught the bull's-eye of her marksmanship slithered quietly away.

Three times a year, once on Quintin Bell's birthday, the second at the village Christmas party and the last at his annual political fund raiser at the Country Club, Mayor Quintin Bell's behavior turned Wanda's life and her legs into quivering jelly. When she at last completed extensive damage control caused by His Honor's intoxicated behavior, both mental and physical exhaustion reluctantly forced her into taking a day off from her day-to-day regimen of running the village of Glen Forest on the Water Course. She once remarked to her friend and confidant, Margaret Farnsworth Pepperwall Jones, owner of Mildred's Ennui Latte Emporium, after too many glasses of dandelion wine, "His Honor's life style will be the death of us both."

Quintin Bell appreciated his secretary's efforts; knowing he needed her efficiency and her pit bull like tenacity of acting as a smiling, polite buffer deflecting the unwanted from bothering him, often interrupting his enjoyment of a piece of candy. Still, Quintin Bell treated her almost as indifferent as he did all the others in his life, including his wife and his supposed best friend, John "Scats" Brown. Quintin had a special cure for what ailed his secretary. His cure wasn't exclusively for Wanda, but he made her think it was a special pick-me-upper designed for her and her alone. His cure always worked. It was a smile and a nod that preceded a simple statement. The first time the mayor appeared at the front door of Wanda's apartment situated on the second floor, rear, of Shake's Mortuary, she almost needed the mortician. The mayor smiled and nodded without ever setting foot in her apartment. His simple remark: "Get well quick," oozed compassion and caring. His seductive smile was followed by a goose bump producing whispered request, "I need you." He smiled, nodded again, turned and left.

Wanda never heard the last part of his statement: "The Village needs you." Her knees were knocking louder than a Hitchcock swarm of angry woodpeckers. That first visit and the mayor's kind words of need set off an on-going series of risqué fantasies churning through the intelligent, creative horny brain of Wanda Mensch.

The mayor's secretary may have appeared to live the life of a matron dedicated to her job and her boss, but Wanda Mensch had more of one thing in life that exceeded what her boss, John Brown and ninety nine percent of the world had together. Her Mensa IQ was imbedded in a mind that was a steel trap. Only the best computers could fight her to a draw in a contest. One thing she knew about the mayor that he wasn't even aware of was the powerful non-verbal signals attached to his nods and the particular reactions affixed to each. Those reactions produced almost frightening supernatural results. One nod in particular stood out in Wanda's mind bringing eternal admiration from her and giving birth to a special desire. She wished to be like Peter Pan's Wendy, never growing old and having the eternal blush of youth in her cheeks. If that were possible, and she prayed it would be, then she knew that one day Quintin Bell would be hers and hers alone. That is, when Quintin Bell reached an age where other women didn't find him or his money attractive and he was filling out his application, with help from her, for his assisted living residence. Then Wanda would be there for him, all young and vibrant, ready to meet his every need. He would finally be hers. Her prayers to be Wendy, which she believed would be answered, had her adding thigh high, black patent leather boots and a riding crop to her compendium of fantasy apparel.

The nod that intrigued Wanda Mensch, the one in question, was tied to a voodoo doll with Mayor Bell's likeness.  The grotesque image of Quintin Bell was the sophomoric effort of several garbage collectors.  They worked for a firm that had exchanged tits for tats with the Mayor.  A long hat pin protruding from the doll's groin area had evoked laughter, most muffled, and enough dark rumors to satisfy a zombie jamboree. The doll had been mounted on the hood of a garbage truck and was spotted in the garage of the waste disposal company after hours.  Several workers were found gaping at one another in stunned silence the next morning trying to figure out why they were unemployed.  They had no idea a nod was involved. Wanda knew, but she wasn't talking, only sporting a subtle smile.

One of the waste disposal collectors once lived in Glen Forest on the Watercourse, renting the front apartment above Shake's Mortuary.  The worker, Sam Someone-or-other, and his new bride were model tenants.  Sam worked for the village as did his wife, Amanda, who was the high school's librarian. Wanda, however, renting the other apartment above Shake's Mortuary, her's having a view of the mortuary's back parking lot, knew another side of the model tenants thanks to thin walls and the efficient use of a drinking glass.  The walls in the two upstairs apartments were so porous Wanda could even tell what brand of toothpaste the newlyweds used by the sound of the cap being removed.  She had carefully categorized and filed her first hand views, she detested the word, eavesdropping, into her computer brain.  Sam's bride gave birth to a baby girl. Wanda knew the baby's name before the mother first saw her child.  She even knew the moment the baby was conceived. Paper thin walls couldn't conceal the librarian's moans and pleas to her husband to, "put the pedal to the metal," an expression that had somehow activated her passion button after viewing, "Smokey and the Bandit" with her husband. The librarian's pleas for speed did, however, conceal Wanda's own sounds as she listened through the wall.

A second plea by the librarian, another passion driven order, "Geronimo," confused Wanda. She could never get the couple's last name straight. "During the day their name is one thing and at night another," she complained to her friend Margret Farnsworth Pepperwall Jones, the complaint coming after the dandelion wine had run out and the two ladies were forced into slamming shots of what remained from her father's collection of bathtub gin, a reminder of the Prohibition Era still stored in one gallon red gasoline cans. "At night, I hear what sounds like a Native American war cry, "Geronimo," interspersed with pushing a pedal against metal. During the day I hear Germono. Sometimes I think that school librarian of ours is engaged in an extra-marital rendezvous with an Apache warrior instead of her husband."

"Oh, Wanda," Margret would say, her hands held in prayer, the finger tips at her lips as she feigned a blush, "you're so naughty." She would smile and say, "Do tell me more."

Wanda was seldom confused about anything and detested any lack of clarity in her life. She was not about to abandon her lack of information gathering through thin walls because of name recognition so she originally categorized her neighbors as the, "Someone-or-other couple." That was soon changed to the, "Geronimo-Germono couple" and finally shortened to the, "G-G Two."

Sam and Amanda Geronimo-Germono had named their baby girl, Matilda. Father and mother appeared elated. Wanda was also elated and envious. She loved children; her love also coming from the story of Peter Pan. Her envy, on the other hand, was tied to the librarian's passionate cries. Those cries should have come from her and been directed at Mayor Quintin Bell as she used her riding crop to urge him on along with her calling

His Honor, Mallet Man in reference to his love of croquet.

Then Sam Geronimo-Germono left his wife and little girl who was nearing two.  Shock filled the second floor rear apartment of Wanda Mensch.  Even General Pepperwall's bronzed charger couldn't believe what happened.  Wanda, stunned and numb, could.  She knew the juicy details. Sam had left his statuesque and buxom wife, the provider of literature to the town's high school students, for another lover.  Wanda quickly discovered the juicy details of the divorce, getting the particulars from her drinking buddy, Mildred who had a pipe line of information coming from her younger brother, Judge Ransom Jones of the Cook County Courts.  She shared those choice tid-bits of information during several imbibing meetings during the week where the two would catch up on what they called, "P.U. in the Glen."

Each Sunday afternoon, Officer Noel Jones of the Chicago Police Department and grandson of Judge Jones, would visit his aunt at her coffee house in the town square.  Mildred had opened her Ennui Latte Emporium for formal British Tea on Sunday afternoons much to the disdain and criticism of Reverend Rufus Puffin, Pastor of the United Church of the Glen for not keeping holy the Lord's Day.  Before leaving, Noel would place a reinforced canvas tote bag sporting a tasteful logo of the "Daughters of the American Revolution" behind the counter at the front door.  The bag contained a liter bottle of Gentleman Jack for his grandmother.  Noel would pick up a second identical bag, this one empty, to be used the following Sunday.

Wanda discovered how much she enjoyed a formal British Tea on Sunday.  She also enjoyed sharing a taste of Gentleman Jack after Mildred had flipped the, *Sorry; We're Closed* sign to the street side of the front door.  Wanda didn't give a hoot about what Pastor Puffin thought and she also enjoyed visiting Mildred's Emporium on Mondays and Tuesdays, her visits coming in the evening just before sign flipping occurred.  Many

Sunday, Monday and Tuesday evenings saw Wanda leave Mildred's Emporium walking in a wobbly direction across the square to her apartment above the mortuary. As she past the General's statue she would mutter, "Up yours, pervert." Wanda knew General Glen Forest Pepperwall's history better than he did. She knew everything thanks to her expertise on the Internet and access to world class university libraries.

Wednesday evenings saw Mildred cross the town square after she had closed the "B", as she referred to her coffee house, the "B" standing for any associated words that could be attached to Ennui. Mildred preferred, Blah, as in a case of the blahs or, if she were in a particular foul mood, the word, "Bitch" would be used. There were several reasons attached to Mildred's visit to Wanda Mensch's apartment. First and foremost was to sip dandelion wine with her friend, Mildred's supply of Gentleman Jack having run out. The second reason being to share any new P.U. either may have uncovered during the brief interim of less than twenty four hours since they last socialized, their polite way of saying, "getting drunk." The third reason for their visit was to place matching water glasses up against the common wall separating Wanda's apartment from that of the librarian's checking to see if there was any news besides her legally discarding her married name—Geronimo or Germono—and switching back to her maiden name, Newton. They were hungry to hear a possible reoccurrence of any sounds referring to Geronimo and his skills with an accelerator pedal. The only thing they ever heard through the wall was the sounds of Broadway show tunes or the evening news. One night they heard a giggle they associated with Amanda's teenage daughter, Matilda and the expression, "two cents, please." That was followed by what sounded like the pleas of a subdued male voice asking, "Could I please see four cents worth?" They gave up trying to determine that meaning for a third glass of dandelion wine and continued with embellishing their P.U. list.

On their last Wednesday night together Wanda became upset with Mildred for not having any new information from her brother, the judge pertaining to Sam or anyone else.  There was nothing from, who Wanda called, "Your baby faced, flat foot nephew," as she referred to Officer Noel Jones.  Wanda had opened a new file in anticipation of Mildred's visit and the latest P.U. gossip.  There was none.  Mildred drank and Wanda seethed.  She detested having an empty file.  She knew Sam's lover's name, Geoff Bartholomew, Meow for short, but what she didn't' know was what had happened to Geronimo Germono after the divorce.  He and his lover disappeared and Mildred's pipelines of information were dry. That distressed Wanda. What distressed her even more was that Mildred, now about to finish her fourth glass of wine, hadn't contributed any new information that evening, P.U. or otherwise.  In a huff, she removed Mildred's almost empty glass from her hand and shoved her out the door of her apartment.

* * * * *

As several more years went by, Wanda became even more distressed.  She was still Wanda wanting to be Wendy.  Her wanting continued, prayers mounting along with her consumption of her father's dandelion wine, bathtub gin and countless tea cups of Mildred's Gentleman Jack.  Her wanting continued while her wrinkles expanded.  Then Wanda's world crumbled to fine dust.  Quintin Bell was dead.

Quintin Bell's body had been found next to the eighteenth green of the Glen Forest on the Watercourse Country Club.  The side of his skull had been crushed by several blows from a croquet mallet found lying across the back of his neck, his personal engraved mallet.

# Chapter 3

## John "Scats" Brown

### (Arvia, Bo and Ben Bell)

Quintin Bell's gluttonous appetite for power under the guise of civic mindedness; his untiring efforts to line his pockets while projecting a public image of altruism and élan in the promoting of community spirit contributed to his status and his death. Because in part of his progressive dynamic and openly corrupt leadership, Glen Forest on the Watercourse held the reputation for being the premiere community in which to reside.

Many of the rich and famous, self-anointed, self-appointed or *wannabes* saw Glen Forest on the Watercourse as Camelot. Visible corruption or not they wanted in to King Quintin's domain. The King, however, wouldn't let them in, his draw bridge chained up, locked by his sneer and his castle's moat filled with flesh eating creatures while he satisfied his sweet tooth with a never ending supply of bon-bons. The King took sport in keeping out of his palace undesirable elements or, as he called them, "Scum sucking social climbers." He often remarked to his friend, Scats, "Do you know what those phonies and snobs are?" His answer followed in an instant. "They're lower than whale crap. And, Scats, you don't get any lower than whale crap 'cause that's on the bottom of the ocean." He gave a smug look to his attorney and added, "I can't tolerate crap in my kingdom."  He paused then said, "Don't you dare remind me of my brother-in-law, Scats.  He lives here because he's my wife's brother and that's the only reason."  He shook his head and said, "The imbecile's a schmoe."

The line of phonies, snobs, suspended piles of whale crap riding the currents and a single schmoe spurned and rejected by Mayor Bell didn't take lightly to his arrogant disdain.  Being humiliated was a new experience for most; not for Berthold Pepperwall.  They didn't know that Quintin Bell thrived on humiliation and, all but Bo the Schmoe, kept trying to find ways to gain access to a prized Glen Forest on the Watercourse exclusive address and status zip code.  Their attempts knew no limits.  Money could buy whatever their money wanted to buy, at least in their circles, and humiliation be damned.  What they didn't realize was that Quintin Bell was an expert on the behavior patterns of the phonies, snobs and drifting piles of whale crap who stalked him; he knew their environments, their feeding habits, what they purchased and especially their breeding habits.  He had bedded down with their spirited mares, their shy frightened does and assorted frisky bitches.  Quintin Bell did, indeed, know the scum social climbers better than they knew themselves.

Many outside the walls of King Quintin's realm still believed money could buy anything.  An ugly incident based on fact, not fiction, dispelled that belief.  The episode pointed directly at several of the same garbage collectors who had lost their jobs years ago because of finding humor in a voodoo doll.  Some of the dismissed drivers were sought out and each offered a handsome stipend by one of the rich and almost famous who wanted a prized Glen Forest on the Watercourse address.  The stipend was for a clandestine undertaking designed to embarrass Mayor Quintin Bell.

The drivers were given a simple order: Drive a large dump truck, the vehicle painted with the official seal of Glen Forest on the Watercourse, and deposit a partial load of hazardous waste in the center of the town's square.  Then, with the tailgate left down, drive up Sheridan Road and deposit samples of the hazardous waste into the center of each town that made up Chicago's North Shore communities.  The truck, filled with a glowing, smoking, noxious smelling cargo, never made it across the village limits of Glen Forest on the Watercourse.  Truck, waste and the three men in the cab disappeared.  Shortly after, the personal injury lawyer who had formulated what he thought was a perfect plan to acquire the perfect address found himself disbarred and placed in what government officials referred to as a Civil Protection Arrangement.  The lawyer's family continued living where they were.  The family received supplemental incomes in the form of unlimited debit cards while the head of the household was never seen or heard from again.

His Honor's efficiency so impressed his secretary that she contemplated adding a black leather bra and panties to her fantasy ensemble.  The thought of wooing the mayor while wearing a wig fashioned after Wendy's hair simmered in her mind.  Dreams of Wendy's youth kept Wanda's hopes of a life with His Honor on the front burner of her fantasy stove.  Now, however, her flames of passion were being smothered and choked by Quintin Bell's obituary.

Until his untimely and mysterious demise, Quintin Bell's thirst for power couldn't have been satisfied by all the prestige tequila in all of Mexico.  There weren't enough sensuous, sexy couriers wearing candy apple red accents delivering securely taped stuffed envelopes to his steam room to please him.  He took whatever he desired; humiliated whoever he pleased, including his wife, Arvia, and thumbed his nose at life.  As he said to John Brown, "I'm like Little Jack Horner.  I stick in my thumb, or whatever, and always end up with a plum."  Suddenly his eyes glazed over as if he had taken on an ice storm with his face.  "The problem, Scats, is there ain't enough plums to satisfy me."  A sheet of ice seemed to distort his face, his eyes barely visible.  "One of these days, John I'm going to squash every plum in the world.  If I don't, one of them, I fear, is gonna squash me."

Quintin Bell didn't dwell on the negative.  His thumbs were always on the lookout; hormones were in a constant state of simmering, taste buds and a parched throat constantly butted heads and his excuses for a celebratorial evening centered on one other aspect of his life besides power.  Quintin Bell loved debauchery.  His birthday, the town's Christmas party, political fund raiser and re-election gala were all held at the Glen Forest on The Watercourse Country Club.  Liquor always flowed well into the night at those social gatherings; tequila being the drink of choice.  Most of the guests hated tequila, but they drank it, tolerating that liquor, mostly in the form of a strawberry or mango flavored Margarita.  They gave boisterous toasts to the mayor with His Honor's favorite adult beverage.  After several choruses of, "For he's a jolly good fellow," by the smiling, jovial, backslapping party goers, much of the tequila found its way into the sand trap bunkers surrounding the eighteenth green.  With Mayor Bell out of sight and turning up the flames under his debauchery pot, the remainder of the tequila became part of the eighteenth holes water hazard with its plume of water spray separating the tee box from the green.  Tequila was as close as anything or anyone from Mexico or any other Central American or Caribbean country ever got to the Glen Forest on the Watercourse Country Club except to cut lawns, prune trees and to apply environmentally dangerous chemicals to the golf course.

The entire town of Glen Forest on the Watercourse looked forward to Quintin Bell's annual Christmas party.  The festive day was split into a noontime gala complete with a gift-giving Santa Claus for the children of Glen Forest and their parents.  The mayor made sure there was plenty to eat and drink as well as mountains of candy, in all forms, for the kids.  His sick, demented soul grinned at the sight of the children, wired on gluttonous amounts of sugar, running their parents ragged. Mom and dad, under the influence of too much alcohol, chased their children around the eighteenth hole and its hazards. Quintin laughed like a roaring jungle beast saying to Scats Brown, "They look like stumbling skid row wino's navigating an obstacle course while trying to round up their spoiled brats to go home." Many a child, wet and sand covered, was led kicking and screaming to the parking lot clutching their presents from Santa, their pockets stuffed with soggy sand coated candy.

The evening portion of the Christmas party also had its share of stumbling winos. A unique Santa Claus appeared, this one replacing the town's Chief of Police's rotund, red-nosed brother, Sean, who was passed out drunk sleeping on the floor in front of the entrance to the mayor's private steam room. The evening edition of Santa was a stripper who had been hired by Quintin Bell and John Brown from a topless bar they frequented in an isolated unincorporated, unnamed triangle bordered by Stone Park, Maywood and Bellwood. The bar was miles away from Glen Forest and ideal for maintaining anonymity. Santa, Ivana Rasputina, her real name according to her contractual arrangement with the mayor, was hired to be more than a terpsichorean dressed like Santa shouting out, "Ho-ho-ho's" in an accent that appeared to come from the Russian block. Contractual terms had her shedding her Santa suit at a designated time. The designated time was usually when Mickey Finn, the Chief of Police, was drunk enough to yank off the Velcro fastened, form fitting Santa suit. Rasputina, the pole dancer, known by her name appearing on the blinking marquee of Tony's Pink Pony, Ivana the Slider Glider, would show off her tattooed breasts, one displaying a bearded winking Ivan the Terrible and the other, a profile of Lenin. When Chief Finn's staggering turned to stumbling he didn't need Greenwich Mean

Time to tell him duty called and he should rid Santa of her attire.

Another part of Slider Glider Santa's pact with Quintin Bell and John Brown was to wear a red G-string under her suit. "Hell, John, it's Christmas," said Quintin reprimanding his friend who had balked at the costume's addition. "Have some decency," he said with a wink to his friend who was standing with a forward lean in front of a seated Slider Glider looking like he was about to fall in her lap. A green tassel with a puffy white ball dangling from the end of the G-string was a visible part of the Santa's under garment. A tiny bell hung from the puffy white ball that Santa rang without the use of her hands.

"I don't want to be the guy responsible for taking Jingle Bells out of Christmas," said Quintin, as he gave John Brown a nudge sending him on top of the Glider Slider; the tiny bell sounding like it came from an alarm clock.

The G-string always ended up being a part of Chief Finn's uniform, appearing around his neck like a lanyard making him look like a strung out, Geritol Hippie. Santa, wearing nothing more than ankle high, red vinyl boots with a flashing red light bulb on each toe, brought howls of laughter from the crowd, a Margarita glass was in one hand and a nacho chip dripping green salsa in the other made no attempt to conceal her private parts. Choruses of, *All I Want For Christmas Are...*Santa's body parts, one of many categories, substituted for two front teeth.

During one Christmas party, after Santa's disrobing, Wanda followed the female Santa to the ladies restroom and stripped her of her red, ankle-high boots with the blinking red toes while waving a small imitation pistol in Santa's face. The gun was made of licorice and coated with sand. Santa was too scared to notice. "You look even askance at His Honor's manhood and I'll be forced to dispatch you to the North Pole from the ejection seat of my Astin-Martin," said Wanda using the latest 007's voice. The frightened Santa, a trace of what looked like white powder under her nose, began pleading for her life. Wanda waved the candy pistol, the barrel starting to droop, in the girl's face and said, while handing her an envelope with her salary for the evening, "Show time is over, Miss Glider Slider. Take your silicone boobs, tattoos and pierced body parts, hop into your Kremlin sleigh and make tracks for Siberia."

Quintin Bell and John Brown later heard the story from an agitated Glider Slider on a subsequent trip to the western suburbs. When Quintin walked into the office the next morning he greeted his secretary with the biggest smile she had ever received.

* * * * *

John Scats Brown never appeared bored from his friend telling him the reasons for his success. Quintin Bell's success did more than trickle down to the attorney. Money, in the form of retainers, was dropped off at his office weekly, the envelope handed to his latest secretary who had a bra size greater than her IQ.

"Scats, the cardinal rule is to use the other dumb bastard's money," Quintin had said so often that John Brown, Attorney-at-Law had the reason and accompanying mannerisms memorized. He would slap his right knee, let out a hyena type laugh and shake his head in agreement with his friend's rationale. His laugh and body language were a polished act. John Brown secretly hated Quintin Bell; his hate incubated and hatched while they were teammates in college playing football. Scats, like Quintin Bell, made the college All-American football team. His selection was to the second team, and that back seat recognition to his teammate became a cocklebur buried in his backside. He had been dubbed, Scats by Quintin the first time he carried the ball during his freshman year. Scats ran like a crazed water bug. His walk was also similar but not quite as crazed. The nickname was multi-faceted. As a child, Scats discovered his father's record collection.  A large segment of the collection was devoted to Ella Fitzgerald.  Scats fell in love with the great singer.  In no time, nestled up against his parents Hi-Fi, he could match his new love, Ella note for note singing, *A Tisket a Tasket.*

John Brown was better looking than his friend.  The only blemish to his bubble gum card hero's face was a scar across the bridge of his nose, a memento from his football helmet saying, "Don't believe everything you hear about a face mask protecting you from injury."  His gridiron statistics received accolades and rumors of a possible Heisman Trophy nomination and, at the very least, a guaranteed All-American first team selection.  He got neither.  Then he discovered that his friend and blocking back used a series of romantic encounters before, during and after the football season with the female editor of the college's newspaper.  Quintin Bell got headline press releases touting his feats on the football field from the editor, a doctoral candidate possessing the appearance and shape of a bookworm burrowing into a discarded, tattered pulp fiction magazine.  John Brown, the touchdown-record-setting running back, got nary a mention.  The homely bookworm discovered Quintin Bell's interpretation of patriotism after Saturday's games, after the playing of the National Anthem and after the flag had been lowered from the stadium flag pole.  She got her face covered by Old Glory and the rest of her by Quintin Bell.  John Brown got her tears on his shoulder once the All-American teams were announced and the Stars and Stripes lay in a crumpled ball on the floor of the editor's office.  It was at that point that John Brown decided he wanted to kill Quintin Bell.

* * * * *

Arvia Pepperwall was named after her great, in a long line of Pepperwall greats, original grandmother.  Arvia even resembled her namesake and relative, a mulatto with Native American blood, possibly Mohican. Her face, surrounded by black, lustrous hair tied in a single braid hanging down her back almost to her waist, could have appeared on an early cigarette pack. Her large dark eyes always wore a tinge of sad even when she laughed. She lacked but one quality of her ancestor. There was no trigger finger. Like her greatest of grandmothers, she possessed one quality all Pepperwall women had and the late General and all subsequent males lacked. She was a fighter. This was something the town's founder knew nothing about. Arvia Pepperwall became even tougher when she added the name of Bell to hers. No one knew, not even Quintin Bell who made the colossal mistake of misjudging her and publicly humiliating her with his indiscretions.

Quintin Bell wanted Arvia Pepperwall for his wife for one reason and one reason only. The Pepperwall fortune, that in the form of the palatial Pepperwall mansion known as Dogwood. The jealous referred to it as the Dog or, in extreme fits of envy, Dogshit.

Quintin Bell got what he wanted and more. The Dog was now his along with two others; a pair of German Sheppard's belonging to Hans the main gate guard and a new title for Quintin, being called the spouse of Arvia Pepperwall. That title he quickly discarded in the arms of Alice Nell Puffin, Pastor Rufus Puffin's wife and Linda Ann Finn, wife of the Chief of Police. Lucia Gunderson, the newly appointed principal of the Glen Forest on the Watercourse Country Day School, also eased the pain of his new title. The major source of Quintin's new stress came in the form of Arvia's super intellectual brother, Berthold Bo Pepperwall. Bo the Schmoe, as he was known throughout the village because of his erratic behavior and constant ideas for amassing wealth, catapulted Quintin into fits of rage that even Scats Brown couldn't understand. "I agree he's a schmoe, an idiot, the biggest loser I've ever encountered and he couldn't pour piss out of one of your golf shoes if I read the directions to him," said Scats to his friend in an effort to calm him down. "Is that dolt worth having your luscious half breed wife locking you out of your own wigwam?"

Quintin didn't care about being kicked out of his bedroom. He would just kick some other unlucky husband out of his bedroom, mainly Chief Finn who he once ordered to sleep on the couch. "I'd like to interview your wife for a new position I'm creating," he had said to the Chief, presenting him with a bottle of his favorite Scotch. After observing his Chief of Police down his third water tumbler of Johnny Walker Blue, he continued with the reason for his visit. "I think your personable, intelligent versatile wife would be a nice fit for this idea I have for a public relations liaison for our town." Mrs. Finn, also known as Two Drink Linda, was well into her second tumbler of Scotch neat and listened intently to the conversation taking place in her cluttered living room filled with uncomfortable Swedish modern furniture. As the Chief began to slurp through his fourth drink and stumble for the sofa, Two Drink Linda suggested moving the interview into her bedroom saying, "I think we should let Michael," referring to her now snoring husband, "get his rest. He does work so hard for you, Mr. Mayor," she continued while brushing her breasts against Quintin's arm. "I have so many questions about this exciting job and I don't want our discussion to disturb him." She offered her hand to Quintin as she led the way, her too wide spaced brown eyes showing the affect of the Scotch by blinking what looked like a Highland Fling.

Quintin Bell eventually listened to his friend, Scats, and sired a son, Benoni, now sixteen. His son was an incredibly handsome and intelligent young man destined for the Ivy League, but not as a football player to his father's chagrin. Benoni wanted to be a rock musician, a bass player. Ben progressed through his teen years pursuing his dream and imitating the sound of his bass while fingering the imaginary strings of his equally imaginary bass and attempting to ignore his father's demeaning remarks.  As Ben grew up, his father distanced himself more and more from his son and his wife. Rumors ranging from divorce to King Quintin abdicating his throne ran rampant through the town.  There were even rumors, factual data for the statistically pure of heart, of Quintin Bell's satisfying his manly needs to such an extent that the population of Glen Forest on the Watercourse both grew and decreased at an alarming rate. As a new birth was recorded increasing the population by one, a family, or at least one adult moved away from Glen Forest on the Watercourse.

Quintin Bell never believed the story of how General Glen Forest Pepperwall met his fate.  He should have.  Until the early morning hours when his body was found on the lawn of his custom designed croquet course bearing his name at the Glen Forest on the Watercourse Country Club, Quintin Bell viewed himself as omnipotent and omniscient.  Then he met St. Peter and discovered what it was like to be kicked out of more than a bedroom.

* * * * *

Quintin Bell's death came as no shock to the community.  No one, not even the coroner, questioned the cause of death: blunt trauma to the right side of his skull and severe bruising and discolorations to his groin area.  A croquet mallet, complete with red, white and blue stripes and the inscription in bold print, *Hands Off, QB* etched at each end, was labeled as the possible contributing cause of death.  Another weapon suspected was the size forty D bra found near the body. According to Police Chief Finn: "Fill those two cups up with sand from the eighteenth green's bunker and swing it hard enough, why I bet you could put a dent in an armored car."

Linda Ann Finn, Amanda Newton, Alice Nell Puffin and

Lucia Gunderson all wore the same bra size. Lucia Gunderson breathed a sigh of relief because her bras all had a custom wire uplift-push feature for maximum cleavage display. Her bra couldn't be the possible murder weapon. Further examination of the body by Chief Finn showed no additional dents and no evidence of strangulation marks made by either nylon, wire or both.

Chief Finn slurred on with his investigation. Standing with one foot on the deceased's posterior looking like Daniel Webster debating the Devil, his questions, most unintelligible, spilled out along with him drooling on himself. Answers to his questions were equally slurred and contained nothing out of the ordinary. Questions starting with, "Did you see? Did you hear? Did you smell anything out of the ordinary?" Variations of, "No" or what sounded like the negative cut short Chief Finn's investigation and had him ordering Bo Pepperwall to bring him another Johnny Walker Blue. "Make it three fingers and neat, you schmoe," he said, his order sounding like, "tree dingers with meat, use snow."

During his questions and drink order refills Chief Finn's right index finger spun around a pair of women's crotchless panties. The panties had been clutched in the deceased's right hand.

Everyone in attendance at the fatal party knew the scanty undergarment, a monogrammed "W" on the cheek of each side, came from the mayor. It was his way of jokingly stating, "WOW" and embarrassing his secretary, Wanda Mensch. The joke, like all of the mayor's humor, was in bad taste and in no way indicated any sexual desires for his secretary. Quintin Bell would never give plain, blah Wanda Mensch a glance. If he did, the panties would spell out, "MOM" instead. The crotchless panties, however, opened up an entire series of questions pertaining to Wanda Mensch as a possible suspect in the mayor's death. Everyone, except Wanda, laughed at that rumor. She hugged and savored every innuendo and variation. But, Wanda wasn't in attendance the night her boss was killed. At least, that's what Johnny Walker whispered in Chief Finn's ear. None of the revelers remembered seeing her. Even if she had been in attendance, most of the people wouldn't have noticed the plain, matronly secretary. Then the panties disappeared. The next morning Chief Finn couldn't remember crotchless panties but Wanda did. So did Alice Nell Puffin. Many at the party concluded that Alice Nell was the swinger of the croquet mallet. She had enough reasons. So did Lucia Gunderson. So did Amanda Newton, but she hadn't been seen at any Quintin Bell party since the one and only time where she had walked home vowing to get even with the mayor. Her vow was so loud even General Pepperwall atop his charger in the town square had to put his fingers in his ears.

One Quintin Bell social gathering ended identical to all other Quintin Bell social gatherings. The next morning after the country club's grounds keeper, Raphael "Rip" Repeater and his crew repaired the massive damage to the eighteenth green, the course sported its immaculate look for the first foursome's early morning six thirty tee time. Rip knew exactly what to do after the mayor's party. He and his crew were doing it before the sun came up. Rip, a former professional baseball player, his promising career as a catcher cut short by an injury, respected manicured lawns and impeccably trimmed hedges. When he took a naked jump from the second floor bedroom of a female fan in an obscure Appalachian League town he landed on neither. The fan's husband, a surprise intruder, heard the clatter of Repeater bouncing off the garbage cans in the parking lot below. So did the neighbors. Rip, his Friar Tuck's bald spot glistening in the moonlight, disappeared limping into the Appalachian night, the limp never leaving him, but his baseball career did along with his dream of playing on a lush, green playing surface in the major leagues.

With the sun's eastern glow ready to spill a creeping blanket of gold over Lake Michigan, Repeater and his crew began fishing out numerous articles of clothing, mostly undergarments, women's outnumbering men's by a seven to one margin, from the eighteenth hole water hazard. The hazard's bubbling water spout also needed to be unclogged. A second black bra, this also a size D reinforced with wire, had a hole cut out of each cup, and was found stuffed half way down the spout. Rip and his crew knew the risqué bra belonged to the Glen Forest on the Watercourse Country Day School Principal. She had showed it to them one morning after the Mayor's re-election festivities. Hung over, a blinding sun making her squint, Lucia Gunderson awoke to see Rip and his crew looking down on her as she stretched, yawned and literally rubbed sand from her eyes. She had passed out in the eighteenth green sand bunker. Wearing only her bra and her skirt from the night before, the skirt backwards and inside out, she looked up, saw Rip and his gawking crew, cupped her bra, gave it a good push toward the sun and said, "I bet you Spics never saw a set like this before."

Where the police chief's wife sported the nickname, Two Drink Linda, the elementary school principal was known as Three D Lucia. After three Dirty Vodka Martinis on-the-rocks, with an Oliver Twist (Lucia's way of incorporating literature with alcohol and sex), she openly blabbed about having bedded down with several elected public officials. She never mentioned municipalities or names. The vodka and her east coast accent, complete with a lisp, made her sound more incoherent than normal.

Rip's crew, after enjoying a view of the prior night's devastation, waded into the large water hazard wearing one piece, chest-high rubber waders and carrying trout nets. They sloshed out, trying not to laugh, with bulging nets containing an array of items ranging from a high heel wedgie, a large stuffed pimento olive stuck on the heel, to numerous liquor bottles, tequila outnumbering vodka, wine and beer bottles. There were also lone empty bottles of Chartreuse, Goldschlagger and Malort, the twig missing from the bottle of Malort. The trout nets never found a fish of any species, only a dozen and a half condoms, a Smurf doll, the cause of the jam to the spout of the pond's water aerator and a Chicago Cubs T-shirt caked in mud. The nets of Repeater's crew also captured a collection of floating Styrofoam cups, several baseball caps with the logo of Chicago's professional teams and an old fashioned white cap worn by nurses. Also hauled out were the usual hats belonging to the Chief of Police and Forest "Smokey" Bearren, the Fire Marshall. The nurse's hat belonged to Fire Marshall Bearren's wife, Gwen, a retired R.N. who worked at the high school as the health clerk. She detested modern nurses and their wearing scrubs for giving her profession an image to the outside world of being made up of, in her words: "Slobs in smocks." She reported to work every day dressed in her white uniform, enough starch to ward off a tornado, white nylons complete with a matching garter belt, shoes covered with a coat of white liquid polish and her immaculate hat placed on a mountain of grey streaked hair.

Rip's crew also floated to shore three ornate carved, high-back walnut chairs. They were rinsed off, sanitized, polished and returned to the dining room. Two once-white and starched waiter's jackets and several serving trays that had been used as Frisbees ended up on the grass area at the edge of the water hazard. A surprise find was the bottom half of what looked like a belly dancers costume, the sheer nylon legs charred to the knees. Four golf carts were also pulled from the water. The water hazard had been designated as the finish line for the golf cart drag races, one of many highlights of Quintin Bell's summer political fund raiser. The annual drag race, called the Best of the Breast, had the carts driven in reverse by four of the leading village citizens: Chief of Police Finn, the perennial winner; Rodney "Bird Dog" Pointer, the Head of the School Board, Fire Marshall Bearren and Attorney-at-Law John Brown, head of the local Republican Party. Quintin Bell didn't allow Democrats at his party unless they had money. Each cart had a passenger or passengers; one or two partially nude female party goers strapped on the back of each cart in place of the golf bags. The bag straps were around their waists holding them in place. Whichever cart went into the water first was declared the winner. Chief Finn and his wife, Linda Ann, the daughter of a slain Cicero, Illinois mobster, always won. The Chief's wife suffered from a dual identity crisis. She believed she could sing like Barbra Streisand. She couldn't. Each time she looked in a mirror she thought she looked like the late Hollywood actress, Jayne Mansfield. She didn't. Her breasts were the only thing she had in common with the late movie star, the rest of her body, from head to toe, resembled an inverted mop handle punctuated by a boney rear end and a pair of big bouncing boobs courtesy of the medical profession. When the Police Chief's cart took its usual victorious splash in the water hazard, Linda Ann could be seen raising both hands above her head in victory, her breasts oozing out of her scooped, sheer top. As the golf cart turned into a submarine and sank, Chief Finn's puffy red cheeks and severely pitted, bulbous nose disappeared from sight while each of Linda Ann's index fingers shot up above her head as she sang, "Don't Rain on My Parade." As her screeching rendition turned to the sound of bubbles gurgling to the pond's surface, guests politely stated, "It's Mop Handle again by a pair of noses."

So, when Chief of Police Finn, his blue blazer still dripping, looked at Quintin's lifeless body sprawled on the well manicured Croquet Course of the country club, his only comment was, "Drank too much again, didn't you, you perverted crotch cannibal." His statement was followed by his right barefoot applying an old fashioned football place kick in the area of Quintin's groin and a silent statement, "That'll teach you not to lust over my wife's boney ass." Then he looked at those surrounding the lifeless form of Quintin Bell--some of them still able to stand--and asked in a soggy slur before limping away, "Doesn't it look like the mayor drank too much?"

Replies to the Chief's question bordered on, "He always drinks too much", to "leave the drunk rot" or "Rip will take care of him in the morning." Other slurred comments suggested Rip or one of his crew should drive any of a variety of pieces of machinery used to maintain the fairways and greens over the mayor's body. A lawn mower, the low, fine cut one for cutting the greens, was a popular choice of equipment. Someone also mentioned a weighted roller along with the soil aerator with its series of pounding spikes. All the suggestions received scattered applause. Rip and his crew, appreciating the well paying jobs Quintin had given them, concentrated their efforts on getting the country club's lush greens and fairways into immaculate playing shape and a nod of approval from Yips McDermott. Running over their deceased boss was against one of the thousands of rules of golf.

* * * * *

The Chicago area's late August weather, according to those residing near the lower end of Lake Michigan in northern Indiana and southern Michigan and to those communities adjacent to the lake all the way north to Milwaukee, Wisconsin, expressed their feelings in an identical manner: "Chicago weather sucks!" Glen Forest on the Watercourse with all its wealth and Mayor Quintin Bell's back room political candy samples couldn't change the stifling glue-like oppressive air that seemed to relish making human beings miserable. The town's original Indian name, Bastard's Manure Swamp arose from the grave to sneer at the misnomer, Glen Forest on the Watercourse, as Quintin Bell's wake and funeral collided with the sultriest of sultry days in decades.  No one heard the faint warning rhythm of beating tom-toms or saw the smoke signals rising over the Indiana Dunes.  The usual cooling Lake Michigan breezes stayed blocked by a permanent stagnant wall of dripping Turkish towels similar to the ones the mayor enjoyed leaving scattered around the floor of his private locker room.

Quintin Bell's life had ended three days after his fiftieth birthday.  He was a handsome corpse.  Even in death there was his sly, come hither smile still coaxing victims to his web.  Shakes, the mortician, tried to remove the smile but, even with rigor mortis, the deceased's lips kept curling up.  Perhaps if Quintin knew that almost all of his community's residents and those of surrounding municipalities were smiling at the news of his demise, his lips would have had a different curl.

Two people, however, were not smiling, at least not on the outside.  His forty five year old, raven haired wife, Arvia and her younger brother, Berthold projected a professional mourner's somber image.

The inside of Arvia's cheeks showed two swollen ridges of teeth marks.  She sat on a sofa placed strategically in front of her husband's casket.  She had no choice but to be forced into greeting well-wishers.  After all, she was the wife, now widow, of Mayor Quintin Bell.  "Thank you for coming," she said sounding like a broken record without the click as she watched a blurred sea of faces that gradually changed from the familiar to the anonymous as the evening crawled along.  Anonymous faces then gave way to a bizarre collection of strangers.  The bizarre transformed into an erotic parade of curvaceous women with Victoria's Secret bodies held in by black form-fitting dresses that seemed to love caressing their forms.  High heels were high and hem lines even higher.  Black nylons hadn't been worn for mourning and Arvia hated each of them for their legs, her thick ankles a genetic curse passed on to her by some female, southern plantation worker or Mohican squaw, neither related to Vivian Leigh. Each shapely mourner sashayed by Arvia offering nary a glance or a word of condolence to the widow who pretended to grieve. Before each left, however, Arvia had heard every whispered farewell to her deceased husband. Brief forms of good-bye ranged from, "I've always loved you, Q"; to, "Quintin, you lying prick"; to, "Thanks for sticking me with the abortion bill, you bastard;" to, "You could've told me you had the clap."

Arvia watched and heard, trying not to listen, saying nothing. The ridges inside her mouth grew until they screamed at her telling her to use language she detested. She didn't. One thing she knew that none of the female mourners knew the one's she dubbed, "Black veiled trollops," there was no need for her to resort to coarse language. The days of insults and her husband's infidelities were history just like her husband's steam room she knew was called, The Candy Store. For the first time since her son was born, Arvia Bell embraced her new life. Quintin Bell was dead and Arvia was glad. So was her relieved ancestral trigger finger.

* * * * *

Bo Pepperwall was also glad Quintin Bell was dead. He was glad for a multitude of reasons. The most important for Bo was not the value of the deceased's estate, but what percentage of the deceased's estate he would inherit. His ship had finally arrived and he was convinced wealth was only days away. All he had to do was wait patiently for the reading of Quintin Bell's Last Will and Testament.

Patience wasn't one of Bo's virtues. Not with what he knew. Not with an incredibly high IQ that was superior to Wanda Mensch's. Bo didn't know Wanda or her Intelligence Quotient and had only vaguely heard of her as the Mayor's Secretary. He didn't care. What bothered Bo was for the first time in his life he was faced with a dilemma and he didn't like dilemmas.

They baffled him, albeit for only a moment or two before his brain, spinning like a mini-cyclotron, pulverized the dilemma into either inert dust or a solution that satisfied him. Now as he counted down the hours waiting for the reading of his brother-in-law's Last Will and Testament, he found himself forced to choose between right and wrong. Good and evil stared at him as did morally correct behavior and upholding the Ten Commandments. He found his patience was locked in a tug-of-war. Had he ever held a job longer than two days (he had a habit of telling his bosses how their business should be run) he might have had money in his pocket instead of lint. He had waited all of his life for a break. Now he had his break and it was a big one. Bo wasn't sure of what to do. Pulling on one end of his tug-of-war rope was greed. He didn't believe he was greedy, just deserving. He was a dreamer believing that, according to the story his mother read to him as a little boy, the story telling him that happy thoughts would make his dreams come true, that they would. As a child, he tried thinking happy thoughts so that the other kids would play with him. They didn't. What he got were name calling, practical jokes and bullying. The other kids had no concept of IQ's and Stanford-Binet tests. All they saw was a boy their age named Berthold who was different, acted different and that difference made him strange in their eyes. They made fun of him until they drove him into his own little world of pretend and make believe.

Bo had never been formally versed on the real history of his ultimate ancestor, Glen Forest Pepperwall, his of soiled trousers fame and a double blast of buckshot to his posterior. Even Bo's mother didn't know the entire story. If she did, she kept it quiet possibly fearing that the statute of limitations might not have run out on some of the General's criminal activities, those activities masked as civic accomplishments that involved large sums of money.

Bo had received his fair share of buckshot wounds during

his life. So, he thought. Now his sense of justice had him facing his desire for wealth with a newfound sense of morality. He never had money before, but his mother and Peter Pan had taught him their versions of morality. Bo didn't like the collisions going on in his brain. When he realized those collisions were not caused by a croquet mallet, he smiled.

Everyone from Chief of Police Finn to the Country Club's cadre of Hispanic lawn and grounds keepers speculated that Quintin Bell's death was an accident. He had, as usual drunk too much, fell and accidentally hit his head on a hard object. His head hitting three times was logical. His head and body had to have bounced like a golf ball chipped on the eighteenth green by Yips McDermott, a couple of bounces and roll to the cup. Chief Finn felt his theory made sense. He had Yips as an expert witness. He also had numerous scenes from his favorite "Three Stooges" movies, "Caddy Shack" and "Tin Cup" and an episode of Herman Munster on a golf course.

Only one person thought he knew the mayor's death wasn't an accident. That person was Bo Pepperwall. He believed he was the only witness, recognizing the killer. He was wrong. Not quite a handful of others had also seen or heard the croquet mallet colliding with bone.

Chief of Police Finn had ignored Bo when questioning the revelers after the mayor's body had been discovered. The intoxicated Chief wasn't about to waste his time dealing with Bo, who had originally come forward with his evidence of witnessing his brother-in-law's death and knowing who committed the murder.

"Here's the drink you ordered, Chief Finn," said Bo politely as he handed the on-the-rocks glass, minus the ice cubes, filled to the brim with Johnny Walker Blue Label.

It was the only time Chief Finn could afford to drink the best Scotch which he did in great amounts saying silently to Quintin Bell: "Violate my Linda Ann and I violate your wallet." The

Chief gave a nod to indicate his appreciation for Bo's prompt service. There was a second nod, this one with a twitch, which was supposed to send Bo on his way. He didn't leave. "What's on your mind, Schmoe?" asked the Chief, his question, an order and a dismissal all in one.

"Chief Finn," started Bo politely, articulate and soft spoken. He tried to ignore the Chief's indignant glance. "Chief Finn, I know who killed my brother-in-law."

Chief Finn took a gulp of his Johnny Walker Blue Label, smacked his sweaty lips and said to Bo, placing his facial expression two rungs below shunning him, "What could you possibly know, Schmoe?" He took another gulp of Scotch and handed the glass to Bo. "Here, Schmoe, do what you do best and get me a refill." He paused and said, "Then you can haul your worthless self out of here." He licked at his lips that were sweating even more. "Don't forget to clean up first." Chief Finn staggered, caught his balance and said, "Where in the hell is my Johnny Walker Blue?"

* * * * *

"Sometimes being a schmoe has benefits," said Bo to himself as he lay fully clothed on his mattress the night before the wake, his backside and the mattress touching the floor. He knew all the facts pertaining to the death of his brother-in-law. He didn't want to, but he did. He saw it all from behind the large trash Dumpsters concealed by a row of arbor vitae outside the Country Club's banquet hall. He saw the croquet mallet make contact with Quintin Bell's skull; not once, not twice but three solid times. Then he saw the tell-tale walk he knew so well.

As he lay fully clothed in bed waiting for morning and the trip to downtown Chicago for the reading of his brother-in-law's will, he contemplated about how much money he would inherit. He knew what he had to do. Anticipating how rich he would become gnawed at Bo's insides. He had been around money and wealth living at Dogwood, the Pepperwall family estate his entire life. He liked wealth. His forthcoming wealth meshed with his morally correct option to do right. His decision seemed so easy. He would choose both options. It was a win-win situation for him. "Berthold, old chap," he said to his empty room, "keep your information to yourself." He thought for a moment. "In a few short days you'll be a rich man." The worn out bed springs groaned. "Bo the Schmoe," he muttered, picturing himself zooming along the winding streets and roads of Chicago's North Shore driving each of his late brother-in-law's expensive toys parked below. He saw himself racing up Lake Shore Drive skidding into the turn at Hollywood, a delectable piece of Quintin's candy seated next to him.

Berthold Pepperwall didn't want or need candy. He wanted money. Besides, there wasn't a female alive in Glen Forest on the Watercourse, not a one who he called the "V and V" ladies, the "V's" standing for valium and vodka, who would get near him; even with money. Money wasn't the root of all evil. Being penniless, having only a ball of lint in one's pocket was evil. What Bo craved was to do the logically correct thing. "I'll pick up a few dollars in the process," he had said to his cracked ceiling. Then smiling added, "After, I'll go to the police and tell them who was responsible for the impetus behind the croquet mallet."

* * * * *

Quintin Bell's teenage son's emotions, drastically opposite from those of his mother turned widow and his troubled uncle, bubbled up like the caldron of lust synonymous with his father. His lust, however, was subdued and respectful. Benoni "Ben" Bell sat in the front seat of his mother's Mercedes. The sixteen year old All-American boy look-a-like grieved in a way only unique to adolescent males with over-active hormones. Even though he held no respect or love for his father—he didn't even like him—Ben Bell felt the loss of his blood, but not very much.

His mother's Mercedes was parked in the small lot behind Shake's Mortuary that had space for three cars. One of the slots was reserved for the hearse; a second spot for the funeral director's 1949 Cadillac and a final spot, the largest, for handicapped parking. The Mercedes covered the marked diagonal strips of the handicapped parking space.

Matilda Newton, the high school librarian's seventeen year old daughter, snuggled next to Ben in the lush leather front seat of the Mercedes. She was curled up under his soothing, protective right arm. Plain and non-descript, she wore aviator style tinted glasses, her one and only attempt at flirting with a simmering identity. The two teens possessed a unique fondness for the other. Matilda liked Ben because, behind his shy demeanor, he treated her, she felt, like a female should be treated with old fashioned respect and manners. He never made her feel homely and when they were alone he looked at her as if she were the grand cliché of being the only girl in the world.

Ben liked Matilda because she was, indeed, the only girl, his mother included, that didn't turn him into a petrified door mouse when he was around females. He also liked her because nature and genetics had blest her with immense breasts that, on occasion, she would show him one or the other, never both at the same time and never out of her bra. She referred to that as her, "Both Rule," placing a price tag of two cents for a look. That night in the Mercedes, even though Ben was at his most persistent pleading self, Matilda held fast to her rule.

The straining buttons on Matilda's blouse barely enforced her Both Rule yet kept Ben at bay. His fingers shook so badly he almost poked Matilda's eyes out several times at the faint sight of her white, bulging bra. "I've got to get home," she said to Ben, her voice soft and sweet as cotton candy as she nestled closer to him. She loved the feeling of his arm around her, oblivious to the stifling humidity that made their clothing stick to damp flesh and the leather upholstery.

"Not yet," he pleaded, his breath uneven and a familiar ache in his groin, a cross between pain and abject pleasure, giving him thoughts and urges he had before, but never acted on. "Besides, you only have to walk across the parking lot and you'll be home." A button on Matilda's blouse gave up and mysteriously popped open. Ben's pleasure and pain increased tenfold. "Just a few more minutes," he pleaded. "I'll explain to your mother that you were paying your last respects to my father."

"I never met your father," she said, the fingers of her right hand caressing the fatigued button then returning it slowly to doing its designed job. "I came because you're my friend, because we're friends, well, almost more than friends." She took a nervous inhale and asked, "We are, aren't we?"

"You know we are," he said, excited and disappointed in the same breath as he watched another button return to its intended use.

She smiled.

Ben truly liked Matilda, thought he loved her, but after watching his mother and father for so long, didn't want to be in love. His heart sagged as he saw the last of the buttons cover her with what he thought was the sound of a giant lock snapping shut. Then he laughed as she held up two fingers in the sign of a *V*.

"Two cents, please," she said, a business like tone to her statement making her sound like her mother collecting fines for overdue books in the high school library. Two cents was her private joke to him, his standard response the holding up of four fingers and saying, "Both please." Their finger symbolism always evoked giggles.

"I'll pay you when I get back to school," he said, laughter in his voice that was contagious and they both found themselves laughing out of control.

Matilda had used the expression, two cents, please the first time Ben unbuttoned several buttons on her blouse.  She had blushed so hard that she invented the deepest shade of red known to the art world.  Two cents was her way of wanting to know how unsavory women felt when asking for money for sexual favors.  Ben's four finger sign was his way of saying, "Please show me both.  Oh, please, pretty please.  I'll do anything for you."

The sexual favors never did materialize into Ben's seeing both and never exceeded passionate French kissing or her feeling his arousal through his trousers that he managed, sometimes like a contortionist, to press against her thigh. Matilda was still a virgin and an eternity away from losing her amateur standing and violating her, *Both Rule*.

"I'll walk you to the door," said Ben, then starting the Mercedes.  "Thanks for being with me tonight," he said sounding out of breath.  "When can I see you again?"

"I'll be working in the library tomorrow helping my mother," she said, adding a look in hopes he would join her.

Ben sighed, "Funeral's tomorrow."  A depression spread through him that was not caused by the death of his father. "No way is my mother going to let me miss that."

"Day after tomorrow then," said Matilda, her words sounding like an invitation he couldn't refuse.  They hugged for what seemed like an hour not wanting the evening to end. Then Ben put the Mercedes in reverse, backed out of the handicapped parking zone and drove ten yards to the back door of the mortuary where a flight of wooden steps led up to the second floor apartment where Matilda lived with her mother.

* * * * *

Bo stood alone in the back of the funeral parlor staring at the teak wood coffin.  He had but one thing in common with his late brother-in-law.  That one thing began and ended with the love of money.  Quintin Bell had the money while Bo garnered his version of love, a ball of ugly lint in his pocket representing his assets. There was actually a second commonality that Berthold Pepperwall and Quintin Bell enjoyed. That was in the hatred they harbored for one another. Insurmountable jealousy fueled Bo's hatred even though his incredible intelligence sent him conflicting messages, all logical; telling him that one day his brother-in-law would see the light, share the wealth, give him a piece of the pie, if even a sliver. Now there was no light in his brother-in-law's life and a private lobe in Bo's brain kept telling him he would soon shed his mantles of a schmoe and loser.

Quintin Bell had hated Berthold Pepperwall because it was easy. Even more so, it had provided Quintin Bell with humor. A wealthy Quintin Bell had a *GQ* cover looks that radiated charm. He was a college graduate, an All-American football player. It was easy for him to look down on the uneducated, "The great unwashed of America," he called them. It was even easier to do the same with the poor and the needy, even upper middle class striving people and Quintin Bell did just that. He laughed and humored himself at the expense of others. More so, he detested the fact that his wife's brother was alive and breathing. Quintin Bell didn't know that his wife's brother possessed an earned doctorate from the University of Chicago, receiving it in abstentia on his sixteenth birthday, choosing to go to Euro Disney with his mother instead.

Arvia knew of her brother's accomplishment. She also made the trip to Europe. Now there was too much drama and trauma in her life, thanks to her husband's philandering behavior, to ever mention Bo's accomplishment. A doctorate, however, was not the ticket that needed to be punched to be accepted into the Glen Forest on the Watercourse social register.

Over the years, Bo had changed from a cute kid who mothers would fawn over to an adult that only his mother and sister would love. Bo's physical appearance, not his spirit and being, had matured into what appeared to be a stand in for the star of one of the original grainy black and white B porn films complete with bubbles burned into the film. He had straight black hair with too much gel that made him look like an advertisement for Dixie Peach Pomade. He couldn't afford either gel or pomade so he used engine oil that he stripped off the dip sticks of Quintin's cars. He preferred the Jaguar. His hair was always combed back, and he sported a pencil thin mustache that lay at a horrific slant across his upper lip. He thought the mustache gave him a touch of distinction. It didn't. It looked like an undernourished prehistoric caterpillar had gone to die below his nose. His intense eyes, almost a sinister black, appeared to be calculating and plotting. They were.

Bo seemed oblivious to the other mourners in the funeral parlor. There were a steady series of annoying, CLICK/SNAPS that came from the metal cap of a scratched Zippo cigarette lighter in his hand. The lighter was his combination good luck charm and security blanket, his original blankey having gone through a disintegrating process that ended up as the lint in his pockets. A day didn't pass where his sweaty fingers didn't trace the inscribed words to an almost obliterated insignia on the Zippo stating: "Screaming Eagles". Bo didn't smoke. He knew all about the negative sides of smoking having devoured all of the research on the subject. Besides, he realized that cigarettes cost an exorbitant amount of money and he couldn't afford the butt of a filter tip. Tasting menthol flavor was out of the realm of his pocketbook. Tobacco was the farthest thing from his mind as he stood alone in the funeral parlor, nary a mourner acknowledging his presence. Money, however, wasn't. "How much, dear daisy-pusher-upper?" he muttered to himself. "How much did you leave me?

* * * * *

Family, Quintin's one friend, John Brown, Raphael Repeater and his crew, the curious, a line of women wearing even tighter fitting black dresses and Quintin's numerous enemies attended the grave side service. Surrounded by more flowers than the Holland, Michigan Tulip Festival, they listened to Pastor Rufus Puffin, the borderline morbidly obese, bald minister of the United Church of the Glen, pray for the soul of the deceased. Pastor Rufus McDowell Puffin, yellow sweat stains soaking his white clerical collar, never referred to Quintin Bell by name, only as the Deceased. When he finished his final prayers at the grave site, prayers that made the mourners feel they were at a revival meeting in the Scottish Highlands; he was embarrassed at the anger surging through him. Anger of any kind was reserved for Satan, not a dead man who had allegedly violated a man of the cloth's wife as well as other wives. Pastor Puffin glared defiantly at a smiling Satan and silently stated: "I'm glad the bastard's dead. Now he can fornicate with your wife." Pastor Puffin resembled the bird. His wife, Alice Nell looked nothing like someone resembling who a Puffin would have for a wife. She was twenty five years his junior and gorgeous enough to earn a banner displayed diagonally across the perfect mounds of an hour glass figure stating: *I Know You Want Me.* There was no patriotic top hat visible on her cascade of peroxide blond tresses although viewers, especially males, thought they saw her index finger pointing at them saying, "Alice Nell wants you." When Alice Nell appeared in her husband's new church– The United Church of the Glen–male worshipers broke out into a nervous sweat. Even nearby Lake Michigan showed signs of emitting steam vapors when Alice Nell Puffin walked along its sandy shore wearing a selection of provocative beachwear from her wardrobe of revealing selections. Alice Nell dutifully assisted at the grave site handing out single long stem roses to each of the mourners.

The Puffins had arrived without fanfare to Glen Forest on the Watercourse from somewhere south of the Mason-Dixon Line, somewhere near the retreat course of the very late General

Glen Forest Pepperwall, his foul aroma all but dissipated by then.   Rufus McDowell Puffin, an ordained minister from Aberdeen, Scotland, had heard a rumor about an empty and forgotten Glen Forest Unitarian Church.  The new church had been abandoned after a severe lightning storm; one particular bolt broadsided the church's name carved above four Gothic columns.  The lightning strike obliterated and blackened over half the church's name leaving only the letters spelling out, GLEN S UNIT visible.

Mildred Farnsworth Pepperwall Jones was one of the original parishioners of the church.  She was a distant relative of General Glen Forest Pepperwall, on her father's side and a decedent on her mother's side of one of the many founders of the Daughter's of the American Revolution.  She swore on a stack of King James Bibles that she saw the words, Church of Satan visible on the face of the church after the storm.  The reported sighting took place the morning after spending the previous evening drinking Gentleman Jack and dandelion wine with Wanda Mensch.  Mildred's hangover state had her seeing only the S in Glens Unit and she knew it was a sign from Satan.

When Satan took up residency in Glen Forest on the Watercourse, the church became an abandoned eye sore until the arrival of Rufus McDowell Puffin and his wife.  In a matter of days, Rufus McDowell Puffin had chiseled the name, United Church of the Glen above the entrance.  Then he cleared out the nests of birds and bats that invaded his temple with a blast from an antique muzzle loader he bought at a Savannah, Georgia American Revolutionary War memorabilia store, the engraved inscription, "Pvt. GFP" barely visible on the butt plate of the stock.  He held his first service that following Sunday.  No one in town knew what the church was united in, but the town's women, especially Mildred Farnsworth Pepperwall Jones were thrilled to have their church back and their men couldn't wait to attend services to get a glimpse of the pastor's shapely blond young wife, Alice Nell.

Quintin Bell and John Brown also began to attend church on a regular basis once they saw the shifting Lake Michigan beach sands in Alice Nell Puffin's hourglass. After hearing Alice Nell's favorite expressions in her southern drawl, they went after her like twin hounds of the Baskerville's. The first time she spoke to them was at a Christmas church social where they had spiked the cranberry punch with Southern Comfort and Everclear grain alcohol. When she drawled, "Ya'll funnier than sheeeet," Quintin Bell and John Brown found religion and stepped into a fantasy world, one that the mayor's secretary prayed to trod if only for a few moments.

Alice Nell loved the attention of handsome men, especially wealthy handsome men. She accepted their donations to the church after allowing the two to savor her charms in the back of the organ loft by stating in her thick syrupy southern accent, "How did ya'll know that dancin' the horizontal rumba to *Tico-Tico* is ma favorite dance in the whole world?"

With Pastor Puffin's grave-side eulogy ended and secretly craving a giant, frosty gin and tonic, he indicated to Alice Nell to start the mourners filing by the casket to pay their last respects to the man few respected. Several of the sexy women from the night before dressed in even more revealing attire, brought out a seldom seen side of envy from Alice Nell. She silently said in her southern drawl, "Beyeeytch!" as she handed each a long stem red rose, being sure to add a yank on the thorny stem.

The annoying sounds of a series of CLICK/SNAPS could be heard coming from a clump of trees behind the mourners. Most of the mourners ignored the rapid clicking and snapping sounds as they tried to stay cool in the oppressive heat and humidity that had hung like a soggy black velvet curtain over the funeral service. A few mourners did cast annoyed glances toward the clump of trees, but when they recognized Bo their attention returned to the teak wood casket of Quintin Bell while they muttered: "Schmoe."

Arvia softly fingered a gold and diamond studded pendant fashioned with the intertwining letters Q and A hanging from her neck.  Her red, bitter eyes were hidden by too large, out-of-fashion sun glasses once suitable for a breakfast at Tiffany's.  She scrutinized each of the mourners until they all became unidentifiable blurs.  Her fingers carefully hooked the gold chain around her neck holding the pendant.  A quick tug followed and no one noticed the pendant drop to the ground.  No one, that is, except her brother.

Bo Pepperwall also scrutinized the mourners, his eyes resting briefly on the physical endowments of the women.  Each of the women showed a quick, questioning feeling of pain as Alice Nell Puffin placed a rose in their hands with a subtle tug.  "Well, dear brother-in-law, tomorrow is D-Day," muttered Bo, unable to keep his excitement in check.  "You know, D as in dollars."

* * * * *

The mourners and well-wishers, free-loading funeral fans Bo called them, had long since departed from the reception hosted by Arvia by the pool at Dogwood.  Bo paced his bedroom floor like a nervous duck in a shooting gallery.  The floor boards creaked in tempo with the metallic CLICK/SNAPS coming from his lighter as his footsteps filled the bland, unadorned room with a metronome beat.  A magazine cover picture, the torn edges ragged, stuck out on an angle from the side of his dresser's yellowed mirror.  Malcolm Forbes smiled at Bo.  He was dressed in a leather biker's outfit as he straddled his favorite Harley.  Bo smiled back at the picture.  "You told me the only way I could be a success like you was to have happy thoughts," he said.  "To think positive," he stated, looking at the worn picture.  Then he let out a sigh, sat down on the edge of his messy bed, put his head in his hands and said, "Look at me. Look at how I live. Look at this dump I live in."

"Look at where your dump is situated," a voice said to Bo.

Bo cautiously looked up. His black eyes scanned the room once to the left and again to the right. His head never moved. He was the only one in the room except for the picture on his mirror. Bo blinked. "Malcolm," he asked. "Is that you?" Bo studied the magazine picture. "What's going on?" he asked, his words heard only by him. "Stop messing around with me, Malcolm. A minute ago you were straddling your motorcycle and now you're butt's resting against the leather seat, your legs stretched out. Come on, Malcolm, stop messing around."

Bo's head soon returned to resting in his hands. In a minute he fell slowly backwards and lay fully clothed, his suit coat still buttoned, looking like he was reclining on the contour of his ancestor General's original sway back plow horse. Bo stared at the ceiling, cob webs spreading in all directions from the tarnished brass light fixture, its imitation crystal cracked in as many directions as the cob webs. He clutched his cigarette lighter in his hand and heard a voice again, the same voice as earlier, ask: "Have you ever bothered to look at where your so-called dump is located?"

Bo's hand turned so clammy that his lighter slid from it. His eyes zeroed in instantly on the picture and saw Malcolm looking back at him. The man and the motorcycle hadn't changed positions. The picture's head, however, was nodding toward the main house. "So close and yet so far," said the picture. "So close to carrying out your strong sense of justice and yet you let the root of all evil keep you from achieving your dream."

"And, what's that?" asked Bo, his frustrated words coated in sarcasm.

"Come now, Berthold, if you don't know by now, you'll always be a, well, I hate to say it, but you'll always be a schmoe."

Bo felt his mattress touch the floor.  "No, I won't," he said, softly, all traces of frustration having vanished.  "You'll see." His right hand felt dry and he wrapped his fingers around the Zippo.  "Just a few more hours, Malcolm, old buddy, and Bo will make you proud," he said, his eyes closing, a series of determined CLICK/SNAPS drowning out his final statement. "No more Bo the Schmoe," he said, then his CLICK/SNAPS got replaced by his snoring, a trickle of saliva coming from the corner of his mouth.

# Chapter 4

## <u>Berthold "Bo the Schmoe" Pepperwall</u>

### (Lucia Gunderson)

Weird and exciting sensations raced through Bo Pepperwall as if he had been doused in pixie dust. No one would have noticed since he always had a jaundiced shade to his exterior. Never before had he experienced being arrogant and insolent. He had never said, "In your face, Sucker," to anyone. Both his mother and Peter Pan frowned on the use of degrading expressions although Peter's cocky behavior sometimes brought a raised eyebrow from Bo's mother. Bo was puzzled. "Did people with money, lots of money, say, 'In your face' and use a word like, Sucker?" he asked himself.

Bo knew he was inches away from finally having more than his lucky Zippo and lint in his pockets. His leaking, listing ship was about to dock. Captain Hook and Smee would be under his command now. That thought alone made him jittery. Another thought added to his inner turmoil confusing him. For the first time in his life, Bo found himself having to choose between right from wrong. His mother always made decisions like that for him. She was always right and he was always wrong. Then she died, but by then, he was an adult and wrong was eliminated from his life. Years later, Bo discovered another strange feeling. He was confronted by a moral dilemma and the feeling of guilt.  Even Malcolm Forbe's picture on his dresser mirror didn't bring him comfort.  "That's easy for you to say," he had said to the picture of his idol after he thought he heard Forbe's say, "It's a process, Bo.  Be patient."

* * * * *

Bo sat with his sister and nephew surrounded by the plush walnut paneling of attorney John Brown's opulent office, Scats being the executor of Quintin Bell's estate.  Though once apparent best friends and kindred spirits on the outside, John Brown despised Quintin Bell.  Memories of college where he had scored the touchdowns but his teammate and friend got the recognition, glory and scored with the coeds never left him.  Twice divorced, John Brown's libido was on a constant boil, his lust making him look like a panting sled dog after finishing the Iditarod.  If Quintin Bell were a sled dog on another sled, he would have finished first.  Scats always came in second.  John Brown could still hear Quintin Bell's drunken laughter, his mocking words a sucker punch to the solar plexus:  "You'd really enjoy her, Scats.  I just did," he boasted, his right forefinger and thumb forming a circular symbol of approval.

In the beginning, Scats was only jealous of his friend.  Jealousy had long been replaced by a smoldering revenge.  Now, John Scats Brown, wealthy Attorney-at-Law, savored the moment.  As he sat in his hunter's green, high back leather swivel desk chair, his role as executor was farthest from his mind.  His sights focused on the very wealthy and classy widow of Quintin Bell.  His index finger was coiled, patient and ready to squeeze his trigger.  Unlike his loins that ached for her, he was in no hurry to fire off his best shot of all time.  He thought: "You were so right, my late friend.  I will enjoy her." He paused then continued with a hidden smile, "Again and again and again," he repeated, his right thumb and forefinger formed in a circular mocking symbol of approval for his late friend.

Outside of her late husband, Arvia Bell saw John Brown as one of the most despicable human beings ever to walk the earth. John Brown may have been aroused by the mere mention of Arvia Bell's name, but Arvia Bell's feelings for the attorney were inversely proportional to his. "That man is a total disgusting ass," she had often said to her image in the large, golden gilted mirror on her dressing table. A migraine sent her to bed by just hearing John Brown's name. In her most private inner self, she harbored anger towards God after her husband died, saying to the Almighty: "Would it have been so hard for you to provide a second croquet mallet? Surely you offer a two for one special to those of us who pray."

Ben Bell sat in a matching green leather wing back chair next to his mother bored with the proceedings. Ben and preppie were synonymous. From his blue blazer to his oxford cloth button down collar shirt to the orange and navy blue striped tie to penny loafers, sans pennies and socks, he was destined for a top tier college and four years as a fraternity man. He wanted none of it. Shaggy in hair, but not dress and behavior, he continued his dream of being a rock star. No musician alive could send fingers flying over the strings of an imaginary Gibson like Ben Bell. He had the moves, the jumps, the bobble head doll bounces and two left feet in black, high top Converse All-Stars to tap out rhythm like most rock musicians. He even had his Grammy acceptance speech, complete with a series of "F-bombs", memorized. He was ready. The only elements missing for stardom were he barely knew how to play an instrument, his singing voice was suspect and his mother wouldn't allow him to own a pair of black, high top Converse All Stars. Ben had secretly taken guitar lessons, but after six weeks, he had learned just enough to finish *Mary Had A Little Lamb*. Yet he persevered, advancing to do a masterful job of butchering *Three Blind Mice* and slaughtering *Jingle Bells* for the Christmas season making it sound like *Jungle Boogie*. A pair of tiny yellow head phones jutted from his ears like miniature hearing aids, the nondescript music of a rock band, Jammin' Jamie's Joint, blared in his ears causing irreparable damage to the delicate mechanisms of anvil and stirrup. He didn't care. All he wanted was to go home and spend the day in Dogwood's swimming pool.

Ben Bell was at the reading of his father's will because his mother ordered him to be there. Although a senior in high school and barely sixteen, he had been promoted one full grade in grammar school. His then principal at the Glen Forest on the Water Course Country Day School, Miss Lucia Gunderson, had done the promoting, that after Ben's father had promoted her.

Head Mistress Gunderson was a tall, Rubenesque woman who talked with a strong New England accent punctuated by a slight seductive lisp. Her words came through luscious, ripe lips that tilted on a severe angle from right to left, her bright orange lipstick in jeopardy of dripping off. She had a nervous right eye that made her appear to be leering at whoever she talked to. Her praise for Benoni Bell's academic achievements was lisped to his parents at a private meeting in her office that resembled the decor of a Victorian house of ill repute. Two days after the meeting, Arvia received a note from Miss Gunderson stating that Ben would by-pass the sixth grade and be promoted directly to seventh. The day before Ben came home with his note of promotion, Miss Gunderson had met in private with Quintin Bell asking him to apply his governmental accounting expertise in helping her solve, as she put it with her tilted New England accent, *a seven thousan dolla erra in er school's extracurricula activities fun.*

Quintin Bell came to the aid of the Principal with an innovative shifting of debits and credits that bordered on embezzlement. Miss Gunderson then showed her appreciation, her lazy, beckoning right eye stating her thanks and offering Mayor Bell her own private blend of candy. The Mayor accepted, utilizing the Victorian decor of her office to savor her sweets, her first candy sample presented on a desk top cluttered with her collection of globes that showed snow when shaken. A blizzard, a massive nor'easter, struck her office. Another taste of candy found her swivel chair almost spinning off the polished brass casters of its base. The last piece of candy in her box culminated with loud, crashing thumps of her frosted glass office door vibrating to a Bossa Nova beat. For an encore, Quintin, unable to take his eyes off the beckoning right eye of Head Mistress Gunderson, almost drowned her in the large aquarium taking up one wall of her office. The aquarium was filled with graceful angel fish, two of the fish riding a tidal wave over the top of the tank and onto the principal's fake Oriental rug where one of them was found dead a week later.

Bo Pepperwall lounged, almost in exile, on a faded chocolate brown colored, cracked leather Chesterfield chair that had been brought in from the reception area. He carried it in. Legs crossed right over left, his mismatched socks, one blue and the other black, showed the elastic of each having vanished. His right shoe did a continuous series of counterclockwise circles while his confused mind wrestled with the words, guilt, right and wrong. Like it or not, Bo Pepperwall was surrounded by the four walls of John Brown's office. Guilt, right and wrong were related to the law and Berthold Pepperwall knew it. What he also knew was he would soon be a rich man.

John Brown sat behind his desk as if he were the captain of a forty foot sail boat in the Monroe Street Harbor. He was; the boat visible from his high rise office window, the name, *Ella Scats* in graceful gold letters across the gleaming brown teakwood stern. The only changes in Scats Brown from college was hair that became salt and pepper and his water bug gait taking on an ever increasing limp thanks to the pounding his hips and knees took during his football days. Age fifty was good to him. He was tall, muscular and he still drew subtle looks of approval from females.  Now he wanted but one look of approval, that coming from Arvia Bell.  He wanted to savor her body even more.

Bo Pepperwall saw in John Brown everything he wanted. Being the caretaker of a stable of glamorous women also intrigued him but he didn't rank female companionship on the top five of his wish-list.  Bo may have been perceived as a flighty, scatter-brained dolt by most everyone who met him, but they, like John Scats Brown made the colossal mistake of believing that he was a genuine schmoe.

John Brown put down Quintin Bell's Will and looked at Arvia, lust dripping from his deep brown eyes.  "Arvia, do you have any questions?"

"I don't believe so," replied Arvia, her voice parrying the attorney's lust.  "Quintin seems to have crossed all of his t's and dotted all of his i's to perfection," she said, an uncharacteristic chill filling the room that made her brother thrust his hands in his pockets and her son glance up.  "Just like always."

"You're a very lucky lady," said John.  He replaced the Will in a grey enveloped embossed with "Last Will and Testament" in old English script.  "Quintin made sure that you and Ben will be quite comfortable."

"Yes," said Arvia, not holding back her sarcasm.  "My son and I should be comfortable considering it was my money to begin with."

John raised his perfectly trimmed eye brows and started to speak, but was interrupted by Bo.

"That's it?" Bo asked in dismay.  "There's no mention of me?"

John Brown cleared his throat and tried not to smile.  "Well, Mr. Pepperwall," he said, making Bo's name sound like a joke. "Mr. Bell did leave you a message."  He fixed his gaze on a grey envelope, his fingers caressing the flap, a guffaw bottled up.  He didn't laugh and maintained his professional aplomb.  More than anything he wanted to tell Berthold Bo Pepperwall why, according to his favorite quote relating to filling golf shoes with urine, that Bo Pepperwall was indeed the consummate Schmoe.

Bo tried to speak. He couldn't. He tried to swallow. That didn't work either. All he could do was reach for his Zippo lighter, pull it out of his front pants pocket and begin nervously rattling off a series of CLICK/SNAPS that brought a look of disapproval from his sister. He slipped the lighter back into his pants, but several muffled Click/Snaps followed. When he finally got control of himself he stammered, "Jesus Christ, will you give me the message already."

"Mr. Pepperwall," said the attorney, an insulting formality in his tone that made even Arvia feel bad for her brother. "Mr. Pepperwall, I've been instructed to read Mr. Bell's message to you in private. And I...."

"Forget privacy," snapped Bo, his stomach thumping like an agitator in a washing machine. "We're family." He glanced at his sister but she didn't look back.

"As executor I must carry out Mr. Bell's wishes," said the attorney, enjoying his role. "I don't...."

Bo snapped the metal lid of his Zippo lighter and slammed the lighter on the cracked leather arm of his chair catching his thumb between the arm and the scarred metal of the lighter. "Read the fuckin' message already," he shouted; a grimace across his face as he tried to put the horse back in the barn. "Sorry, Sis," he said watching the horse gallop away. His pleading, disbelieving eyes looked at John Brown while his begging heart tried desperately not to let go of his dream. He could see the word, right gasping for breath, wrong's fingers encircling its neck.

"If you insist," said the attorney, a single sheet of business size letter head paper slipping out of the envelope like the Glider Slider disrobing on the Pink Pony's claustrophic stage; the bar smelling like a cheao, generic pine scented cleaner. His fingers gently smoothed the creases from the Glider Slider trying to minimize her stretch marks; the entire production appearing to be rehearsed; which it had.

"I do most certainly insist, Mr. Brown," said Bo, growing more intense; his lighter finding his pocket. "How much did he leave me?"

John Brown slowly lifted the single page as his lips curled in. He cleared his throat and nodded, his eyes still fixed on Arvia's knees that were crossed, and began to read.

"Mr. Pepperwall, this letter was drafted by Mr. Bell with the instructions that I read it to you verbatim and in private. Since you insist, and Mr. Bell thought you might, I will read this to you per your insistence." He cleared his throat again. "Dear Scats:  As for that imbecile, Bo..."

A series of CLICK/SNAPS stopped and Bo's eyes reflected disbelief. He couldn't speak. His eyes began to water and he couldn't control his sniffles. "He's joking, right?"  His eyes went into a convulsion of blinks then he blurted out, "Peter, say it isn't so. Mom, help me."

"I'm afraid your brother-in-law was not joking, Mr. Pepperwall," said the attorney loving Bo's reactions, his legal demeanor in check. "There is, however, one last thing Mr. Bell wanted me to tell you." The attorney's stare caused the frayed threads on the neck of Bo's undershirt to unravel even more. "He was most insistent that you understood the meaning of his words."

Bo scooted to edge of the Chesterfield chair and almost slid off. "What?" he asked, his rekindled hopes ignited. "What is it?"

"A warning," said John Brown so slowly everyone in the room, except Bo, thought they heard the church bells from Holy Name Cathedral far to the north ringing a funeral dirge.

"A warning," Bo asked, dumbfounded?

"Yes, Mr. Pepperwall, a warning," said John Brown as he

was about to send Berthold, Bo, Bo the Schmoe, Pepperwall into the hereafter. "According to Mr. Bell, and I'm quoting." He paused and continued with the look. "This is Quintin speaking to you from his grave." There was another pause that he inserted for effect. "Bo, if you try and get one penny of your sister's inheritance for some hair brained, get-rich-quick scheme, I will come back from the grave and use your head for a croquet ball." John Brown flashed a smile of total enjoyment. "You know all about croquet, don't you, Bo? It's played with a wooden ball and a long handled mallet. Like the one that supposedly ended my best friend's life."

Bo refused to believe what he heard. He wanted to challenge the letter, but couldn't. He gave a frustrated CLICK/SNAP to the Zippo lighter and looked at John Brown as if he were staring at a cardboard silhouette of the attorney. He knew his sister and nephew were looking at him, but his head and eyes wouldn't move, couldn't move. He began to cry, his tears turning to twin tropical waterfalls spilling onto the barely visible series of parallel creases of his stained, threadbare trousers. He coughed and managed to look anxiously to Arvia and even to Ben for support, for the comforting shoulder that always avoided him. There was no support and no shoulder. Another series of rapid CLICK/SNAPS emerged from his pants pocket and he coughed again, a choking, sniffling, nauseating outpouring starting somewhere south of his esophagus. Trembling fingers, the nails chewed to the cuticles, wiped at the tears like the worn out windshield wiper blades of a used car as he cast a forlorn look to Arvia and Ben. Before they could conger up a sympathetic reply, his tears stopped. He began to sniff, a puzzled look coming across his ashen face. He sniffed some more looking at his sister first and then his nephew. The puzzled look disappearing in an instant and replaced with one of panic. Smoke drifted up from his pant pocket. His eyes darted from his sister to his nephew to his pant pocket and even to John Brown, panic now being replaced by horror.  "Oh, shit," he cried out as he started beating at his pocket.  "My lucky dollar!" he shouted.  "Washington's on fire!"

# Chapter 5

## <u>Schmoe vs. Scats</u>

## (Malcolm Forbes)

Bo knew humiliation. They were kindred spirits addressing each other on a first name basis. His late brother-in-law made sure of that, telling him almost daily using his favorite analogy, "Schmoe, do you know you're lower than whale crap?" Bo didn't like hearing that his human existence was viewed by another as being equated to a massive mammal's bowel movement riding a current bouncing along an ocean's floor. None of the combined derogatory remarks that riddled his entire life, not from playmates he knew growing up, not the searing jabs from his brother-in-law that mocked him and not being ignored by almost the entire population of Glen Forest on the Watercourse could compare with the epitome of degradation that he experienced in John Brown's office earlier that day.

"That arrogant egomaniac laughed in my face the whole time he read that letter to me," he said to his picture of Malcolm Forbes on his dresser mirror. His right hand was deep in his pant pocket squeezing the life out of his Zippo lighter, his dislike of the attorney molting into more than hatred. "He mocked me with every word, Malcolm; friggin' mocked me." Bo inhaled as if he were about to blow up a balloon. Before the surge of air escaped his lungs, he found his lips in a twisted smile, the air forced through his lips making him sound as if he were playing a kazoo. He began darting around his tiny cubicle playing a solo game of tag with his walls and two pieces of furniture. "You're it," he stated with each tag. "Mock away, Mr. Barrister," he said, his eyes joining his smile. "Enjoy it while you can."

Tired of playing alone he plopped down on his bed. He was still dressed in his lone, worn, stained suit from that afternoon; the suit once midnight blue, but now looking like a gaudy plaid from a variety of stains. Sleep avoided Bo, his smile having been driven away by a returning anger that jumped out at him like the ugly claw replacing Captain Hook's hand. The illumination of a full moon managed to fight its way through the dirt covering the one window of his room casting a depressing shadow on his picture of Malcolm Forbes. "He didn't leave me a lousy red cent," he said to the picture. "Not a farthing," he muttered. "Nothing," he continued as his smile crept back. "You're going to regret mocking me, Mr. John Scats Brown," he said, his statement flowing through a broadening smile, the words being absorbed by the grey, depressing walls of his room. "One might say, Mr. Shyster lawyer, when you least expect it, you're going to taste mockery Berthold Pepperwall style.

Bo no longer cared about being cut out of the Pepperwall fortune. There were many ways to get his hands on some of his sister's inheritance, money that belonged to her and her ancestors, even him, originally. The money wasn't important now. His computerized brain fired off charged impulse after charged impulse, ideas flowing like the spouting fountain at the country club highlighting the approach to the eighteenth green. There was something now more important to him as his heavy eyes closed, sleep finally telling him who was boss. Rest did not come with sleep. Instead, he found himself submerged up to his nose in Dogwood's Olympic size swimming pool in his suit.

The stains from his suit turned into solid blobs and he watched them float to the surface. He could see a pool surface of swimming faces grinning at him, making little kid nah-nah-nah sounds at him; sounds he had heard so many times before. All of the faces belonged to John Scats Brown.

*"You ain't got no money,"* the John Brown faces sang to him, substituting money for nobody. *"And nobody cares for you."* The faces disappeared under water, a massive collection of powerful kicks splashing water into Bo's face.

"I care for me," said Bo to the disappearing attorney's feet. "So does Peter Pan."

The John Brown heads popped above the surface, giant mouths replacing the faces and grinning at Bo. *"You and that faggot fictitious character are the only ones,"* they said. Then they broke into a violent laugh that bore into Bo's soul.

"You wouldn't be so nasty if you knew what I knew," said Bo to the sea of attorney faces that replaced the giant mouths. He coughed and a stream of water and snot gushed from his nose. "You're forgetting I was at Quintin's party the night he died."

*"I know that,"* said the John Brown faces. *"You were cleaning up the trash; garbage working with garbage."* The faces echoed a tidal wave of laughter that washed over Bo's head like waves crashing over the bow of the Jolly Roger. Bo gagged and coughed again.

"You'll be laughing out of the other side of your face if I ever told the police what I saw while picking up that garbage and taking it to the Dumpster," he said, surprised that the mocking smile didn't budge from the faces.

*"Oh, and what did you see?"* asked the faces that had now turned to painted dark red lips as if in an overhead shot of a Busby Berkley musical. *Was it your little green friend flying around? You know, green like green with envy."*

Bo parried the mockery, slamming it back into the faces the

way his late brother-in-law once did to him in the one and only tennis lesson he received on the Dogwood all-weather court. Bo had two black eyes after that lesson. Now his eyes were aglow as he said, "I saw what I saw. Make no doubt about it, Mr. Attorney. We garbage collectors see plenty. We're sticklers for details."

*"Plenty?"* echoed the faces then peeling off to form a circle around Bo, water splashing in his face the entire time. *"Was it Pastor Puffin trying to grab the Police Chief's wife, Linda Ann by her boney ass?"* they asked, their laughter louder. *"Shame on a man of the cloth showing his lust after too many gin 'n tonics,"* the faces continued, the laughter growing more raucous. *"But oh those hooters on the Chief's wife; ain't they somethin', Schmoe?"*

"Hooters," Bo repeated. "They're nothing but surgically implanted pseudo mammary glands; over-rated protuberances that human beings with small to no minds find themselves slaves to," he said, then splashing water at the faces in front of him. "Who cares?" He felt himself being sucked under the pool's surface and he gasped for air only to come with what seemed like half the pool's water in his mouth. He popped to the surface coughing and gagging, water spraying from him in all directions, sounding like he was singing, *Nobody Knows the Trouble I've Seen.* Then he muttered, "How does my being a spectator at a croquet match interest you?" His question was met with even louder mocking laughter.

*"What match was that?"* asked John Brown, the circle of faces vanishing. He turned on his side and did a series of powerful strokes and kicks that made him resemble a shark sizing up his next meal, waiting for the instinct to attack, to kill. *"Was that the match that Quintin and I had with the high school's librarian?"* he asked, his stroke and kick not letting up. *"That goody-two shoes erudite broad had boobs bigger than the Dewey Decimal System and a body that was a lethal weapon. Stupid broad didn't have a clue."* His head went from side to side, the look on his smiling face

indicating he remembered the night he and Quintin sent the disillusioned angry librarian walking home barefoot from the country club. *"Perhaps you saw our croquet matches, if you could call them that, with Alice Nell Puffin," "There were lots of those. No, you didn't see any of those matches. If you had, you'd have locked yourself in your bathroom ignoring your mother's remarks about going blind if you didn't stop what you were doing. Gee, I guess you could blame Quintin's untimely demise on Alice Nell and her variety of tricks with a certain croquet mallet. Your brother-in-law gave her plenty of reasons to kill him."*

Bo felt a surge of bravery. "I don't need to know what the pastor's wife did with a croquet mallet," he said defiantly. "What I know is something nobody else knows." He paused. "Do you know what that is, Mister Big Time Attorney?" Now it was his turn to answer his question as he began to tread water with increasingly powerful movements from his sculling hands and arms. "I heard the three whacks to my brother-in-law's head. That's one-two-three," he said, putting an emphasis on each of the numbers. "I also saw the croquet mallet on the ground."

John Brown continued swimming in a circle around Bo, his laughter returning, this time not quite as loud, the mockery gone. "Everybody knows Quintin got hit in the head three times. Everybody saw the croquet mallet. Even the coroner knows about the bruising to Quintin's balls. So did the Chief of Police, good old Mickey Good-For-Nothing Finn and his screeching wife, the poor excuse for a Barbra Streisand wannabe. I bet you didn't know that Alice Nell Puffin and even Pastor Puffin could count to three. Well, the pastor could. Tell me something I don't know." The grin suddenly disappeared, replaced by a scowl that caused Bo to move his hands and arms, even his legs, harder to keep his head above water.

"What you don't know, *Scats*," he said, the bravado in his voice increasing, surprising him. "I saw who did it."

The attorney stopped, faced Bo and began treading water. He glared back at Bo.  *"Oh," said John Brown.  "And who might that be?"*

Bo's face turned to stone as if he were holding Aces and Eights.  "Wouldn't you like to know?"

"As an officer of the law, I have every legal right to know."

"You're not an officer of anything, Scats," Bo shot back.  "If you had a brain, you'd be dangerous.  You should have been disbarred before you were even admitted.  As for legal rights, heck, a charlatan has more rights than you."  A surge of energy raced through Bo and he pushed up at the water with his palms, dropped to the bottom of the pool, his knees bent, feet flat on the pebble surface of the bottom.  Then he uncoiled his legs and exploded to the surface.  He shot out of the water like a guided missile from a submarine, his knees almost clearing the surface before he settled back into the pool.  How did you like my little exhibition of physics, Scats?  It wasn't too difficult for you to comprehend, was it?  I mean you being a college football player.  Did my missile demonstration metaphor confuse you, Scats?  I'm sure the police wouldn't be confused when I launch another missile and tell them what I saw; when I lay out my evidence.  I don't want to confuse your Second Team All-American grade point average, Scats, but aren't the police officers of the law?"

*"Stop the bullshit, Schmoe,"* ordered John Brown, shades of his arrogant scowl returning as he inched closer to Bo.  *"Personally, I don't think you saw shit."*

"How does a unique walk sound, Scats?"

"Walk," he repeated.  "Are you talking about the Police Chief's bowl legged stomp?  Perhaps the cheeks of his wife's tight, boney ass squeaking together with her baby step gait; or how about Pastor Puffin's waddle?  And, don't forget Alice Nell Puffin's ass rotating like an erotic ball bearing when she walks.  Oh, and don't omit Miss Protuberances the Librarian.  When she walked she moved mountains, those twin granite peaks of hers.

Now there's a lady who hated old Quintin bad enough to want him dead." He paused appearing to be in deep meditative thought. "Even though Goody Two Tits wasn't invited to the party that doesn't mean she could've dropped in unannounced and provided the impetus to your brother-in-law meeting his maker." John Brown's smile returned like a flashing neon sign. "Oh, and while I'm on education, how about Principal Lucia the Lisper, the Rubenesque nymphomaniac?" he asked. "She was pissed at Quintin for killing one of her angel fish." His head went under, popped up and he spit a stream of water that landed just short of Bo. "And, how 'bout your sister, you schmoe?" he asked. "If there was anyone in this town who wanted Quintin Bell dead it was her. The poor lady was perceived as being an idiot for putting up with all of the women her husband violated, many under her own roof." He let out an ugly laugh and said, "Several of those pieces of candy left their wrappers behind on your sister's sheets."

"You should know," said Bo, not the least bit shaken. "You held the camera for most of his, how did my sister describe them, oh, yes, indiscretions."

*"Put your cards on the table, Bo,"* said John Brown, his words more of an order than calling a poker hand.

Bo continued treading water, staring back at John Brown, not backing down. "Some of my cards are on the table, Scats, and some of them aren't," he said, his eyes boring into the attorney. "You know what I've got up my sleeves, Scats?" he said, pausing long enough for his question to sink in. "I know that Police Chief Finn was thrilled that Quintin was dead. I saw him kick your best friend in the groin to help the killer's handy work along. What was it he said about getting back at the two guys who took undo advantage of his wife multiple times." He relished the look he saw on John Brown's face. He had struck a nerve. Bo smiled like a sly fox poised in front of an open hen house. "I think the only two people at the party who didn't want to see Quintin dead were Smokey Bearren the Fire Marshall and Bird Dog Pointer, President of the School Board. They were both appointed by Quintin.  They'd lose their jobs when the next mayor came along."  He then did something he never thought he'd do in twenty lifetimes.  He splashed water in John Brown's face a second time and shouted, "Hey, Malcolm how do you like the way I brought money and morals together? Now, is that a happy thought or is that a happy thought?"

# Chapter 6

## <u>Arvia Pepperwall Bell</u>

## (Dogwood, Hans, Schickle and Gruber)

Coveting Arvia Pepperwall's wealth and then marrying her for what he jokingly said to John Brown, "Her assets and her ass," gave Quintin Bell a moment of satisfaction, but not for long. Arvia and her family mansion were merely things to him; pleasures filling an abyss; one satisfaction in a never ending line that lasted about as long as an orgasm. Once the parade passed by, boredom set in and he returned to his one true passion in life. To his credit and unbridled flaunting of political corruption, the late mayor parlayed his wife's financial portfolio into a staggering cache of assorted dollar signs, his amassing techniques on par and, in some cases, besting the ruthless land and feminine pulchritude grabbing days of General Glen Forest Pepperwall. Somewhere in the fiery recesses of Hell, General Glen Forest Pepperwall was proud of Quintin Bell, boasting to his Robber Barron colleagues: "That ruthless, money grubbin' ass bandit might not have Pepperwall blood flowing through his corrupt veins, but I'm proud he married into the family." Now the General and the Mayor chatted face-to-face.

Berthold Pepperwall and Wanda Mensch knew how Mayor Quintin Bell made his fortune. Wanda's knowledge being first hand far exceeded Bo's. They both understood how one rotted branch on a family tree aped all of the other rotted branches on the family tree.  Each had heard the hand-me-down stories that had been sanitized and pared over the years.  Wanda, in between glasses of dandelion wine and tea cups of Gentleman Jack, had a front row seat to the mayor's deals.  She also scoured the Internet, made copies of all his communiqués, kept a scrapbook of his newspaper clippings and had transferred all of that information to a computer flash drive.  Actually, she had three flash drives with the information, keeping one on her at all times pinned to her underwear.  The other two were under lock and key in two different places and only Wanda knew the locations.  She knew more about Quintin Bell than he did.

"Malcolm," said Bo to the dog eared magazine picture of his idol grinning at him from the scratched and yellowing bedroom dresser mirror, "I'm not like the others."

The picture's facial expression showed doubt.

"I'm not, Malcolm.  "I'm really not."

The picture's facial expression didn't change.

"Malcom, if I really were a schmoe, I wouldn't be going to the police.  I'd grab the money first.  Maybe I'd never go to the police."  He winked at the picture.  "Well, I am going to take a little money to get this idea I have rolling before going to the authorities.  It'll be like doing two good deeds at once."  He winked again.  "I can help my sister overcome her grief and I can prove to everyone that I'm really not a schmoe.  I mean, how many guys named Schmoe would create a project that would eliminate urban blight, would create jobs and make Chicago a more toddlin' town?" he said to his picture of Malcolm Forbes.  "How's that for a happy thought?"

Bo's cheek still felt the sting of his brother-in-law's slap delivered at the hand of John Brown.  That demeaning blow generated thoughts that were new to him, putting a different spin on Peter Pan and enlarging the meaning of happy thoughts.  Revenge greeted him saying: "Hi, Bo, I was starting to get worried that you wouldn't call me. Don't you think it's about time you discovered how to even a score?"

The thought of getting even brought Bo a feeling of exhilaration, spawning off-shoots of creative rationalizing. "Do I really want to go to the authorities and tell them what I saw that night, or should I wait?" he had asked himself many times since he saw the murder. He mulled the question over and over again knowing the answer, but unable to say, "Just do it." After all, he had reasoned, examining the scenario from every conceivable angle, "I'm a Pepperwall. Pepperwalls are politicians. Would a politician tell the authorities about a croquet mallet slamming into a human skull three times? Would a politician, especially a Pepperwall, take the money and run?" He smiled. "Well, maybe not run. Running draws too much attention. And, anyway, I don't want all the jewels in my sister's crown. Peter Pan wasn't greedy, Malcolm. You weren't and I most certainly am not." He gave a shrug. "What would a schmoe like me do with Dogwood?" He looked at his image in the cloudy mirror. "Did I just call myself a schmoe?"

The one jewel in Arvia Pepperwall Bell's crown that came close to rivaling the Hope Diamond; Elizabeth Taylor's jewelry collection and the Crown Jewels of England was the Pepperwall mansion. The English Tudor style sparkling gem would have made a perfect setting for a BBC television series. A thick perimeter of dogwood concealed an iron picket fence guaranteeing privacy for the over one hundred acres of wooded and impeccably landscaped property. Dogwood's lush setting looked down its nose at the rest of the community from its prime location in the elevated northeast section of Glen Forest on the Watercourse. The eight foot fence came complete with a guard house, a full time guard on duty, Hans and his two prized dogs of German Sheppard breeding stock, Schickle and Gruber. Privacy was guaranteed for Dogwood's residents. The northeast section of Glen Forest where Dogwood stood supreme was the only land not a part of the vast swamp, most of it now land fill, which made up the village.  A spectacular view of Lake Michigan could be seen in the distance from the top floors of the mansion.  Among many of the eye popping, drool causing architectural sights surrounding the sprawling, gargoyle adorned palace was a regulation Olympic swimming pool, a shaded Polaroid dome covering half the pool.  Sun worshipers and the fair of skin had their choice of being protected from ultra-violet solar rays or lounging in the shade of an array of eight colorful cabanas at the shallow end of the pool, four on each side and gaily decorated as if ready to welcome Middle Eastern potentates and their harems.  Sun worshippers could sprawl out on floating air mattresses in gala colors or chaise lounges that surrounded the pool.  Six fenced in tennis courts–two each of grass, clay and all weather, lay paired off to the east of the pool and ran north to south.  One extra all weather court was under a similar sun blocking dome that had portable, roll down canvas walls and two large heaters allowing matches to be played even in the dead of winter.  More than one of Quintin's female tennis partners discovered that when the weather outside was frightful; tennis with Quintin meant being bent over the indoor net to add more meaning to the word, Love.  The pool had eight lanes for swimming laps, a diving board and platforms that met all United States Olympic specifications.  The diving platform was added by Quintin for the daughter of one of his female acquaintances, a fellow mayor from a smaller municipality to the southwest who wanted desperately to be annexed by Glen Forest on the Watercourse.  Her daughter, a collegian and aspiring Olympic diver, practiced her pikes, gainers, twists and entries during the warm, steamy summers with the assistance of a video camera and instant replay.  Quintin was also practicing, applying his version of pikes, gainers, twists and entries with the aspiring Olympian's mayoral mother on a padded lounge chair in one of the colorful cabanas, also with the assistance of instant replay. After practice, the mother, completely annexed, enjoyed a relaxing drowsy period of sun bathing on a mattress size float. While the sun reflected off the mother's cocoa butter oiled body in the pool, Quintin practiced more pikes, gainers, twists and entries with the aspiring Olympian on another of the padded lounge chairs in a different cabana. A video camera recorded every precise move for more instant replay.

Guests to Dogwood felt a sense of awe upon their arrival at the divided, one way winding cobblestone road leading to the mansion. The return route was hidden by a median strip of dense shrubs and fir trees. A giant, rather garish black ornate iron gate greeted visitors at the entrance. A gilded gold heart surrounding the letters Q and A had been added and blared out an obvious message from the center of a large black bell sitting atop the gate: *Eat Your Hearts Out, Peasants.*

Hans and his unchained dogs lying next to the open door of the guard house greeted visitors. Schickle and Gruber showed their teeth and let out matching low growls while Hans, dressed like a Nazi storm trooper minus the swastika on his arm, checked his guest lists, one each for Quintin and Arvia, before admitting anyone in. Hans's real name was Sylvester Mendenhal, Hans replacing Sylvester by Quintin Bell because it was more authoritarian. The only visitors Hans challenged were men. All unescorted women were waved through with a smile, courteous nod and the click of the heels of his highly polished, brown knee high boots.

A visitor's vehicle followed the graceful curves of the road, the visitor in awe as he or she appeared to be swallowed up by a dense, manicured forest. The road was lined with a variety of oaks, blue spruce and hybrid Norwegian pines, the curbing outlined to the forest edge in a wide variety of Hosta. A sea of purple flowers covered the ground. A quarter of a mile later, a visitor or visitors would come upon a *U* shaped drive with a branch off to the right leading to a massive garage with a small coach house perched atop.  Because he was banned from the main residence by Quintin, Bo lived in a single room in the coach house.  To the left of the drive was a parking area sectioned and lined for two dozen vehicles and two handicapped parking spots.  The tennis courts and swimming pool were hidden by the house and an orchard of fruit trees, the abundant fruit being donated, according to Quintin, to various food pantries.  Quintin never donated or gave away anything without something in return.  The something ranged from cash kick-backs for future political favors to confectionary favors.  The line of the food pantry female volunteers living in other surrounding communities never ended as long as fruit needed picking.  It was a rare volunteer who didn't accept Mayor Bell's offer for a tour of the house; the tour ending with a quickie.

The desire for a visit to Dogwood and a tour of overwhelming wealth was like pouring gasoline on the fire of curiosity.  A volunteer's view of opulence was, most times, from a prone position and consisted of looking up at one of several ceilings.  They never saw a winding pathway of imported Italian flag stone cutting a jagged course through Arvia's treasured rose garden to the pool.

Arvia's garden was a collection of hybrid blossoms, mostly Tyler Roses, her favorites, which she alone pruned and tended with a greater love than she once had for her husband.  That love now lay dead and interred in the Glen Forest on the Watercourse Memorial Garden in a family plot.  Arvia made sure her husband's remains were kept apart from the good blood family members having them interred with a collection of thieves, bootleggers, half-breeds--two of the half breeds cross dressers—connivers, con-artists and several relatives having died from syphilis.  There was also one lesbian aunt who was rumored to have been a madam.  Those deceased relatives made up the overwhelming majority of Pepperwalls in the Memorial Garden.

* * * * *

The news of Quintin's burial site location brought a silent, "Thank you, Jesus," from Pastor Rufus McDowell Puffin as he worked on his sermon for the coming Sunday. It was a tearful Alice Nell Puffin that had given her husband the news. He never asked why his wife knew about the location of Quintin Bell's burial site before the actual grave side ceremony had taken place. He didn't care. What he did care about was that Quintin Bell was dead. The pastor detested revenge. However, when revenge was attached to revenge of the Lord, as in the case of Quintin Bell's untimely and bizarre death, Pastor Puffin looked up to Heaven and made the Sign of the Cross saying, "Thanks be to God."

Pastor Puffin also abhorred hatred even though he was consumed by the inner fury raging in his soul against Quintin Bell. The pastor loved life, loved it for all of God's creatures, animal, vegetable and mineral. He was like a Protestant St. Francis of Assisi. Then he met Quintin Bell and all he could see was Christ's sandal crushing the head of a serpent. Pastor Puffin didn't care that the sandal that crushed Quintin Bell's head came in the form of a croquet mallet. That thought made Pastor Rufus McDowell Puffin smile as he dabbed the sweat from his balloon shaped face and returned to preparing his sermon, a creative way, he thought, of weaving together the sixth and seventh Commandments. A tall gin 'n tonic also aided his creativity.

* * * * *

Arvia and Bo were in the paneled English library after returning from the reading of Quintin's Will. She looked out through the French doors of her late husband's study, her gaze in the direction of her garden and the pool. She could see her son in the swimming pool sprawled on one of the mattress size floats, his only movement coming from his right foot kicking the water in what appeared to be keeping time to a musical beat.  Arvia's Mercedes had barely stopped in front of the house after returning from John Brown's office when Ben shot out of the back seat, his shirt, tie and blazer left in a trail on the drive as he made a bee line for the pool.  Before his mother pulled the car into the garage, he was on his back lying on a floating mattress, the sun reflecting off his prescription photo grey glasses.  His head phones were plugged in his ears while his left hand splashed to the rock beat of a group calling themselves, *The Mutorcs.*

Bo, a defiant smirk on his face, sat down in Quintin's high-back rich mahogany colored leather swivel chair behind the hand carved teak wood desk and watched his sister.  He was like a giddy kid with a new toy as he pivoted the chair slowly from side to side.  A feeling of being naughty raced through him.  He was in a place that had been off-limits to him ever since his brother-in-law exiled him to the small, Spartan room above the garage.  For the first time in his life, Bo embraced a feeling of legitimate power.  With a sudden surge of bravery, he leaned back in the chair and put his feet on Quintin's treasured writing desk, a gift from a Japanese emissary who got lost during a goodwill tour visit of the United States.

The emissary's itinerary had not included a stop in Illinois or at Glen Forest on the Watercourse.  A nasty, flight cancelling fog at both O'Hare and Midway airports, plus a confused limo driver who didn't understand a word of Japanese had the emissary coming face-to-face with a bronzed statue of a saber wielding warrior on a horse.  "Ah, Samurai," muttered a pleased, but very lost emissary.  Several circuits around the town square by a shaken and now totally disoriented limo driver, along with a left turn that should have been a right and a right that should have been a left, had the emissary emerging from his vehicle on the manicured croquet course at the Glen Forest on the Watercourse Country Club.  Quintin Bell's annual political fund raiser in full debauchery greeted him. The pastor's wife, Alice Nell with a Rob Roy in one hand and her black bra in the other, was his welcoming committee. The emissary didn't understand Dixie southern drawl or Yankee hospitality but he did understand bare boobs and cocktails. "Ah, biggu oppai," said a pleased emissary as his translation of Alice Nell's well endowed upper anatomy tied his tongue. The desk had been his way of expressing his appreciation for the royal treatment he received at the hands of Mayor Quintin Bell and, especially at the hands of Alice Nell Puffin who had him shouting from the back of his limousine: "Tora, Tora, Tora!"

Bo loved his feet on top of the desk his brother-in-law had cherished. He glanced at his scuffed, brown wing tip shoes with the knotted black laces and made a mental note that when the time was right, he'd find his way to Quintin's closet and take several pairs of shoes from a collection that would have held its own competing with Imelda Marcos. Quintin never wore a pair of his custom shoes with the hand sewn stitching more than a half dozen times tops. It made no difference to Bo that Quintin wore a size thirteen extra wide and his own shoes a nine narrow. He was on his way. Besides, he could stuff the toes with rolled up paper and no one would ever know. He looked at his sister, folded his hands over his stomach and felt as if he were on the clichéd top of the world. Out of habit, he made a nervous glance at the library door expecting Quintin to barge in and start screaming before throwing him out bodily, his point of egress ranging from a conventional door, to being jammed out a window to, once, being hurled through the French doors. His nerves died down, but a trace of fear lingered, the result of Quintin's letter and the threat of his head being used as a croquet ball. If anyone could come back from the dead, it would be Quintin Bell.

Bo knew the damage a croquet mallet could cause to the human skull, especially with a foot planted on said skull and the mallet brought forward with the force of a medieval battering ram.  He also knew who the impetus behind the battering ram was and who belonged to the foot on the back of Quintin Bell's head, forcing his face into the manicured lawn, suffocation being a contributing cause of death.  What no one saw was Alice Nell Puffin slipping several "ludes" and two Viagra capsules into the mayor's snifter of tequila.

Since that memorable night at the country club and what followed at the wake and funeral, Bo couldn't believe the number of people who indicated that they were elated at the passing of Quintin Bell.  Some openly expressed their disappointment at not having been the culprit who dispatched His Honor into the hereafter.  About the only one who seemed genuinely sorrowful at Quintin Bell's passing was Wanda Mensch.

Amanda Newton had heard Wanda's continuous forlorn sobs through the walls of her apartment and had walked across the hall to offer her comfort.  Wanda wasn't answering her door.  She was incapacitated, an empty red gasoline can wrapped in her arms as she lay on the floor cursing Peter Pan, Wendy, Margret Farnsworth Pepperwall Jones, dandelion wine, Gentleman Jack, bathtub gin, fate and, most of all, Quintin Bell.

Bo removed his feet from the desk, leaned forward in the chair and watched his sister gaze out the window.  His right hand slithered like a stalking serpent in the direction of the center desk drawer.  His eyes stayed glued to his sister as he slowly pulled the drawer open, his right hand worming its way inside, anticipating, sensing.  For a moment he felt like the cat burglar who once tried to make off with his sister's jewels only to be cornered by Schickle and Gruber during his escape.  Charges were never pressed against the burglar.  The police weren't even summoned.  Rumors quickly spread via Wanda and her pipeline of information.  Mildred Farnsworth Pepperwall Jones's younger brother, Judge Ransom Jones had started the flow of information to his sister through his grandson, Police Officer Noel Jones of the Chicago Police Force. Officer Jones had a friend, an ER doctor at Cook County Hospital. The juicy details included two jaw sized chunks that had been torn out of the burglar's ass. The chunks matched the jaws of two large animals. Schickle and Gruber were never mentioned. There was another rumor, one that Wanda Mensch couldn't squelch, that the burglar's black ensemble had been soiled by excited bowels and a surprised bladder. The bronze statue in the town square wore what appeared to be a frown. Wanda Mensch wanted to shake the hand of the E.R. Doctor and provide her friend Margaret Farnsworth Pepperwall Jones with her own red gasoline can of bath tub gin. The message was clear. Screw with Quintin the Bull and you end up with parts of your anatomy gored or missing. Now Quintin Bell was gone and Wanda would never experience shouting, "Ole," while being ravished by her boss.

The top of Bo's soft, clumsy hand scrapped against a sharp splinter on the inside corner of the desk drawer drawing blood. His eyes watered as he bit his cheeks to muffle the sound of his pain. The hand was out of the drawer and being sucked on by his pale narrow lips. He felt relieved that his sister hadn't noticed. Several sucks later, he took his hand from his mouth and returned to exploring the desk drawer contents. His heart began to race as his index finger came in contact with a solid, cool object that turned out to be a metal lock box. He tried to carefully slide the box from the drawer while avoiding distracting his sister but, being true to his nickname, the heavy, awkward box slipped through his sweaty hands, a sharp corner making contact in his lap. Besides feeling clumsy, Bo felt two other things. First was his left testicle being crushed by the lock box and, the second, air rushing out of him while his eyes grew bigger than a couple of Kennedy silver dollar coins. A look of choir boy innocence froze on his face as he forced a painful smile at his sister who had glanced at the sound of escaping air. His smile vanished when he saw her return to watching her son out the windows of the French doors.  Bo thought his heart would jump out of his chest as he glanced down at the green metal box.  "My money," he screamed in silence.  "Oh, thank you, God.  Thank you, Malcolm."  His trembling fingers tried the lid and, to his surprise, it opened.  His eyes still fixed on his sister; greedy fingers Brailled the contents.  He froze, his brain questioning, asking:  "Who puts something smooth and silky in a metal lock box?"  His right thumb and forefinger pinched shut around the object and, with his eyes still glued on his sister; he removed the silken object and placed it atop the box in his lap. He glanced down and then, equally as fast, shot a look in his sister's direction before glancing down again.  He blinked several times.  A black bra was staring back at him.  Curious and struck with the belief that the bra could be hiding his money, he considered stuffing it into his left pants pocket, the right one having a hole burned in it at John Brown's office.  Bo examined the bra more closely by using a series of quick alternate glances, one glance at the bra and the other at his sister.  He surmised that the bra belonged to Pastor Puffin's wife.  His right index finger slid slowly across the material disappearing momentarily and then reappearing through a hole in one of the cups.  Bo's eyes stayed on his sister as both hands continued to examine the bra.  He seemed amazed to find the other cup had an identical hole.  His index finger transferred holes and he couldn't help himself from playing the transfer game several times.  Bo's black, calculating eyes blinked at his index fingers that waved playfully back at him, first one, then the other and finally both at the same time.  Realizing that game playing wouldn't lead him to money, he gently slid the bra onto his lap.  He kept glancing back and forth from his sister to his new found treasure.  He remembered seeing the bra at Quintin's final party.  He had hidden behind the massive row of arbor vitae watching Quintin Bell and John Brown playing keep-a-way with the bra from a giggling Alice Nell Puffin who gave a half hearted attempt to get it back. The last he saw of the bra was when it dangled from the hand of someone walking hurriedly away from the prostrate figure of Quintin Bell on the croquet course; someone with a unique walk.

Bo's analytical brain had recorded a number of unique walks throughout his life. His photographic memory now clicked off human gaits pairing them with the undergarment that had showed up in the lock box. His first comparison was to the Police Chief's wife. Since she envisioned herself as the 1950's movie star and pin-up girl, Jayne Mansfield, her breasts, one or the other, sometimes both, would accidentally spill out from her low cut dress, the accident usually occurring in front of a group. To hide her blushing faux pas, Linda Ann would cover herself with cupped hands, turn and walk away with her baby step gait, thighs squeaking together and her head looking over her shoulder with an, "Oops, I'm so embarrassed," smile on her face. Then, as if on cue, her imaginary piano player accompanist tickling her ivories, she would screech out a chorus of, "The Way We Were."

Bo's profile had also categorized the unique walk of Amanda Newton, the high school's librarian. Bo thought she walked with an authoritarian gait that would make the heels on Hans's boots fill the Dogwood gatehouse with crackling thunder. She had been seen without her bra at a Bell fund raiser. But that had been only once, an accident bordering on molestation. That lone episode took place in the eighteenth green sand bunker. She had screamed and cursed at his brother-in-law and Scats Brown telling them both in a dignified manner, "May both you perverted animals take the primrose path to the everlasting bon-fire." Her suggested guided tour was followed by her failed attempt to neuter Quintin Bell, her knee bouncing off the Mayor's quick reflexes and catching John

Brown instead.  The lawyer hit the sand like John Wayne in "The Sands of Iwo Jima" wondering who had circumcised him with the shattered end of a tequila bottle.  Amanda was last seen walking barefoot back to town.  Her walk was a painful, bleeding limp the result of her having stepped on a shard of glass from the Mayor's snifter that had been dropped as part of his reflex reaction to her knee.  The snifter broke on a rake head lying at the edge of the bunker, the rake head having been discarded earlier by Alice Nell Puffin who had found it too clumsy, although curiously erotic, for game playing.  That night, Amanda Newton's walk would have received a single, polite click of Hans's heels.

Bo's profile of walks also listed the pastor's wife.  She had more than a wiggle in her walk.  His recorded analysis showed that Pastor Puffin's wife had become somewhat enamored with the belly dancer who had been hired that night.  He remembered the belly dancer storming out of the party in mid gyration after the shaft of a croquet mallet invaded her veils.  She was last seen splashing in the eighteenth green water hazard putting out a fire that was clawing up her veils.  Her walk and accompanying sprint to fire prevention was more of a hop skip and jump; her belly, dancer's athletic prowess and agility combining for a gait that would have puzzled Hoyle.

Arvia interrupted Bo's analysis.  His choir boy innocence returned when he saw the questioning look on his sister's face as she stood at the French doors.  He gave a guilty, sickly smile back.  As Arvia returned to looking out the doors, his hand crept back into the open lock box.  His heart rate picked up again as his fingers came in contact with something else.  Stretching out his fingers and pressing down he slowly slid out his new find.  A quick glance revealed several Polaroid photographs.  His sister's image returned but he couldn't help himself.  He had to have a closer look at the photographs.  Sweat popped out on his upper lip above his narrow, tilted mustache as he studied the top picture. A grinning Quintin Bell was standing next to a woman who was wearing the same hole-in-the cups bra. She smiled seductively at the camera. It was Alice Nell Puffin and, for whatever reason, she was wearing a green G-string with a white tassel hanging down. If the Polaroid picture had sound, it would've delivered Alice Nell's message of, "Ho-ho-ho," at least that's what Bo thought the message was judging from the oval shape of her lips.

Bo's right hand did a shuffle of the pictures. He was sweating like the lone time he had snuck into Quintin's private steam room one night as he took an unauthorized break from cleaning up at a Country Club party. That night he had drained the half empty glasses he had collected by drinking the contents of each. Then, enjoying his newfound state of inebriation, he admitted himself into the Pro Shop and made his way to the steam room. Switch on and fully clothed, he entered the cedar lined room, sat down and promptly fell asleep. When he awoke with a start he felt like he had just climbed out of Dogwood's pool which he was never allowed to use, but snuck in late at night when Quintin wasn't around. Back outside, his clothing soaked, he returned to doing his cleaning job. The debauchery phase of the party had wound down into spilled drinks, powdered sugar and smudges of chocolate icing on chins courtesy of the sweet table and couples staggering toward the parking lot. No one had missed him.

Bo studied each Polaroid pose. His grinning brother-in-law adding creativity to each picture with the changing position of his head in relationship to Alice Nell's anatomical parts and a different leer flashing back at whoever took the pictures. For whatever perverted reasons, Quintin Bell preferred the old Polaroid camera over modern digital technology and Bo was glad he did. When Polaroid film was on its way to joining the dinosaur, Quintin bought up every box he could in Illinois and surrounding Indiana, Michigan, Wisconsin, Iowa, Minnesota and even Ohio, Kentucky and Tennessee.  Bo took one last curious look and slid the pictures back into the box, gently closed the lid, eased the desk drawer shut and cast a sympathetic look at his sister.  There were more items in the box and Bo planned a return trip to the private study for a more thorough investigation.

Bo leaned back in the high back leather chair again feeling like a newly anointed mogul.  "Sister, dearest," he said, breaking her tranquil spell.  "How would you like a cup of tea? I hear it's good for what ails you."  Before his sister could answer, he pushed back on the reclining leather chair.  The choir boy innocence evaporated as the brass caster wheels slid forward and Berthold, Bo, Bo the Schmoe, Pepperwall found himself falling backwards, his head hitting the floor and the heels of his shoes ending up on the edge of the antique Japanese writing desk.

"Bo," said Arvia, alarmed at hearing the crash and a moan coming from the soles of her brother's shoes.  "Are you alright?"

"I'm fine," stated Bo from his prone position as he tried to act as if nothing had happened.  He jumped up from the floor and hit his noggin on the corner of the antique desk.  "Your husband should've invested your money in a chair that didn't tip over," he said, rubbing the start of a goose egg, his right index finger still inserted through the hole of the black bra.  "He had enough damned money."

"Bo," said Arvia, a polite reprimand in hear voice.  "You know I hate the use of vulgar language."

Bo sighed.

"Didn't you learn your lesson yesterday in Attorney Brown's office?"

Bo sighed again and shook the bra from his finger, the intimate lingerie item falling to the floor under the desk.  He seemed to turn into a frightened kitten with the thought his sister might have seen the bra. "Sorry," he muttered, then quickly adding, "How 'bout that cup of tea?"

"You know I hate tea," she said.

Her reply made Bo feel as if his sister was in the process of drowning the kitten.

"If there was anything ailing me," said Arvia. "I wouldn't want tea to cure it."

Bo shrugged. "Well, you just don't seem like your normal perky self and I thought you might need a little pick-me-upper." He looked down and could see one strap of the bra sticking out from under the desk.

Arvia turned her attention back to looking out the window and saw that Ben had paddled his way under the shade of the dome. "Bo, I'm more than perky," she said, her eyes focused on Ben. "I'm alive. More alive than I've ever been." She paused and then added, "I have an inner peace. I never knew such tranquility existed." She stopped. A combined sound of disgust and thanksgiving came from her. Then she went silent, a pensive look on her face. "It wasn't there while my philandering husband was alive."

Bo bent down, picked up the bra and hit his head on the corner of the desk again. Tears came to his eyes as he stuffed the bra into the left front pocket of his pants causing an obvious bulge. He walked over to his sister and put his arm around her shoulder. "Death affects each of us differently," he said trying to be philosophical as he looked out the French doors and saw Ben on the colorful raft. Both he and the raft were not moving. "I've had different feelings since the accident that night at the country club." He stopped when he saw his sister's questioning look. "Don't take this wrong, Sis," he said, quickly changing the subject, his hand caressing his sister's shoulder. "But, Ben kind of reminds me of Quintin." He was taken aback by the look his sister shot at him.

"He does look more like his father every day," she said,

reflecting.  "I pray to God that he doesn't grow up to act like him."

Bo knew better than to grin, but what he knew and what he did were always, without fail, different.  He let out a chuckle that resembled a cross between clearing his throat and a choke.  "Can you believe that Ben will be graduating from high school this coming year?"

"I know," said Arvia, a melancholy in her voice.  "And then he'll be in college.  And then...."

Bo gave his sister's shoulder a squeeze.  "Don't worry, Sis, I'll always be here for you."

"I know," said Arvia.  "And your coach house room above the garage...."

"You're too kind," said Bo, his plan to move back into the main house, to have his own bedroom with closets, a bathroom complete with walk-in shower and hot tub, being placed on a demeaning hold by his own flesh and blood.  He did not like knowing that his sister was content with his living arrangements.  "But I'd still be here for you and for Ben too. One of these days you and I will be watching him on that air mattress reading the Wall Street Journal and amassing a fortune from his cellular phone.  He'll be another Malcolm Forbes; a Donald Trump or a Warren Buffett or even a Bill Gates.  Heck, he may even become the owner of one of those professional basketball teams.  Those guys have billions."

Arvia reached up and stroked her brother's hand.  "I would hope not," she said.  "Money was all Quintin ever thought about."  She paused and saw the parade of female mourners passing by once again.  Then she scanned the pool area with its cabanas, the heated tennis court and the diving platform. Anger began to bubble up as she looked at the Oriental desk. Then her thoughts shifted to the master bedroom suite.  That room had become a demeaning scene for her husband's trysts, articles of women's under attire having been collected by her.

The bubbles increased into a rapid boil as she remembered the risqué behaviors of some of the town's prim and proper females under her roof at their annual Dogwood Christmas party. There was no Christ in Christmas at those parties. Anything holy was also absent during the other three hundred and sixty four days in her late husband's life.

Arvia's boiling pot began spilling over as she recalled a comment made to her by Alice Nell Puffin. In her honey dripping drawl, Alice Nell pierced Arvia's mind and soul at one of the Dogwood Christmas parties: "Honey, ya'll's husband reminds me of my late grand pappy's bull." Her statement was accompanied by a look of envy and followed by, "I bet he really makes ya'll go, moo."

Arvia slammed the lid on her pot and Alice Nell's words and said to her brother, "Money, dear Berthold, is the root of all evil." She glanced at Bo and then out the French doors. "Quintin was obsessed with money and ruling with an iron hand." She let out a sigh that appeared to have been bottled up since she discovered the first pair of bikini panties under the king size bed in their bedroom. "His iron hand cost him a son," she continued, a sigh following her comment and then joined by: "All he needed to be totally evil was to have a hook for a hand. Just like the one that dreadful captain had in the story mother would read to us when we were children."

Bo reached into his left front pocket, slid his fingers past the bulge of the bra and pulled out his lighter.

CLICK/SNAP!

"I feel bad about Ben, Sis," he said. "But, on the bright side of things, I don't have an obsession with money. I really don't," he said, trying not to sound defensive. "I'm more the respectful type. I appreciate the little things in life. Like in a penny saved is a penny earned." He hated what he just said knowing most times all he had in his pocket besides his good luck charm Zippo lighter and a ball of lint was a penny.

Arvia's finger tips continued to trace the top of her brother's hand on her shoulder, her eyes still on her son in the pool. "I pray Ben doesn't get caught up in any money mania or dreams of fame," she said, her statement sounding like a prayer. "So many of those pitiful people are gone and forgotten; their money vanishing like an auctioneer's words of, Going once, going twice," she said." Arvia sighed. "And pray, dear God, that my son puts behind him that insane desire thathe has to be a rock musician."  She paused and looked seriously at her brother. "Do those people really think they play music?"

"I guess," he said with a shrug.  He looked at his sister and said, "You know, Sis, money's the farthest thing from my mind."  Then, never knowing when to keep his mouth shut, he blurted out, "I just want the best for you, the best for Ben and the best for us."  He paused.  "I worry about you."

"No need to worry, Bo," she said softly.  "I'll do just fine."

CLICK/SNAP!

"I've really been thinking about a great idea for you," he said, his excitement beginning to churn.  "It could make us, I mean, you, rich.  It really could."

"Bo, sweet Bo," she said, making his name sound as if she were back being his big sister trying to comfort her first grade brother the first time he had been called, "Booger Bo" by the other kids at school because both his little fingers were constantly buried in his nostrils.  "I'm already rich.  There's not a material thing I want or need."

Bo's hand slid from his sister's shoulder and he tried not to look astounded.  "I'm not talking about things," he said, feeling his frustrations spilling over and unable to dam them up.  "I'm talking about real live money; lots and lots of cold, hard cash; cash for you, cash for Ben and, of course, a pittance or two for me, if you'll allow me to be your financial analyst and manager."

"Oh, my sweet, sweet Bo," she said, her soothing words to her first grade brother now pouring out sympathy and understanding as she walked away from him heading toward the French doors. She opened the doors, stopped and took a deep breath. Her eyes closed and she folded her arms across her chest as if hugging the day. "Bo, why would anyone want more money when they have this beautiful day?" she asked, pausing, her eyes embracing the manicured grounds. She inhaled deeply and stated, "Money couldn't make my beautiful rose garden anymore beautiful."

CLICK/SNAP! CLICK/SNAP! CLICK/SNAP!

Bo reached in his right hand pocket and pulled it inside out. Then, waving the pocket with the burned out area at her he said, "Here's my beautiful day, Sis. See it?" He waved the tip of the burned hole at her. "Every day of my life is as beautiful as this. How do you like that beauty?" His eyes welled up with tears.

Arvia smiled at him, her head moving ever so slightly from side to side. "You worry too much about the wrong things in life," she said. "Do you know what you need right now?" she asked, not giving him time to answer. "What you need is a long ride so you can enjoy this beautiful day." She nodded in the direction of the garage and said matter-of-factly: "Take Quintin's Corvette for a jaunt. You always liked it." She stepped out through the French doors, looked back and smiled lovingly at her brother. "And, Bo, be sure you fill it up with gas."

Bo watched his sister turn and walk toward the pool. "But, my idea," he muttered softly, pleading. "It's custom made for you. I bet John Brown would like it. It reeks of money. I could call him, invite him over, we could talk. Scats has a case of the hots for you." He could feel his insides melt away as he watched his sister walk toward the swimming pool. "You'd really like my idea!" he shouted after her. "You really would." He began to follow her feeling like a stray puppy. "I know you'll like it."

She didn't hear him.

Then Bo turned on himself for trying to use John Brown to influence his sister.  "She hates that jerk," he said to the empty den.  "I hate that jerk," he continued as he squeezed his Zippo. "I hate him enough to make me a rich man."

CLICK/SNAP!

* * * * *

Her son was the only thing on Arvia's mind as she neared the edge of the pool.  She waved at Ben trying to get his attention and called out.  "Ben, honey, don't you think you'd better come in out of the sun before you get burned?"  She paused and called out again.  "I don't want you getting skin cancer."

Bo, the stray puppy, followed his sister to the edge of the pool deck.  He stood like the statue of General Pepperwall in the village square, feeling the warmth of a new coating of fresh bird droppings covering his head and shoulders. "But, Sis, it's a great idea," he said to himself.  Then without warning and surprising even himself, he lost his temper.  "Damn you," he muttered.  Every muscle in his body grew tight and his world turned the color of his eyes.  The next thing he knew his scratched Zippo cigarette lighter sailed over the pool and skipped across the all-weather surface of the domed tennis court.  "Dammit, Sis, don't be so stupid!"  Then, realizing what he had done, he ran towards the tennis courts.  "My good luck charm," he muttered.  "Shit!"

* * * * *

Arvia sat at an ornate metal patio table at the edge of the pool reading the latest issue of *House Beautiful*.  She looked up and saw her brother walking quickly down the slightly curving flag stone path toward the pool.  He was carrying a paper grocery bag.  "Did you enjoy your ride in the Corvette?" she asked.

"You might say that," he said, placing the bag on the table.

"I see you bought yourself a little something," she said, giving her open magazine a subtle point at the bag sitting on the table.

"Actually, dear sister," said Bo opening the bag, "I bought you a little something." He reached in the bag, pulled out a white oblong package and, with a clumsy nonchalance, opened it, spilling half the contents on the table and said, almost boasting, "And, a bit of sustenance for my nephew and yours truly."

Arvia's nose crinkled as she observed the foot long hot dog sandwich coated with mustard, green pickle relish, diced onions, wedges of tomato, a cucumber spear, hot sport peppers and a liberal sprinkling of celery salt. Her brother had spilled half the condiments on the table top; a grease stained bag of French fries nestled up against the sandwich. "And what is this supposed to stimulate?" she asked, the crinkle turning into borderline disgust, "An advertisement for by-pass surgery?"

"The hot dogs are for me and Ben," he said, his never-say-die excitement at full tilt as he separated three more unopened packages from the bag. "Hot dogs are good for what ails a person. They're American. They're patriotic. They're part of capitalism and making money."

"Bo, darling," she said politely, "an avocado salad and a glass of Perrier would be divine. Besides, there's nothing ailing me."

"Exactly, dear sister," Bo said, as his hand disappeared inside the bag reappearing in a moment with a white plastic knife and fork, a handful of brown paper napkins and a square Styrofoam container. Acting like a waiter, he placed the container in front of her. "An avocado salad for madam," he said, a dignified air accompanying his serving, "Compliments of Berthold Pepperwall, loving, thoughtful, brother." He reached into the bag again. "And, direct from France, a glass, oops, sorry, a designer Styrofoam cup of your favorite beverage, with a lemon wedge." He set the cup in front of Arvia. "Bottoms up, Sis," he said, minus all signs of dignity. "No belching allowed." A smile formed as he reached in his left pocket, the bulge gone, and the bra hidden safely in the bottom drawer of his dresser where he put it on the way to the garage. He pulled out his lighter and rubbed it against the side of his pants. "I hope you don't mind, but I put this on your account at the deli."

* * * * *

Arvia, Ben and Bo sat around the scalloped, metal table with a matching aqua marine umbrella shading them from a hotter than normal noon day sun. Arvia wore a pair of jeweled Gucci sunglasses while Bo squinted, his black eyes no bigger than tarnished, corroded B-B's. She gently rested her plastic fork along the edge of the plastic container and dabbed at the corners of her mouth with a brown paper napkin. "Will you two please show some resemblance of manners by chewing your food, "she said, annoyed at the eating habits of her son and brother. "Did you two ever hear of the word, masticating?" she asked. "That means you use your teeth to chew your food before swallowing." She sighed. "Schickle and Gruber in the gatehouse have more manners than you two."

A pair of muffled grunts met her initial question and subsequent comments.

Arvia reached over to where Ben was seated next to her and removed his ear phones with two yanks. "Manners, Benoni," she said sternly. "Please slow down. No one's going to steal your sandwich." A look of disgust followed the word, sandwich.

Ben glanced at his uncle and said, "Yeah, sure, Mom." He wiped some mustard and a glob of relish caked between his fingers on a pool towel he had around his neck. He plugged the ear pieces to his head phones back into his ears. "Hey, Uncle Bo, do you want that last hot dog?"

Bo hesitated.

Ben's hand shot out and, before either his mother or uncle could blink, a large portion of the hot dog vanished into his mouth, a tomato wedge and some diced onion falling to the table. Without taking time to chew, the fingers of his other hand pinched his spilled food and funneled it into his mouth.

* * * * *

Arvia and Bo relaxed on two chaise lounge chairs by the side of the pool watching Ben float on his mattress. The remains of their lunch, crammed into the brown paper grocery bag placed in the middle of the table, jutted out, a small fly darting around the paper.

CLICK/SNAP!

"Sis, have you thought about what you're going to do with your life?" Bo asked, weighing each word of his question. "I mean, you can't just sit in this house forever."

"But, Bo," said Arvia, peering at her brother over the tops of her sun glasses. "You know I love this house. I'm content here. And, besides, our ancestors built this beautiful edifice. Dogwood is who I am. It's Pepperwall."

Bo slowly reached under his lounge chair and partially opened a package that was identical to the ones that contained the lunch he had brought home. "I'm still hungry," he said defending his tactic. "And besides, Ben would have taken this one too if I hadn't hidden it from him. The kid eats like those vultures who attended Quintin's parties."

Arvia removed her sun glasses and gave her brother a look of disapproval. "Do not equate Benoni with the likes of those parasites who attached themselves to his father."

Bo gave a sheepish shrug then took a large bite of his hot dog sandwich that puffed out the sides of his cheeks while mustard, relish and a wad of chopped onions spilled into his lap. He tried to talk.

Arvia slowly raised her right hand and crinkled her nose. "Manners, Berthold," she said. "Did you ever ask yourself why you were never invited to attend any of the social functions that were held in this house?"

Bo swallowed, his neck sticking out as if half the hot dog went down whole and sideways. He gave another attempt at swallowing, put the remainder of the hot dog in his lap and got mustard on his pants, the mustard adding to the collection of stains he acquired since the last time he washed them. Bo's eyes began to water and grew wider than they did in John Brown's office at the Will reading. He coughed and then gasped momentarily for air. "Sis, you need more than being content in this house," he said, his sales pitch refueled by the hot dog. "That's boring, he continued. "You need a project. You need some excitement in your life." He gasped again.

"I have excitement," said Arvia, her sun glasses back in place as she rested the back of her head on the lounge chair cushion. "I have Ben. I have you. And I have this beautiful day. That's all the excitement I need."

"Heck, Sis, I know I'm not exciting," Bo stammered. "But I have an idea that will put some real excitement into your life," he said, then licking a blob of mustard off his thumb. And, I'm talking real excitement. That's excitement with a capital 'E'."

"Bo, I have no desire to take tennis or golf lessons," replied Arvia, sounding bored with the conversation. "Those things don't interest me. If I want exercise, I have this beautiful pool for swimming." She nodded toward the mansion. "I have a completely furnished gymnasium with every workout machine ever designed." She let out a sigh. "I hate knitting and sewing and, if I want to dabble in painting, I'll take the commuter train to downtown Chicago and spend a relaxing afternoon at the Art Institute admiring the masters."

Bo's stomach was tying and untying knots so fast he thought he was a participant in a Boy Scout Jamboree contest. He coughed without covering his mouth, part of his hot dog spraying out, the taste of stomach acid burning his throat. "Look, Sis, you can't sit around in this big old barn of a house all day doing nothing. You'll go batty. Quintin isn't around anymore. Hell, he never was. Too busy chasing his tramps who wear bras that have holes in them." He wanted to take back his statements about Quintin, to apologize for using the word, Hell, but knew there was no way. "Oh, you know what I mean."

"I know exactly what you mean, Bo," said Arvia, her words like the warmth of the sun. "You don't have to apologize for Quintin's indiscretions. At least you told me to my face. My friends never did."

"Oh, those weren't indiscretions," continued Bo, unable to keep from sticking his foot in his mouth along with another bite of hot dog. "Those were..."

"I know what they were," said Arvia, uncharacteristically interrupting him. "Just as I know about the contents in that metal box in Quintin's desk drawer that you found so intriguing."

Bo's normal bleached complexion burst into flames. "I don't know what metal bra you're talking about."

"Bo, you don't have to protect me," said Arvia, her words filled with sunny warmth.

Bo thought his cheeks were going to melt from the heat. He lifted the hot dog sandwich that had been sitting in his lap creating a new stain pattern on his pants and jammed it into his mouth.

"Dear, sweet, Bo," said Arvia as she paused while reaching for a tube of sun screen alongside her lounge chair. "Perhaps you're right. Maybe I do need something to keep me busy. What has that impossible brain of yours created for me?"

Bo couldn't believe what he just heard. He also had a hard time believing that he couldn't breathe while feeling undigested chunks of hot dogs and greasy French fries smothered in catsup fighting to see who could lead the charge out of his stomach.  A muffled choke came from him along with a partially chewed slice of tomato.  He pointed at his mouth trying to get his sister's attention, a gag coming out.  Waving his hands and arms frantically, he let out a sound that resembled a clogged toilet after one too many flushes.  Suddenly, he toppled off the lounge chair his head hitting the side of Arvia's lounge chair.

Arvia bolted upright and looked at her brother lying on his back on the pool deck his black eyes rolled back in his head, his hands groping at his throat.  "Bo," she said alarmed looking at her brother appear to strangle himself.  "Oh, my, God" she said as she stepped to the edge of the pool and shouted, "Ben!"  Her hands and arms waved in a very lady like manner as she repeated his name, "Ben, help!"

Ben looked up from his mattress, waved back to his mother, adjusted his headphones, turned up the volume and put his head back down.

Arvia looked bewildered at her son and then at her brother who had struggled to his hands and knees.

Bo gasped and wheezed, color creeping into his cheeks, his eyes watery.  "Oh, God," he moaned.

"Are you going to be okay?" asked Arvia, her adrenalin level returning to only slightly above normal.  She saw her brother nod.  "Good," she said softly.  She bent down and said, "Now you'll listen to me the next time I talk about manners and chewing food."  Her head did a sympathetic move from side to side.  "Heavens, for a minute I thought you were having a heart attack."

"Heart attack," repeated Bo out of breath and feeling queasy.  "Nah, the ticker's fine."  He tried to catch his breath by inhaling deeply several times.

"Are you sure?" asked Arvia still holding onto her brother's arm.  "Should I call nine-one-one?"

"No need," said Bo, his answer no more than a wisp of

breath. "If I had been choking to death or having a heart attack, I'd have been dead by the time they got here," he said with a sarcastic grunt. "Especially if you had told the paramedics it was me." He looked at his sister. "Did you say you'd really like to hear my idea for you?"

She nodded in the affirmative. "Of course," she said still showing concern, but wanting to reprimand him. "Ideas don't cost anything." She placed her hand on her brother's shoulder and asked, "Are you sure you're okay?"

"I am now," said Bo standing up, placing his hands on his hips and taking a giant inhale. He smiled, exhaled and then threw up down the front of his shirt and pants splattering the new pair of shoes that he had taken from his brother-in-law's closet. He swallowed, made an ugly face, picked up the last of his hot dog sandwich lying next to the puddle of vomit on the pool deck, placed the last of the sandwich in his mouth and swallowed. "Do you really want to hear about my idea I have for you?" he asked his sister while the toe of his right shoe tried to slide his regurgitated food under the patio table.

* * * * *

After Bo had sloshed back to his room above the garage and cleaned up, he returned to the pool area where his sister was sitting under the patio umbrella. He was wearing one of Quintin's bathing trunks, a red, white and blue stripped model complete with a circle of thirteen white stars around the front and back. He had intended to clean up the mess he thought he made, but discovered that Hans had been summoned from the gate house and had the pool deck immaculate when he returned. Schickle and Gruber appeared more than content.

CLICK/SNAP.

Bo looked at his sister, apologized for his accident and reassured her he would now chew his food before swallowing. "Did you say you wanted to hear about the idea I had for you?"

he asked again, his heart beating so hard its outline pushed out from his chest like a vibrating war drum of one of his sister's ancestors.

"I did," she said nonchalantly.

"There's something else, Sis," he said, the staccato beat of his words rushing out.

"More ideas of yours that don't cost anything?" she asked, her question more of a tease than interest.

"It's the Mayor's office," he said, his black eyes almost circling like twin pinwheels. "You're in line to fill Quintin's seat as mayor."

"I know," she said. "General Pepperwall wrote that law to keep power in the family."

"I didn't know that," said Bo. "I only heard this mayor succession thing when John Brown mentioned it in his office."

"I don't pay much attention to what John Brown has to say," said Arvia looking at her brother over the top rim of her sunglasses. "Never have."

"You should," said Bo. "John Brown and many of the others in town, I've heard, want you to be mayor."

"Dear, Bo, I heard the rumors," said Arvia, seriously joining interest. "Do you know why they want me as mayor?"

CLICK/SNAP!

"They think that because I'm a woman, that they'll be able to control me, to get what they want," she said. "They feared Quintin."

There was a look on her face Bo had never seen, and he never heard her sound so serious. Suddenly, Bo realized his sister was Quintin and he got scared. "You don't believe the town fathers would take advantage of you, do you?"

"I do," she said coolly. "But they won't."

CLICK/SNAP!

"They're forgetting that I'm a Pepperwall."

# Chapter 7

## <u>Sam, Heckle and Jeckle</u>

## ("Pecker" Peccarino and Undercover Cops)

Bo, his eyes looking like two burned out charcoal briquettes, squinted at the glistening majesty of the Pearly Gates. "Let me in I hear music," he sang softly knowing St. Peter would be waiting behind those gilded, sparkling doors. The stubby, calloused fingers of St. Peter's right hand crushed Bo's as he greeted him with a handshake, his saintly words stating: "Berthold, now you see what happens when you think beautiful thoughts."

Bo's feeling of rapture dissipated like the fine silken clouds outlining a halo around the Pearly Gates. He felt as if he were being stabbed in the right cheek of his rear end. He opened his eyes and saw the cracked, dirt smudged cob web laced ceiling of his room and knew that an errant bed spring had been the culprit and not an errant spike used in crucifixions or Captain Hook's hook.

What Bo Pepperwall once dreamed in his wildest of creative dreams on his lumpy, sagging mattress was about to happen. His enemies, critics, those who passed judgment on him, even those from his childhood who taunted and teased him, now lay prostrate at his new, highly polished, designer calfskin shoes. Gone were his scuffed wing tips with the warn heels, slips of cardboard covering a hole in each sole from the inside, knotted and mismatched laces barely doing their job.  He could see a panorama of pleading faces dwarfed by his shadow looking up, begging forgiveness.  His right arm pointed to Heaven, the index finger extended as if poking a hole into a pure white, puffy, cumulus cloud above him.  His left arm and index finger pointed at the worshipers sprawled at his feet and he said, sympathy and sarcasm coating his words: "Oh, ye of little faith."  He added a sad shake of his head saying, "Bo the Schmoe indeed."

* * * * *

Shock ripped into Arvia like a spring tornado tearing through the southwest suburbs heading for a taste of Chicago's skyline.  As despicable a human being John Brown was to Arvia, that didn't prevent her from clutching at his arm for protection.  Ben stood next to his mother and the attorney gaping. Then he uttered to his mother, "Gee, Mom, is this place cool and rockin' or what?"

Arvia had no reply to her son.  She wanted cool, but in the form of air conditioning and a tall frosted glass of iced Perrier, a lemon wedge smiling up at her.  The only rocking she felt came from trembling knees.  "Dear, Berthold," she managed to say, unsure of whether or not to let go of John Brown's arm, jump in her Mercedes and speed off to safety.  "Whatever possessed you to endanger our lives by bringing us to this....?"  She paused, gave her free wrist a slight flick to cover the general area and finished with, "slum."

"Slum," repeated Bo, still picturing himself in front of the Pearly Gates.  "This is no slum, Sis."  His hand made a sweeping motion over the crumpled black top where they stood.  "This is urban renewal.  This is gentrification.  This is your golden goose crapping fourteen karat golden eggs, sunny side up."

Arvia wasn't listening.  John Brown listened, but was

thinking about how he could turn this apparent fiasco in his favor to finally capture his elusive treasure, Arvia Bell.

Ben's eyes were wider than the yolks of his uncle's perceived golden eggs. "Cool, Uncle Bo," he said, shuffling like a rock star being interviewed, hand gestures, their meanings known only to him, punctuating his limited excited statements with, "Like, wow, man," before adding, "Totally epic."

Bo, oblivious to the blistering Indian summer sun, surveyed his new world that dwarfed Neverland about which his mother once read to him. He was staring at King Solomon's Mines, the Hanging Gardens of Babylon and the gates to Fort Knox. They now belonged to Berthold Pepperwall. His name was on the deed. In his good pocket, the one without the hole, nestled the key to a rusted padlock. The padlock fastened a chain securing a corroded, bent and disfigured accordion gate in front of the entrance. His lottery balls were falling into place, each of his numbers smiling back at him, their painted lips puckered, each ball singing, changing one word to their song, his altered version, *"Give me a buck to build a dream on and my imagination will build upon that buck."*

The trio of eyes, one pair in disbelief, another scared stiff and the third, Ben's, embracing what was perceived as, "out of sight awesome," scanned the littered parking lot. Discarded, battered and rusted household appliances, their original functions barely discernible, were strewn about like cemetery headstones courtesy of marauding vandals. Piles of rubble and tiny mountains of broken concrete dotted the crumbled black top that once was a parking lot; an abandoned railroad spur, the rails flush with the pavement, ran down the center of the lot.

"Wow," muttered Ben, sounding like a small child with a sand pail in one hand and a shovel in the other on seeing a Chicago beach for the first time. All Arvia and John Brown could do was stare and silently question the rusted hulks of several stripped, abandoned cars, their makes and models obliterated. "This is beyond epic," blurted out Ben.  "Man, the art teacher at school would love to get his hands on those junk cars for a sculpturing project he told us about."

The questioning eyes weren't thinking about art.  They wondered how they could escape the jungle of junk punctuated with a variety of grotesque weeds, some taller than they were.

Bo never heard about mad dogs and Englishmen as he kept enumerating the benefits his sister could derive from his idea. "Sis, this is an incredible architectural gem," he said, his arms waving like a butterfly on designer amphetamines ricocheting off the glass walls at the Garfield Park Conservatory.  "This cornucopia looming in front of us," he said then beginning to stumble on his words.  He reiterated about his golden goose, this version having a gaggle crapping his golden eggs.  "Those golden eggs have my name on them," he stammered.  Then he caught himself, apologized and continued.  "I mean, your name, Sis.  Those fourteen karat, sunny side up eggs are exclusively yours.  You'll be famous."

All Arvia saw was a decrepit, abandoned factory building appearing to have been erected just after the O'Leary cow leveled Chicago.  She swore the building was making eerie faces at her as she tried to gain control of her knees.  Her feet shuffled in place, but her stomach sent her an alert that a horde of poor people, evil people, certainly people minus all manners and the social graces were about to swarm down upon them.  She let go of John Brown and wrapped her arms around her son.  "Benoni, I think it's time to go."

"Go," repeated her son.  "Mom, we just got here."  He looked at his mother almost pleading and said, "How can we go?  We haven't even been inside that dungeon looking building.  I wanna see if any vampires live there, maybe some zombies."

"How can we go," muttered a sweating and disgusted John Brown.  "Young man, that's easy," he said.  "You just start walking toward your mother's car."  He took a glance at Arvia and silently said, "Lady, you owe me an all-time romp in the hay for today."  He stepped toward Arvia and Ben.  "Your mother is right, Ben," he said, issuing his legal directive.  "It's time to go."

Ben felt his mother tug on his shoulders, but he kept moving toward the factory's front entrance, repeating: "Come on, Mom," he pleaded.  "Just one teeny look inside and I promise I'll go.  Honest.  That place is looking so cool."

"Cool it is, Benny Boy," said Bo, a feeling of euphoria having taken him over.

Arvia and John Brown still couldn't believe that Bo spent Arvia's money buying an abandoned steel making foundry and warehouse, the building erected about the time America discovered The Great Depression.

John Brown glared at Bo.  "Are you for real?" he asked, his head going slowly from side-to-side.  "Do you have a brain in your head, Schmoe?"  He wanted to grab Bo by his stained, long sleeved white shirt, the buttons missing from the cuffs, and shake him. "Tell me, when do Bonnie and Clyde come speeding around the corner of that building with Tommy Guns blazing?"

"Stop being a pompous, ignorant ass," Bo shot back, catching Ben, Arvia and, especially the lawyer, off guard.  "Your body's not going to be converted into a Monty Python character searching for the Holy Grail."  Bo looked at his hands and blinked.  Fists looked up at him. "Vincent Price, Bella Lugosi, the Mummy, Lady Ga-Ga  and the Creature from the Humboldt Park Lagoon won't be charging out of that architectural treasure," he said, a defiance in his voice that startled his sister and landed a second blow to a totally surprised lawyer.  "They wouldn't lower themselves for the likes of you, Scats."

"Whoa," muttered John Brown.

Bo glanced down and still saw fists.

"Oh my," muttered a shocked Arvia.

"Awesome," said Ben, unable to hide his grin.

Bo couldn't believe he had just talked to John Brown the way he did.  He felt great.  Almost as great as when his sister had said to him the day he threw up all over himself at the pool: "Bo, if you feel your idea will provide me with an emotional and recreational outlet, I'll advance you the necessary funds."  She had paused, gave him a look that caused a mountain of goose bumps and added:  "Of course, I'll have to charge you interest."

It had been so simple.  No questions asked.  Bo had formulated an elaborate presentation filled with the benefits his sister could garner.  He had done more than research.  His brilliant mind plugged in data, calculated percentages and studied societal trends while applying the concepts of probability and chance.  He started out his plan by informing his sister:  "I can get this prime piece of Chicago near north real estate for a song.  Trust me."

She did.

Arvia never heard the rest of her brother's presentation after she had said the magic words—necessary funds.  There was no need for Bo to elaborate on his idea to resurrect a 1960's discotheque complete with go-go dancers.  That part and the rest of his presentation ended up sitting on the worn, chipped dresser in his room above the garage.  "Why bother?" he had said to his picture of Malcolm Forbes.  "I got the money."

Bo had paid the delinquent property taxes, a handful of city, county and state fees and walked out of the County Building the owner of a decayed building with an array of broken windows, most caused by rocks, some by stray bullets.  He didn't care about the layers of graffiti and that his future discotheque was surrounded by mountains of garbage and urban squalor.  He was on his way.

Arvia's trust in her brother now turned into fear for her life and that of her son.  She looked at her brother and didn't want to see what she was seeing.  There stood an ecstatic Berthold Pepperwall fawning over what was to be her great escape from tedium.  Instead, it was her brother's dream.  Where she saw rusted metal window frames that hadn't seen glass since the combined terms of three U.S. Presidents held office before she and her brother reached the age of reason, he saw spotlights and neon signs flashing in the Chicago night.  Arvia saw spray paint scrawls; the artistic meanings known only to the index fingers that held down the buttons of the aerosol cans.  Bo envisioned the factory's entire exterior and interior painted with the theme of his business venture, his spinning brain applying colors and décor to his visions of reality. "Isn't this a gem of a place," said Bo, the rapid clicks of his lighter shouting out his excitement like a telegraph operator's key.

Arvia heard her brother, but she's wasn't listening.  She couldn't listen.  Her attention was riveted on a scene that made no sense to her.  A man wearing a heavy winter parka and a black ski mask covering his face, walked along the sidewalk across from where they were standing.  "What's that strange man doing?" she asked John Brown.  "I can't believe what he's wearing in this heat."

The lawyer wasn't listening.  He had Ben by one arm and Arvia by the other.  "Time to go," he repeated, applying a slight pressure on their arms.  "His mind was whirling, "Time to go and get you between the sheets," he thought, unable to stop looking at Arvia while almost drooling.

Arvia didn't budge, her inner voice kept sending out a warning:  "Ski mask plus Indian Summer equal Trouble."  Trouble came in the next second as she watched the masked parka stop alongside a shiny, new BMW convertible, the top up, parked directly across the street from them at the curb in front of a housing project.  Arvia watched the masked parka remove a metal bar from under the parka.  In a flash, the BMW's passenger side door popped open, the masked parka was inside joined by the car's alarm system screaming out to anyone within a mile radius.  The masked parka disappeared from Arvia's sight for a moment and then she heard the car's engine hum into action.  The masked head popped up followed by a screech of spinning tires trying to grip the cement pavement.  The fading sound of the car's alarm offered the only evidence that a high priced, shiny new silver colored convertible had once been parked on the street.  "My, God, John" she said, her words starting and ending with a gasp.  "Did you see that?"

"I'm sorry, Arvia," said John Brown, the noise of the screeching tires and the alarm making him more tense.  "See what?"

"That masked person...," said Arvia, almost unable to talk and pointing in the direction the car had sped away.

"You've gotten too much sun, Arvia," said John Brown, his attention shifting from the high rise public housing project across the street back to the factory's exterior and then to where Arvia was now pointing at an empty street.  "I don't see the Lone Ranger.  Maybe you should get into the shade."

"I'm not talking about the Lone Ranger, you idiot," she snapped.  "I'm talking about someone wearing a mask and stealing a car."

"Oh, shit," said John Brown, looking quickly in both directions.  "That's where I parked my Beamer."  He let out an angry groan.  "I knew I should've taken a damned cab," he muttered as he looked at Arvia's Mercedes parked within an arm's length of them outlined by rubble and brown weeds. "Oh, shit.  Some bastard stole my car."

"Please don't use vulgar language in my presence," Arvia snapped back.  "You sound worse than my brother with his description of golden eggs and my late husband's depictions of the female anatomy."

"Oh, relax, Miss Frigidaire" said John Brown, the anger and

frustration of knowing his car had been taken from under his nose snuffing out his lust. He knew it was impossible to retrieve his crack about his late friend's wife. Quintin had described Arvia Pepperwall Bell on too many occasions, most fueled by multiple shots of tequila, that she lacked the pepper part of her name. According to Quintin Bell, "Sex with my wife is like drinking tequila on-the-rocks with no tequila and no rocks."

"Both of you relax," said Bo, before Arvia could retaliate.

"Relax" replied Arvia, her voice uncharacteristically harsh. "How can I relax when I'm standing in the middle of a ghetto? My, God, we could all be shot."

"You're not going to get shot," said Bo, still full of enthusiasm. "Just listen to the rest of my idea and..."

A car backfired and Arvia, Ben, John Brown and Bo ducked down and threw up their hands and arms to cover their heads.

"And what about my car?" asked John Brown, peeking out from under his right arm pit.

"Stop worrying," said Bo, his aggressive tone to John Brown still in force as he peeked out from under his arm pit. His peeking brought into view a rattle trap, four door sedan belching blue smoke pulling up across the street and parking. The car's passenger side front tire had bounded up on the curb. Its rear end angled out on the street blocking one lane of traffic. Before the blue smoke had time to evaporate, a hooker resembling a cross between a pit bull with blond tresses and an obese Lena Queen of the Jungle wobbled over to the driver's side window on a pair of six inch heels with four inch platforms of clear plastic. The pit bull held a commanding edge over Lena and her two piece revealing outfit barely covered her discretions and several rolls of flab in leopard print.

The hooker caught John Brown's attention. "My god," he muttered. "She's got goldfish in each of the platforms."

"Goldfish," repeated Bo in a shout. "I'm not planning a pet shop here."

"Okay, okay," said John, not taking his eyes off the hooker. "Whatever," he muttered. "The way I see it, Schmoe your planning days are over."

"Butt out, Scats," snapped Bo.

John Brown wasn't interested in what Bo said. He watched the woman lean her head inside the car and talk to the driver. The entire time her oversized backside wiggled her inventory in more directions than calibrated on an average compass. After a few seconds, she removed her head from the driver's side of the car, walked around to the passenger door, got in the car and slid out of sight. Suddenly, a noise sounding like a gun shot came from the car. Arvia, Ben, John Brown and Bo ducked back down as a black smoke ring billowed from the car's dangling exhaust pipe. The bald tires of the rattle trap had no problem bettering the squeals made by John Brown's BMW that had just been stolen. A choking trail of grayish blue smoke hung in the sticky hot air as the car sped away, no sign of the woman in the car.

"Dearest, Berthold," said Arvia mildly. Then she startled her son, John Brown and her brother by shouting, "Did your Mensa brain boil away in this godforsaken heat and humidity?" Her mild voice returned and she asked, "What is this awful place?"

"Your project, Sis," stated Bo, his excitement back, roaring like a bon-fire. "It's your key to perpetual perkiness and the start of your new life." He couldn't contain himself. "Feast your eyes on the U.S. Treasury."

Arvia's right arm swung around, her hand accidentally slapping John Brown across the face. She didn't apologize and gestured toward the factory building. "This is your idea for my new life?" she asked Bo, her growing ire now attracting the attention of the people watching from the housing project across the street. "I was perfectly content with starting a new life without Quintin," she said. "Then you started all of this drivel about making my life more exciting." She pointed at the decaying building. "What happened to the exciting life you painted for me that afternoon by the pool?" she asked, her stare failing to jolt her brother's confidence. "What happened to Michigan Avenue?" she asked. "Where are the *Mag* Mile and the Gold Coast? I don't see that trendy boutique on Rush Street I could dabble in when I wanted. I don't see Rush Street period."

"Relax, Sis," said Bo, the inner flames of his excitement reaching up to touch the sprawling mountain of cumulonimbus clouds overhead. "Can't you picture this lot filled with Jags and Mercedes, Caddy's and BMW's? Valet parking only. Twenty or maybe thirty bucks a car."

"And my car if I ever get it back," said John Brown, his head almost twisting a full three hundred and sixty degrees as he looked for the police.

"I can't believe your idea was to bring me into a slum so I could stand sweltering in the middle of a refuse pile," said Arvia, her hands and arms now waving as if she had joined Bo's drug stimulated butterfly. "I'm sure the Native Americans who stood here several centuries ago never envisioned this repulsive rape of their land."

"Sis, my idea was to get you to be your own person. Make a name for yourself. Make us, I mean, you rich."

"How am I going to make a name for myself?" she asked, pointing at another scantily clad woman standing on the corner doing a bump and grind routine at the passing cars. "My goodness," Arvia managed to mutter. "She's almost naked."

Heads turned to witness what appeared to be another hooker, this one wearing pasties, a rhinestone thong and a pair of stiletto heels that looked like they came from the same shoe store where the other hooker shopped. A bell hung from each pasty. Arvia's hands quickly went over her son's eyes. "I'm definitely going to make a name for myself surrounded by the likes of that," she said, pulling Ben closer to her.  "A name that will make me the laughing stock of Glen Forest and a one term mayor if I'm not escorted out of office in shackles before that."

A CTA bus came to a reluctant stop and the hooker got on. Moments later she exited from the rear door laughing as she held out what looked like a man's toupee.  As the bus pulled away, she could be seen rubbing the toupee across her crotch with her left hand and waving at someone on the bus with the other.

"Disgusting," said Arvia to her brother, failing to see John Brown's grin.  "Does this look like Boul Mich to you?"

"It will, Sis," said Bo.  "Trust me.  My idea will make The Loop look like one of those cookie cutter drab suburban strip shopping malls by the time I get through."  He paused and cleared his throat.  "I mean by the time you get through with my idea, Sis, Chicago Magazine will name you entrepreneur of the year for what you'll bring to the City of Chicago.  Heck, for the whole world."

John Brown, a faint smile still on his lips, watched the hooker disappear into the housing project entrance.  He had no idea, but Bo did, that the hooker was an undercover cop. "Arvia," he said seriously, "I think your brother's idea will work for you."  He paused, looked at Bo and continued.  "In twenty or thirty years and once the dust settles from the atomic attack. Personally, I..."

Two taggers appearing to be no older than eighth graders startled them as they sprinted out from behind the factory building and began to spray graffiti on what appeared to be the last bare spot on the building's concrete wall.

"...think you're out of...."

"No I'm not," Bo shot back defiantly, startling the others, especially John Brown.  His index finger was inches from John Brown's nose.  "Look.  One year's rent on the Gold Coast for some little bitty shop is what it would cost to turn this building into a trendy cash cow." He faced his sister. "Sis, you and Susan B. Anthony are soon going to be the best of friends."

"Gee, Uncle Bo," said Ben, pulling out the ear plugs to his head phones and watching the taggers put the finishing touches to their whirlwind creation of swirls and geometry gone awry. "Do you think that paint will help keep the building from falling down?"

Bo watched the taggers disappear around the corner of the building. "Benny Boy," he said to his nephew, pointing at the factory, "do you know what I plan to do with that falling down building?"

Ben shrugged and readjusted his head phones.

"Well, Mr. Future Fortune 500 member," said Bo, taking a step to Ben and carefully removing his head phones, "I'll tell you exactly what I plan to do with this falling down building." He looked at Arvia and John Brown who were having a hard time watching and listening to the new, assertive, confident Berthold Pepperwall. "Tell me, Nephew," Bo continued. "Have you ever heard of the words, Go-Go?" He placed his hands on his hips and glared at Ben. "Well, have you?"

"I have," said John Brown, reaching out to take Arvia by the hand as he continued, "As in go-go, going, going, gone. Come on, Arvia let's get out of here before the sniper fire starts again. I hope you'll get me to a safe area so I can get a cab back to my office and call the police about my car."

"None of you are going anywhere," said Bo, a firmness in his voice that held the others attention. "Don't go jumping to any conclusions, conclusions that could keep you from making a ton of money."

John Brown gave a sneer, but gently let go of Arvia's hand.

"And stop worrying about your car," said Bo, nodding towards the high rise housing project across the street. "I've gotten to know the cops in this area and they'll have your car back pronto."

"Yeah, right," said John Brown, reaching for Arvia's hand again.  "I'll get it back and it'll look worse than those abandoned heaps sitting on this gem of yours."

"Did you see that hooker get in the car before?"

"So?" snapped the attorney.

"An undercover cop," Bo snapped back.  "I know what you were thinking when you saw her disappear.  She was squatting under the dash calling in the theft.  That was her partner driving that unmarked car.  His name is Pecker."  He turned away and said, "For a lawyer you sure lack street smarts."

"After seeing all of this I have all the smarts I need," said John Brown, his defiant, arrogant demeanor returning in full force.  "Quintin was right about you."

"My arrogant, power-hungry, womanizer brother-in-law never took the time to get to know me," said Bo, his anger being directed at another human being instead of his reflection in his bedroom mirror.  "How could he?  Always too busy giving orders to everybody.  He was always ordering Arvia like she was the hired help.  That monster almost crushed the life out of his son not to mention what he did to me.  And, yes, Mister Brown, he played you like a Stradivarius and you were supposed to be his friend.  Do you know what you really were, Scats?"

"Time to, pardon the expression, scat," John Brown said to Arvia, yanking on her hand.

Arvia yanked back.

"Mr. Brown, all you were was another pair of hands to hold the camera for your so-called friend's photo sessions," said Bo, then catching himself, the words, croquet mallet lodged in his throat.

"You're out of your mind," replied the attorney, still involved with trying to get Arvia to leave.  "What photo sessions?"

Arvia's hands were on her hips.  If her glare at John Brown

consisted of daggers, ten thousand rays of sunlight would have blazed through his body.

"At least listen to my idea," said Bo assertively, his bold, new demeanor continuing to flabbergast the others as well as himself. "Sis, you told me to exhibit manners. Well, you can at least give me the common courtesy to listen to what I'm trying to do for you and you alone."

John Brown, avoiding Arvia's skull and cross bones blazing eyes, pointed at the factory building. "I thought LSD went out with some nut job by the name of Timothy Leary," he said. "Obviously not," he continued glancing at Ben. "I think you should escort your mother to her car."

Before any of them moved, two unmarked police cars screeched into the far end of the parking lot where four adults, two males and two females were involved in what appeared to be a shouting match gone awry. A handgun and switch blade knife flashed into view. Four car doors exploded open and an equal number of undercover cops, guns drawn, ordered the four adults down on the hot pavement, spread eagled and face down. One police officer held his gun on the adults while two others handcuffed the group and confiscated to small brown paper bags. The fourth police officer walked over to John Brown, Arvia, Ben and Bo.

"Oh, God," said Arvia in a frightened whisper, we're going to jail."

"Cool," replied Ben, removing his head phones and stuffing them into his pocket. We're going to be busted by the Pigs."

"They can't arrest us," said John Brown, slipping into his attorney demeanor.

They're not here to bust us," said Bo, giving a wave to the approaching undercover cop that consisted of his right index finger going into a quick crook and then straightening out from its position by his side. Bo gave a subtle nod. "Hey, man."

The undercover cop nodded back stopping in front of the

four.  He gave a quick glance, his eyes settling on John Brown. "You the owner of the Beamer rag top?"

"You found my car?" asked John Brown sheepishly.

"Two blocks up the street," the undercover cop said, his baseball cap setting on his head at an awkward angle, the bill almost pointing to the side.  He pointed in the direction of where John Brown's BMW was found.  "Car's fine except for a scratch or two where the jimmy bar entered and exited and, oh, yeah, you'll need a new ignition switch.  Nanook of the North in his parka disguise did a number on that."  The undercover cop glanced over to his partners about the time a Paddy Wagon pulled up on the lot.  'If you want, we can give you a ride to your car and you can start the paperwork to press charges against the perp."

John Brown glanced at Arvia.  "Thank you, officer, but I can get a ride to my car," he said, hopefully.  "I'm an attorney and I'll pursue the necessary details to assist you in being sure the thief gets his just reward."  He paused, "What station are you assigned?"

"Chicago Avenue," replied the cop.  "Ask for Pecker; short for Peccarino.  Here's my card."

John Brown took the card, glanced at it and put it in the pocket of his white dress shirt, the collar unbuttoned and his tie pulled down.  "Thank you, Detective Peccarino."

The cop gave a quick nod and looked at Bo.  "How's your project comin', man?"  He took off his baseball cap and ran his fingers through his thin dark brown hair, his fingers accomplishing the same thing as a comb minus most of its teeth.

"Everything's cool, man," said Bo, with an equal quick nod. "My sister here," he said glancing at Arvia, "likes my idea."

Officer Peccarino looked at Arvia, his brown eyes seeming to dance with glee.  "Your brother has set you up with a can't lose idea, Lady," he said, giving another glance at the building. "Glad you like what your brother's got up his sleeve.  You're sitting on a genuine gold mine. A bunch of us at the station are providing security in return for a piece of the action." He put his forefinger to the bill of his baseball cap, "Nice to meet you," he said, turned and walked back to assist his partners with loading the four adults into the Paddy Wagon.

"Pecker's a great guy," said Bo to the others who seemed to be in a trance.

"You're doing business with the police?" asked Arvia, puzzled. "What kind of business?"

"More like monkey business," said John Brown, reaching for Arvia's hand again. "May I have a ride to my car?"

"Wait a second," said Bo, now totally annoyed with John Brown. "This isn't about monkeys, simians, rhesus or whatever. It's not about your car, Scats, and it's not about you." His black eyes had turned red. "Remember Whiskey A-Go-Go? That was right here in Chicago; nineteen fifty eight, just north and east of here on Rush Street."

John Brown shook his head in disgust. "Sure I remember," he said, his arrogant sneer beginning to come out of hiding. "On second thought, I'm not sure. I think I was just out of diapers at the time." His sneer grew. "And do you know what happened to it, Bo? It became, like I said before, a-gone-gone. Just like..." He nodded to Arvia and Ben. "...the three of us."

Arvia reached for her son's hand and pulled Ben closer to her. "I think Mr. Brown is right, Ben," she said, her words covered in caution. She gave a discrete glance toward the housing project where a man decked out in a lime green, double breasted pin striped suit, matching dress shirt and shiny tie sat behind the leopard skin covered steering wheel of an old purple Cadillac convertible, it's tail fins as big as Ben and decorated in flashing, yellow, bulbs shaped in what appeared to be a phallic symbol. "Besides, that man is staring at me."

"Uncle Bo, are you talking about old time dancing?" asked Ben, acting as if he didn't hear a word his mother said. "Like I see on cable TV, reruns of...."

"I'm not talking about Arthur Murray," said Bo, trying not to let his impatience take over.

"Who's Arthur Murray?" asked Ben innocently. "I never saw him dancing with those girls in the white boots, the ones who jump around in those short skirts and their hair never moves."

"You saw that on TV?" asked Bo, his impatience shoved aside by an emerging grin.

"Yeah," said Ben, his body beginning to move into a series of gyrations that sent a series of chills racing up and down his mother's spine. "They do all kinds of wild dances. The kids at school dig them." His dance moves came to a halt when he saw John Brown's annoyed look, a look on par with the one's he used to get from his father. "Kind of cool if you ask me."

CLICK/SNAP.

"I think it's time we leave this awful place," said Arvia, taking her son by his hand.

"Leave," Bo blurted out. "Didn't you hear a word your son said?"

"I heard and I saw," said Arvia, her nose in a crinkle. "I can't believe you'd think I'd get involved in something like...."

"A Go-Go club, Sis," said Bo, interrupting. "As in retro disco, dear sister; listen to your son. Go 'head, Benny Boy, enlighten your mother."

"Ben, it's time we...." She stopped and stared across the street. "Oh, my God," she muttered, as a teenage boy wearing a trench coat stopped by a bicycle chained to a No Parking sign. The boy quickly removed a bolt cutters from under the overcoat, cut the lock and peddled away on the bicycle before any of them could blink.

"Oh, my God, John did you see that?"

"See what, Arvia?" asked John Brown, showing a curiosity to Ben's dance moves and his explanation. "I hope you didn't see the Lone Ranger again."

"Oh, my God," said Arvia, wrapping her arms around her son with a protective hug.

"Chill out, Mom," said Ben, weaseling out of his mother's arms. "The dance shows are neat. Disco I think it's called and I really dig the way those girls move and never smile. Sometimes it looks like they wear long t-shirts instead of short skirts."

"They only wear t-shirts?" John Brown asked, his interest growing. "Are they wet t-shirts?"

"John," screamed Arvia! "Tender ears are present."

"Those aren't t-shirts, Benny Boy," said Bo, the palms of his hands rubbing frantically against his Zippo cigarette lighter. "Those were the first mini-skirts back then; mini-skirts and white boots in a changing time of the sixties, a time folk singers used to ask about where all the flowers had gone."

"And, that's exactly what we're going to do," said the attorney. "We're gone from this garbage dump."

CLICK/SNAP.

"Well, they look like t-shirts that are too long," said Ben, trying to free his right hand from his mother's vice-like grip. "I mean the girls I see on MTV and the Playboy Channel, man, they don't wear anything."

"Benoni Bell," said Arvia!

"Ah, Mom, take a chill pill," said Ben, freeing his hand from his mother's. "Most of the girl's at school wear less than that." He paused, thinking, then said: "Hullabaloo, Uncle Bo. That's the name of the show on cable, Hullabaloo. And those go-go dancers, they do the Frug, and the Mashed Potato, the Stroll and the Watusi. Most of the kids at school think it's awesome."

"See," Bo said to his sister and John Brown, a look of don't-tell-me-I-don't-know-what-I'm-talking-about flashing back at them. "Did you hear that? Did you hear the magic word; the money word?" His look went from flashing to sparks flying. "Awesome. The word is awesome. What more do you need?"

"A Go-Go Club?" asked John Brown, not knowing what else

to say.  "Am I hearing you right?  You're going to turn this property into a Discotheque?"  He looked at Arvia.  "Mrs. Bell," he said, addressing her with a formality he saved for his clients. "Cut him off.  Don't give this lunatic another penny.  Don't even give him the time of day."  He glared at Bo and shook his head. "When's the last time you saw girls wearing white boots?"

"Excuse me, Mr. Brown," said Ben, politely interrupting. "The girls in our high school marching band honor guard wear them.  So do the girls in the flag corps.  They get cheered and whistled at a lot at the football games.  And, that's by the parents and spectators."

"Benoni Bell," scolded Arvia.  "You should be...."

"Gee, Mom, they do," said Ben.  "Wouldn't you whistle at girls wearing white go-go boots, Mr. Brown?"

"John Brown, shame on you," said Arvia, noticing the look in his eyes.

"Well, if I recall," said John Brown, a smugness in his voice, "didn't the wife of a friend of mine once wear a pair of white boots to the Country Club's Halloween Masquerade Ball way back when?" asked.  "Seems to me I heard a number of whistles that night," he said his smile more of a leer.

"That was a social function totally void of manners and appropriate behavior," said Arvia, indignant.  "The entire evening was filled with bad taste depicting a time in our history of exceptional bad taste, a time that I'd just as soon forget," she said, her indignance growing.  "If it hadn't been for charity, I would've never attended dressed the way I was dressed.  Go-Go boots," she muttered, "How silly."

John Brown wasn't annoyed.  He remembered the costume party and how he had cornered an intoxicated Arvia Bell in the Club's cloakroom and stole what almost amounted to more than a single kiss.  He also remembered being interrupted by a sweating and panting Quintin Bell dragging a giggling Linda Ann Finn, the Police chief's wife, into the same cloakroom.

Sobriety quickly returned to John Brown but not to Mrs. Arvia Bell. He had held his breath and watched as the Mayor sent coats, cloaks and capes flying everywhere. John Brown had Arvia by the hand dragging her out of the cloakroom door without being noticed and not hearing the Mayor telling Linda Ann, after laying the Police Chief's wife down on the service table, about what she could buy with the pay raise he was considering giving her husband for his service to the community.

"Not silly, Sis," said Bo, correcting his sister who didn't take being corrected lightly. "Awesome, trendy, a fad, as in a money making fad," he said, his words coming in rapid fire. "Today's in-crowd is a generation on a nostalgia kick. They've heard about the Sixties and now they want to experience it firsthand. Trust me. I know. Retro is the new in word."

"You want me to spend my money on a Go-Go Club," said Arvia in disbelief. "You want me to become a common saloon keeper?"

"Not exactly, said Bo, his confidence still at a hundred percent. You and your trendy new, awesome club won't be common."

"Is there a difference between nostalgic bad taste and any other type of bad taste?" she asked, arms folded across her chest. A warning sign to anyone she disagreed with.

CLICK/SNAP.

"That's exactly it, Sis," said Bo, seeing his opening. "Nostalgia, but with class; class like you have and your patrons will have the same kind of class. No one but the best will be admitted; the best as in the upper crust of society. Your place will be exclusive. You'll be one of the most famous entertainment providers in all of Chicago. The Pepperwall name will be linked to the Palmers, McCormicks, Burnhams, Fields and that chewing gum magnet." He paused and threw out his arms. "Heck, Sis, the Pepperwall name will stand alongside of the founding fathers of this great country of ours."

Bo paused, beaming. "Sis, forget being famous in Chicago, he said. His hands turned into raised fists thrust as far above him as his arms would allow and he shouted, "Today Chicago; tomorrow the world!"

John Brown gave a pleading nod to Arvia indicating they should leave. "I still have to retrieve my car," he said, sounding almost meek.

Bo ignored him. "Sis, your discotheque will have dancing, a live rock band complete with pyrotechnics, flashing strobe lights and a hi-tech sound system that will make your customers' ears bleed. You'll have a five star restaurant with a line of chefs waiting to grace your kitchen. If you wanted a trendy shop, I'm giving you a trendy shop in the form of a boutique. All the latest fashions for sale; and with your name on them. Your exclusive logo," he continued beaming. "And, now don't go getting Puritan on me, there will be dancing girls in cages, wearing you-know-what, and there will be other girls in special costumes, attached by wires, soaring across the ceiling, and then we'll have a hair salon, maybe a computerized dating service, and, can you believe, even a Starbuck's."

"Berthold," said Arvia concerned. "And you were worried about me going batty?"

"Sounds totally excellent to me," said Ben.

"See that, Sis," said Bo quickly. "That's totally excellent as in awesome, as in other classy people who will think it's awesome; as in those classy, awesome people spending cold hard cash to be one up on their friends. It'll be more than nostalgia. It'll be daddy-o, groovy, the bee's knees, the snake's hips and hubba-hubba coming back from the dead and wilder than the roaring twenties and the Great Gatsby. Oh, man, Sis you'll not only be the Mayor of Glen Forest on the Watercourse, but a trend setter. You'll be rich beyond your wildest dreams. You'll be beyond cool."

CLICK/SNAP!

"Do I look cool to you, Mr. Brown?" asked Arvia. "Cool at my age? Me, the mayor and a trend setter being referred to as awesome?" She shook her head ever so slightly. "I don't think so, dear brother."

Bo stepped in between John Brown and his sister. "You can look however you want with all of the money you're going to make, Sis," he said. "Before you know it you'll be hob-knobbing with Donald Trump. I can see a President of the United States stopping in. Secret Service agents everywhere as the President and the First Lady do the Watusi."

Before Bo could muster up a single, nondescript, spastic dance step, the quartet of heads turned at once. Four different coats of fear covered their faces; reflexes ignited and they scampered for safety barely avoiding being hit by a large, rusted dump truck that had bounded up over the curb in a series of jolting crashes and headed straight for them. The truck driver, no apparent desire for slowing down visible on his face, accelerated the truck leaving them standing in a cloud of dust and diesel exhaust fumes. Before fear could switch to bewilderment, brakes screeched and squealed and the truck skidded on broken asphalt and gravel before coming to a crunching stop. A battered tailgate banged open and the loaded bed began to tilt. Tons of broken concrete laced with twisted strands of reinforcement bar slid down the truck bed with a roar crashing to the ground in a giant, dusty mound. A nervous looking driver with no more than six strands of hair pasted to his sweaty head, six gaudy gold chains around his neck and a huge wad of chewing tobacco jutting from his cheek, looked nervously out the truck's open window. He quickly cranked the window shut as a warm breeze forced a cloud of cement dust around the truck's cab obliterating the driver from their view before engulfing them, burning their eyes and searing their throats.

John Brown spit out a blob of dust and shook his head in

disbelief.  "I'm assuming, Mr. Schmoe," he said with a sarcastic cough, "that this project you concocted for your sister will include hiring that same truck driver to haul away the rubble he just dumped on your go-go soon to be gone-gone venture?"

"It's not my venture," said Bo, sputtering and coughing as this knuckles gouged at his stinging eyes.  "It's Arvia's.  I'm merely the guy who sees to it that the details are handled.  I'm the guy who will do all the dirty work so my dear sister can be in the glow of the spotlight.  My dear sister has earned the right to garner all the glory a Pepperwall decedent deserves and, above all, reap all of the profits."  He paused for a moment before adding, "Especially after what my late brother-in-law put her through."  He leered at the attorney.  "Of course, he didn't put her through it alone.  You were there helping, you and your skills with an old Polaroid camera."

John Brown's look had one message:  "Bo, you're a dead man."

The look didn't deter Bo.  "And you, Mr. Brown, as an attorney-at-law should know that I'll be protecting my good sister's political future and reputation by keeping her name off the deed."  He paused and looked left and right and then back to John Brown.  "Politicians can't own bars in Chicago or in Glen Forest," he continued with a smile. "This here schmoe checked that out all by his lonesome self."  He increased his smile for affect.  "That's why my name will be on the deed." His smile broadened.  "Now is that awesome or is that awesome?"

"Dirty details about sum up what I'm seeing," said John Brown, spitting again on the pavement.  'Oh, yes, do add filth, squalor and decay," he glanced across the street, "and that includes human as well as physical decay."  He looked at Ben. "Young man, I think you should escort your mother to the car."

Bo's right hand shot out as if he were a clone of Hans at the Dogwood Estate main gate stopping an unidentified vehicle.

"None of you are going anywhere until you see the inside of the building and hear the details of my plans for my sister's grand and glorious new and soon-to-be famous life," said Bo, his voice exceeding authoritative and dictatorial, scaring them all, even himself. "Now, follow me." Like the three blind mice expecting carving knifes in the forms of stiletto switch blades, the three followed Bo until they were standing in front of a twisted iron accordion gate that hadn't seen a coat of paint since before President Roosevelt declared war on Japan. Bo wrestled with a large, corroded lock trying to force in the key while fighting a too long unruly chain that seemed to possess serpent like qualities as it coiled around his wrist and arm.

"This structure of yours, Berthold, does not appear to be safe," said Arvia, tucked behind her brother's shoulder. "I think..."

"Oh, don't be such a scaredy cat..."

They nearly jumped out of their collective skins as a section of sheet metal fell from the roof and landed just to the side of them with a clanging, dusty crash. "Of course it's safe," said Bo, taking a glance up. "Like my astute, intelligent nephew said, 'it's awesome'."

* * * * *

Arvia, Ben and John Brown stood behind Bo wedged in the rusted front entrance, the scarred, open door sporting the last vestige of a grey paint barely clinging to life. They stared, mouths wide open, barely breathing and not saying a word. Their combined brains tried to formulate a sentence describing their reactions to what their unbelieving eyes saw. The cavernous foundry cast eerie shadows, giant ghoulish silhouettes of discarded machinery and a jagged mountain range of abandoned equipment once used to create shapes and forms cast of steel. The steel shapes and forms were no more leaving tragic signs of a once healthy business succumbing to a slow, agonizing death by economic and sociologic strangulation. Floors, walls and ceilings that once gave birth to metal castings sending them from the molten to the wooden crated proud final product, now resembled the set of a Frankenstein horror movie. Debris was scattered from wall-to-wall.

Bo stood in the middle of the factory, his voice several octaves above what causes glass to break, and talked to the others who were still wedged in the door. "And that's where my flying girls will zoom down over the dance floor," he said, pointing at a moveable hoist suspended from a steel monorail seventy five plus feet above the floor running the length of the buildings skylight minus most of its panes. "Visualize it," he said, his right hand and index finger tracing the imaginary course of the hoist as it traveled through the route of his mind. "Bosomy beauties wearing sequined costumes leaving nothing to the imagination will soar above the crowds. They'll wear glittering masks, and their sensuous bodies will make giant, curvaceous arcs from one end of the club to the other." He stopped, glanced at his nephew and asked, "Ben, what's greater than awesome?"

Just how revealing are these costumes?" asked John Brown. He winced, glanced at Arvia wondering why her elbow had rammed into his rib cage. "I was only asking to see if your dimwit brother had taken into consideration the fact that the City of Chicago might also have legislation pertaining to decency. I'm only thinking of you and your reputation, Arvia. You're the new mayor of Glen Forest."

Ben, apparently more excited than his uncle and intrigued by the remains of the abandoned equipment, eased away from his mother and John Brown. His curiosity led him behind an old fork lift truck, and he disappeared into a cavern of chipped wooden pallets stacked eight feet high, some of the stacks leaning at precarious angles.

Bo still pointed, his excited voice echoing throughout the factory. "And over there will be our bar. We'll serve drinks in giant glasses. Of course, the bottoms of the glasses will be thicker than the platform heels my friend, the undercover cop, was wearing. We'll pack them with crushed ice and the customers will think they're getting a bargain when they watch our bartenders pour straight from the bottle." He stopped, smacked his wet lips and grinned. "No shot glasses here," he continued. "No siree. The booze hounds will think they're getting a triple. Ha, crushed ice makes singles appear to be triples." His eyes had lost their red cast and looked like a pair of giant, shiny pearls. "How much do you think a glass of ice costs, Scats?" The pearls glowed. "How much, Mr. Attorney?" he asked. His mouth clamped shut, lips sucked in, then, almost shouting, he said, "Ice don't cost a thing; not a farthing; nary a red cent; nothing! Does it look like I'm squandering away my sister's money?"

Arvia and John Brown still stood and stared. Then Arvia said to her brother: "Ice doesn't cost a thing, Berthold. Then she politely added to her correction quietly stating: "Not don't."

Ben, now completely out of sight, continued to explore the dilapidated machinery, crates, barrels, and piles of scrap metal. "Gee, look at all this neat junk," he said.

"Junk?" repeated Bo, hearing Ben's remark coming from behind the wall of pallets. "Young man," he shouted to the teetering stacks of piled wood, "those are artifacts of a past generation. Those are relics of decades in turmoil, priceless gems. Those will be music to our ears. You know music, Benny Boy, you're a musician. You strum whatever that thing is you strum. You make music. That junk, as you call it, will be part of our music, our retro scene and our bringing back memories. It will be our way of telling our customers that we know where all the flowers have gone." Bo imitated his nephew strumming his imaginary electric bass as he began to hum the song's melody. His humming stopped abruptly and he said, "Some of this junk, Benny Boy will be part of our decor.  Those priceless gems you're so fascinated by will make up this here discotheque's theme, its name will make all of us famous and rich beyond what my buddy, Malcolm Forbes, could ever fathom."

CLICK/SNAP!

"Sounds epic to me, Uncle Bo," Ben's voice stated drifting over his concealed location.

John Brown and Arvia had inched their way close to Bo until they were almost crouched down behind him.  "And how much is this epic theme, more like a scheme, going to cost?" asked John Brown.  His question was draped in caution, a caution learned from the time he and Quintin had attempted to force the high school's librarian, Amanda Newton into playing their version of Nude Croquet in the Country Club's eighteenth green's sand bunker.  John Brown never forgot the game that never was.  Amanda Newton had slammed the head of the croquet mallet she had wrestled from the Pastor's wife into the attorneys groin; a striped wooden ball preceding the mallet's head.

"That's theme, not scheme, Mr. Brown," said Bo politely, but still projecting that he was in command.  "And that theme won't cost my sister one extra red cent.  Everything I need is right here.  Free.  I even have the graffiti blaster's truck from the Mayor's office coming tomorrow to clean the building.  That's a freebie.  And, the day after that, I have some high school kids taking a shop course at the Joseph Kennedy Magnet High School for Overachievers coming here on a field trip with their teacher to replace all the broken windows.  The teacher just happened to mention he likes cognac.  I've got a friend who makes imitation cognac in his basement.  Just like when Scotch was made in sick bay on that cargo ship in *Mr. Roberts*.  My friend will put his concoction into any shaped bottle and glue on any brand label I want.  A whole case we'll cost be no more than twenty five bucks.  Twenty if he's drunk and I haggle with him.  Not a bad price to get all these windows replaced.  One snifter of that rot-gut and that shop teacher will think he's lying on a scaffold doing a stained glass creation in the Sistine Chapel."  He pointed to another area of the factory.  "See that partitioned space over there?  That's where this here factory's office used to be and that's where my sister's trendy boutique will be.  She'll sell T-shirts, sweat shirts, baseball caps, jackets, all knock-off designer copies made in some sweat shop in Bangladesh at low tide and all with her logo on them.  We'll sell mugs, stuffed animals and dolls modeled after my theme flying girls.  Can't you just smell the money coming in from your boutique, Sis?  Oh, dear god, I don't want to forget your personal line of jewelry, the Dogwood Collection."

"Bo," whispered Arvia, still huddled against her brother's back in a slight crouch.  "What I smell is not money.  What is that nauseating aroma?"

"Oh, someone I talked to in the County Building mentioned something about some toxic waste," replied Bo, sloughing off his sister's concern.  "Don't worry.  The North Branch of the Chicago River is right out the back door.  We'll just dump the whole mess in there.  No problem."

"Excuse me, Mr. Pepperwall," said John Brown after clearing his throat.  "Did you ever hear of the EPA?  The mayor of this city has taken great pride in cleaning up the Chicago River.  He wouldn't take too lightly to having someone pollute one of his pet urban projects."

"EPA, DNA, DAR, DOA," stated Bo, not seeming to care.  "Come some dark night, the back door opens up at the loading dock and a bull dozer will push all of that stuff into the river, maybe with a drunken bum or two," he giggled, knowing he had been ridiculed his entire life for  what many saw as his eccentricities.  "Am I gonna tell the Feds?  Not I."  He paused and said: "Ask me if I can tell right from wrong?"  He glanced at John Brown and saw the attorney looking back at him. "Right from wrong," he repeated in an angry whisper.  "Yeah, I know right from wrong and what I'm doing is right."  He paused, tried to exhale away his venom and, without taking his eyes off John Brown's, he pointed to another corner of the factory. "And that's where our restaurant will be, right on the site of the old employee cafeteria.  We'll clean up those old picnic tables, hose down that serving line, polish it up and we'll specialize in comfort foods; things like chili, beef stew, meat loaf, mashed potatoes and gravy.  The mashed potatoes will have real lumps.  And, Sis, do you know your undercover cop investors will also be our waitresses, waiters and bartenders?" He cleared his throat and grinned.  "And, do you know how those waitresses, waiters and bartenders, those officers of the law, will be dressed?"

"Berthold," said Arvia using his formal first name.  "You're using law enforcement personnel to wait tables?"

Bo spun around facing his sister, almost knocking her over. "Of course," he said excited.  "They're part of my theme," he managed to say his grin exploding while his eyes began to puddle up.  They're our antithesis.  The police officers will be pirates.  They'll be dressed in unbuttoned shirts tied at the navel, the waitresses in cut off short shorts.  They'll wear bandannas and one big, brass loop earring.  They'll have tattoos, real or glued on, and wear an eye patch over one eye."  He paused and almost chocked as he said, "All over the right eye." He smiled and asked, "Do you know why?"  He didn't wait for an answer.  "Because the class people you'll be catering to are conservatives and have money.  Right is for right wing. Republicans, get it?"  Then, not knowing why he said what he said, "Right is for doing the right thing."

John Brown and Arvia looked at each other in disbelief.

Bo was far from finished.  "My, I mean, your waitstaffinvestor cops will cut our security costs to nothing, Sis," he said, gasping for a breath of air. "They'll serve our customers while wearing roller blades. That will speed up service. The right people, the classy people love fast, efficient service. They like being waited on hand and foot. Just like Upstairs, Downstairs or Downton Abbey or way down south in Dixie. If we didn't have pirates, we'd have slaves and I'd change the theme to Gone with the Wind. Republicans love slaves."

"Pirates?" asked Arvia cautiously, while trying to once again position herself behind her brother. "I can understand a security detail of police officers but what do pirates have to do with my club?"

CLICK/SNAP!

"How short will the female police officers' short-shorts be?" asked John Brown from a distance just out of the range of Arvia's elbow.

"Short enough to plunder and steal and loot," said Bo, spinning around again to face his sister. "And who steals money besides politicians, Sis?" he asked, without giving her time to answer. "Pirates steal money. "And where do you find pirates who plunder and loot and commit outrageous indecent acts?" Again, he didn't give his sister a chance to answer. "In Peter Pan, Sis," he continued. "That's in Peter Pan as in the story our mother used to read to me." He paused, brushed at his eyes with the knuckles of his index fingers and said, "The way she used to read to us." His tears increased. "A Peter Pan theme will allow us to plunder and loot the pockets of our customers like a ship full of pirates, in good taste, of course. People loved to get fleeced." He grinned at his sister, his tears like a leaking faucet splashing to the concrete floor. "And who makes getting fleeced so much fun?" he asked, his grin managing to get bigger. "A loveable character," he gushed. His mouth closed making it sound like a cap had been inserted over an air leak. "You can't get much more loveable than Tinker

Bell." He gasped for his next breath. "Our Tinker Bell will be part of the French aristocracy." His chest began to swell up. "Sis, congratulations," he said like a proud impresario. "You are now the owner of La Tinkerbelle's a Go-Go."

Arvia could barely mouth the name she just heard. "La Tinkerbelle's a Go-Go?"

* * * * *

Bo looked like a music box ballerina pirouetting and pointing to various areas of the foundry. He stopped and pointed to another corner of the factory. Several quick strides had him standing proudly beside an old roller conveyor system.

CLICK/SNAP!

The palm of his left hand tried to spin the rollers. Half cooperated. "Is this conveyor awesome and cool or is it cool and awesome?" he asked his sister and the attorney. "This unique contraption, along with our pirates in the short shorts, will help us get our drinks, even our bar snacks and appetizers to the customers. Heck, even the meals to the dining room. Our sexy, little pirate waitresses will shout out their orders and the bartenders will put the drinks on a tray and send then down the conveyor. The whole process will be computerized. When you see your first quarter's financial statement you just might experience an orgasm."

"Berthold," hissed Arvia, an accompanying look showing she was not pleased with her brother's language even if Ben was still out of sight somewhere behind the pallets.

"How much?" asked John Brown, a business tone to his question that Bo liked.

"A mere pittance," said Bo, recalling a phrase he thought he read that Malcolm Forbes may have used. "I mean, people will have to pay an admission to get in. Can you imagine people being stupid enough to pay to get into a bar? I can. Then, after several cocktails, when Mother Nature says it's time to relieve themselves of their drinks, they'll have to pay to use the rest rooms.  It'll be just like the old days at the bus station downtown or like some modern airlines are thinking of doing."

"How much?" asked John Brown, showing a growing interest in what he was hearing.  "Talk dollars to me, Mr. Pepperwall.  How much is all of this going to cost before your sister becomes more rich and famous than she already is?"

Bo polished his lighter on the side of his thread bare slacks, a small safety pin keeping his fly closed.  "You sound exactly like Quintin, Mr. Brown," said Bo, visualizing that he was at the helm of the attorney's boat, Ella Scats berthed in the Monroe Street Harbor.  "You're totally like him.  From your love of wine, women and song, if you can call the singing that comes from Chief Finn's wife's mouth singing, to your drunken croquet matches."  He gave a knowing smile to the attorney. "You even used the same mallet when you played each other.  I think that was the same mallet Quintin mentioned in his letter, the same mallet that killed him."

John Brown cast an innocent look in Arvia's direction.

"Mr. Brown," Bo continued.  "Or should I keep on calling you, Scats?"  He didn't give the lawyer a chance to react.  "Do you know that this is the next hottest development area in the city of Chicago?  We're smack dab in the center of a real estate bonanza, surrounded by a booming Lincoln Park, River North, Buck Town and a creeping downtown moving both west and south.  Man, kick out the poor and the street people and bring in the real estate developers, the yuppies and their gentrification mentality.  An army of entrepreneurs looking to make a killing will all but trample the others to get in on the parade.  Just sit back and watch the great white flight to the suburbs reverse itself. La Tinkerbelle's can't miss."

"This all sounds so awfully expensive," said Arvia to her brother.  She looked at John Brown.  "And a bit too risky and risqué to suit me," she said, pausing, then adding:  "And also very troubling.  I just can't envision being responsible for displacing poor people.  Our mother, as tight fisted as she was, always came to aid of the poor, the social outcasts and the downtrodden."

"Just like Peter Pan," said Bo, not missing a beat.  "Pirates were poor, Sis," he said, the enthusiasm in his voice growing once again.  "So was Peter Pan.  Heck, all he owned was that stupid green hat and a handful of golden fairy dust."  He paused, his chest heaving.  "How can you put a price tag on pirates, Sis?" he asked, inching closer to his sister and pointing to the steel rafters above them.  "Picture this.  Six cages will be suspended over the bar with Go-Go girls.  The cages will look like treasure chests and they'll hang from what will look like a pirate ship's rigging.  The girls will be like the one's Ben watches on reruns of Hullabaloo.  Patrons can buy tokens, expensive tokens in the shape of keys and, if they buy the lucky key that fits the lock on a cage, they get a hug from one of the girls, maybe a dance and maybe more."

Arvia's eyes started to narrow.  "More?" she asked.

"More?" repeated John Brown, a twinkle in his eye.

"You know, more like in a kiss," said Bo, totally missing the content of the two inquiries.  "Didn't movie stars once sell kisses to raise money to support some kind of war or some nonsense like that?"  Bo disregarded his comment and kept on explaining.  "No need to fret.  "The keys will never work.  What might work is an idea I have for dancers using brass poles.  I haven't figured that out yet, but I'm getting there."  He pointed in another direction.

CLICK/SNAP!

"But, what does all of that have to do with displacing poor people?" Arvia asked, interrupting her brother's sales pitch.

"The poor people will be fine," said Bo without a care.  "The government will take care of them.  They always do."  Without coming up for air he pointed in another direction.  "The band will be there."   He pointed up again.   "And above us, suspended by wires, will be our special flying Peter Pan pirates swinging above the dance floor in special harnesses, dropping discount coupons on the patrons for specials at the bar or the restaurant or the boutique.  Oh, Sis, you're going to be bigger than Liz Taylor, Jay Lo, Paris Hilton and whatever a Kardashian is combined, even bigger than Elvis and Michael Jackson in their prime."

"Bo," said John Brown in almost a whisper, "the startup cost; how much?"

Bo looked at John Brown as if to say, who cares.  "My economic projections indicate that the money we take in from the coin operated movies in the washroom stalls will wipe out any debt in a few weeks.  Trust me."

"Movies in the restrooms," repeated Arvia, sounding flabbergasted.  "Where did you ever get such a disgusting idea? Who in their right mind would watch a movie in a stall?"

"I got the idea from Hans in the guard house at the front gate," answered Bo.

"Who," asked Arvia?

"You know, Hans, that guy with the two dogs.  He's the one who wears the German uniform and stands guard over Dogwood.  He told me about going to a book store on his afternoon off where they had coin operated movies in private booths," explained Bo.

"What kind of a bookstore would have coin operated movies?" asked Arvia, having no clue.

"That's not important, Sis," said Bo, a look of pleading coming to his face.  "The important thing is do you like my ideas for your new life?"

"Bo," said Arvia, hesitancy in her voice.  "I don't want to be Liz Taylor or whoever those Jay Lo, Paris and Kardashian people are."

During the group's conversation, Ben continued exploring

the foundry.  "Uncle Bo," he said, still hidden by stacks of debris, "you'd better come over here.  I think I've found your toxic waste."

Bo, Arvia and John Brown looked at one another alarmed.

"Toxic waste," John Brown repeated, a concerned tone in his voice making him take several steps back, leaving Arvia with her brother.  "What's the kid talking about?"

"You'd better come quick," Ben hollered!

"Ben," Arvia called back.  "Honey, are you alright?"

"I'm fine," said Ben, his voice sounding as if he were holding his nose.

Bo headed in the direction of Ben's voice with Arvia close behind him.  John Brown was several paces back as they made their way behind the equipment and through the canyon of pallets into a maze of boxes, barrels, and crates.  The moment they saw Ben their nostrils slammed shut.

"Oh, my God," said Arvia grabbing her brother's arm.  "He's surrounded by poison."  She squeezed Bo's arm and pulled him toward Ben, the stench increasing with each step.  "Be careful, Ben," she warned.  "Don't touch anything."

"Listen to your mother, Ben," said John Brown, still several paces behind Arvia and Bo, his football instincts ready to kick in if he had to sprint for the door.

"What the heck is that?" asked Bo, his question coming from behind his left hand that was covering his mouth.

CLICK/SNAP!

Bo looked down and saw a man wrapped in a torn wool blanket lying on a bed of newspapers.  "What the," he said, as he inched forward, his hand still covering his nose and mouth.  "Heck, I mean who are you?"

The man pushed the worn wool blanket down to his waist exposing a tattered red and black checkered lumber jack shirt that looked like it had been on the receiving end of more axe chops than trees.  He picked his head up off the floor, a stream of grey light exposing a dirt smeared face sporting a shaggy, grey beard. The man was in is his forties, but looked sixty. He yawned, exhaled and belched then looked at Bo and then to Arvia and Ben. He stretched again, farted, yawned and stretched some more. He studied each of his visitors and asked: "Whadda you people doing trespassing in my domicile?"

"You're what?" asked Bo, taking a step back.

"My domicile," said the man, farting again. "This is my residence, my home, you imbecile."

Arvia took several steps back, grabbed hold of John Brown and dragged the both of them away from the derelict looking man. "My heavens, John, I think I'm going to be sick."

The man stood up, stretched and yawned again, his torn soiled pants dropping down until a pair of muscular thighs stopped them about the time Arvia's hand was on its way to her mouth. "Hey, Lady, don't you go gettin' sick in my house."

"Your house?" repeated Bo sounding as if he were interrogating a suspect in a stereotypical damp basement of an old Chicago Police Department lock up. He nodded at Arvia. "That lady standing over there just happens to own this place." He forced a tough-guy look that didn't work. "Now, before Mrs. Pepperwall-Bell gets upset, I suggest you take yourself, your stench and your belongings out of here. If you know what's good for you."

The man pulled his pants back up and fastened them with a length of knotted window sash cord. Satisfied with the knot, he walked up to Bo until his bearded face was almost touching Bo's nose. "Look, big shot," he said with a hissing defiance coated with halitosis that could remove the rust and corrosion from the entire foundry. "You don't scare me with your threats."

Bo stepped back without inhaling. "Just get out of here," he said, his words muffled by his hand across his mouth. "And take all your junk with you."

"Oh, and now for something entirely different," said the man as if he had used the phrase dozens of times before. "I'm being thrown out of my own house again by another collection of big shots." He gave a glance to Bo and the others then shook his head and farted. "There's no end to you big shots, is there?"

"Look, I don't have a clue who you are or where you've come from," said Bo, his hand clamped tighter than ever to his mouth and nose. "And, I don't care."

"That's because you're a big shot and big shots don't bother to know the people they steal from," said the man, still unruffled. "You took my business, my building and even my wife."

"Your wife?" repeated Bo, making the mistake of dropping his hand from his mouth. "What wife?" he asked, his hand clamping shut once again over his mouth and nose.

"Yeah, my wife," the man said, his demeanor unchanged. "Actually, she was my second wife. Left me for the same Mr. Big Shot who took my saloon. I guess that's what second wives do." He paused and belched again. Bo and the others stepped back. "But that lyin' cheat got hers in the end. Mr. Big Shot cast her off like a lone, discarded sweaty gym sock," he said. He let out a sarcastic grunt that sounded like a cross between a laugh and a cough. "Then Mr. Big Shot died and left everything to his wife. My two timing, gold digging wife ended up with nothing. Just like me."

"I can see why," John Brown whispered to Arvia.

"I heard that, Mr. Big Shot Number Two," said the man, stepping closer to John Brown and Arvia and stopping when he was almost on top of them.

John Brown and Arvia held their breath and stood petrified, unable to move.

The man stared at John. "Hey, don't I know you?" he asked casually. "Yeah, I know you. You were with that other big shot who took my bar when I was a day late with the money I owed you two guys. Yeah, I know you.  How could I forget?"

"From the color of your eyes, how could you remember anything," said John Brown, his eyes communicating with Arvia's while his hand stayed forced across his mouth.

The man brushed a cockroach off his sleeve then gently gave it a nudge with the right toe of his torn running shoe, the mate a different, size, make and color.  "Very funny, Mr. Big Shot," he said, while being sure that the cockroach was safely out of sight. "I bet all those old poor people you and that other big shot threw out of my building aren't laughing.  All those nice people being evicted from their apartments because it was impossible for them to pay the higher rents you two guys jammed down their throats.  Did it on purpose, didn't you?  Money grubbin' plans for a mini strip mall.  You two didn't care.  You didn't even care about that sweet, young girl, that social worker you two guys ridiculed, the one who worked with all of those sick, crack babies and the old folks living in the apartments above my bar.  Do you think she's laughing?  Do you think they're laughing?  Are those babies giggling and going goo-goo?"

Arvia let go of John Brown's arm, her eyes wide open, and a concerned look barely visible in the grey of the foundry.  "You didn't really do that, did you, John?"

"Of course not, replied John Brown, indignantly.  "Why would I waste my time with someone and something like this?"

"You didn't think I was a nothing something when you took everything I had in the world," the man said.  For the first time his eyes showed a glow of fury.

"Get your belongings and get out of here," ordered John Brown.  "You've got a minute."

"Don't worry, Lady, I'm leaving," said the man.  "You and your big shot friends ain't gonna take anything else from me." He gave a sarcastic laugh.  "Nothing to take, he said then leaning forward until his nose almost brushed John Brown's nose and sneered.  "Not even Heckle and Jeckle."

"You mean there are others living here besides you?" asked Bo, as he tried to get his derailed presentation to his sister back on track.

The man put his two index fingers in his mouth and let out a shrill whistle.  Two black cats cautiously emerged from underneath a wooden pallet.  "Well, guys," the man said lovingly to them, "looks like we're getting kicked out of our palatial digs.  Don't worry, we'll find another place."

The two black cats brushed against Arvia's legs, one on each, and she bent down to pet them.  She looked up at the shaggy looking, foul smelling man.  "Which one is Heckle and which one's Jeckle?"

"What do you care, Lady?"

"I care because I love cats," said Arvia, stroking one then the other under their chins.  "My late husband hated them."

"Nice choice for a life's mate," said the man as he knelt down alongside the two cats opposite of Arvia.  "Jeckle's the gimp with the bad front paw," he continued, giving the cat's paw a gentle massage with his grimy fingers.  "He got stepped on by a druggie when a bust went down across the street.  He's kind of a refined sissy, if you know what I mean.  Very picky about what he eats."  He turned his attention to the other black cat.  "Doesn't stop him from killing rats though," he continued as he stroked the other black cat.  "Now, Heckle here, he won't kill a thing.  But he eats anything dead or alive."

Arvia straightened up.  "Did you say alive?"

"Don't worry, Lady, both guys are cleaner than all of us put together."

Arvia slowly knelt down on both knees and continued to stroke the cats using both hands while talking softly to them in cat lover language.

"Don't you guys go taking a bite out of this lady," said the man as he got up and went back to his makeshift bed.  He rolled up his blanket along with the newspapers and stuffed all of it into a black, plastic garbage bag that was spread out under the newspapers. He set down the garbage bag, walked to another stack of wooden pallets and pulled out a grocery shopping cart that was out of sight behind the pallets, the cart having three good wheels. He pushed the cart, wheels flapping and grinding, back to where the plastic garbage bag rested and carefully secured it to the cart which contained other filled plastic bags. He walked back to Arvia who was still engrossed stroking the two cats that were beyond content. "Sorry, Lady," he said politely. "But you can't have the guys. They come with me." He gave a nod and Heckle and Jeckle gave a last brush to Arvia's knees and were on top of the shopping cart in a blink. The man looked at John Brown. "Yeah, you're the guy. I never forget a face. You're a lawyer, right?

John shrugged.

"Worked for that Bell guy didn't you?"

"Did you say, Bell?" Arvia asked with a gasp.

"Yeah, lady, you know him?"

"Quintin Bell?" asked Arvia cautiously.

"Yeah, that's him," said the man as if he didn't care. "A real big shot, a bigger shot than this double breasted pin-striper here," he continued nodding at John Brown. "The two of them took my saloon, took everything I had. They even violated my wife, if you can call mutual consent violating. The Bell guy promised her everything; so did I once-upon-a-time. That was a big mistake on my part. Never promise a woman anything when you're on the rebound. Material things can never take the place of what matters the most in life." He paused, his eyes beginning to show a trace of sad, and then he gave a shrug.

"What was it that mattered?" Arvia asked, as she stepped to the shopping cart and began petting the two cats.

"Mandy and my little girl, lady," he said, melancholy coating his statement. "I really fucked up," he blurted out then glancing at Arvia. "Sorry, Lady," he said, apologizing. "That's a memory that just won't go away.  Not even in the sanctuary of this here domicile of mine."

"My husband took your business?" asked Arvia, pausing for a moment.  "And the other things you mentioned?"

"I only cared about my saloon and my tenants, lady," the man said, a sad respect coating his words.  "As for the other things, well, they were only things."  He stared at John Brown.  "You had your way with my wife.  She showed me the Polaroid pictures you two perverts took.  Told me about the creative ways you used a croquet mallet."  His head went from side to side.

"Croquet mallet," repeated Bo aloud.

"No offense Lady, but you're better off having a late husband," said the man as he went back to his shopping cart and rechecked to see if his belongings were secured.  "You'd be better off without this sleazy pinstriper as well."  He looked at Arvia.  "Sorry again, Lady, but this guy had better keep his distance from me or I'll rip a board off of one of these here pallets and put it in that part of his anatomy where the sun doesn't shine."

"If you know what's good for you, you'll think twice about threatening me," said John Brown, shifting into full legal mode.

The shaggy, foul smelling man walked to John Brown and got in his face.  He exhaled and said: "I'm really shaking in my Nike cast-offs, Mr. Big Shot."

"But, John," said Arvia.  "I thought you said...."

"Obviously this man's a derelict and doesn't know what he's talking about," said John gruffly, startling Arvia.  He turned his attention back to the man.  "If you know what's good for you, you'll take your belongings and those two flea farms you call cats and leave."

CLICK/SNAP!

"Did you say you owned a saloon?" asked Bo.

"Sure did, the man said with a touch of pride.  "Sam's the Workingman's Saloon.  "Best bar in Chicago.  Not too far from here."

CLICK/SNAP!

"Then you should know something about running a bar, right?"

"Now, Bo, wait just a second," said John Brown.

"What makes for a good saloon; a good bar, a good cocktail lounge?" asked Bo looking at his sister. "What makes those places classy?"

"What difference does it make to you?" asked the man, his hands gripping the handle of his shopping cart.

"All the difference in the world," said Bo, sensing something good was about to happen. "That is, if you want to get back to doing what you do best."

CLICK/SNAP!

"What makes for a classy gin mill?" the man repeated. He didn't waste a second thinking about his answer. "The same things that make for a good dive or the old Top of the Rock in the Prudential Building or the Tip-Top Tap in the old Allerton Hotel," he said sounding as if he had taught Business 101.

"Those things are?" asked Bo.

"Three simple things," said the man. "You don't need magic. You don't need money. Heck, you don't even need to belong to Mensa."

"What three simple things?" asked Bo, his curiosity and excitement rising.

The man looked quizzically at Bo and then at the others. "Why do you want to know?"

"Just curious," said Bo, trying to maintain his businesslike demeanor.

The man glanced at his four visitors then shook his head. "You planning to turn this place into a bar?" he asked Bo, "You and the pinstriper big shot here and this nice lady?"

"Could be," said Bo, trying to keep the lid on his excitement. "And could be I'm looking for the right man to run it. Now what three things make for a good bar?"

The man gave Bo a curious look and shrugged. "First, you need a bartender who listens. Second, you don't pour drinks from any Las Vegas type computerized dispensers." He raised his eye brows. "And, third, you don't allow broads working behind the bar. You can have an army of 'em in front of the bar, but never, never, never behind."

"I beg your pardon, said Arvia, taking a step toward the man and then retreating from the stench.

"Beg all you want, Lady," said the man, not taking his eyes off Arvia. "But broads don't belong behind a bar." He paused, farted, pointed at himself and said: "And this is one guy you ain't never gonna find behind a bar working with some broad."

"Women are every bit as capable as men to be bartenders, said Arvia, knowing she had descended from a long line of saloon keepers.

"You don't drink, do you Lady," stated the man.

"Well," was all Arvia managed to say before the man cut her off.

"Look, Lady," said the man, a matter-of-fact in his tone that took them all by surprise. "Broads don't belong behind a bar because broads don't know why men go to bars. Broads don't know how to listen, they talk too much, they steal more from the till and tip jar than male bartenders and their main interest is in meeting a meal ticket."

"I beg your pardon," said Arvia indignantly.

"Lady, you sure do beg a lot," said the man, a twinkle in his eye that caught Arvia by surprise. "Do you know that men only say twelve thousand words a day while you broads yak twenty five thousand?" He paused. "And that bit of psychological data came from a study before all of this cell phone stuff."

Arvia shook her head. "Oh and where did you hear about such sexist tripe?"

"That's psychology, Lady," said the man, making an

infinitesimal adjustment to his belongings in the shopping cart. "It's fact. Look it up. I did. Read it in a psychology journal I took from a garbage can."

CLICK/SNAP!

"Speaking of facts," said Bo. "I'm assuming that since you called your saloon, Sam's, I suppose that's what your name is."

The man adjusted his belongings on the shopping cart. "Very profound," he said as he looked at Bo for a moment. "Your IQ must be at least in the third standard deviation from the mean. Don't know in what direction, but, yeah, Sam is what my parents called me."

"Nice to know you, Sam," said Bo, extending his hand. "And my IQ just happens to be in the third standard deviation from the mean. With that Mensa group you referred to a moment ago," he said pausing. "Tell me, Sam the bartender, have you ever thought about becoming a pirate?"

Sam stared at Arvia and asked: "Hey, Lady, is this guy related to you?"

# Chapter 8

## <u>Amanda Newton</u>

### (Ben and Matilda)

en cut a diagonal path across the front lawn of the Glen Forest on the Watercourse High School ignoring the, *Keep off the Grass* signs. The manicured lawn looked like an extension of Rip Repeater's labors on the Country Club's fairways. Several hurried strides had Ben sprinting up the school's ten marble steps, each engraved with one of the Commandments. The separation of Church and State had been tailored by one of General Pepperwall's mayoral ancestors to fit the taxpaying wants and needs of the Glen Forest on the Watercourse citizenry. The General, once a Bible thumping, page flapping disciple of the Lord when he wasn't swindling, conniving and fornicating through his political world, would have been proud.

At the top of the vast polished landing Ben grabbed the handle of one of the massive twin brass front doors and pulled. Each door had a life-sized, raised etching of Socrates and Plato on the left and right respectively. The two philosophers glistened in the late morning sun from their daily buffing. Being the first Saturday of the start of school, there were a scattering of students registering, late incoming freshmen and transfer students trying to distance themselves from overly protective parents. Ben approached the library counter where

Amanda Newton was sorting through stacks of periodicals.

Amanda Newton didn't look like a librarian although she tried. She was tall, slender and blest with a figure that had all the right ins and outs in all the right places. Her fashion model's cover girl features were down played by a pile of strawberry blond hair pulled back in a too large bun. At work in the high school's library, she covered herself with a daily change of baggy, colored frocks that ended just below the knees of her slacks. Amanda Newton knew what her alabaster body looked like and that her facial profile had been likened to The Bust of Nefertiti by her former husband. More than one high school male student, especially the juniors and seniors, walked into a wall when the librarian was on duty sans one of her frocks. Small groups formed to watch her stand on tip-toes to replace books on top shelves. Eyes bulged out if Amanda Newton wore a skirt on those rare occasions.

"Hi, Mrs. Newton," said Ben as he bounded up to the counter. "Is Matty around?"

The librarian's alluring deep blue eyes peered at him over the top of her Benjamin Franklin style reading glasses resting on the tip of a perfect nose. She barely acknowledged Ben's presence, her expressive eyes indicating a disapproval of her daughter's nickname. "Matty?" she repeated coldly.

"Matilda," said Ben, not losing his eagerness. "I'm sorry, Mrs. Newton. I forgot."

Amanda Newton nodded and accepted his forgetfulness as a sign of adolescent immaturity and being a product of Mayor Quintin Bell's loins. She didn't correct him, however, for using Mrs. with her name even though she had been divorced since Matilda was four; the divorce dragging on for almost two years. She mistrusted most anything under the masculine gender heading and the titles "Librarian" and "Mrs." offered her protection, she felt, from all living adult males who graced her comprehensive mistrust list that was topped by her ex-husband.

Two names on her list received special treatment, those accented by a red highlighter. The names of Quintin Bell and John Brown were buried under bold crimson smudges. She did not include on her list of the damned the newly born, the prepubescent innocent, Benoni Bell and the school principal, Melvin "Overcoats" White.

Amanda Newton had made two mistakes in her life. Mistake number one, her husband, headed her list. He had violated her trust, took her virginity, defiled the purity of her womb then abandoned her for another. The second mistake encompassed the names of Quintin Bell and John Brown. That mistake took place when her daughter, Matilda was in the agonizing process of going through the *Terrible Twos*, and age that lasted as the *Frustrating Fours* were about to change over into the *Futile Fives*. Amanda was a struggling, single mother who could turn heads. She saw Mayor Quintin Bell's turned head and accompanying overtures towards her during his quarterly inspection of the school's physical plant as more than professional, polite and well meaning. She had heard the rumors about the Candyman; tried to ignore the whispers of his marital infidelities and never gave credence to the demeaning forms of behavior that took place at the Country Club during parties hosted by the Mayor, his wife most times absent. After all, she surmised, he was the town's mayor, a pillar of the community and a gentleman married to a descendant of the town's founder. After the Mayor's inspection, Amanda Newton found work difficult. Mayor Bell's small talk, his large, smiling eyes and boyish grin had seduced her. She tried to shake the tingling embrace. She couldn't. Little did she know that the Candyman had struck again.

Amanda was an educated lady, a Phi Beta Kappa Vassar graduate with New England roots fertilized by old line money; that money looking down arrogant collective noses at the concept of divorce. Divorcees were shunned even though many of the collective noses relished the experience of adulterous conduct with the formerly married. Amanda Newton, ignored by blood to the east and isolated in the Midwest, embraced the protection and anonymity of her transplanted New England roots in Glen Forest on the Watercourse. She was devoted to her daughter and her job. That was her life until Quintin Bell, along with Rodney Pointer, president of the school board and Fire Marshall, Forest Bearren, examined more than the high school's physical plant. "I'd be honored if you'd attend my annual fund raising party at the Country Club next week," Mayor Bell said to her in the privacy of her office, the Board President and Fire Marshall staying out in the hall. There was his coy smile and impish grin as he asked, "Have you ever played croquet?" Before she could reply that she had, many times growing up by vast, well manicured lawns along the eastern seaboard, she heard him say, "Cocktails at six, followed by a buffet at seven. Your name will be on the list." He smiled, winked and finished saying, "Games begin at eight."

Had Amanda Newton known what kinds of games were played at Mayor Quintin Bell's fund raiser, her thrill of being invited by the mayor himself would have been replaced by a plan to flee Glen Forest on the Watercourse in the same manner General Glen Forest Pepperwall fled Georgia. Amanda Newton, like most of the residents of Glen Forest, had heard rumors about the mayor's party games. She did not entertain rumors. Valid, reliable data, she knew, were the only sources of fact. Drunkenness, debauchery and demeaning behavior were the ammunition that kept small minds in small towns firing at tedium. It wasn't so much the invitation to the fund raiser that caught her attention but the way it was presented. She remembered his every words, "Your excellent work, dedication and professionalism have not gone unnoticed. Please join me at my private party."

Amanda Newton had kept a secret since first becoming the

librarian at Glen Forest on the Watercourse High School. She wanted to be a principal. Specifically, she wanted to be the principal of Glen Forest on the Watercourse High School, home of the Slashing Rapiers. Her belief that hard work and dedication, combined with the fact that the current, long time principal, Melvin "Overcoats" White was passed retirement age, would be recognized as the basis of her hoped for promotion. Now, with the Mayor's words of recognition and assuring smile, her confidence exploded.

Amanda Newton didn't know that the Mayor's private party would be attended by several hundred or so of the more affluent citizens of Glen Forest on the Watercourse and well healed contributors to his campaign. Mayor Bell made her feel what she hadn't felt since her wedding night, that of being special. Now she did something she rarely did. Fantasize. Mayor Bell made her feel like she was being anointed as queen of the ball. She would be escorted by a handsome king up a long red carpet leading to a golden throne, her glass slippers gliding along the carpet, the size tens, her only physical imperfection, skimming across the plush, scarlet runner. She quickly learned that a devoted public servant, pillar of the community and married man was fascinated by her size tens; fascinated enough, so that as the evening progressed, Mayor Quintin Bell, Attorney-at-Law John Brown and Pastor Puffin's wife, Alice Nell sipped tequila from them. Mayor Bell savored the right one and Attorney Brown the left while Pastor Puffin's wife made sure that the heels of both were covered with salt and the toes smeared with lime juice, her tongue working overtime.

Amanda Newton's handsome, royal escort had turned into a urinating toad and she felt ashamed that she had let her mind fabricate the outcome of an elegant, social evening. Mayor Quintin Bell and John Brown lacked schooling in the same social graces that she learned growing up in New England. Bar

Harbor, Newport and Hyannis Port were second nature to her and unheard of by the mayor and his attorney accomplice. A croquet mallet, an antique Polaroid camera and Pastor Puffin's wife's sick, erotic orders punctuated with her southern laced giggles were not chapters in Emily Post's bible on etiquette that the librarian had memorized early on in life. The mayor's innocent, confectioner's sweet coaxing quickly turned to not-so-innocent orders, groping hands and a camera's popping flash bulbs that had her fleeing the party.

Cinderella had walked home barefoot that night, her carriage never arriving, never having a chance to turn into a pumpkin. She limped home minus her bra and had no idea of how she ended up without it. Alice Nell Puffin would have been glad to tell her had she only asked. A hot shower, followed by a second hot shower couldn't wash away the filth she knew covered her. The next morning Amanda awoke and went immediately to Matilda, holding her and vowing that no man would ever be allowed to cause her harm. That same morning Amanda Newton asked her Fairy Godmother to grant her one wish. That wish was to protect her daughter, Matilda, from any and all males of the town of Glen Forest on the Watercourse. Protection was all inclusive. Any inappropriate gesture aimed at her daughter, inappropriate included saying such things as, "good morning" and "have a nice day" would be met by a harsh reprimand. Ashamed of waiting too long to prevent a section of pages from being ripped from Emily Post's book, she made a silent vow for revenge. Quintin Bell and John Brown would certainly feel one or both ends of the same croquet mallet that she managed to avoid that infamous night at the Country Club.

Amanda Newton kept her memories of that night many years ago until one morning she awoke from a bad dream nauseous and with a headache. Nausea and the headache turned out to be a massive hangover. The bad dream ended up with a sugar coating.  The morning news had applied the sugar. Quintin Bell was dead; a croquet mallet found alongside the deceased.  The news confirmed what she knew all along.  She had been a witness to the mayor's demise.

* * * * *

Benoni Bell was a rare exception to Amanda Newton's wish to her Fairy Godmother.  "Apology accepted, Benoni", she said, a librarian's businesslike tone greeting him.  "And what brings you to school on a Saturday?"

"When I saw Matilda at my Dad's wake she said that you might need some help.  You know, with the start of school and how crazy it can be around here," he said, his boyish eyes volunteering.  "So, here I am."

"That's very thoughtful of you, Benoni," said the librarian, her guarded trust slowly lowered when it came to her daughter's friend and fellow senior classmate.  "Shouldn't you be at home looking after your mother in this her time of need?"

"Oh, Mom's okay," he said, as if his father's body had never been found on the back lawn of the Country Club.  "Mom's working with my Uncle Bo on starting her own business."

The thought of Berthold Pepperwall helping anyone with anything made the hair on Amanda Newton's arms snap to attention.  "Your uncle," she repeated.

"Yes, Mam," he said, his enthusiasm evident.  "Uncle Bo has this real cool, awesome idea for Mom," he said.

"Awesome and cool," repeated the librarian, sliding her glasses up over her forehead resting them on her hair.  She had never heard the words awesome and cool used in any sentence describing Benoni Bell's uncle.  The hair on her arms stayed rigid.  "I sincerely hope your mother is feeling well enough after the ordeal she's experienced.  Please extend my deepest sympathies to her."

"She's fine," said Ben, pausing and looking quickly around

the library. "Mom doesn't need sympathy. I've never seen her happier." He took another look around the library. "Is Matilda here?"

"Matilda's working in back in the Reference Section," she said, pleased that Ben had continued to use her daughter's Christian name. "You may go back and help her if you'd like."

"That would be cool, Mrs. Newton," he said, his smile on the same level of a choir boy's. He waved and walked behind the counter into the back room but saw no evidence of his girlfriend. He spotted another open door and walked into a small lighted room surrounded by floor to ceiling book shelves. Matilda, her back to him, was kneeling on the wall-to-wall beige carpeting that appeared never to have been walked on, sorting papers into file folders. "Pssst," he said, sneaking up behind her and making her jump.

Matilda turned, gave him a dirty look for scaring her and then broke into a grin. "You really came," she said, straightening her light beige summer skirt that hid her brown and white saddle shoes from sight. "Just the way you promised." She smiled and added, "And, on a Saturday."

"I told you I'd come to help you," he said, his angelic smile punctuated by the *V* he made with two fingers.

Matilda's face almost caught fire. "Ben, my mother," she said, her voice hushed as she pointed in the direction Ben came from. "My mother has eyes in the back of her head and she can hear a butterfly blink."

"I'm just teasing," he said, talking in a normal conversational tone. "I just spoke to your mom and told her I was here to help you."

Matilda nodded her appreciation. "How are you?" she asked, her eyes darting back and forth to the open door. "You seemed like the normal you when you gave me a ride home from your father's wake. Are you still okay?"

"Everything's cool, said Ben, glancing at the shelves of

books, stacked magazines and a section of old 33 1/3 LP's.  He smiled at her, a care and concern for her showing that he was more than a friend.  "Hey, have I got some hot news that I think you'll be interested in."

"Oh, and what do you think I'd be interested in?" she asked, turning her attention back to her sorting various stacks of papers.

Ben held up two fingers in a *V* then quickly jumped back putting his hands in front of his face as a stack of papers sailed at him.

"Don't joke about that, Ben," she said in a whisper.  "You know that has a special meaning to me."  She paused, her blushing increasing, "And, I hope, to us."

"I'm sorry," said Ben as he started scooping up the papers Matilda had thrown at him.  "I was just teasing."  Then he held up the four fingers of his right hand.

Matilda's eyes darted again to the open door.  "Our special moments are nothing to joke about," she said, still whispering.  "I think they're sacred and should be treated as such and not like some smut gestures and the inappropriate language most of the girls in this school use."

"And what smut gestures do you know about that I don't?" he asked, the choir boy in him radiating.  "Oh, and I didn't know that the girls who attended our prestigious home of the Slashing Rapiers used inappropriate language.  Like what?"

"You're teasing again," she said, snatching the papers he had picked up out of his hands and throwing them back at him.  "You know darn well how they talk and how they flaunt their bodies and what they do with the boys in this school.  If their parents only had a clue to how their innocent children behave when out of their sight they'd faint."

"You worry too much," said Ben, turning serious.  He paused and looked sincerely at Matilda, the sight of her made his stomach do flip-flops with his heart.  "What we do is also sacred to me," he said. Then whispering he said, "And, very special."

"Honest?" she asked, feeling a tinge of nervousness as she continued to keep her eyes on the door.

"Honest," said Ben, crossing his heart with his right index finger. He could hardly hear what he just said his voice was so hushed. "Hey, it was the first time for me too. I mean, I never did." He stopped, lowered his eyes and couldn't control the heat he felt racing through his cheeks. He tried not to look at her, shifting his gaze to the books on the shelf just behind Matilda's head. "I mean, when you unbuttoned your blouse and showed me." He stopped again, his eyes now on hers and not on the book shelf. He cleared his throat. "You know, showing me how beautiful you are in your bra." He smiled. "Then," he continued breaking into a grin, "I had to pay you two cents."

Matilda continued to blush but never took her attention from the open door. "I don't know why I did that." Her gaze dropped to the papers in front of her on the faded marble floor. "I guess I just wondered what it would feel like to get paid for doing something considered naughty," she whispered nervously.

"Naughty," repeated Ben. "But Matty we didn't do anything except play some show without any tell."

Matilda continued to look down. "You haven't told anyone have you?"

"Never," said Ben, telling the truth. "Hey, come on, you know that's our secret. I would never tell...."

Matilda glanced up and turned ashen.

Ben didn't have to turn to know that Matilda's mother was standing in the open door behind him.

"Tell what?" asked Matilda's mother, sounding as if she could break the alibi of a serial killer.

Ben turned slightly so he could just see Amanda Newton

standing in the door entrance, arms folded across her chest, a quizzical look on her face.  "I promised my mother and uncle that I wouldn't tell anyone about my mother's new business until it opened."  He paused.  "I did tell Matilda a tiny part though and she swore she would never tell another living soul. Honest," he said, as he crossed his heart again.  "But, I can tell you this...."

# Chapter 9

## <u>Benoni "Ben" Bell</u>

### (Mister Sam, Princess Matty and Tinker Bell)

The driver's side door to the Mercedes popped open as if it had been kicked from the inside. It had. Ben was out of the car and around to the passenger side door as if he had jumped up and skidded across the hood. He had, but not before slamming the door shut with his hip. "Come on," he said to Matilda sounding almost frantic; his excitement about out of control. He grabbed her hand and almost yanked her out of the car.

"Ben," said Matilda, her warning accompanying the pain on her face. "Calm down. You almost dislocated my shoulder."

"Sorry," said Ben as he continued to squeeze Matilda's hand while pulling her across the once cluttered parking lot toward factory building. "I thought Saturday would never get here," he said. "That first week of school really sucked." He couldn't control his excitement as his grip tightened and his pace turned into a jog. He blinked when he realized the maze of rubble and debris was gone. "Watch your step," he said over his shoulder, tugging at her as if she were a stubborn puppy. He headed toward the propped open iron accordion gate, his grip on Matilda's hand tightening. "You can't believe the wild things that my uncle and my mom have done to this place," he managed to say, his eyes jumping like Hullabaloo dancers. He felt a tug on his arm. "Don't be scared," he said, trying to reassure her as they stopped in front of the gate.

"My hand," said Matilda, agony flashing back at Ben. "I can't feel my fingers."

He turned, looked at her and blinked. "Oh, I'm sorry," he said releasing his grip. His head now joined the dance card of his eyes. He winked at her. "This is the most awesome and coolest place you'll ever see."

"Are you sure it's safe?" she asked flexing her aching fingers and watched them change back to pink. "Am I in a real slum?" she asked, her head turning slowly back and forth, the aviator sun glasses she wore were unable to conceal wide disbelieving eyes. "I've only seen pictures of places like this in newspapers and magazines," she said, her eyes speaking volumes about the buildings surrounding the factory across the street. "I can't believe your mother is," she said, pausing and searching for the right words. "I can't believe your mother is a Slum Lord."

"She's no such thing," Ben said, slipping his arm around her shoulder again for reassurance. "Mom's the owner of a night club not a housing project. Besides, she digs helping poor people. Just like I heard my late grandmother used to like doing. I heard mom tell my uncle that she plans to offer jobs to some of the people living across the street from here." He nodded at the high rise apartment building across the street, its balconies showing a smattering of curious onlookers. "Some nice people live there. I've met a few. They're not like most of the people in that phony baloney place where we live," he said.

"Aren't you afraid of being in this place, in this terrible neighborhood?" she asked, her hand latching onto his arm.

"Nah," he said. "There's nothing to be afraid of. People around here are cool."

They both squinted as they squeezed sideways through the propped open, rusted steel front door that had, *Deliveries for La Tinkerbelle's* scribbled across it in yellow chalk. Ben waited for

Matty's eyes to adjust to the dark interior. He needed little acclimating. His daily trips after school to pitch in with his uncle and Sam had the entire layout etched in his mind. School had become a bore for him and he couldn't wait for the bell to ring to end the day. There would be Principal White's monotone announcements followed by his second quote for the day that was drowned out by students communicating in shouts. No one ever listened to Principal White. Students never listened to reminders by other students about some important activity taking place at school. Ben could never figure out who the activity was important to, surely not to him and most certainly couldn't compare with his working in a discotheque.

The bell to end school was a quarter through its dismissal ring and Ben was racing down the hall toward Plato and Socrates to give one of them a shove. If there had been a third door, one with his father etched on it, he would've have given that one a kick. He kept thinking of the rhyme he first heard when he was in kindergarten: *School's out! School's out! Teachers let the monkeys out!* He was the first monkey out the doors and on a suburban bus heading to the CTA train station in Wilmette. He took the El transferring at Howard Street and riding both above and below ground into the city for another bus ride, the bus stopping a half block east of La Tinkerbelle's. He was oblivious to the surroundings. He didn't care who looked at him or how, and didn't care what they looked like. Benoni Ben Bell never felt more important or wanted in all his young life. No one his age was doing what he was doing and, above all, he didn't have a father to shun him. Excitement embraced him and he embraced excitement back. Then his mother drove a stake in his heart the next morning before he left for school.

"You're not going anywhere, young man, until I see signs that you're doing your homework." his mother said, scolding him for the first time in his life. "You'll be lucky to be accepted by a second tier college at the rate you're going." He didn't believe his mother could sound like his gym teacher, Coach Speede, who ordered students and faculty alike in a coarse, baritone growl as if they were Marine Corps recruits to: "Toe the line, Jar Head!" That was followed by, "Drop and give me twenty!" Coach Speede's snarl and bulldog like stare once had the new librarian and newlywed, Mrs. Amanda Germono in a pushup position obeying his orders. Mrs. Germono got to the count of two before she stopped, stood up and said to Coach Speede, "You Cretin, you should be a physical education instructor, whatever that is."

Benoni Bell wasn't an honor roll student because of his looks; he wasn't promoted a full grade in grammar school because he conned his teachers with small talk. He was, like his uncle, brilliant. Accompanying his intelligence was a combination of savvy when it came to understanding human behavior. He also had a natural instinct for being street smart. His mother's harsh orders had him agreeing and obeying on the outside. Inside, he formulated a plan to appease her before her last words, those having to do with his going to college, smacked his ears. Nothing was going to keep him away from La Tinkerbelle's. Seeing television reruns was one thing. Being in the company of real live go-go dancers who had hair that didn't move, well, that was something else. Besides, Ben Bell wasn't a Jar Head.

Ben placed his hand on Matilda's. He wanted to tell her about all the work he had done for his uncle and new friend, Sam, but so much progress had been made since being exiled to an island piled with textbooks he barely recognized his efforts. He kept blinking knowing that he was in the same building. The concrete floor came into focus. "Look at that," he said to her. He pointed at a giant emblem resembling a skull and cross bones centered in the middle of the factory's floor. "Is that beyond awesome or is that beyond awesome?" he said to her. The floor had been painted in a flag blue with two wide stripes, one red the other white around the perimeter. The florescent lime colored skull and crossbones glowed in the dark and spread out ten feet in all directions like a giant octopus. Beneath it his uncle had added a portion of the logo from the Glen Forest on the Watercourse High School, an identical copy of the *Slashing Rapiers*. Ben's hand slid from Matilda's. He turned his head, looked at her in disbelief and said, "Wow, Matty, I can't believe it. I don't recognize a thing. It's totally epic!"

Matilda stood more rigid than the statue of General Glen Forest Pepperwall in the town's square. She peered over the top of her glasses, her eyes like an owl.

"You okay, Matty?" asked Ben, his question almost a whisper.

She blinked once.

Ben and Matilda gawked at stacks of black plastic chairs. Their chrome legs reflected the light from several bare bulbs used by his uncle and Sam, the light casting an eerie glow to the edge of the floor before losing to darkness. Each stack stood at attention in military precision waiting for the command to march. One end of the dance floor was strewn with white, molded plastic tables, the majority square in size seating four. There were rectangular tables that seated six and four large round tables that seated eight to ten patrons. Four miniature Jolly Roger's replicas were embossed at each of the corners of the square and rectangular shaped tables. Skull and crossbones peered out from the center of the large, round tables, all of them waiting to be arranged and placed with the appropriate number of chairs. "Keen," said both Ben and Matilda, their voices hushed. Then, in unison, their eyes traveled up marveling at the sight of six cylindrical cages suspended from the ceiling each by a separate cable. Each identical cage resembled a cross between a home for a giant parakeet and a medieval torture device. There was no resemblance to his uncle's original idea of a treasure chest and no signs of brass poles.

"Well, if it isn't our long lost Master Ivy Leaguer," said Sam, startling Ben and Matilda. He had crawled out from under the side access to the bar and was on his hands and knees, a large red adjustable pipe wrench in his right hand. "I see you decided to honor us with your presence. Enjoy your vacation?" Sam stood up, brushed off his knees and walked toward the couple. "Call me Sam," he said to Matilda, switching the wrench to his left hand and offering his right to shake hers. "You must be the reason Master Ivy Leaguer took a vacation from here." He smiled at Matilda. "Now I understand why he talked about you all the time while he was pretending to pitch in and help us."

"I'll be glad to pitch in and help," Matilda blurted out, then thankful for the building's darkness that hid her blush. She reached out and shook Sam's hand and felt that she somehow knew him. Welcome was written all over his smile and she embraced the warmth. Then another embrace latched onto her. Actually, two embraces. Sam's black cats had laid claim to her ankles the way they had with Arvia. She was down on her knees hugging and stroking the two scrawny felines, the trepidation of being in the factory gone and a curious attraction for a man named Sam warming her heart.

"The one on your left is Heckle," she heard Sam say to her before she could ask. "The other guy's Jeckle." Index fingers stroked under soft furry chins that had Heckle nestled comfortably on Matilda's left breast and Jeckle on the right one.

"Awesome," whispered Ben to his uncle.

"They're cats," Bo said to his nephew, his response coated with, *who cares* and frustration that the progress on the factory building's transformation to his dream seemed to hang in mid-air like his go-go cages. "Okay, folks," he said, clapping his hands twice. "Today's meeting of the Anti-cruelty Society is officially over." Two more claps of his hands followed. "Back to work, he ordered. "Go-Go's don't get done-done by playing with the guys," as he referred to Heckle and Jeckle. "And, young lady," he said to Matilda. "If you'd care to join us and pitch in, we'd appreciate your help."

"Best obey the boss man," said Sam, as he got back on his hands and knees and crawled under the bar to continue working on stopping a leak in one of the large stainless sinks. "Your uncle's been riding the mood swings lately and has been a real grouch. I wish I knew what was on his mind besides getting this old eyesore transformed into a disco."

"He's been like that since after my dad's funeral," said Ben, shrugging his shoulders. "Sometimes I see him lost in space. Other times I catch him talking to himself. God, I even saw him pointing once, but there was no one there to point at. I heard him say to this invisible whatever something about, 'You bet I know'."

"Know what?" came Bo's question from somewhere behind the stacks of chairs.

"I don't know, Uncle Bo," said Ben in the direction of his uncle's voice.

"I don't know either," shouted Sam from under the bar. "All I know is there's a leak that needs fixing."

"What can I do to help?" asked Matilda, the cats still nestled against her purring softly.

"Uncle Bo will find something for you to do," said Ben. He couldn't get over how Sam's appearance had changed. From the time he left with his mother after his first visit to the run down building then returning several days later, the dirt and grime had vanished from what had once been a derelict called Sam. The derelict also disappeared. In his place, a new Sam; a trim, clean cut, dapper and handsome man that greeted him and Matty. Ben caught a glimpse of his uncle and noticed the motion of his arm. "Matty, I'm going to help my Uncle Bo for a minute," he said to her. "I'll find out what he wants you to do."

She smiled, her attention focused on the two contented cats as she continued to sit on the floor in the same manner she had in the library's periodical room. Besides Heckle and Jeckle, Sam commanded her attention. At least the noises of metal on metal coming from behind the bar did. She felt a strange fascination for him. A feeling that she knew him kept shifting her attention back and forth from the cats to the clanking. "Mr. Sam," she found herself curiously calling out.

"Ouch," was the reply from behind the bar as Sam, rising up, hit his head on the sink. He stood up and placed his hands on the bar, the large wrench gripped in his right hand.

"Mr. Sam," continued Matilda, her fingers working the ears of both cats who had found a home most human males would die for. "Does your wife work here?"

Her innocent question caused Sam to let go of the wrench. "No wife, Princess Matty," he said, adding his nickname for her that seemed natural and the thing to do.

Matilda's fingers froze. "Why did you call me that?" she asked, a nervous politeness to her question.

There was a shrug from Sam and the words, "I dunno." There was a second shrug. "I guess because you look like a princess to me." Sam disappeared for a moment then reappeared on his hands and knees as he crawled out from under the bar. He stood up, brushed at his knees and said, "Once-upon-a-time I had a beautiful little girl like you."

"You did?"

Sam nodded. "I was married before," he said. Suddenly he found himself searching for words. "Well, I was married three times," he said, his explanation becoming a collection of stutters and a stammer. "Correction, I was married only twice. Neither of them worked out." There was another pause with more word searching coupled with word weighing. "What happened between my marriages to two women was a huge mistake." He paused again, reflecting. "I still miss my first wife." He looked at Matilda. "We had a daughter. That was the beautiful little girl I mentioned. She was two. Pretty as a princess and I loved her dearly. Her mother, however, wasn't too thrilled with my reason for leaving her. Never let me see my princess again."

Matilda's fingers twitched on the cats' ears and her next question came out in a whisper. "Why did you leave your princess?"

"Because I thought I was in love with someone else," he whispered back to her. "It turned out what I thought was love wasn't. My life turned into a sick joke. Besides losing my Princess, I got fired from my job because of a rumor someone in town spread about me laughing at a joke about some politician. Later, that same politician took my business away from me."

The conversation between Sam and Matilda didn't go unnoticed by Ben and his uncle. They had been arranging tables around the perimeter of the dance floor when they both stopped.

"Your wife wouldn't let you see your own daughter because you fell in love with another woman?" asked Matilda bravely, her fingers making the cats purr and nuzzle.

Sam could feel his hands tremble. He reached for the wrench on the bar top and squeezed the thick red handle as if he were trying to choke the life out of it. He was returning to a territory that once caused him more pain than he ever knew existed. "I thought I fell in love with a man," he said.

Matilda lifted each of the cats and rubbed her nose against Heckle's first and then a jealous Jeckle's. "That's no reason for anyone to be prevented from seeing their child."

"Beware of the wrath of a woman scorned, Princess Matty," said Sam, his fingers allowing the wrench's handle to breath. He closed his eyes and saw what he once thought was Paradise turn into Hell. An ugly divorce ended with his being labeled a pervert unfit to be near children by his wife's attorney, a well paid friend of the politician who fired him. Then, the one who he thought loved him, turned out to be someone who loved many, often in groups. Sam didn't like being one of many and said so. He was told to join the real world and live in modern times. That discussion took place on the Eisenhower Expressway nearing seventy angry miles per hour. The heated discussion was joined by a nasty chunk of jagged concrete that got tired of riding on the back of an overloaded dump truck and decided to join Sam and his companion in the front seat of Sam's car. In the process of making a surprise entrance through the windshield, the concrete chunk removed most of a human head from a neck thereby ending both a relationship and a discussion about behavior in modern times.

"So, Princess Matty," continued Sam. "In a few short months after losing my little girl, I found myself unemployed and attending a funeral. After the funeral I bought a bar," he continued. "It seems that my love with the roving eye named me the beneficiary of his life insurance." He thought back for a moment. "I named my bar, Sam's and made it a place for the common working man and woman to come in and unwind after a day on the job. That's where I met my second wife. She was divorced, had lost custody of her two sons and was unemployed. Gee, I thought, likes attract. And then Master Ivy Leaguer's father and his old man's shyster lawyer buddy had other ideas about likes attracting."

Matilda looked at Sam, tears in her eyes. Both cats reluctantly found the floor as she stood up and walked to the bar where a calm Sam was standing. "I'm so very sorry," she said, tears trickling down each cheek. "Did you say it was Ben's father who took your business away?"

Sam nodded. "That and my second wife who turned out to be more demented than my, for lack of a better way to express it, boyfriend."

Matilda looked at him confused. "Didn't you say you were," she paused and blushed. "Gay?"

"Good question, Princess Matty," said Sam, reflecting. "Thought I was," he said, his fingers tracing the outline of the wrench. "Guess I wasn't. Don't know." He lowered his gaze. "Maybe I didn't want to be after what I went through." He looked at the wrench as if he had just picked it up off of a shelf in a hardware store. "All I know is that I think of my Princess Matty and her mother often." He started to squat down to get back under the bar then stopped when he heard Matilda call out his name.

"Mister Sam," said Matilda, not wanting to see their discussion end. "If you knew Ben's father, did you ever live in Glen Forest on the Watercourse?" she asked with polite trepidation.

Sam's squatting down had stopped, his chin even with the top of the bar. "A long time ago, in another life, I drove a garbage truck" he said.

Ben and his uncle glanced at each other.

"My then wife and I had a nice apartment that was above the town's mortuary. She was the librarian at the Glen Forest on the Watercourse High School."

* * * * *

Ben and his uncle watched tears and hugs; their own tears joining in until Bo clapped his hands twice and said, "Shiver me timbers, me hardies. This here pirate ship ain't gonna float on a sea of crocodile tears."

"We'll talk later, Princess Matty," Sam said to her as they hugged and then he picked up his wrench and disappeared under the bar. "Captain Hook is cracking his cat-o-nine-tails again."

Matty joined Ben and his uncle as they continued to set up tables. "May I help?" she asked stepping in without waiting for a reply.

"You bet," said Bo wiping his runny nose with his shirt

sleeve.  He waved his hand in the direction of the stacks of chairs.  "Four chairs each at the square tables, six at the rectangular ones and eight at the bigger round size tables," he ordered.  "Four, six and eight, who do we appreciate," he chanted, a tone of leadership in his voice that Ben had never heard.  "Croquet!" shouted Bo then repeating his cheer of, croquet two more times.  He grinned at Matilda.  "Your boyfriend and I will get the tables set into place for you."  He paused.  "Be careful not to slide the chairs.  Don't want to scratch the new floor and put scars on Jolly Roger's face before the paying customers do."

Ben gave his uncle a gentle nudge on the arm.  "You know, Uncle Bo, I told Matty about your idea for the girls flying across the ceiling," he said, ever so cautious.  "She says she wants to audition."

Matilda swatted at Ben's arm and shouted, "You never told me about any auditions, Benoni Bell!"  Her voice blushed like her face. "Mr. Bell," she continued. "Your nephew's lying."

CLICK/SNAP!

"Ben," said Bo, his voice sounding as if he were about to close a multi-million dollar Hollywood film deal.  "Did you let the, pardon the expression, cats out of the bag about our little secret to make some very special young lady the biggest star ever to shine over this great city of Chicago?"  There was a nervous pause, the cap of his cigarette lighter slipping in his sweaty hand.  "That is the biggest star ever to fly across the heights of La Tinkerbelle's ceiling."  He looked more than serious as he glanced at Matilda and then his nephew.  "We're talking bigger than two of Chicago's greatest stars ever, the ravishing beauties, Kim Novak and Ann Margret."

"I don't know who those people are," said Matilda interrupting Bo, her words coming out so fast they created a breeze.  "Ben Bell you only asked me if I wanted to come down to see your mother's business," she said, the words continuing to race out. "You never told me about auditioning to fly across some ceiling, like some..."

"Like Tinker Bell," said Bo nonchalantly, cutting her off and lifting a square table from the stack in front of him. "You know, the famous character from Peter Pan," he said, unable to keep from leering at Matilda, his narrow, crooked mustache appearing to slide back and forth under his nose. "Your mother's a librarian, and I'm sure you've grown up around books," he continued, his tongue digging at his lips in a hungry lick. He already had Matilda attired in a black leotard as he set another table in place.

CLICK/SNAP!

"Well, show biz doesn't appeal to everyone," continued Bo. "I'm sure there is some woman in the entire city of Chicago who would like to wear a sequined costume and soar above a crowded dance floor bathed in a spotlight, all eyes feasting on her, the star attraction, other women envying her, fans adoring her," he said, inserting a nervous pause. "But then, there's a life of books, a life lived hiding in a library or above a mortuary with a view of my ancestor, the town founder, covered in bird poop."

Matilda looked nervously at Ben and back to his uncle. She buried her face in her hands and turned away.

"Think about what I said, young lady," said Bo, his tongue working across his lips on some unknown mission. "It's a chance of a lifetime."

Matilda slowly looked up at Ben's uncle. "But I couldn't. My mother would find out."

"I'll never tell her," said Ben, trying to keep his eagerness from bubbling over. "You know how I am with secrets," he continued, holding up his index and middle fingers in two *V*'s.

His nephew's symbol went over Berthold Pepperwall's head. "It would be impossible for your mother to know you were the star of a show bigger than Hullabaloo," he said, his acting nonplused in high gear.  "How could she?  You'll be wearing a mask."  He dug his hand into his right front pants pocket and felt his bare leg.  His left hand went into the opposite pocket and he pulled out a cardboard cutout resembling a cat girl mask.  "Nifty, don't you think?  And it'll match your costume.

"What kind of costume?" Matilda asked, her voice barely audible.

"An ordinary leotard worn by dancers the world over," he said, trying to be blasé.  "Little girls in ballet class wear them. I'll make a few modifications for you, but that's something I would only do because you're a friend of my nephew and, besides, you're Sam's flesh and blood."  He turned and pretended to realign the table he was standing next to.  "Your custom costume will be black like the mask and covered with sequins.  You'll sparkle like the stars in the Milky Way on a clear night.  The patrons will only see the graceful sparkles as you swing back and forth above their heads.  You'll be wearing a bandana around your head like a pirate and, oh, yes, as a lady pirate, you'll have on black patent leather, thigh length boots." He paused again while continuing to straighten a chair that didn't need straightening.  "Every lady pirate I've ever seen in the movies wore boots and a bandana.  With your special mask even your own mother wouldn't recognize you." He acted as if he were in deep thought.  "Sam wouldn't even recognize you."

"Recognize what?" Sam's voice echoed from under the bar.

"Nothing," said Bo calmly.  "Concentrate on fixing that leak."

My Uncle Bo digs pirates," said Ben to a more than curious, but still very leery Matilda Newton.

"You won't be an ordinary pirate, young lady," said Bo.
CLICK/SNAP!

"You'll be my flying buccaneer; my pirate version of Tinker Bell.  I just might give you a stage name like Tink for short.  Just picture yourself flying across this here ceiling like a graceful black swan," he said, pointing up, his hand following an imaginary course. "And, you'll have nothing to fear because you'll have two companions soaring with you, one on your right and the other on your left."

CLICK/SNAP!

"If I could only come up with a novel name for your companions, said Bo aligning a single chair."

Matilda politely cleared her throat. "May I make a suggestion, Mr. Pepperwall?" she asked.

"Suggest to your heart's content," said Bo, catching his cigarette lighter as it slipped from his sweaty palm.

"I know this might sound a bit corny," she said, her nerves no match for the excitement she felt. "You could call one Peter and the other Pan."

CLICK/SNAP! CLICK/SNAP! CLICK/SNAP!

# Chapter 10

## <u>Sam Geronimo Germono</u>

## (John Cinderella)

His once despised room above the garage he often rereferred to as, "Monte Cristo's exile without the iron mask," now seemed like a penthouse to Bo; a plush oasis; a personal sanctuary he never thought he'd call home. Smidgens of hatred still seeped out of his pores. John Brown reading Quintin's mocking letter made up one smidgen. What he was about to do finished off the other smidgens. He began to sweat. Berthold Bo Pepperwall was about to do something he never believed he was capable of doing, something for which Mensa could never prepare him. He was going to turn in the killer of his brother-in-law while making his fortune at the same time. That was his decision; a logical conclusion looked at from every conceivable angle. As usual he knew he was right and, as usual, he wasn't.

For several weeks after his idea received the financial green light from Arvia, he seldom left La Tinkerbelle's. He opted to sleep on the harsh concrete floor cushioned only by old newspapers that Sam had hauled from garbage cans behind the housing projects across the street. The sagging mattress in his Spartan room, spear shaped broken springs jutting out and stabbing him like Captain Hook playing Pin the Tail on the Donkey with both cheeks of his ass now felt like a feather bed.

He stared at the glow from the security lights outlining Dogwood's driveway. Once an annoyance, they now provided an ambiance to the coach house room. The cracks and waves in his water stained ceiling, a silver dollar size chunk of plaster hanging on for dear life aimed at his forehead became a lustrous gem, a priceless artifact that Malcolm Forbes might covet. Bo didn't care. Only one thing mattered to him. He was in love and his love was named, La Tinkerbelle. That's all he thought about. Well, almost.

He should have been more elated at the discotheque's progress. The sketches stored in his fertile mind made the transition to reality faster than if he were a child playing with an Etch-a-Sketch. Shape and dimension joined elevation while width and depth incorporated his subtle uses of black, white and chrome colors. He had resuscitated a foundry and taken it off life support. Out of the graffiti covered decay emerged a vibrant venue shouting out, "Hey, people, this is where all the go-go's have gone!"

Bo's new sense of morality cast a slight tarnish on his emerging creation, but barely. Tinker Bell had exceeded what he had imagined for his star performer and namesake character. Matilda Newton was born to be bathed in a spotlight. During her first rehearsal flight she caused the roller skate and roller blade wheels of the undercover cop waitresses and waiters to freeze. All eyes in La Tinkerbelle's were glued on her except the bartenders who were receiving a master's degree in mixology from the master, Sam.

Tarnish did not touch Bo's elation toward his waitstaff and bartenders. They had crafted their own costumes from old Levis cut off above the knees, some costumes being cut off so short the next visible body joint was at the hip. He didn't lay out a dollar; not even for roller skates and roller blades. The cops had furnished their own, paying visits to area big box sporting goods stores where their pitch was: "Would you like to make a donation that will benefit Schmoe Research?" The charity mattered not when there was a police shield attached to the request. On top of it, Bo had become friends with the officers, first name basis friends. They were the first real friends he had since the fourth grade. Back then he had tried to steal a kiss from a red headed and pig-tailed, cross eyed, freckle faced Peggy O'Shaunessy in the stair well between the first and second floor of Immaculate Heart of Mary grammar school. Peggy had moved away half way through the school year just after biting Bo on the lower lip and drawing blood. To emphasize her displeasure with Bo's attempted kiss, she poked him in both eyes and threatened to tell her mother that he had molested her. Peggy wasn't sure of what being molested meant, but she knew she could get Berthold Pepperwall in trouble by uttering that one word. Bo feigned being sick and stayed away from school for a week. When he nervously returned to school, one eye still black and the other inflamed, he found Peggy gone.

Then there was Sam. He was more than a friend to Bo. Sam was like a brother, buddy, guidance counselor, confessor and mentor. He was also the father he never had. Bo and Arvia's father, Malachi had run off with a cabaret singer named Kitten Amore who he had met at Joker Joe's in Niles. Her rendition of a *Slow Boat to China* as she sang and played the piano had the elder Pepperwall resigning his mayoral post. He turned that and the Dogwood estate over to his wife before the courts took it from him. Then he drove off to Las Vegas with Kitten, her real name, Esmeralda Como, her father an Italian immigrant and her mother Costa Rican. Malachi Pepperwall, like most of his ancestors, shunned religion, but when he saw Kitten he knew that what his parents had explained to him about the meaning of his name was true. Malachi, manipulating the translation of his name between the New and Old Testaments and comingling it with raging hormones, knew he was being led away to a new life by the hand of an angel. Arvia had just turned ten and Bo seven.

Sam understood. He knew more about angels and demons from his own life and experiences in the bar business than all of the bartenders in Cook County. From the first moment he met Berthold Pepperwall, he saw someone who desperately needed a friend. He didn't know he would be Bo's first friend. Then Sam found his little girl, his Princess, and Bo had to share his new friend. He didn't care. If Sam had his Princess, he had La Tinkerbelle's.

Bo's long time ongoing dreams of no longer having lint in his pockets now included his palms overflowing with gold doubloons. All he needed was to close his fingers around his soon-to-be wealth and his years of being a penniless Schmoe would vanish forever. He tried to keep the doubloons from spilling to the floor and rolling away. His fingers wouldn't work; they wouldn't curl, wouldn't clutch. The scene of a croquet mallet crashing into the side of his brother-in-law's head clouded his own head with guilt.

CLICK/SNAP!

His hand slid from his left pant pocket leaving the scratched cap of his metal security blanket. "If you go to the cops," he said to the ceiling, "it could mean the end of everything you've dreamed of. The cops are your friends, but they're still cops." His hand shot back into his pocket.

CLICK/SNAP! CLICK/SNAP!

"Don't act hasty, Berthold, old buddy," he continued, the ceiling appearing to listen. "Play your cards right and you could kill two birds with one stone." A smile crossed his dry, narrow lips, his left hand sliding the lighter from his pocket. He interlaced his boney fingers together around the lighter, the nails gnawed to the cuticles. His hands slid down resting on the gold plated belt buckle that was out-of-place on his stained pants. The Masonic logo glistened in the darkness of his room. It was the first belt he owned that hadn't been made of simulated leather crafted by slave labor on some Pacific Island atoll. He really didn't own it. He took it from his deceased brother-in-law's massive walk-in closet. His sister had surprised him by saying, "Take whatever you want, Berthold. Take Quintin's suits, his shirts and shoes; take it all. I'll have them tailored for you." Bo took and Arvia paid. He took shoes, though too long and too wide, his feet feeling like they were wearing snow shoes. Bo took shirts with collars two inches to big and sleeves so long they had to be rolled up. His lighter rested on top the belt buckle. He chuckled. "An American Eagle in the hand is worth more than the buzzard I saw from behind the bush that night," he said, his head then turning toward the worn chipped dresser. He could see the outline of his picture of Malcolm Forbes but couldn't see his hero's face. "I will do the right thing, Malcolm, old buddy," he said with contentment. "But, as I think you know, it's important that the checks clear first before the money gets counted." Another contended sigh followed. "Who knows? Time magazine might make me Man-of-the-Year." His lips turned up at the corners. "Can you see old Berthold here on the cover after I turn a slum area into a gentrified neighborhood? My late brother-in-law would spin in his grave." He shut his eyes and visualized the magazine cover. His entire body quivered. Then a shiver turned his spine to ice. Standing behind him on the Time cover was the murderer, a defiant smile flashing: "I dare you." Then the silver dollar chunk of ceiling plaster lost hold and hit him on the bridge of his narrow nose.

* * * * *

"Have you told your mother yet?" asked Ben as he took a stack of *Time* magazines from Matilda. She was sitting on the floor in the high school library's Periodical Room.

"Ben," she whispered, a look of fear staring back at him.

"I'm sorry," he said in a hushed voice. "You were just so

excited when you found out Sam was your father."

Ben," she whispered again. "Please."

"I can't help it," he said, arranging the magazines in a neat pile on the top shelf of the back wall that was floor to ceiling shelves. "God, I can't believe it. Sam."

Matilda looked as if she were about to cry. "Ben," the whispering of his name continued. "Please."

Ben reached for another stack of magazines and saw the title, *Forbes*. "Who reads this junk?" he asked, searching for the letter *F* on the tags beneath each of the shelves.

"Nothing in a library is junk," said Matilda, sounding as if she were her mother.

"Looks like junk to me," said Ben, sliding the stack in its appropriate spot. He turned away from the bookshelf and looked down where Matilda was sitting. "Can you believe it, Matty? Sam." His eyes jumped to the doorway where Amanda Newton stood, a look on her face that made Ben quiver. The question that followed could have made the iceberg that sunk the Titanic melt.

"Sam who?"

* * * * *

Sam sat on one of the black, cracked and scratched leather high back swivel bar stools that had just been delivered to La Tinkerbelle's front entrance by John Cinderella, the junk man. John Cinderella looked like a junk man who was the twin of W.C. Fields. Bo discovered him, or John discovered Bo about the time John ran over Bo, or Bo, daydreaming, walked in front of John's pick-up truck after getting off the bus the second morning he and Sam were to start working on what was to become La Tinkerbelle's a Go-Go. John had slammed on his squeaking brakes about the time Bo found himself in mid-air getting ready for a landing on the pavement in front of his dream. John's top heavy load in back surged forward bouncing off the cab and hood of the pickup joining Bo on the pavement. Both Bo and John had the exact same thought after the accident: "I'm going to sue that careless bastard for all the money he's got." Then they looked at one another and struck up a deal that only kindred spirits could concoct. There would be no law suits only Bo buying select merchandise from John and John furnishing every alternate load at no cost. They were both happy.

A handshake saw Bo reading the hand drawn words in three slanted lines on the truck's door: *John's Junk Store* 1411 W. Chicago Avenue HA 1-0800 before heading into the factory building. "I just might need that tid-bit of infor later," mumbled Bo as he watched the top heavy load on the truck teeter more than before.

John had made dozens of trips to La Tinkerbelle's, mostly to pick up anything that resembled being metal from the parking lot area. John eventually cleared the lot of all debris. His greatest contribution to the disco was a delivery of bar stools about the time Sam discovered his daughter. "Hope you like these beauties," John had said to Bo. "They're on me."

Bo knew they should be after all of the tonnage John had removed from the factory's floor and sold it to a scrap metal dealer for a small fortune.

"Sorry about not helping you unload these stools, Boss," said Sam to Bo. "Since my little princess is back in my life, I'm having a hard time concentrating on this business venture of yours; at least not today."

"Aw, a little work will take your mind off of seeing your daughter after all these years," said Bo, casting an eye at the remaining twenty chairs waiting to be positioned along the curving bar. Even seeing Sam down-in-the-mouth couldn't dampen his spirits. "Great stools," he said with pride. "Got 'em gratis from John."

Sam nodded. "Yeah, they are great," he said, as he swiveled ever so slightly on the stool. "I remember stools like these in a couple of nice joints downtown years ago. I'm not sure, but I think the old London House or maybe Mr. Kelly's had stools like these."

"Doesn't matter," said Bo, not knowing what he was feeling for his newly adopted brother and number one employee. Maybe if we got these stools organized then you can take some time to clear your head and think about having a daughter again."

"Guess so," said Sam, his voice hushed. "But, that's not why I'm feeling down in the mouth, Bo."

Bo looked but didn't say a word. He didn't have to.

"What am I going to do when my little girl's mother finds out?"

CLICK/SNAP!

Bo's thought did a, "Hello" and "Goodbye" in an instant. Sam's dilemma didn't matter. He had his own. "I wonder what Sam's going to do when he realizes that his princess is my Tinker Bell?" his nervous brain asked in silence.

* * * * *

John Brown sat in his leather Chesterfield chair, an ever-so-slight twitch of a swivel visible as he stared out his office window looking at the boats moored in the Monroe Street Harbor. Soon the harbor would be nothing but depressing, icy water, the boats gone into their winter hibernation spots, his Ella Scats bedded down like a bear in a forest den. "You got what you deserved, Quintin, you two-bit, cheatin' bastard," he said to his view of Lake Michigan. "Use and abuse, use and abuse, use and abuse, that's all you ever did to people; one for all and all for you, Quintin. Didn't make any difference who you used or how you used them. You always got what you wanted; never ever thought that someone you took from, someone you abused and humiliated would get even. Now you know what it feels like."

* * * * *

Pastor Rufus McDowell Puffin sat on his threadbare Lazy Boy Lounger in the cramped corner of his office that looked like it was shared with Sir Walter Scott. He couldn't take his eyes off his wife, Alice Nell. He had never seen her so forlorn. His heart made an attempt to go out to her but it didn't quite make it. "You know the Lord punished him for a reason," he said to her, his worn Bible open and face down in his lap. "It was the Lord's way of having him pay for his sins." He closed his eyes and let out a sigh. "Oh my, so many sins," he continued, sounding sympathetic but not feeling that way. "I do believe he's the only soul I've ever come in contact with who enjoyed adding Commandments so he could find unique ways to break them."

Alice Nell Puffin sat on a converted bench that had once been a pew in the original Glen Forest Church before the Puffin's had arrived. Head down, hands folded in her lap, a combination of feelings seeming to crush her spirit; she heard her husband's words but longed for the virile strength and stamina of Quintin Bell. "He was indeed a unique sinner," she muttered, not noticing the agreement in her husband's eyes. Her own feeling of sadness was sprinkled with a mixed sense of gladness that Quintin Bell was dead. "Ya'll were askin' for it," she said to herself. "And that's what ya'll got for your cold, cold heart cheatin' on little ol' me," she sighed. "I worshiped you more than I did the Lord," she continued. "No man, and I mean no man, mocks little ol' Alice Nell and gets away with it. No man."

Rufus Puffin tried to feel sympathetic toward his wife, even forced a sympathetic look. The look was more of a gloat. His hands folded in prayer against his sweaty lips. "The Lord is all knowing and all forgiving," he said to his wife, the faintest of a faint smile on his thick lips.

"Amen," replied a reverent Alice Nell.

* * * * *

Arvia stood gazing out the open French doors of the den she had reclaimed as hers. The center drawer to her late husband's antique Oriental writing desk stood pulled open, the metal lock box that had commanded so much of Bo's attention sat atop the desk, the lid open. The weather had turned cool; a brisk fall chill in the air caressed her as she continued to stare out the glass doors.

"You had no idea the Golden Rule worked both ways," she said to the well manicured landscape sprawled out before her that seemed to understand. "Oh, poor Quintin," she continued. "You certainly did do unto others. And you had those others do unto you only what you wanted them to do; what you ordered and even bullied them to do."

She could feel the years of repressed humiliation converting to a rage that had her reaching for the handle of the French doors to let in the autumn air. Quentin's ill-gotten money and the lavish gifts didn't bother her. Ill-gotten assets had been a part of the Pepperwall legacy. They were taken for granted. Public humiliation, although a part of the Pepperwall family behavior for well over one hundred years, had resulted in the demise of several male family members. The General leading the pack, buried with a load of twelve gauge buckshot buried in his posterior courtesy of his wife, the first Arvia. The last Arvia wife enjoyed a different anatomical view; perfect outlines of a croquet mallet on the side of a crushed skull.

A faint smile came to Arvia's lips. "Public humiliation has its down side," she said aloud to her garden. "You found that out, didn't you, my dearest Quintin." She forced out a laugh coated with sarcasm. "Do you know who's doing unto you now?" she asked, the cool breeze rushing into the den through the open door, and then laughing even louder. "Bo!" she shouted, giving herself a hug. "Bo, the person you despised, the

Schmoe, the loser with the neon letter L on his forehead has everything of yours but your women.  He has your money and your cars.  He's even wearing your shoes even though they don't fit him.  And with my blessings and a hefty check to the country club, he's even using your private locker area and steam room."

She hugged herself even harder.  "And, dearest Quintin, do you know what else I'm doing?" she asked, her arms loosening up.  "I'm even giving him your money."  She clapped her hands together several times as if to congratulate herself.  "It was all my money to begin with so you shouldn't feel too badly."  She could feel her rage butting heads with the evening chilled air.  "How does it feel?  How does it feel to have the Golden Rule tossed in your face, crumbled up and scattered on your grave?"  She was back to hugging herself.  "I hope you didn't mind that I had you buried in the derelict side of the family plot," she said, the evening air winning the pushing contest with her anger.  "It's a fitting place for an evil human being like you who used and abused more people than all of my ancestors combined."

Arvia glanced at the top of the Oriental desk.  There were two stacks of photographs sitting near the edge of the desk top.  Along side of the photographs was a digital camera complete with a wide angle lens and rapid fire shutter release.  She clicked the French doors shut and walked slowly towards the desk, her rage returning, increasing with each step.  "I hope you felt the pain of that mallet against your head," she said, her jaw clenched so tight she could barely get the words out.  She snatched up one of the stacks, several of the pictures spilling out and landing on the circular Oriental carpet protecting the teak wood floor under the desk.  Her fingers shuffled through the stack, the pictures a blur, but the scenes burned into her mind.  She tossed the stack of pictures on the desk as if tossing in a bad hand of poker.  Her left hand scooped up the remaining stack, her right hand peeling off each picture and tossing it back on the desk. She paused as the last photograph hit the desk top and skidded off the top onto the seat of the leather desk chair. Her hands were in tight fists. "Too bad there wasn't the flash of a camera to record your final moment," she said every muscle in her body taut. "There were so many other flashes you seemed to savor, you and that demented friend of yours, John Brown." She unclenched her hands. "You violated so many people, including me, so many times. I bet you could never guess in a million eternities the person who killed you." Her head made a single trip from side to side. "Who would mistake your head for a wooden ball?" she asked, her fingernails gouging into her soft palms. "It was a mistake, wasn't it?" She stopped to ponder, almost playing a game with her words. "Gee, was it your Chief of Police's weird wife? You gave her many a reason to detest you the way you made fun of her being anorexic while violating her.

Her murder-quiz word game covered the pain of her nails digging into the soft flesh of her palms. "Maybe it was the slut married to our pastor who did you in. She played all of your games more than the combined parade of trollops who waltzed in and out of the country club carrying your envelopes. If the pastor's tramp spent as much time at the country club taking golf lessons than in your private steam room, she could have been a scratch golfer instead of you scratching her itches and vice versa." The fingers of her right hand abandoned their gouging and reached for a photograph nearest to her. There was the teasing, seductive smile of Alice Nell Puffin, the handle of Quintin Bell's croquet mallet happily hidden where no croquet mallet had ventured before. Her sound of disgust was swept away by the photograph being shredded into confetti size pieces.

"And what about the school librarian, Mr. Mayor?" she asked the empty den. "She had every reason in the world to get even with you." She picked up another photograph from the desk and pressed it against her breasts. "And, dear Quintin, don't forget Wanda Mensch. You made your poor secretary an accessory to your perverted madness by stringing her along. You even had her keep your calendar organized for your candy deliveries and the letters of entry given at the gate house so those heavily sealed envelopes and whoever delivered them could be escorted into our home. Too bad Schickle and Gruber were always chained up. Wanda had every reason to be the one to crush your skull."

Arvia sighed again as she glanced down at the digital camera, saying: "I'm fearful of what I might find if I ever learned to use this perverted gift you received from John Brown." She walked back to the glass doors and looked at her faint image reflecting from the glass and said: "Above all, dearest Quintin, I had more reasons than all of them combined to see you dead."

* * * * *

Bo sat next to Sam at the bar, the stools all aligned according to his plan and asked his disconsolate new brother, "Feeling any better?"

Sam's head barely indicated the negative. "I don't know if the pain was greater by not being allowed to see her or seeing her again after all these years." His sad eyes glanced at Bo pleading. "What am I going to do about her mother?" His plea went up a notch. "Worse yet, what's her mother going to do about me? The lady knows how to administer pain." He closed his eyes and felt something he had never felt before. Sam Germono was face-to-face with doom.

"Pain sucks," muttered Bo.

"That it does, Mr. Pepperwall," said Sam, without looking at Bo. "Now that things in your life are looking up with this here retro night club of yours slowly taking shape and, looking pretty good if I do say so myself, you don't have to worry about pain."

Bo looked out of the corner of his eyes at Sam. "If that were really the case," he said a blob of phlegm showing on the end of his tongue. He made a face and swallowed. "I've got to do something that might cause me more pain than I've ever experienced in my life."

It was Sam's turn to look out of the corner of his eyes. "Bo, "what pain is that?" he asked.

"Well, it ain't always hurting the one you love, as the old song goes," Bo said slowly, trying not to answer Sam's question.

"Kind of depends on what version of that old song you listen to," said Sam, his understanding bartender's look locked in on Bo. "When I was a little kid my grandfather had an old record about hurting the one you love by Spike Jones that made me laugh. My wife's version, on the other hand, didn't have anything to do with love. Can't say that I blamed her, but not being allowed to see my daughter?" he uttered, his face and words showing anguish. "Ouch, man. Now that's the ultimate in hurts."

"I don't know about ultimate hurts," said Bo, unable to look at Sam. "All I know is there's a chance I could lose all of this," he said, watching the reflection of his right hand making a slow sweeping motion in the mirrors behind the length of the bar. "I could lose it, Sam, before I even finished what I had planned. Now that I have the chance to finally be somebody, to be respected, to not being called Bo the Schmoe anymore and then have that yanked away, well, Sam my friend, that's going to really hurt."

"And what would cause that?"

Bo looked at Sam and felt he wanted to die. "I know who killed my brother-in-law." CLICK/SNAP!

Sam didn't blink. "Boss," he said, his voice the epitome of peace. "It looks like the two of us are up the well-known creek in a cement canoe without the proper means of locomotion."

Bo blinked.

CLICK/SNAP!

"Now is the time for two good men to stand up for what is right and just," said Sam.

CLICK/SNAP!

Sam reached under the bar and said, "Forgive us, Father for we know what we do."

# Chapter 11

## <u>Charles, Franco and Captain Hookette</u>

### (La Tinkerbelle's a Go-Go)

The concrete floor ignored the newspapers Bo was lying on and took a sadistic pleasure in turning the marrow of his bones into popsicles. He felt like death; an entirely new feeling for him. A lifetime of humiliation had been transformed into one of exhilaration and really being able to fly like Peter Pan thanks to Sam's suggestion the night before. As he slowly moved his toes first, and then his fingers, he realized that the foundry's dim light wasn't trying to drill through his eyes to burn his brain away. That thought didn't make him feel any better even though he was thankful that death had passed him by. Bo didn't need his Mensa IQ to surmise that he had a hangover. He didn't need to weigh and consider his options before reconsidering death, the lesser of his evils. "For gosh sakes, Sam," he muttered, each word coated in pain. "What did you do to me?"

Sam also felt awful and knew that his was not to reason why. Too many experiences with the grain and the grape; too many promises and too many ways to avoid temptation had been a big part of his past life. He should have known better to heed the warning being preached to him as he uncorked the Tullamore Dew: *Keep the cork in the bottle, Germono! Keep the cork in the bottle!*

Bo only drank when he worked at his late brother-in-law's country club affairs waiting tables, cleaning up and emptying partial glasses. His emptying method was to drink what was left over. After all, he had concluded, "It's free." Wiping his mouth he would add, "Waste not. Want not." He and Sam wasted not early into the morning.

Sam, who had corked his own bottle years earlier after losing two wives, his Princess Matty, his bar and almost the desire to live, aired his personal woes with Bo. Sam had been in the midst of unpacking the disco's first shipment of liquor, taking inventory and stocking the back bar when the vision of seeing his Princess Matty again got the best of him.

Bo, visualizing his wealth evaporating in front of him before he had a chance to spend it, climbed up the ladder of the Dogwood Estate's diving platform and took a not very Olympic caliber plunge into despair. Coupled with a possible sentence behind bars that he was sure to get for concealing a murder, he did a swan dive into the swimming pool that had been drained.

An entire bottle of Tullamore Dew was the culprit responsible for their morning agony, every Irish drop exploding between their ears like the pounding base drum of the Shannon Rovers marching in a Chicago St. Patrick's Day parade. One bottle would have been enough, but then Sam uncorked a bottle of Drambuie, laughing and saying, "Laddie, I think the Scots and the Irish get along." They didn't.

"Oh, my God," muttered Bo, his mouth tasting like a giant wad of surgical cotton soaked in a generic balsamic vinegar and sprinkled with compost from his sister's rose garden. "Did I die in my sleep?" He looked at Sam through two slits and politely asked, "Why did you try to kill me last night?" The two slits returned to a painful crust grinding close. "I've never felt so bad in all my life."

"I didn't try to kill you," replied Sam. "And, I have felt this bad before." His eyes looked like two pools of contaminated blood in matching algae clogged ponds. "Don't take this in the wrong way, Boss," he continued. "But I ain't ever drinkin' with you again for as long as I live."

"I ain't ever drinkin' period," said Bo, his hands massaging at his temples as if he were trying to force his fingers through his ears. "What am I going to do, Sam?" he asked in a whisper. "Besides going to jail and losing all of this, I've got two candidates to interview this morning for the Boutique Manager's job." He tried to let out a moan but couldn't. "I'm not capable of interviewing myself." The moan finally won. "Besides, my sister is supposed to be here to sit in on the interview. If she sees me like this, I'll by-pass jail. I'm passing *Go* and not collecting two hundred dollars. Arvia will see to that. She'll bury me alive in the derelict section of our family cemetery."

"Boss, you worry too much," said Sam, his hands pulling up to the elbow rest of the bar where his chin grabbed hold. "I've got the cure for all of your troubles." The knuckles of both index fingers scraped away the loose particles of a sand and gravel mix from around his eyes.

Bo jumped back.

"Boss, ain't no man alive whose seen the troubles I've seen. And there ain't any man alive who knows how to get the hair of the dog that bit him like yours truly."

"I didn't get bit by a dog," Bo managed to say. "There ain't any dogs here. Only Heckle and Jeckle." He watched Sam's head disappear behind the bar and then saw him crawling along the factory's floor on his hands and knees toward the kitchen area, a bottle in one hand. "I never had a pet, Sam," he said, pressing the palms of his hands up against the sides of his temples. "My mother said they cost too much money."

* * * * *

Bo and Sam sat on the floor with their backs up against the

bar when Arvia appeared at the entrance to La Tinkerbelle's. She walked across the spacious factory floor and stopped in front of her brother and the bartender. "Well, now," she said, a visible annoyance coating her short statement as she looked down at them. "Breakfast?" she asked.

Sam held up the tall tumbler with a half eaten celery stick peeking out over the rim of the glass. "My Mother Nature vegetable juice cocktail," he said. "Miss Arvia, you're looking upon the mortal remains of two industrious gentlemen who spent last night in its entirety laboring for the greater glory of your soon to be new and elegant bistro, La Tinkerbelle's." He nodded at Bo. "These two industrious gentlemen seated before you have added another Go in your Go-Go."

"Indeed," she repeated, doubting.

"Vegetable juice cocktail," Bo repeated, holding up the glass in a faux toast to his sister. "Not as good a breakfast as a Chicago style hot dog, but one that won't choke me to death." He took a sip of his drink, coughed and sprayed tomato juice all over himself.

"Yoo-hoo!"

Arvia turned and looked to the front entrance. The eyes of Sam and Bo also managed to find the front door where two silhouettes outlined the noon sun.

"Anybody home?" asked an effeminate voice. "I mean, can any of you pull yourself away from casting ball bearings or whatever you're doing on the floor in this god-awful place and direct us to a Mr. Pee-pee Pot or Petermill or Pepperwall or whatever his name is? Franco and I have an appointment to meet with him. And, I might add, we are prompt-o. Like on time-o, as in punctual-ozo." There was a pause followed by a sound that resembled the word, "Icky" and then, "We are ever so polite, prepared and ready; ready, ready, ready to rock 'n roll. Now where is this boutique we are supposed to create with our magic?"

Sam and Bo glanced at one another, gulped their Bloody Marys and managed, with the help of the bar, to stand. Arvia forgot how to breathe. They watched the two shadows take shape as they sauntered toward them. Bo wanted to speak, but couldn't. Sam didn't know what to say so didn't, while Arvia's lungs remembered how to inhale. Speaking would have been a waste of time as one member of the approaching duo started and dominated the conversation.

As Bo, Sam and Arvia quickly learned their two visitors each sported several names calling each other those names multiple times. Frank, also known as Franco and Werewolf, but only by his companion, introduced himself as Frank. He would never be mistaken for one of the world's ten best dressed men. He wore a wrinkled Hawaiian shirt, Levi's and a pair of tasseled black loafers with thick, black crepe soles. He had an incredibly polite voice that sounded as if his words emerged from the depths of a gravel pit. A pair of kind eyes was set in a football shaped head that was topped with an out-of-control crew cut, gel coating a dozen or so coagulated clumps of spiked hair that looked like a neglected lawn. "Please forgive, Charles," he said, the gravel spilling down a metal ramp into a deep pit. "His public school education neglected to teach him about the word, polite. The poor soul is also completely void of people skills, manners and appropriate behavior."

"Pull-eeze," replied Charles, his remark sounding as if it came from someone who was auditioning for La Cage Aux Folles. His delicate hands graced by too long, slender fingers began moving like two white doves with acute cases of hiccups. "Do excuse Franco's loutish behavior," he said. He glanced at Bo, Sam and Arvia. "Which one of you is this Mister Pee-pee Pot person?"

Bo, Sam and Arvia glanced at one another. None of the trio had ever encountered the likes of someone like Charles. They had seen albino white curly hair before, but not pierced eyebrows, the studs resembling the sailor boy on a box of Cracker Jack. Flashing lime green colored eyes, the result, they learned, of colored contact lenses were set in a perfect face that could grace fashion magazine covers, the covers sporting gorgeous models with make-up that looked like they had been born with it. Charles wore eye-liner. It was perfect and he did look like he had been born with it. His lips caught the attention of Sam, Bo and Arvia. The upper was thick and full, the lower pencil line thin. As they learned later, Charles had taken advantage of what he thought were cut-rate Botox injections. Cut-rate was just that. Half price for half the lips, the upper puffed and full, the lower looking non-existent. Charles or Charlie Chuckles, a name that sent him into flitting rage, insisted at times as being called Bella. That name was used after he had consumed one too many crème de menthe frappes and believed he was a vampire. At that transitional point, he expanded flamboyance and bizarre behavior to unheard limits.

Before Charles got half way through introducing himself and stating: "Franco, that dear sweet boy who couldn't find his fly if I didn't help him," Sam had managed to work his way behind the bar taking Arvia with him. Bo was left to fend or defend for himself.

Bo didn't seem to mind. Charles, Charlie Chuckles or Bella had made his hangover disappear and a new surge of energy sparked him. "Am I to assume that you gentlemen are here about the boutique manager's position?"

"Oh, assume away, dear boy," said Charles, his fluttering white dove hands appearing inebriated as he talked. "Go ahead and make an ass out of you and me." He stopped for a moment to laugh at his joke then continued, "That's the managers' positions, I'm sure," he said, his hands acting as if they had been nipping on some kind of hallucinogenic drug. "You know, *S* apostrophe with a plural. Franco and I are a team and there is no I in team. We are a we and we are what you get."

Bo opened his mouth but that was as far as he got.

"Now what is it you want Franco and me to do?" he asked, the white doves appearing to circle for a landing on Bo's shoulders. "No, don't tell me, there's nothing you can tell us to do. One look around these dismal surroundings tells me you made the right choice by summoning the expertise of the Tandem Two." He nodded at Franco who hadn't said a word. "You prayed for a miracle, Mister Pee-pee Wall and we, the Dynamic Dyad, are your saviors. Your prayers have been answered. Two for tea and tea for two and lucky you get we, Mr. Wee-wee."

"Pepperwall," said Bo just managing to correct Charles.

"Oh, whatever," said a flustered Charles. "A pee wee is still a wee pee. Pepperwall it is."

Bo seeing his opportunity started walking in the direction of where the new boutique would be located in the old foundry building. "Follow me, Count," he said, "and don't trip on your cape."

"Touché," said Frank, a tone of admiration in his voice.

While Charles groused as he followed Bo, Sam held Arvia's hand and kept her from joining the others. "Miss Arvia," he said in a half whisper. "Let your brother handle this." He gave her an assuring nod.

"Sam, please tell me my brother is not seriously considering hiring either of those two to manage my boutique."

"Don't fret, Miss Arvia. Your brother is a lot smarter than people give him credit. We both know about his IQ and a Schmoe he's not. He'll do well."

"Dearest Lord, I hope so," she said, her hand sliding from Sam's, "But I think I'd better join him. No telling how much money he might spend on those two."

"No worry, Miss Arvia," said Sam, his dissipating hangover allowing him a smile. "After talking with your brother into the wee small hours of the morning, I can assure you that your brother has a good handle on finances."

Arvia smiled back at Sam. "I dearly hope so," she said, as she turned and headed to join her brother and his two job candidates. "He dips into my bank account like he used to jam his hand into our mother's cookie jar when he was a little boy."

One of Bo's hands helped him emphasize and explain his plans for the boutique. His other hand was in his pocket caressing his cherished Zippo. "Now the designer t-shirts, baseball caps and sweat shirts should be on display over there," he said, his hand pointing in several directions at once. "Do you think we should carry hoodies? Perhaps monogrammed hoodies with the La Tinkerbelle's logo?" he asked, then suddenly wheeled around and pointed in the opposite direction. "I believe the leather whips, boots and spurs should go there." His index finger jabbed at the air like Victor Borge doing his punctuation routine. He pointed in another direction before Charles could butt in. "And the oils, body lotions and the condom variety display assortments should be right there," he said, his finger making an exaggerated point. He smacked his lips and said: "Can't say that we're not socially responsible." He spun in another excited direction. "Then the alternative life style section should be there," he said, his pointing and spinning now at a feverish pitch. "You, Charles, appear to be cognizant of alternate life styles."

"Touché again," said Frank with a slight nod of approval.

Arvia watched her brother in silence, amazed at seeing her bloodline act like a wheeler dealing Pepperwall putting bait in the jaws of his trap. She continued to listen.

"And our religious paraphernalia will go..." He paused then jabbed his index finger at a spot that only he knew. "There!" There was another brief pause. "That should please Jesus, don't you think?" A pleased look was painted across his face. "Do you think this will fly in Transylvania?"

Frank and Charles stared at the space that Bo had just

described, analyzing.  Charles, his distorted lips in a pucker, wasted no time saying, "Just leave it to us, Mister Weewall. Franco was an architect in his other life; the Frank Lloyd Wright School in Arizona, a born genius.  Of course, gave up everything for little ol' me.  Can you blame him?"  His eye lashes fluttered as if on cue.  "Our creation will be the talk of the clichéd Windy City.  Leave it all to us."

Arvia politely cleared her throat.  "Excuse me, gentlemen, but what do you estimate the cost will be for your expertise to develop the La Tinkerbelle's a Go-Go boutique?"

"Dearest Lady," said Charles, his hand coming to a stop in mid-air.  "Artistic creativity, especially ours, knows no financial constraints.  No limitations.  No boundaries."  He paused, fluttered his eye lashes at Arvia and asked, "Dearest Lady, did you say La Tinkerbelle's a Go-Go?"

Arvia smiled.

"La Tinkerbelle's, Franco," said Charles, his eyes flashing excitement.  "How divine, dear lady, a real authentic retro disco," he said.  "Isn't it divine, Franco?  It brings back memories of your reading Peter Pan to me when I was in the hospital recovering from that life threatening disease."

Frank gave a frustrated sigh.  "You had your tonsils out, Queen Victoria."

"No matter," said Charles ignoring Franco's barb.  "Your reading Peter Pan to me saved my life."  He looked at Arvia. "Dear lady, this is kismet."

Frank looked at Bo and Arvia apologetically.  "Miss Bell, Mister Pepperwall, I do apologize for the domineering behavior of Charles.  He can be an embarrassment at times.  Actually, most times, but if he doesn't get carried away and try biting our customers on the neck or other parts of the human anatomy, you'll be pleased with his efforts; our efforts.  And, yes, Miss Bell, money is only a minor concern of ours.  You and Mr. Pepperwall will be pleased with our finished product."

"Oh, dear, sweet lady," said Charles, his hands exploding. "How can you think about putting a price tag on your becoming the talk of this here toddlin' town?"  The back of his right hand went to his lips for an instant and he said:  "Oh, my, did I really use the word, toddlin'?"

Frank gave an approving nod.

Bo pursed his lips.

CLICK/SNAP!

"But, dear lady, before you can toddle along with us, we have to do something with that hair of yours."  His puffed upper lip almost swallowed his wrinkled nose.

"And what's the matter with my hair?" asked Arvia, an indignance in her voice traced back to her late ancestor, General Pepperwall.

"Nothing that our colleague and dear, sweet friend, Ramon, can't repair," Charles said, then pausing as if in a state of meditation.  "Given the time, Ramon could make even you the talk of the town.  The man is a maestro when it comes to hair and his salon is always SRO.  But for us...."

The ire coming from Arvia stopped Charles cold.  "And what's the matter with my hair?"

"Dear lady, you are the owner of a soon-to-be-famous bistro."

"What about my hair?" she asked again, her voice up two octaves.

Charles gave her a flustered look.  "Shelve the Pocahontas look, dear lady and make believe you're sophisticated and special.  Go back several decades and try to be like Jackie O giving a TV tour of the White House."  His hand reached out to touch Arvia's single braid and a repugnant look came across his face.  His hand jerked away as if Arvia's hair had become vile. "Oh, forget Jackie O.  No one could pull that off.  Try Nancy. That would be so much easier.  I mean, even I could trying to out-class the Queen of England and get away with it."  The repugnant look at been replaced by one of growing frustration.

"Pull-eeze," he said, reaching out and giving Arvia's braid a flicker of a touch with his index finger, "Middler is out and so are single braids touching your derriere. Ga-Ga's in so, go-go and get-get with the times."

* * * * *

Sam still stood behind the bar, his eyes glued to the interview session taking place across the factory floor; the quartet subdued by the sun's rays trying to force their way through the grime coated skylight. Sad memories of his past collided with his hangover. He glanced down and saw the empty bottles of Tullamore Dew and Drambuie and thought about digging another bottle out of the case, cracking the seal and repeating last night's performance. Instead, he plucked a pair of bottles out of the case and placed them on the new glass reflected back bar. The collision in his brain was like a pinball bumping and being pushed in a never ending series of ricochets. Princess Matty was one of the pinball machine's rubber bumpers. His ex-wife, Amanda was a flashing blinding light positioned next to her daughter. There was a *Tilt* sign flashing on and off. The sign was centered in the crushed face of his illicit love. Charles and Franco were two more flashing lights joining the worries of Bo's pending confession; his mug shot blinking with the others. There were flashing neon pictures of his second wife posing in the nude for Quintin Bell and John Brown. He slowly squeezed his eyes shut. The pinball machine disappeared. He opened his eyes a crack hoping he was in a dream. He wasn't. The others were still in animated conversation with Charles leading the way and Arvia catching up. Sam heard her say, "And just what in Hades is wrong with my hair?" He tried to move his head from side to side but it hurt too much. A sigh escaped from him and he said in a hush, "Set 'em up, Joe. I got a little story you ought a know."

* * * * *

Matilda and Ben sat on the library floor in the reserve book section after school.  Piles of periodicals scattered around them waited to be sorted and shelved.

"I'm going to do it, Ben," she said, a hush to her voice.  "I don't care if my mother finds out.  I know I'm homely and...."

Ben's head jerked up.  "Don't you ever say that; you're beautiful."

Matilda gently touched Ben's hand.  "That's sweet of you, Ben, but I know that these..."  She shyly glanced down at her breasts.  "...are the only thing boys and the dirty old men that run our town notice about me.  If that's what they want, then let them pay to look.  And more than two cents."

Ben shook his head.  "Are you sure you want to do this?"

"Before I finished your uncle's audition I knew," said Matilda, holding up the index and middle finger of her right hand in a *V*.

* * * * *

After her encounter with Frank and Charles, ninety nine percent Charles, Arvia was relieved to see them leave.  She glanced at her brother and asked, "Are you really considering those two?"

Bo was beyond elated.  "Sis, they're perfect.  They are the epitome of boutique."

Arvia raised her eyebrows and said, "If you say so."  She excused herself saying her good-byes to Sam and left.  Her head spun like a child's top.  No one had ever criticized her as blatantly as Charles.  "There's not a darned thing wrong with my hair," she muttered to a light breeze that swept across the factory's parking lot.  "Not one darned strand."  She stopped at her car and studied her reflection in the driver's side window.  "My hair style is perfect you rude, ill-mannered imperfect excuse for a human being," she said, examining the lustrous single black braid that ran more than half way down her back. "It's who I am." On rare occasions, mostly for formal gatherings, she coiled the black braid on top of her head. La Tinkerbelle's was not a formal gathering. She let out a huff, got in her silver Mercedes and started it up. As she backed out to turn the car toward the gouged out, steep drop off of the parking lot ramp, she noticed Charles and Frank. She spun the steering wheel, aimed directly for Charles and stomped on the accelerator. Just as she saw extreme fear wipe away the look of flamboyant arrogance on Charles's face, she spun the steering wheel hard in the opposite direction. The rear end of the Mercedes fishtailed, the tires throwing up an ugly conglomeration of gravel, dirt and assorted trash in a dense cloud as the back tail light came within inches of shortening Charles's height by two and a half feet. Arvia smiled when she caught the look on Charles's face in her rear view mirror. "Ramon," she hissed at the disappearing image in the mirror. "Whoever you are, kiss my backside."

* * * * *

Sam thought he had experienced every form of human emotion possible after watching Quintin Bell and Attorney John Brown destroy his rebuilt life and the lives of so many around him. Then there was the shock of his daughter coming back into his life in, above all places, a discotheque and as a teenager. He hadn't been prepared for that just the way he wasn't prepared for Charles and Frank. He didn't know what would happen next, but he knew his daughter's mother would soon join the bizarre parade marching back into his life. Sam took pride in recognizing that he was a realist. He congratulated himself for storing his old shopping cart, newspapers and plastic bags in a broom closet behind Bo's makeshift office. "Experience is the best teacher," he muttered knowing that life back on the street was a real possibility. He stayed busy with taking inventory and stocking the bar even though his mind was centered on his Princess Matty. His eyes began to water as he tried to picture her growing up. She was two when he last saw her and now she was a senior in high school, a young woman. His self pity was put on the shelf of the back bar along with the liquor bottles when he heard Bo talking to himself a mile a minute about the boutique.

"Berthold, you genius, your idea to locate the boutique in the glass enclosed office cubicles is sheer borderline brilliance," he said to the factory's vast space. "If I didn't need the help of that inane Charles and his unfortunate friend, I'd run the place myself." He kept talking to himself. "And, I wouldn't have to pay out a dime in labor costs."

Heckle and Jeckle ignored Bo, as they did most times, and joined Sam who was forcing himself to keep his mind on getting the bar ready for what Bo had called his Grand Celebrity Opening Night.

"It can't miss, Sam," he had said to his friend late one evening as they were on their hands and knees affixing masking tape to the perimeter of the dance floor. "Big shots mean big money," Bo continued non-stop. "That translates into big, big free publicity for us, free advertising. You know how big shots like to tell other big shots how big they are."

Sam gave a grunt. "Are you forgetting that I wrote the book on big shots," he said. "Be careful with this idea of yours, Boss," he continued. "If I know one thing about big shots, it's that their arms are too short to reach the bottom of their pockets."

* * * * *

Promptly at two, Bo's candidate for a belly dancer squeezed her way through the rusted gate opening of the front door. Bo blinked, Déjà vu blinding him for an instant. He thought he knew her but didn't know from where. The factory's dreary light hid her face, but he was sure he had seen her walk. It was a shuffle punctuated by a skip and a swaying of the hips. "Where do I know her from?" he asked himself. "Welcome," he said to the woman standing in front of him. "I assume you are Miss Schmitt," he asked. "It is Schmitt?"

"It is Schmitt," the woman replied with a slight Chicagoeze accent. "And you must be Mr. Pepperwall," she said. "At least I hope you're Mr. Pepperwall, the gentleman I have an interview with this afternoon."

"I am indeed that gentleman," answered Bo, savoring being referred to as a gentleman in a positive way for one of the rare times in his life.

CLICK/SNAP!

Bo's mind wasn't cooperating with his role as interviewer. It kept tickling the jammed computerized Roll-a-dex of his brain. Bo saved every experience, every encounter with each person he came in contact with from birth to present, both good and bad. Ninety percent were bad. "That walk," he thought. "If John Brown were a woman it would be his walk."

"Mr. Pepperwall," the voice repeated again, as she came into view. "I hope I'm not late." She stopped in front of Bo, extended her tiny, almost frail hand, and shook Bo's hand.

Bo grimaced. "Strong handshake for a woman," he said.

"For a woman," she repeated, sounding offended.

Bo ignored her comment. "Welcome, Miss Schmitt," he said, letting go of her hand. Then more than Déjà vu took a swipe at Bo. Close up and in the light Bo saw his belly dancer; a faded blue sweatshirt, sleeves cut off at the elbow and a worn out, *Dance Chicago* printed across the front in old English Script caught his eye for a split second. Déjà vu was on a roll when Bo saw the woman's eyes. They were a faded blue, so light they cast a hypnotic affect. They also sparkled. Bo was certain he knew her; at the very least, seen her. He stared at the woman so hard he almost absorbed her. She had a trace of Fatima's belly but not the heft. The upper and lower parts of her body appeared to be separated by a sensuous ball bearing that didn't stop rotating.

CLICK/SNAP!

"You've got the job!"

"What," she blurted out.  Her mouth hung open, her jaw appearing as if it had a sign dangling from it saying: "Temporarily out of service."

"The job is yours if you want it."

The out of service sign didn't reply.

"Excuse me, Boss," said Sam, wiping his hands on a dirty rag that was once his plaid, lumberjack shirt.  He squinted at Bo's new belly dancer and said in a surprised voice, "Naomi?"

"Oh, dear God," blurted Naomi.  In the next instant, she and Sam were hugging each other like middle age twins who had been separated after pre-school graduation.

Bo felt as if he were being swept away downstream, the last survivor of the Johnstown Flood, a torrent of rushing water battering his body against rocks and tree limbs.  "You two know each other?" he asked.  After the hugging, cheek kissing, sobs, tears and choking gasps, Bo had his question answered.  Naomi Schmitt and Sam knew each other, old friends from once happy times that had turned heinous.  They had met before Sam had lost his bar to Quintin Bell and John Brown.  When it became evident that Quintin Bell and John Brown were going to evict the elderly tenants living in tiny apartments above the bar, Naomi Schmitt made the mistake of butting heads with the two impeccably dressed connivers. She lost.

A social worker for a neighborhood coalition assisting senior citizens, Naomi got slaughtered by Quitnin Bell and John Brown.  She had gone to Sam's bar to drown her sorrows after an emotionally brutal day of wanting to kill Quintin Bell and John Brown.  Seeing one of her favorite elderly ladies succumb to her growing depression, a depression added to by eviction, was too much for a trained social worker.  The too much got added to by a crack baby whose cracks could no longer heal had stopped its agonizing crying. She sat at the bar, despair dripping from her face and said to Sam, "I'll have a Tom Collins." She slowly raised her right hand and extended her index and middle fingers. "Make it a double."

Sam knew the forlorn look. At times in his life, he took credit for inventing it. An untouched Tom Collins and plenty of listening on Sam's part found him volunteering to help Naomi's senior citizens who lived in the apartments above the bar to relocate. "I'll help you in any way I can," Sam had said to Naomi as he nursed a club soda with a dash of grenadine. "Somebody's got to fight for them besides you." Sam and Naomi Schmitt never had a chance to throw a punch. They barely climbed into the ring before the fight was stopped by a TKO. Quintin Bell and John Brown pummeled them. Sam had twenty four hours to get out of his bar, and the seniors had the same amount of time to move from their tiny apartments. Naomi got arrested for leaving four claw like tracks down the side of John Brown's right cheek, a personal pleasure she cherished. She was, however, angry with herself for missing Quintin Bell's unblemished, chiseled jaw.

Good to his word, Sam helped Naomi in trying to aid and comfort the elderly tenants being evicted after a court order obtained by Quintin Bell and John Brown. Nearly broke and out on the street himself, he and Naomi assisted the last tenant to hobble down the back wooden stairs of the building. They booth stood filled with hatred and revenge as they watched a single piece of heavy equipment, its hungry jaws open, tear off a chunk of The Workingman's Saloon and spit it into a waiting dump truck. A strip shopping mall would begin its appearance as soon as a bulldozer brushed away the crumbs of destruction.

Naomi and Sam saw Quintin Bell and John Brown watching the demolition with what they perceived to be arrogant smirks on their faces. He left Naomi, walked casually up to Quintin and John Brown displaying a look of docility and meekness. Then he fired a cracking left hook into the jaw of Quintin Bell. He came back with a right cross that Quintin Bell countered landing a punch under Sam's right eye.  Sam fired another punch. Quintin ducked. John Brown didn't. Naomi heard the crunch and saw John Brown drop to his knees.  She raced to Sam's side as he and Quintin traded punches, their arms warding off the blows.  She let out a scream as she ran full force into the former All-American football player.  He cast her off with a forearm like she was a feather.  The feather landed on a kneeling John Brown knocking him back, the lawyer's head slamming against the pavement.  Before Sam and Naomi realized they were handcuffed and in the back of a Chicago police car.

The strip mall eventually took shape.  A nail salon, fast food take out shop called, "Heroes R' Us", a cut-rate barber shop and a discount store selling everything for fifty cents called the Half Buck being the attractions.  Their only solace came one morning as they watched workers erase an F that a prankster or pranksters had painted over the B on the discount store's sign. Sam and Naomi hugged that afternoon, vowing that they would stay in touch.  They would have if Sam's wife had not filed for divorce, John Brown her lawyer.  That's when Sam found himself wearing mismatched, discarded running shoes and pushing his worldly possession in a shopping cart.  His only motivation to keep from following the depressed elderly tenant who died was his stumbling on Heckle and Jeckle.  He found them while rummaging through a garbage dumpster looking for a meal in an alley behind a Jewish Deli.  The cats were not pleased with the competition until Sam shared his meal with them.

* * * * *

"Why don't we talk in my office," said Bo, eager to get his latest attraction for La Tinkerbelle's in his fold of entertainers.

"My office is over there," he repeated, nodding toward several stacks of pallets forming a cubicle near the closest wall.  He now had an employee, besides Sam, and his undercover Chicago Police officers, who he knew he could trust.  He had his doubts about Charles and Frank; mostly Charles.  Then there was a hair dresser named Ramon who supposedly was going to open a branch of one of his hair salons in La Tinkerbelle's.  So far, Ramon had been a no-show.

"We'll talk after," said Sam, releasing Naomi from their hug.  "Don't be alarmed at what the boss says," he warned her with a smile.  "I think you'll like working here."

Bo led Naomi into his make-shift office.  He sat on one of the two chairs, treasures that Sam once pulled out of neighborhood garbage dumpsters when he first occupied the vacated factory and turned it into his domicile.  "Did you bring your music like you said?" asked Bo.

Naomi's faded blue eyes glowed as she nodded.

Bo watched her unpack a portable boom box from her torn, brown leather dance bag, the shoulder strap knotted through a tarnished brass loop at one end.

CLICK/SNAP!

Moment's later music flowed from two tiny speakers and Naomi Schmitt's figure was causing the tilted mustache across Bo's lip to list from starboard to port and back again before capsizing.

When the music ended Bo's mustache was in a bent handlebar configuration; one end pointing up and the other down.  He said the only thing he could think of.  "How old did you say you were?"

"That's an illegal question, Mr. Pepperwall," she snapped back.  Then, thinking of what Sam had said to her, she replied.  "I'm thirty nine ninety nine."

"Wow," replied Bo, a grin forming.  "If you keep moving like that you'll never reach the big four zero."

Naomi Schmitt was a short, compact bundle of beauty with long auburn hair caressing her shoulder blades and not looking a day over nineteen except around her eyes where too many crows were battling to nest. She possessed a caring smile tipped with a hint of seduction. Her sweat shirt had been shed for the audition leaving her in a halter top, worn bleach spattered jeans cut low at the hips and a white veil that showed what appeared to be singe marks across the bottom. The veil covered her face from the tip of her pert nose to spilling over her breasts. She wore tiny brass cymbals on her thumbs and forefingers that she had clinked together to the beat of the music and the gyration of her hips.

Bo's cigarette lighter had kept the beat with its CLICK/SNAPS!

After the music ended on a scratch and a squelch coming from the boom box, Naomi sat down on the other rickety folding chair, one leg held together with several precarious wraps of safety wire and adhesive tape.

"Miss Schmitt," Bo started, trying to be professional and formal after his mustache had circumnavigated his upper lip, "according to this resume you handed me I noticed the name of Quintin Bell. My late brother-in-law was Quintin Bell. Could it be a coincidence that you worked for him in some capacity?"

She looked at him and said in a cold tone, "It wasn't a coincidence, Mr. Pepperwall," she said, an anger visible in her voice. "It was a colossal mistake. Had I known he was the mayor of that snobby suburb up north along the lake, the low life who did to me and Sam what he did, I would have shunned him like a social disease." She paused then continued. "All I know is that I got a call from some mousey sounding woman by the name of Wanda Mink or something like that. I needed the money so I took the job. God, had I only known." She glanced at Bo and said: "I read where he died. Is that true?"

Bo nodded.

"I thought so," she said, her reply still showing signs of anger, but the anger had a touch of satisfaction attached to it. "That Mink lady I talked to told me I would be performing at a political fund raiser. She even asked me if it would be possible to teach her how to belly dance. She wanted to surprise a friend of hers." Naomi exhaled, trying not to relive that night. "I didn't realize that Emperors Nero and Caligula were also hired to provide the entertainment. Your brother-in-law's fund raiser was pure debauchery. I'll never forget that night. This will probably change your mind about offering me a job, but that man was the biggest swindler, womanizer and maggot who ever walked the face of the earth. I gave up believing in God after working for him that night." She paused, glanced up toward the ceiling and said, "I'm sorry I lost faith in you, God."

CLICK/SNAP! CLICK/SNAP!

"Just a habit of mine," said Bo, trying to get rid of his sheepish look when he noticed her glance at the sound coming from his pants pocket. "Don't worry about not getting the job. I'm a man of my word and the job is yours, if you want it." He paused, felt his lighter and took another long look at Naomi Schmitt. "You're not the only one who ever characterized my late brother-in-law as a maggot. There were many, many folks on that list."

Naomi folded her arms across her chest. "I never even got paid for that night," she said, looking at Bo as if she knew him from somewhere. "Oh, there were several dollar bills tucked in my costume; one character who called himself the Chief of Police slipped in a twenty and then took nineteen in change. Another unique character I remember from that night was some bare breasted floozy who tried to pour olive oil on me while trying to stuff what looked like a striped wooden handle of some kind into the crotch of my costume. She kept warning me in a syrupy southern drawl that I'd better keep my veils to myself because the mayor belonged to her and her alone." She paused and looked way too serious at Bo. "Can you believe that?"

Bo nodded saying: "When it came to my brother-in-law I can believe anything." Vivid images of the fateful night Quintin Bell died raced through his brain, one in stop action. "And, you say you never got paid?"

"I never even got a thank you or an apology."

"Didn't you try to find my brother-in-law after that and try to get your money?"

Naomi carefully removed the music cassette from her boom box and placed it in the side pocket of her dance bag, its torn zipper dangling. "Not with that southern bottle job blond giggling and pawing the bee-jeepers out of me. She was a real sick-o; and two even bigger sick sons-of-guns were your late brother-in-law and that creepy lawyer buddy of his. The entire group needed an army of Dr. Phil's if you ask me; so much for my trying to make a few extra dollars by showing a bunch of Northshore drunken snobs the art form of belly dancing."

"So you were mistreated by my brother-in-law and his lawyer friend, John Brown at the party?"

"Those two, that nymphomaniac nut case married to that pathetic so-called preacher who never had an empty gin 'n tonic glass in his hand all night and a bunch of women acting ever so uppity while putting their boobs on display," she said. "I couldn't wait to get out of there. I never wanted to see any of them again." She paused, blue eyes reflecting. "I thought I was home free until some moron set my costume on fire and I had to jump into a muddy pond so I wouldn't burn to death." She paused, glanced at Bo for a moment, the sparkle gone from her eyes. "Why is it I feel I know you from somewhere?"

Bo gave a shrug. "You say someone set you on fire?"

"Only the lower part of my costume," she said. "And part of my veil." She looked seriously at Bo. "Are you sure the job's mine?"

"Dead sure," he said.

She flashed a look of doubt at Bo, the tip of her right index finger brushed at tears starting down her cheeks. "Sam's a beautiful, caring human being; the best. None better. I often wondered what happened to him and now I know." She looked at Bo trying to regain her composure. "Gee, Mr. Pepperwall, you're lucky to know him and I'm even luckier to work with him again."

Bo couldn't feel his Zippo. He could, however, feel compassion and warmth for his newly hired employee and said, "Well, if you're a friend of Sam and your social work is as good as your dancing, you'll be able to help all kinds of people again." He shuffled several pieces of paper on the top of his pallet desk top. "However, before you can help anyone, you'll have to change your name."

"What's the matter with my name?" she asked, taken back.

"What I meant is that you'll need a stage name, something on our marquee that will create curb appeal and draw in customers. Naomi and Her Seven Veils is cute, but it doesn't cut it; lacks flair, needs pizzazz and, above all, it has to fit our La Tinkerbelle's theme."

"Excuse me, Mr. Pepperwall," said a now annoyed Naomi Schmitt. "When did I ever call myself Naomi and the Seven Veils?"

"I just assumed," he said, then catching himself as he saw a vision of Charles and heard his comment about making an ass out of you and me. He shifted in his metal folding chair and a taped leg gave way sending him into a position where he braced himself against his pallet desk with both forearms. "I'll think of a name," he said trying to appear professional and keep from ending up on the floor. "What do you think of adding an eyepatch and maybe wearing a hook on one hand, maybe a pair of white Go-Go boots with those veils, and do your dance behind a protective front window?"

Naomi's shoulders drooped. She stood up. Very businesslike, she began putting the rest her belongings into her scuffed leather dance bag. "Mr. Pepperwall, hook and an eye patch, plus white Go-Go boots?"

"Now don't be too hasty, Miss Schmitt. The job pays well."

"But, performing from behind a window wearing white Go-Go boots? Are you living in the 60's? I'm not a stripper. I'm an artist. Belly Dancing is an art form. The next thing I know you'll want me to slide up and down a brass pole."

CLICK/SNAP!

"And if you dare allude to my having my crotch tattooed and nipples pierced like some bubble headed coke freak, you'll need a team of surgeons to remove my boom box from your you-know-where."

CLICK/SNAP!

"Most customers who come into bars don't know art from paint by the numbers," said Bo, as he balanced himself into an upright position. "Sam told me that," he said feeling smug. "If you change your bump and grind of the seven veils to the swaying seven seas, you'll be a rich broad."

"I find the term, broad, very demeaning, Mr. Pepperwall."

"Hey, if I were Frank Sinatra, you wouldn't mind being called a broad. And you sure didn't seem demeaned when my brother-in-law, and John Brown tried to rip off your veils when you performed at the Country Club."

"You knew about that?"

"Heard a rumor," said Bo embarrassed. "From my sister, I think." Bo nodded put his hand through his black hair and wiped the oil slick off on his pants.

"Grabbing at my veils was one thing, being set on fire was, well, lunacy. If I ever run into that imbecile again, I'll show him what demeaning is."

Bo carefully slid his hand from his pocket and tried to hide the guilty look on his face. "Well, you won't have to worry about that here. Remember, you'll be in the window protected by a locked door, a door that you and you alone can open.  The glass in front of you will be so thick that a wrecking ball like the one that destroyed Sam's saloon couldn't put a crack in it."

"You want me behind a window dancing in go-go boots; white go-go boots?"

"Of course," said Bo, back to being positive and excited. "This is show business.  We'll call you something that will have pirate overtones, something related to our theme, Peter Pan, something like, Captain Hookette.  You'll be one of our featured attractions at La Tinkerbelle's.  How does that sound?"

"It doesn't," she snapped.

Bo reached for a piece of scrap paper on the top of his make-shift desk and scribbled something in pencil on it.  He handed the paper to Naomi.  "How do you like that offer, Captain Hookette?" he asked, trying to act like he thought an impresario might act.  "Are you sure you won't change your mind about white go-go boots and a hook?"  He saw her raise her eyes and look into his own.  His heart stopped beating.

Naomi Schmitt nodded politely, forced a pleasant smile, glanced down at the paper one more time and then looked at Bo again and said, "Aye, aye, Admiral.  When do we sail?"

* * * * *

After Arvia drove out of the La Tinkerbelle's parking lot at near the speed of sound and nearly ended the life of one half of the newly hired boutique management team, she sped downtown to John Brown's office.  He had told her he had some important documents pertaining to her husband's estate that needed her attention.  Normally, she avoided John Brown as if he was a leper on Molokai, but after her encounter with Charles, she could tolerate a few minutes with the attorney.  At least she would be in his office with the door open instead of his showing up at Dogwood unannounced.  There was no way she would ever allow John Brown in her home again even if she did have a

.38 caliber pistol hidden under her night stand in her bedroom and Schickle and Gruber roaming the grounds at night after Hans had left.

Arvia and John Brown both looked out the window at the boats in Monroe Street Harbor, the fall season continuing its lazy shift to winter. Scats looked at Arvia and asked, "So what's Schmoe up to now? Has he spent all of your inheritance yet?"

"Small correction, Mister Brown," she said. "The money was mine in the first place and I can spend it the way I want."

"Doesn't matter," said John, a smile preceding, "Once a schmoe, always a schmoe."

"I think not," she said softly. "I just left him and we, the Schmoe and I, have hired a management team to run our club's boutique."

"A boutique?" repeated John with a slight shake of his head. "The Schmoe has suckered you into running a boutique?"

Arvia smiled and nodded. "He was also interviewing some woman, a belly dancer I heard him say, for a job. I have no idea for what kind of job so, please don't ask."

"A belly dancer," repeated John Brown, his chair swiveling back so he was looking at Lake Michigan again. "Did I hear you say a belly dancer?"

"That's what I just said, Mister Brown." Arvia paused and looked at the back of her lawyer's head. "Why wasn't there a croquet mallet with your name on it," she silently asked herself?

"He should have hired you, Arvia," said John Brown, lust coating his words.

His comment made her skin quiver with disgust. "Wasn't there a belly dancer who performed at that dreadful political fund raising affair at the Club the night Quintin died?"

John Brown folded his hands as if in prayer and pressed them lightly to his lips. "Oh, the dancer your brother set on fire."

"Bo set her on fire?"

"Schmoe did indeed," he said smiling.  "Only her veils; nothing serious, no injuries or anything like that," he said."  He paused, leaned forward in his chair and said: "Arvia, let's forget about that idiot brother of yours.  How about we concentrate on you and me?  Let me take you to dinner."  He got up from behind his desk and walked up to her.  "We could go to Everest."  He reached out to put his hands on her shoulders, but she gracefully stepped back.  "Everest is five stars just like you."  He tried to reach for her again and she continued to step back.  "But you're more beautiful; more delectable; and, I might add," his tongue licking at his upper lip, "succulent."

Arvia slowly and discretely turned away and walked to the chair across from John Brown's desk positioning herself between the chair and the attorney.  She could feel her skin crawl.  "You asked me to come here so that you can have me finalize Quintin's estate or, more correctly, the financial status of what was my money and my estate from the very start."

John Brown returned to his desk and sat down.  "Ah, yes, your financial status," he said leering.  "The figures," he repeated his words full of lust.  "Let me check your figures."  His eyes traveled over Arvia's body.  "Your figure is in excellent shape."

"I should've known," said Arvia, as she abruptly started for the door.  "I don't find your comments the least bit amusing.  And I don't know why I wasted my time coming down town."

"Now don't be so sensitive," said the attorney, a harshness covering his words.  "I'm paying you a compliment."

"That's not why I'm paying you and, God knows, I'm paying you plenty," she said, now standing at the massive oak door of his office.  "At least I know where my money is going with Bo and La Tinkerbelle's a Go-Go."

"La what?"

"That's what it's called, and he's planning a gala opening night.  He's even gone and invited everyone who attended Quintin's wake as my guests, absolutely everyone.  He says its good public relations; black tie, no less, and gratis besides."

John Brown gave Arvia a blank look and said: "I was at the wake and the funeral."  He paused at stared some more before saying:  "I didn't get an invitation."

# Chapter 12

## <u>Cap'n's Kids, Obadiah and Emerine</u>

## (Juan Ponce de Leone and Izzy Inman)

Had Arvia's earlier wish for John Brown to accompany her husband into the hereafter come true, she would have been denied witnessing the compendium of looks that flashed across his face after telling him about La Tinkerbelle's black tie charity gala. John Brown's lecherous eyes clicked like an electrical switch on Baron Von Frankenstein's laboratory circuit board. Then, in a second, he had turned into a garish neon sign that had just suffered a short circuit after she had said: "Perhaps your invitation got lost in the mail." She knew it hadn't. The feeling of satisfaction she experienced at watching his invitation get swallowed up by her paper shredder before ending up in the recycle bin along with the others she had nixed, made her giggle like a naughty school girl.

John Brown, Attorney-at-Law, Lothario and usurious loan shark sat like a reject mold from a wax museum, the lower half of his body still in the mold, his face a grotesque mask of drooping warm wax. He hadn't felt so stunned since the day he walked into the editor's outer office of the college newspaper to sweet talk her and find out if he had made the All-American football team. He made the team, a copy of the paper on a table outside her closed inner office door so announced. He was second team All-American; Quintin Bell made the first. John Brown had stared at the newsprint until it became a black blur.

Then he heard sobs coming from behind the editor's door.  His knock on the door was soft; his entrance softer and his words tender as he attempted to console the editor.  The bookish editor's soggy, shattered heart lay in pieces atop her desk along with a folded American flag.  "I'm sorry," he had said knowing his statement was directed at him and that his friend had stolen both their dreams.  "Thou shalt not steal," he muttered in the editor's office.  He watched her sob, her tears staining the desk top blotter as he began to plot his revenge.

* * * * *

Arvia Pepperwall Bell's Mulatto blood comingling with strains of Mohican gave her a genetic understanding of human nature handed down from her relatives.  Their dealings with the fork tongued, thieving white man honed that knowledge.  Added to that was a DNA composition based on using wampum, barter and hunting, fishing and trapping skills to survive.  Her bloodline also brought her an inner strength and a sense for financial management that no University M.B.A. programs offered.  The Glen Forest on the Watercourse new village mayor didn't need an advanced business degree.  Neither did she need a back room filled with cigar smoke nor fund raising sex parties at the Country Club to act mayoral.  Acting was out of the question.  The town's power brokers soon found themselves tip-toeing across a vast sea of prairie grass, sidestepping steaming piles of buffalo chips as the new mayor led them into her version of an ambush at Little Big Horn.

There were many looks Arvia savored that day after leaving La Tinkerbelle's and going to John Brown's office, the fear on Charles's face near the top.  Not only did she find the stunned, blinking glows flashing from John Brown's face humorous, but she gave herself several pats on the back for the way she strung him along before walking out of his office.  She had thought about making an exit coated with sexual innuendos, perhaps an exaggerated swaying of her hips as she choreographed her choice of exit strategies. "Too tacky," she had thought. "Too much like Quintin's and John's sluts." She settled on what she hoped was a seductive sounding, "Ta-ta" and the sliding of her sunglasses half way down her nose as if she were going to say to the attorney with her eyes: "Dogwood around eightish for cocktails. Then, who knows." She gave thought to fluttering her eyelashes the way her attonrey's secretary, Bambi did, but that also fit into her too tacky category. Yet, there was no taste of revenge being sweet. Crow in all its roasted perfection sat stuffed on her platter but she had lost her appetite.

When she had taken her first step into the lobby of John Brown's Loop office building she felt soiled. By the time she pushed the elevator's button and stepped out into the reception area of his opulent office, soiled had changed to rancid. An odor more foul that the one she encountered on her intital visit to La Tinkerbelles made her nostrils clamp shut. That odor belonged to John Brown's aftershave lotion. Then she saw the lawyer's secretary and felt sympathy for her. Bambi came direct from the Quintin and John catalogue of Bubble Heads. She was perfect in all physical attributes, her I.Q. the same as her bra size and another in a line of John Brown's here-today-gone-tomorrow secretaries named after cute, cuddly forest creatures. Her job description, as with her predecessors, was to transport sealed envelopes in person to Quintin Bell in the Country Club steam room. John Brown changed secretaries more often than his socks. Bambi, like the others, was a blond direct from the Duh School of Diction and chewed licorice flavored gum that made her tongue and the corners of her mouth black. "Hi, Miss Spell," she said, the gum wad causing the mispronunciation. "Scatsy, oops, I mean, Mister Brown is ready for you." She blushed. "I mean he's expecting you. Go right in." The blond, her tresses doing an obscene dance worthy of one Glider Slider at the Glen Forest on the Watercourse Country Club's

Christmas party, nodded at the door as her chewing gum cracked in time with the sway of her hips.

Arvia couldn't wait to flee the attorney's office. Her mission was accomplished. The dazed look on his face sent its message. She was back in the outer office, ever polite and mannerly, telling Bambi it was a pleasure meeting her and wished her good luck. During her drive north up Lake Shore Drive, she couldn't help smiling at what she saw after she had said to him: "By the way, John, I hear Bo has sent an invitation to the White House for our gala fund raising opening." Her head felt like a flute filled with expensive champagne, the bubbles jumping and exploding with joy.

* * * * *

Outside of scrutinizing her brother's check writing and culling his invitation list, Arvia didn't interfere with her brother's business creation. She was amazed with Bo's ideas and more amazed that he managed to carry all of them off. He exhibited the combined skills of a Broadway set designer, an Arab merchant haggling in a Persian market and a time and motion study expert with distant ties to Frank and Lillian Gilbreth. In the beginning, she was positive he would fail. So she thought. Then came Sam, Heckle and Jeckle, undercover police on roller skates, a gay couple to manage her boutique, a hairdresser named Ramon and a pirate belly dancer. That, she thought, was more than an adequate price to pay for straddling the edge of bad taste. Then her brother's ideas entered into the realm of Edgar Allan Poe. First came the hiring of an octogenarian, three-piece band who he billed as, Cap'n's Kids. Joining Bo's musicians was a teenage champion hog caller from Arkansas, Obadiah Ledbetter. He came complete with freckles; missing his lower four front teeth and arm-in-arm with his common-law wife, Emerine Randall who was the same age as Arvia. Obadiah would be a vocalist for Cap'n's Kids, punctuating old standard lyrics with an occasional championship hog call, "Sueey, Pig! Sueey, sueey, sueey! Ya pig!" Somehow, her brother remembered reading "Lord of the Flies" and equated buccaneers, islands and pigs with his discotheque's Peter Pan theme. Arvia had trouble accepting Emerine Randall, Obadiah's common law wife, who accompanied the band by banging a tambourine off her ample hips.

Emerine Randall, who never wore anything but a sequined, late 1950's style sheath cocktail dress morning, noon or night, had heavy, black penciled eye brows, the result of plucking out, over time, her natural ones that she considered, "Ugly as a briar patch." She cursed fate for bringing her into the world too late to be a Playboy Bunny or a Flower Child; instead she grew up living with her father in the back of a Skelly gas station and general store outside of Magnolia, Mississippi. The store specialized in selling wild boar jerky. Her two biggest thrills in life were waving at Bill Clinton when he was running for President and hearing Obadiah Ledbetter's championship hog calls while she sold wild boar jerky from the back of her daddy's pickup truck at county fairs. She offered Obadiah some free jerky as he walked by holding his latest championship trophy. One bite had him falling hopelessly in love with someone who was twice his age. As the fair ended, they got in her father's pickup truck and traveled across the south selling jerky and Obadiah participating in hog calling contests at every county fair they could find.

Emerine eventually returned the truck to her father a year and a half later. She left it parked behind the Skelly station with a note apologizing for her tardiness and drove off with Obadiah in a newer used pickup truck, a first prize contest award from another county fair.

* * * * *

Bo's ideas continued to spill out. He wanted to paint the

ceiling over the converted foundry's dance floor midnight blue and glue on stars made of silver glitter. Sam convinced him that neither the paint nor glitter would stick to a surface that was caked with decades of industrial grease, soot and smoke.

Bo shrugged off that idea, surged ahead and generated a dozen more. Suspended from the ceiling by cables attached to the foundry's motorized hoist that ran the length of the building on a steel rail was his piece de resistance--six cylindrical shaped wire cages with a go-go dancer in each, wearing little else except a t-shirt resembling a mini-dress, a sequined bikini bottom and white go-go boots. The cages would be lowered and suspended just out of reach of the patrons and would travel slowly back and forth to recorded music from the 1950's and 1960's. It didn't matter to Bo if that music clashed with the old standards from the 1930's and 1940's being played by Cap'n's Kids from an elevated bandstand directly across from the winding bar. He had a tin ear when it came to music. To him, as well as his nephew's generation, loud and unintelligible was a symphony. One of his last ideas, one he considered his most brilliant, was his theme trio. Tinker Bell and her partners, Peter and Pan would soar high above the club's floor suspended by cables from the same hoist that held the cages. Logistically, Bo figured that the more seductive women he could hang from the ceiling, the more male customers, he calculated, would be subliminally directed to the men's room. Upon entering the men's room through a door covered in black vinyl and outlined in brass upholstery tacks, the same tacks used to spell out STUDS at eye level across the door, a man would be greeted by more black. The walls would be black, the lighting subdued and there would be a soundtrack of women breathing heavy and moaning in pleasure. There would be no urinals, only private stalls, each door also black, painted with a textured paint and installed with two tiny lights, one red the other green. Inside each stall was a coin operated box mounted on a side wall that would take quarters and credit cards. A movie projection screen was affixed to the door and had a sign below stating: *Chase Away Your Cares and Woes*. Bo calculated that twenty five cents for a twenty five second showing of a clip of a pornographic movie could make him a bundle of money; at least bags of quarters. Bo didn't concentrate only on his male customers. He also had enough evidence from medical journals that he had read in the waiting rooms of free health clinics as to what turned on a female sexually. He had told his new boutique managers that he wanted to set up a part of La Tinkerbelle's boutique for women only, selling sexual oriented apparel, lotions, creams and various devices, batteries not included. Frank thought the idea was, in his words, "A guaranteed money maker." Charles turned his back and walked away muttering, "Our sisters are not tacky tarts to be equated with the price of a battery." He dismissed his partner with the flick of his wrist saying, "For shame."

"I will not be caught dead having my name associated with such bizarre filth," Arvia warned her brother, unable to think of any other response after she learned of the boutique's section for women only.

* * * * *

Sam didn't pay much attention to Bo's ideas for what he called, "an overpriced gin mill with flashing lights and bedlam." To him, La Tinkerbelle's was first and foremost a saloon serving alcoholic beverages in a myriad of shapes, styles and tastes. If people paid way too much money to get intoxicated in what he called a theme park for the socially inept and culturally deprived, that wasn't his concern. Patrons of real saloons didn't pay an admission fee to drink. They didn't care how drinks were concocted and doctored to erase the taste of the alcohol. Beer was beer regardless of the name on the bottle; so was vodka and gin, foreign or domestic and all whiskeys.

Drinkers drank because booze, in any form, chased away their blahs, blew off internal steam, made them stronger, more virile and gave them an identity of someone on the cover of People magazine or whatever, if only for a few hours.  Sam had witnessed all of the Jeckle and Hyde transformations; saw the recipients of sand being kicked in their faces turn into violent kickers who ended up being restrained, arrested or heading to the nearest emergency room for stitches.  Listen a lot and say very little were the two extra ingredients Sam served with each of his drinks.  That was before he became reconnected with his Princess Matty and before one of  Bo's ideas became personal.

"Sam," Bo started out like he did all the time addressing his bartender and partner by his first name.  "I didn't know your little girl was interested in the performing arts."

"News to me," said Sam, continuing to arrange drink glasses on the back bar.  "Where did you get that little piece of info?"

"A cute little bird named Matilda Newton let it slip out to her friend who just happens to be my nephew, Ben," replied Bo, his Zippo lighter sliding around in his pocket, a film of sweat coating the metal case.  "I guess my nephew told her I was looking for someone to be an aerialist in our show and portray Tinker Bell.  That would be her stage name, Sam; our version of the cute little Tinker Bell from the kid's classic book, Peter Pan. That is, if she decided to be the star of our show.  That is, if you, her father, would give your permission for a young lady to taste stardom at such a young age.  Stardom in its purest form," he said, his well rehearsed sales pitch unraveling.  "Surely you can't get any purer than Peter Pan.  My goodness, Cathy Rigby has made a career out of making children happy.  My mother used to read Peter Pan to me when I was a child."

CLICK/SNAP!

Sam stopped stacking glasses and looked at Bo, his face asking, "Are you serious?"

Bo nodded.  "I think she'd make a wonderful Tinker Bell,"

he said.  "I see her as sweet, pure, innocent and, above all, anonymous."

CLICK/SNAP!

"Her own mother wouldn't recognize her," continued Bo.

Sam didn't blink.  "You think?"

"Of course," replied Bo, his voice less reassuring as it was when he started.  He watched Sam's active hands come together as if in prayer, resting across the waist string of his white apron.  "I mean she would be our version of Peter Pan.  She could be the reincarnation of Mary Martin."

"Sweet and innocent," repeated Sam.  "What rock have you been living under?" he asked, jarring Bo.  "Entertainment today is nothing but modern smut."  He gave Bo a look that would make both a Broadway and Hollywood director drop to their knees asking to be forgiven.

CLICK/SNAP!

"Boss, I'll tell you what I think."

CLICK/SNAP!

"I think if you harm one lovely strand of hair on my little girl's beautiful head, you'll need someone else to click and snap that cigarette lighter you carry in your pocket."  His look now had producers, playwrights, screen play writers and actors joining the directors in prayer.  "Get my drift?"

"Does that mean yes?"

CLICK/SNAP!

* * * * *

Bo couldn't believe that Sam had given permission for his daughter to be Tinker Bell.  At least he thought Sam gave his okay after a mention of her sprinkling golden fairy dust on the customers.  Bo didn't recall giving all the details of the dusting; omitting that the dust would be dropped by his daughter as she swung back and forth across the ceiling suspended by a cable.  He also failed to mention that Sam's daughter would be wearing a black leotard, thigh-high boots and a black mask making her look like a sexy cat. Bo's logical mind also had a difficult time sorting out the rationale for his bartender and friend threatening his life if the slightest iota of bad happened to his Matty. Still, Bo was elated. His plans were almost complete. He could visualize Matilda Newton flying above the crowd between her wing mates, Peter and Pan. He could also visualize what his body would look like after being altered by Sam if anything happened to Princess Matty. Prayers would be of no help to him. Then the right side of Bo's creative, hyperactive brain began generating new design visions of what his soaring trio would wear for costumes. Gone were his good intentions and original ideas. Forgotten were threats of bodily harm causing pain and agony. He was so excited he had to share his excitement with someone. That someone, unfortunately, was Sam.

"Sam," Bo started out, weighing each word carefully. "I have the cutest, most angelic costume for your Princess Matty. It will make her look spectacular."

"Define spectacular."

CLICK/SNAP!

"Spectacular," Bo repeated timidity in his voice. "Well, spectacular like a divine image. Nothing in bad taste, Sam," he said, weighing his words. "Nothing to embarrass you and your family. That's family as in Princess Matty's mother." He paused, his eyes widening, asking for approval. "Today's modern nuns wear less." He smiled at Sam. "Your princess will have the time of her life flying like Tinker Bell." He paused sensing that his life was about to altered. "Trust me."

CLICK/SNAP

Sam returned Bo's request for trust by saying: "Boss, I too hope she will have the time of her life." His eyes were like two dull drill bits gouging into Bo's soul. "If she doesn't, you won't have a life." Both of his hands were clenched around the end of an eighteen inch length of heavy electrical cable that he referred to as his, "Pacifier." He pulled the weapon from under the bar and passed it slowly under Bo's nose. "One quick swat upside the head and you won't have to glue stars on your ceiling. His left eye winked and the homemade sap slapped against an open palm with a sickening pop. "You'll be one of them." A second pop let out an explosion, this one coming from the top of the wooden bar. "I think I'll call this my Tinker, as inTinker, Tinker little star. Get my drift, Boss?"

CLICK/SNAP!

With Bo, understanding came from a different dictionary. So did his perception of a teenage girl having the time of her life. He never mentioned to Sam that his black sequined costumes for Tinker Bell and Peter and Pan were being fashioned in his mind to have holes cut out in the breast areas. Charles volunteered to try on one of the prototype leotards once the holes were cut. He loved the costume even though he could only poke his head a fourth of the way through one of the openings. Frank thought the costumes were demeaning saying to Bo, "Matilda is a sweet, sweet child. She's Sam's innocent princess." He clenched his teeth. "You may be the major domo of this glorious establishment, Mister Pepperwall, but if you turn that sweet girl into a showbiz trollop, I'll personally give you a collection of ugly welts across your back with one of those new leather whips we just received in the boutique."

"Me first," said Charles, his hands clapping as if he were giving a standing ovation at a Cher concert. "And then I'll sink my fangs into you."

Dreams of dollars turned to dignity as his dilemma returned like the insulting slap across the face he received in John Brown's office at the reading of his brother-in-law's last will. His choice of doing the right thing, of turning in Quintin Bell's murderer, had gotten lost with his creating La Tinkerbelle's. He found himself at a tiny dance studio under the Lake Street El tracks in the West Loop buying three new black leotards.  On his return to La Tinkerbelle's, he sat on the dance floor spraying glue on three pairs of too tight leotards and sprinkling them with silver glitter he bought at a Dollar Party Store on a closeout.  His vow to do the morally right thing slowly vanished with each sprinkle of silver glitter.

Bo put his left hand on Sam's shoulder, his right hand clutching his Zippo lighter.  "Your princess is in good hands," he said to him. "Franco and Charles have volunteered to be her bodyguards."

Sam gave Bo a glance that made Bo's mustache turn into what resembled a cluster of pubic hairs.

"You worry too much," said Bo trying to sound reassuring, but failing miserably.  "Besides, I also have an undercover body guard to protect your princess."  He attempted to look smug, almost cocky when he said, "I have Officer Noel Jones of the Chicago Police Department keeping an eye on your Princess Matty."  A poor excuse of a reassuring nod followed as he said, "Officer Jones's grandmother owns the coffee house in Glen Forest on the Watercourse.  Remember?  It was across the square from where you used to live."

"Your point?" asked the protective father of a princess.

"His grandmother's brother is a judge in the Criminal Court."

"And," stated Sam, the two, dull drill bits of his eyes boring twin smoking holes in Bo's forehead.

"My point is she's as safe as a bug in a rug."

"She'd better be."

CLICK/SNAP.

* * * * *

One thing Arvia didn't do and wouldn't do was go along with her brother's idea for the opening night charity gala.  He thought it was the greatest public relations brain storm in the history of show business.  She had other feelings.  "Never!" she shouted at her brother, causing him to bounce backward where he sat.

"Sis," he had started out the way he always did when he wanted something from her as he sat behind Quintin's Oriental writing desk.  "I think your singing a number or two with the band opening night at the charity fund raiser would make you famous."

"Make me what?" she had asked, flabbergasted.

"Famous," he repeated catching himself not to spell out the word for her.  "After you belt out a song or two, you could sail along the Chicago River on Cleopatra's original barge reclining on a cushion of money while sipping your Perrier from a golden goblet."

Her brother had presented her with way too many harebrained ideas in the past but this bordered on the brink of insanity.  "You want me to stand up in front of all of the most important people in Chicago and sing with a freckle faced teenager who resembles Archie Andrews and his common law wife who's old enough to be his grandmother?" she had asked, unable to comprehend what possessed her brother.  "Maybe his great-grandmother depending on what part of the south she came from."

You'll be a sensation," said Bo, caressing his Zippo lighter resting securely in his one good pant pocket. "You'll add a counter balancing exuberance to Cap'n's Kids," he continued, trying to persuade his sister to sing with his three piece band: Reggie on the accordion, Rommie playing the guitar and Regis on the Polish boombass, bongo drums and spoons.  "The guys will play whatever you want to sing.  You'll be buffo!"  He paused sensing that his sister was not buying what he was selling.  "What do you think of Obadiah possibly joining you in a duet?  The kid's got a great set of pipes," he said, his eyes getting wider.  "Add his common law wife's tambourine slapping against those Michelin Tire Boy hips of hers and I can guarantee you a standing ovation." He glanced at his sister and almost pleading said: "You gotta do this, Sis. Your presence up on the bandstand, your face awash in the brilliance of three, count 'em, spotlights, will have an impact on opening night that will cause a ten on the Richter scale. Trust me."

CLICK/SNAP!

* * * * *

The impact of the opening night charity gala at La Tinkerbelle's and the seismographic reading depended on who felt the tremor and where, exactly, the earth's crust shifted. There were only two vibrations felt that night. The first was from the band's amplifier that screeched so loud at one point several pieces of glass vibrated loose from the mirrored ball hanging from the foundry's ceiling. The ball was another acquisition that Bo jumped on while browsing at John's Junk Store, John telling him through the gaps of badly stained teeth, "My good man, that ball used to hang above the dance floor of the Aragon Ballroom." It didn't, but Bo didn't know and didn't care. He felt it would add to the discotheque's aura and aura, according to Bo's way of thinking, would generate revenue. Besides, it was a bargain. John guaranteed it. The mirrored ball did add to the atmosphere but didn't generate a red cent during the gala charity opening.

The second seismographic vibration rumbling through the gala involved Juan Ponce de Leone and the new valet parkers. They were so incensed that evening at not being tipped that they backed patrons' cars against the factory's back brick wall before parking them. They were going just a shade below twenty miles per hour in reverse at impact. Drinks sitting on the bar or on tables inside periodically showed ripples.

Sam felt his pre-opening analysis of a gala charity had been right on the money. It was money that also had him at a near boil the next morning as he went over how much he had given away in food and drink for charity.  "Boss," he said to Bo, his frustration evident after having put a damper about reaching under the bar and using his Pacifier. "Those dead beat stuffed shirts and big shots you invited stiffed the entire crew.  Not a one of them left a tip for the servers, my bartenders or Juan's crew.  Whoever heard of a bartender not getting a tip?  The waiters and waitresses didn't get a dime and those cheap ass politicians and so-called philanthropists didn't buy a thing in the boutique.  I thought Charles was going to throw a kicking, scratching hair-pulling fit when one of them asked to change a hundred dollar bill so he could go to the men's room.  He wanted ten dollars in quarters."  Sam was sputtering now. "You really blew it, Boss with your free parking idea."

"Did anyone empty the coin operated movie boxes?" Bo asked, kicking himself for not remembering.  "At least we made some money."

"Some as in little to nothing," said Sam, as he went back to checking his inventory.  "I gave our gang money out of my pocket for their tips. They deserved every penny after the abuse those snobs gave them."

"But we did make some money," said Bo.  A chilled feeling of possible failure brushing against him.  He felt like a frustrated Heckle and Jeckle coming up on the short end of a hunt with only a mouse's tail for their efforts. Bo's life had been synonymous with failure. Somehow, he always bounced back, writing his defeats off as bad luck, misfortunes or fate.  He never lost his optimism or the supply of lint in his pockets. His brain rarely shut down and, when it did, it was because he had emptied too many glasses while working at one of his brother-in-law's country club parties. Every idea he had to bring him fame and fortune (more fortune than fame) never got off the drawing board; most never made it from pencil point to paper. La Tinkerbelle's was different.  It was real; it was vibrant and filled with life.  He had never been this close to success.  La

Tinkerbelle's cash registers and his pockets would soon be overflowing with currency.  "When?" he asked himself.  "Malcolm, can you give me any idea of when?"

Bo prided himself on being able to distinguish between the smell of cash and plastic credit cards; both caused his heart to palpitate.  There was no aroma of either during and after his charity gala.  He cursed himself for not hearing the sound of coins dropping into slots in the men's washroom stalls.  His optimism quickly shoved aside disappointment and self flagellation.  His day was coming.  Opening day would be that Friday and failure was unthinkable.  Not even the grizzly sight of a croquet mallet slamming into his brother-in-law's head three times could dampen his enthusiasm.  Besides, fairy dust was about to rain down upon anyone who entered La Tinkerbelle's.

* * * * *

Ben offered his own unique views of the night's charity event while driving home with his mother and uncle.  "Uncle Bo," he had said on the ride back to Glen Forest, his very quiet mother driving the Jaguar.  "Those old people sure did spill a lot on themselves tonight.  Gee, and talk about wasting food.  They left enough on their plates to supply our Famine Sucks Food Drive Program at the high school for the next ten senior classes who will follow me."  He glanced at his mother and uncle in the front of the car.  Neither of them said a word, his mother's hands the only thing moving as she steered the Jaguar north up the Outer Drive and making the turn at Hollywood.  "Uncle Bo, I did think the flashing lights were cool.  I was probably the only one.  The band was okay too.  That Obadiah wasn't bad.  I bet everyone could have heard him without those hissing and popping amplifiers you bought from that junk man friend of yours."  He leaned forward in his seat and said to his uncle: "But who was that woman up on the bandstand with the big butt?"  He felt the car jerk to the left and then back to the right.  "I thought your disco was pretty groovy, Uncle Bo.  The only thing I couldn't figure out was why there weren't any urinals in the bathroom.  All you had were those stalls.  Every one of them was occupied for so long.  I really had to go bad and I waited forever."

"We've got almost a week to iron out the wrinkles," said Bo, his voice calm and calculating.  "This was our maiden voyage, so to speak, and we did it without our star, Tinker Bell and her co-star side-kicks, Peter and Pan."  He put his head back against the leather seat rest.  "Nothing will be wasted when our doors open for real," he said.  "Paying customers don't waste."  He closed his eyes and saw a parade of dollar signs march by.  Contentment snuggled up next to him stroking his 10W-40 coated hair.  He couldn't wait for the coming Friday to appear.  TGIF would be SRO.  Money would march through the doors.  Naomi Schmitt would have her wishes come true and be helping all those who needed help.  Sam would be able to take care of his daughter's college education and, somehow, get back his lost years and regain the dignity Quintin Bell and John Brown had taken from him.  The undercover cop waitstaff would supplement their salaries from the City of Chicago helping make their dreams happen; Reggie, Rommie and Regis would finally have a big gig and Frank and Charles would make enough money to realize their dream of opening up a bakery on the north side in the Andersonville.  "We're going to specialize in sticky buns," Charles had said to him.  Before he realized, the parade of dollar signs strutting through his mind was being scattered by the heinous laughter of John Brown.

* * * * *

La Tinkerbelle's first real night of business, a true opening night that Bo and each of his employees hoped for, a night complete with a jam packed discotheque, was upon them.

Money would fall from the factory's high steel beamed ceiling like candy spilling from a giant ruptured piñata; the candy coated in gold dust. That's what the picture of Malcolm Forbes on Bo's dresser had said to him as he left his chilly room wearing the uniform and hat of a cruise ship captain. His feet swam in a pair of Quintin's white cruise shoes. He didn't care. He was dressed to escort his dream to the ultimate ball.

The entire staff toiled like an army of migrant pickers at harvest for the better part of a week after the charity gala. The true grand opening would place the spotlights on the debut of Tinker Bell and Peter and Pan. Cap'n's Kids had rehearsed "Stayin' Alive" so much that Charles became so incensed he began jumping up and down on the boutique's collection of the Bee Gee's CD's. He even turned a poster of John Travolta in his white suit from "Saturday Night Fever" to face the wall. Eye patches were in place, crotches outlined by way too tight shorts, roller skates, roller blades and the food and beverage conveyor spun like a glorified collection of honest roulette wheels. Everyone was nervous, keyed up and coiled like eager greyhounds ready to pounce on the mechanical rabbit. Preparation was about to meet opportunity. All they needed was the first customer to come through the door. That night they got seven and a surprise.

* * * * *

A truck with a large spotlight sat at the back edge of the parking lot, its rear wheels dangling over a drop off above the Chicago River. A single beam traversed the glowing black night as it bounced over a jagged downtown skyline. Bo had wanted three beams, one with a silhouette of Batman, the other two with matching Jolly Roger patterns. When he found out the legal ramifications and the costs involved he settled for the single beam. Bo had been careful in how he spent his sister's money, rationalizing that the more he cut corners, the more would be left for him.  "Waste not.  Want not," he had repeated to himself each time he needed to spend a dime.  That's how his spotlight truck arrived.  He had paid the driver twenty dollars and promises of a free show the driver would never forget if he temporarily borrowed a spotlight truck.  The truck happened to be one of four parked behind Old St. Patrick's Church in the West Loop hyping their Las Vegas night.

* * * * *

Bo only spent money when he thought it would make him more money.  More was one of his five favorite words along with me, myself, I and money.  The factory's parking lot had received a total makeover that would have pleased a wrinkled matron.  Anything that wasn't fastened down had been hauled away by John Cinderella.  His fee was keeping what he hauled away.  What wasn't hauled away disappeared into the Chicago River in the dead of night, Bo lugging whatever he could lift, rolling it down the sloping bank, slipping on three occasions and ending up in the river.  After sloshing up the slippery river bank for the third time, his pants wet and the knees tore out from his tumbles, he gave up his polluting of the river as a bad omen.

A fresh coat of blacktop sealed the lot making it stand out, the glistening black sporting yellow painted parking lane stripes.  There were no Handicapped Parking spaces because Bo felt they took up too much room.  Every car that entered the lot would be greeted by a red and white stripped metal arm dropping across the entrance.  The driver would be approached by Juan Ponce de Leone, captain of the valet parking crew, to collect the parking fee.  One of Juan's three drivers, all dressed in white shirts tied at the navel and wearing tie dyed bandanas and an eye patch, would open car doors for the occupants, welcome them to La Tinkerbelle's a Go-Go in both English and Spanish and wipe the door handle on the driver side with a clean, white towel.  Once the parking fee was in Juan's hand, he would raise the gate and a valet parker would get in the car and speed off to a designated space.  Juan's parking crew were adept at squeezing three cars into two spaces,  four if the fourth vehicle could balance precariously over the bank leading to the Chicago River. After, while customers waited under a canopy decorated with a skull and cross bones, a valet parker would pull up to waiting customers driving the vehicle as if leading a funeral procession.  A soiled, damp, white towel would be guided over the car's headlights before the car doors would be politely opened with a  courteous nod.  The hand minus the soiled, damp, white towel would be presented palm up.  If there was no gratuity, the soiled towel made a swipe across the driver's side windshield and the valet attendant would walk behind the car, a key from his ring sticking out from between his fingers gouging out a path of paint that mirrored the attendant's steps.

Before retrieving a car, each attendant would remove any change or currency from the car's change tray or center console and slide it into a special manila envelope with his name affixed by a white adhesive backed label.  The parking attendant would mark the make of the car, license plate number and date on the envelope then turn it into Juan who would place it in a file cabinet and keep it for thirty days.  If there was no inquiry about the money, Juan would split it with his staff.  If an irate customer did come back claiming he had been robbed, Juan, holding out the appropriate envelope, would say: "Senor, one of my attendant's fond deese money by your car.  He gives it to me for safe keeping.  Meester Bo, de owner, he's an honest man."

* * * * *

Naomi Schmitt stood in the front window of La Tinkerbelle's, the black curtain with the sequined Jolly Roger closed.  She hated most of her costume.  Her pirate hat and black eyepatch she could accept.  The white go-go boots she couldn't.  Above all, she detested the gaudy rubber hook shaped like a male member extending from her left hand.  She was angry with herself for agreeing to Bo's suggestion to make, in his words, "An eye catching embellishment to your costume that will make you more than a belly dancer."  She didn't mind the unbuttoned white shirt, the tails tied at the middle and the specially designed push-up bra that gave some of what had never been pushed up before a nudge in the right direction. What kept her going was that all of Bo Pepperwall's insane ideas were a means to an end for her.  A part-time belly dancing job that made her look like a practical joke from a Frederick's of Hollywood catalogue didn't bother her as much as she had thought; not with a paycheck that provided her with more money than she made as a social worker with a master's degree. She dearly loved helping others.  This job, even with the detestable rubber hook shaped like a penis being gripped by her left hand, the hand covered by the extra long sleeve of her shirt, allowed her to help those who couldn't help themselves.

Naomi Schmitt valued human dignity.  Then her path crossed that of Quintin Bell.  Advanced college preparedness along with her respect for human dignity got thrown into a Roman Coliseum with two ravenous beasts named Quintin and Scats.  Later, after her rude awakening to other forms of human behavior she had only read about, she found herself surprised at the warm feeling she had upon learning of Quintin Bell's death.  She hadn't waited long to get the news that the Glen Forest on the Watercourse Mayor had died.  She got it instantly. Eyewitnesses have that advantage.  She just couldn't believe what she had witnessed.

Naomi had just performed her belly dance routine that night at the fund raiser.  The inebriated audience applauded her gyrations as she glided back and forth along the center of the Glen Forest on the Watercourse croquet court, the back wall of the court used to silhouette her body's movements.  It didn't take her long to realize that more was expected from her than just dancing.  A giggling Alice Nell Puffin being held up in between Quintin Bell and John Brown made sure of that.  So did someone she thought was a maintenance man who leered at her while clicking the cap to a metal cigarette lighter.  What happened to her next was still a foggy nightmare.  She remembered the smell of smoke and realized her veils were on fire.  Something about being on fire stays embedded in one's brain.  Instinct had her jumping into a pond, or lake, or whatever the water situated adjacent to where she had danced.  She remembered howling laughter as she disappeared under the surface holding her nose.  Once she had crawled out of the water hazard that surrounded the eighteenth green she rested on all fours.  She was too mad to think straight.  A series of who and why questions came to mind as she stood up.  She wanted answers to her questions.  As she took her first step, she found herself rolling into the eighteenth  green's sand bunker.  It was the size of Arizona's portion of the Sonoran Dessert.  Exhausted, caked with sand and mad as a wet hen or, in this case, a soaked, singed belly dancer, she lay sobbing in the sand feeling sorry for herself.  No  one came to help her.  Finally, she crawled across the sand bunker on her hands and knees hoping she was going in the right direction of the parking lot.  Sputtering and muttering that she would decapitate the imbecile who set her veils on fire, she heard the ghoulish sound of a solid object against a not-so-quite solid an object.  The sound was a sickening WHACK.  She would never forget it.  She didn't have a chance. There was a repeat followed by a third WHACK.  She scampered forward in the sand bunker, peeked up over the bunker's lip and saw what she didn't want to see.  Then she heard a CLICK/SNAP that sent her scurrying from the sand.  She ran in a crouch, tattered and charred veils flapping, clutching her dance bag while trying to keep her belongings from spilling out onto the well manicured country club's grounds. All she could think of was seeking the safety of the parking lot and her rusted Peugeot with the dented hood tied down by a bent coat hanger. She would never forget the sounds she heard and what she witnessed that night. Now, it was another night and she blinked as she opened the curtain to her glass enclosed stage to recorded soundtrack from Benny Hill playing at an eardrum splitting level. Her hips began to move as did the male member in her left hand.

* * * * *

In the parking lot in front of the main entrance to La Tinkerbelle's a Go-Go and Naomi's window, a cab driver's animated movements caught the attention of the valet parking crew. Juan, picking up on the agitated driver's actions, grabbed his hand-held, World War II type walkie-talkie that Bo had bought from John Cinderella and pushed the Talk button. Bo had explained to Juan about the function of the walkie-talkie. "These beauties, I've been told, were used by Errol Flynn in *Objective Burma*," he had said to Juan who nodded not knowing who or what an Errol Flynn was. "You can give me a heads up notice as to how many customers will be heading to the main entrance by pushing this button." Bo pushed the button on the walkie-talkie and grinned at the sound of the static. "Give the button a push for each customer's car you and your boys park. If you get backed up give two pushes." His finger demonstrated for Juan. "My nephew thinks these are cool, even awesome."

Juan pushed his button, heard the static and nodded his approval. "Cool, but the noise hurts my ears," he said without his accent.

Bo didn't care about possible ruptured eardrums. The walkie-talkie was an inexpensive way to get an accurate car count in the parking lot. One sound of static meant one car. At twenty dollars per car, he knew exactly how many, in his words, "double saw-bucks," were in his parking lot or, better yet, in his pockets. Three quick blasts of static was an SOS. He knew the driving and parking skills of Juan's attendants having witnessed their abilities during a parking practice session led by Juan. He was in awe as he watched them squeeze two cars in between the parallel yellow line spaces designated for a single vehicle. Watching the drivers eject out from an open window was even more impressive.

Juan set down his walkie-talkie and walked cautiously toward the cab driver, his street smart senses kicking in. He could now hear the cab driver and there was no doubt he was in a heated argument, his Middle Eastern accent echoing across the parking lot as he followed his six male fares to the entrance of La Tinkerbelle's.

"But, sirs, dis eeze Planet Hollywood," he yelled. "You wanted me to take you to de Planet Hollywood and I do." He kept right on the heels of the six.

One of the fares stopped, turned and looked at the cab driver. He was a pumpkin-shaped man with a smaller, distorted pumpkin for a head and a complexion to match. A plastic identification tag hung down around a short thick stump that was his neck by a cheap plastic lanyard. "You're nuts," he said to the driver. "You took us on a joy ride. I was born and raised in this city and I know a meter padding con man when I see one."

"Sir, I no run up the meter," said the driver, sweat beading up on his forehead and then dripping off the tip of his brown nose even though it was a cool autumn evening. "Dis eeze Planet Hollywood and you owe me twenty six dollars." He paused. "And a gratuity would be much appreciated."

"Screw you, camel jockey," said the pumpkin-shaped man. He spun around so fast that his identification badge ended up on his back.

The second man in the group of six turned around.  He was the exact opposite of his friend.  The only similarity was the badge he wore.  He looked like the reincarnation of Ichabod Crane and his neck didn't look strong enough to support his lanyard and ID card.  He folded his arms across his chest in an act of defiance and asked: "Hey, man, are you trying to hustle us?"

"Sir, I do not hustle," said the frustrated cab driver, the dripping sweat increasing.  "I am not a cheater.  I own no camels."

"Then where's Planet Hollywood?" asked a third fare who stopped to join the second fare.  He had a head of thick black curls, eyebrows to match and a pair of tiny, silver ball-bearing eyes that blinked non-stop like a video game having a nervous breakdown.

"Dis is eeet," said Juan, who had followed the pack and stepped in to intervene.  "Welcome to da new Planet Hollywood's couzene, La Tinkerbelle's."

The six fares stopped and gave a questioning look at Juan.  Eacg gave his parking attendant uniform with the gold epaulets of a Navy Rear Admiral on the shoulders of his shirt the once over.

Juan continued: "We have de beautiful girls here," he said, cupping his hands in front of his chest and giving the men a knowing wink.  "Come in.  I guarantee you see de biggest, bouncin' chi-chi's your eyes ever did see."  He grinned and said, "Deez girls, she is hot.  They swoop down from the ceiling wit dare big, pointed chi-chi's ready to poke you in da eye."  He crossed the area of his heart with his right index finger.  "Promise and honest Injun," he said, turning and nodding at the cab driver.  "Not you," he said to the cab driver."

The cab driver nodded back, sweat still dripping from his nose.  "Tank you, sir," he said to Juan.  Then he looked at the six men and said, "Twenty six dollars, please."

* * * * *

Arvia's fingers interlocked so tight she lost all feeling from her elbows down as the Jaguar, with Ben driving, bounded into La Tinkerbelle's parking lot, the tortured tires screaming for mercy. She shut her eyes and felt the seat belt harness grab her as Ben slammed on the Jaguar's brakes in front of the red and white arm blocking the entrance. "Nothin' to it, Mom," he said, as the driver's side window hummed to its down position. "And you were so nervous about letting me drive in Chicago traffic. Piece a cake."

Arvia's fingers were still locked, frozen like an ice tray that had been overfilled.

Ben glanced out the window at Juan. "Buenos noches, Senor Juan," he said, his hand in a fist extending out the window making contact with Juan's fist.

"Hey, Ben, my man, and a pleasant good evening to you," said Juan as if he taught diction. He went around the front of the car and opened the passenger side door for Arvia. "And a very pleasant good evening to you, Your Honor," he said. "Excited?"

Arvia freed her fingers, the cracking only evident to her. "Thank you, Juan," she said, "I'm not sure of what I'm feeling. I hope tonight is half the success that my brother thinks it's going to be."

"It's going to be a great night," replied Juan. He smiled at Arvia and said, "If you don't mind my saying, Your Honor, but your new hair-do is stunning. You look like your name should be included on a list of the ten classiest people in America."

Arvia blushed. She had wanted to hate Ramon for what he had done to her single black braid, turning it into a meandering series of a dozen braids, making it resemble an octopus in a bird's nest, but she couldn't. She not only looked like one of the ten classiest people in America but felt like she was number one.

Ben got out of the car leaving the keys in the ignition. "Wow," he said, seeing the searchlight truck, its humming yellow beam clawing at the night sky. "Didn't I tell you, Mom," he said out of breath. "Didn't I tell you about Uncle Bo getting the searchlight? Is this cool, Mom, or is this cool?"

"If you say so, Benoni," she said politely. She glanced up and placed a hand on the fender of the Jaguar to balance herself. "Two signatures on a check do not a safety measure make," she mumbled as she felt her son's hand on her arm.

"Come on, Mom," said Ben, leading her to the front entrance. "I can't wait to see what awesome new ideas Uncle Bo's got for his grand opening. Every weekend when I'd come to work for him there would always be something so groovy new. Where does my uncle get his ideas?"

"God only knows," she said, just as her son stopped at the large, illuminated picture window to the front entrance and saw Naomi dancing, her gyrations complete with her eyepatch, one hand covered by a phallic symbol hook, the white go-go boots shuffling and sliding to the music's beat. A bored, blank look draped over her face as her hips rotated in what seemed like both directions at once and the phallic symbol waved in rhythm to the theme song from *Peter Gunn.*

Old television show theme music was just one of an avalanche of ideas that cascaded out of Bo to embellish La Tinkerbelle's cornucopia of offerings. Naomi had balked saying, "I wasn't even born when some of those shows were on." Then Bo held up five fingers. Naomi may have been a social worker but she understood five hundred dollars for five sessions in the window, each session lasting twenty minutes. Hourly pay like that was only commanded by the likes of a John Brown.

"Is that the social worker your uncle hired?" Arvia asked her son.

"Yeah, Mom," Ben answered back as he waved and smiled at Naomi.  "She's a super, nice lady," he beamed.  "She helps all kinds of people."

Naomi's expression came to life at the sight of Ben and she winked at him with her uncovered eye and gave him a slight wave with her hook.

"Did I just see what I thought I just saw?" Arvia asked her son, then wishing she hadn't asked.

"See what, Mom," Ben asked, as he began to tug on his mother's arm.

Arvia felt herself being pulled along by her son.  "What have I done?" she asked herself.  "When did I lose my sense of propriety?  I'm the Mayor of the most prestigious suburban community in all of Illinois.  I'm in the social register.  I have an image to maintain as a civic leader and, dear, God, look at me, I'm the owner of a saloon with a dancing girl bandying about a replica of the most disgusting part of the male anatomy ever created.  God only knows what else my brother has concocted since that charity fund raising fiasco."  She began harboring regrets for attending the grand opening, but she owed it to her brother who had poured himself into La Tinkerbelle's.  "At least he gave up on that dreadful idea of wanting me to sing with that ancient trio of shriveled up old men and that teenage screamer with his disgusting Granny Clampett," she said to herself.  As she tried to enter La Tinkerbelle's with Ben, their progress was blocked by six well dressed men wearing business suits.  Arvia saw her brother talking to the men in what appeared to be a firm, commanding voice.

Bo stood out like a fresh made snow man on a bear skin rug in his white uniform.  He had a gold patch over his left eye and the erect stance of a sentry guarding the Tomb of the Unknown Soldier.  His hands gripped the sides of a gold spray painted maitre d' stand that had a black Jolly Roger stenciled across the front.  Arvia thought he looked like a real captain, weather beaten hands on the helm, gold scrambled eggs on the bill of his captain's hat contributing to his authoritative image.  The hat tilted at a jaunty angle and his shoes were showroom white.

"There's a ten dollar per person cover charge," Arvia heard him tell the group of six men.

"For what?" one of the men asked in a high pitched, squeaky voice.  He had a miniature paper umbrella behind each ear, one red the other yellow.  "We didn't have to pay a dime at Trader Vic's, and we got these Tiki bowls.  See."  He pulled a ceramic Polynesian drink bowl from under his suit coat.  "Look at the tits on those hula dancers," he said, showing the bowl to Bo. "And we got to keep the umbrellas from our Rum Boogies."  He grinned at his companions.  "Pepe Valdez, the taco king out in the parking lot said you got broads in here with big bazooms.  If they got nicer tits than these hula girls on my bowl, I'll give you the ten bucks.  If not, you can pound a handful of sand from Waikiki up your rosy red."

Arvia couldn't believe what she was hearing as lights flashed crisscrossing patterns above the dark ceiling.  Their reflections bounced off the black and metallic silver walls before colliding with a rotating mirrored ball suspended from the ceiling.  Recorded music blared from the sound system. Speakers hanging above the I-beam ceiling supports were lost in the dark.  The music was, *Money Burns a Hole in My Pocket* and was being sung by Dean Martin.  Arvia saw that her brother had erected an elevated tier not quite making a complete circle of the club's massive dance floor.  He had planned for three levels, but that meant blocking the entrance to the men's room and his stalls with the movie projectors.  That configuration would've shrunk the boutique's entrance in half.  Black and silver, along with red, white and blue painted stripes highlighted with silver sequins were everywhere and, to her surprise, a tasteful blending with the tables and chairs.  There was a gleaming roller conveyor system that wound its way from the bar curving the entire length of the room with stops at the restaurant for picking up food orders by the waitstaff wearing roller skates. The conveyor's curve led her to Sam. It was a different Sam than a week earlier at the gala. She hardly recognized him. His hair had been styled by Ramon as a favor to Charles and his name should've been changed to Rock or Tab or Biff or even Clint. Sam's bartenders each wore an eyepatch, bandana and had their white shirts tied-at-the-waist exposing paunches that had encountered too many tacos, Chicago style hot dogs and Italian beef sandwiches at lunch time while working as cops. Sam wasn't dressed like a pirate or any other character. He was dressed like Sam, a real bartender. "Boss, no offense," he had said to Bo, "but I'm wearing what I've always worn when I tended bar." The cuffs on his white shirt were rolled under the sleeves; his black trousers creased and a white towel was draped over his left shoulder like a sash showing his authority. The bar was his domain and was being run by his three rules.

"That'll be ten dollars each, gentlemen," Bo said again, with no mention of the female anatomy to his six customers who were in Chicago attending the International Disposable House Wares Convention at McCormick Place.

Arvia's feeling of disgust grew when she heard another of the male customers ask: "You're guaranteeing us that we're going to see some nice boob-a-looneys the way Poncho Villa the car parker said we would?"

Arvia did a double take because the man talking to her brother was almost a clone of Bo except for two differing characteristics. The first was the mustache. The man's didn't run on a tilt and appeared professionally trimmed. The second was the man's hair; it was coated in styling gel not motor oil.

The men looked at one another and, almost in unison, reached into their pockets. Three removed wallets, two fingered polished money clips and the sixth had a wad of bills, torn receipts and three holy pictures of the Blessed Mother held together by a knotted rubber band.

"Enjoy the show," said Bo to his first customers. He looked like a cat that had just eaten an entire pet store out of all birds.

"Doz broads better have nice tits," muttered one of the men as they passed by Bo and headed into the cavernous La Tinkerbelle's. "I got a brudder-in-law who lives on da west side dat will turn youse Captain Kangaroo head into a botched plastic surgery job if we don't see some hot tooty-fruitys."

"TGIF," Bo shouted after them, his eyes flashing with excitement, the six ten dollar bills worming their way into the pocket of his white pants. His eyes lit up even more when he saw Arvia and Ben. "Oh, Sis, this is going to be a fantastic night. We just opened the door and already we have six paying customers; they look like conventioneers which means they're all on expense accounts." He raised his eyes and glanced at the black sparkling ceiling. "Thank you, God for this Friday." He wanted to cry for joy when he saw two of the conventioneers enter the men's room.

* * * * *

Ben led his mother to the bar where he saw Sam was working. "Cool costumes, uh, Ma," he said, seeing one of Sam's bartenders that had a stuffed parrot mounted on his left shoulder. All, except Sam, wore multiple gaudy purple and gold plastic necklaces around their necks. The necklaces were provided by Charles and Frank, a good luck gift of several thousand pieces of fake promotional jewelry donated by a friend who supplied the New Orleans Mardi Gras Parade.

Before Ben or his mother could say a word to Sam they heard a shout of, "HEY!" It was Bo. A strong, polite business expression peered out at them from under the brim of his white, gold adorned captain's hat.

They looked, their faces asking.

"That'll be ten dollars each," shouted Bo.  "La Tinkerbelle's guarantees the finest in entertainment."  His thin lips showed a faint curl up.  "If we don't tickle your tickler, we will refund double your money."

"Berthold," Arvia replied in a borderline huff and bark.

Bo blinked.

CLICK/SNAP!

"That's okay, Sis," he yelled back with a polite wave of his right hand.  "I was just joshin' you."

* * * * *

When the waiters and waitresses, who had been practicing balancing empty serving trays while on their roller skates, saw the six customers they headed for their stations.  The eyes of undercover police officers–one eye each; the other covered by a black patch etched with the rhinestone outline of a skull and cross bones–scrutinized the six conventioneers as if they were possible terrorists.  Trays and order pads were at the ready.  So were handcuffs and tightly woven leather blackjacks.  Mace and pepper spray were frowned upon because too many innocent people might be harmed.  A quick flick of the wrist aimed at a temple would have the blackjack doing its job and the unruly customer being escorted from La Tinkerbelle's as if he or she had too much to drink.

* * * * *

Frank, poised and ready to serve their first paying customers, stood at the entrance to the boutique, an almost life size elegantly framed Erte hanging from the wall behind him.  "Will you stop flitting around like our logo, Tinker Bell," he said to Charles.  "Forget putting the hangars equidistant from one another.  Get your tight little tush over here and get ready to greet our customers."  He heard a, "humph" from Charles and switched on his friendly smile, choked back his excitement and said to his partner: "Don't even think about biting anyone on the buttocks tonight."

"You're so overly gay you're sad," said Charles, as he joined Frank in the entrance to the boutique.  "Speaking of sad, have you seen Ramon?"

"You mean the Sheep Dog?" Frank asked, his eyes checking and double checking the boutique's display.  "The poor fellow should practice what he creates."

"Now don't you go getting into your bitter mood, Sweets," Charles said, his eyes also double checking the inventory.  He scooted back into the boutique, adjusted two hangars sporting sequined t-shirts that made the statement: "My Peter Digs Your Pan."  His adjustment was a fraction of an inch and produced a pleased look.  He rejoined Frank and asked, "Have you checked on Ramon since he moved his new salon annex in the cubicle next to our boutique?"

"I checked," said Frank.  "He's worse than a homo Tinker Bell the way he's flitting around his new shop complaining that nothing's right and that he's made a terrible mistake opening up a branch that will never have any customers."  Frank laughed.

Charles also laughed.  "No customer's indeed.  Already he's done the hair of every waitress working here as well as two waiters, three bartenders and Sam.  He told me he even has two phone numbers."  Charles let out a sigh.  "That's two more than poor, poor me."

*  *  *  *  *

Ben's head swiveled back and forth so fast it looked like his neck was a ball bearing.  He marveled at the transformation of what was once a rundown building pleading for euthanasia. The pleas had been answered and changes beyond Ben's wildest imagination had taken place since the hot sultry day when he first met a homeless derelict named Sam behind a stack of chipped wooden pallets.  His excitement had him saying to his mother: "Have you ever seen anything like this, Mom?"

Arvia didn't answer, her eyes unbelieving the way they were the night of the charity gala.

Ben watched Sam work a damp, white cloth in slow deliberate circles over the top of the polished walnut bar. The bar, an antique, was another of Bo's finds, the bar was actually a collection of elegant hardwoods taken from four defunct neighborhood corner saloons, two from before the Prohibition era. One of the neighborhood establishments once offered a free meal to those in need but then was forced to lock its doors because of dealings with Quintin Bell and John Brown.

"Sakes alive, Benoni!" Arvia said to her son. "Will you please calm down?" She couldn't conceal the frustration in her voice. "I wish you'd show as much enthusiasm preparing for college."

"Sorry, Mom," he said, as the sound system began to crackle and pop, the noise making the six conventioneers and all of the employees cringe, sending their hands racing to their ears. A series of deafening hissing noises followed as Reggie, his accordion at ready, bellows closed, shouted into the microphone: "Testing, testing, testing one and a two and a three."

Arvia's hands pressed against her own ears but that didn't shut out the shouts and clapping coming from the table in front of the bandstand where the six conventioneers sat. The table was covered with a dozen drink glasses, their two drink minimum order urged on by their waitress. "It'll save time," she told them, leaning forward to show them two of the reasons why they came. I'll bring extra ice and I'll have your bartender, Sam the Procurer," she stopped, winked and let her tongue travel across her upper lip in slow motion before finishing her statement, "pour your second one clean. You can add ice later."

"Does this mean the tits are coming?" one of the conventioneers shouted at her.

She smiled and gave her breasts a jiggle, her Chicago Police Department shield popping out from her blouse. She quickly covered it and said: "My ID badge.  Kind of like the ones you gentlemen are wearing.  The City says we have to be licensed to serve alcoholic beverages."

"And tits" echoed the conventioneers.  The six began to rap on the table top with their heavy drink glasses and started to chant: "Tits, Tits!"

Ben shouted at Sam.  "Wow, Sam," he said, his head from the shoulders up looking like it belonged on a bobble-head doll.  "Is this place awesome or is this place awesome?"

Sam leaned across the bar and said to Ben: "It's only a bar, Ben, but it's definitely an awesome one."  In the next breath he said: "Good evening, Miss Arvia, nice to see you.  May I bring you a champagne cocktail in honor of opening night?"

"Thank you, Sam," Arvia tried to say without shouting to be heard.

Sam smiled and said, "Nice hairdo, Your Honor."

The subdued light couldn't hide Arvia's red cheeks.

"A one and a two and a three," Reggie said into the microphone again, the hissing, popping and crackling toned down.  The bellows of his accordion, the words, *Dick Contino* in sparkling white appearing across the black folds, spread open. Rommie's pick bounced over the strings of his Les Paul guitar and Regis started a lively beat with his boombass as they began to play and sing, "Sailing, sailing over the bounding main."

"Does the music have to be so loud?" asked Arvia.

"The boss wants it that way," said Sam, pointing at his ears and flesh colored ear plugs.

"I told you it was awesome, Mom," Ben shouted to his mother.

"Awful is right," she said to her son."

"Champagne cocktail?" Sam shouted again.

"What's a chimp's tale?" Arvia hollered back at Sam.

"Could I have a bottle of that root beer Uncle Bo gets from Wisconsin?" Ben shouted to Sam.

Before the root beer got uncapped, the three of them saw Bo get up on the bandstand.  He was resplendent in his captain's uniform, the spotlights elevating the white of his starched uniform to eye squinting brilliance.  He took the microphone from its scratched, polished slightly bent chrome stand while the trio continued to play, their song's volume just audible.  "Ladies and gentlemen," Bo announced, the PA system vibrating so the ice cubes in the conventioneers' drinks rattled.  "Arvia Bell welcomes you to the gala grand opening of her world famous night club, La Tinkerbelle's a Go-Go."  He pointed the microphone in the direction of the bar.

"Dear Lord in Heaven," she uttered in dismay.  "He's linked me, the mayor, to being the owner of an establishment that serves alcoholic beverages."

Bo continued.  The spotlights reflected what looked like a blinking star coming from his uncovered eye.  "Tonight Arvia Bell and the staff of La Tinkerbelle's welcome you to the world premiere performance of the one and only Tinker Bell and the sultry swinging arcs of Peter and Pan."  His voice became low and gravely turning him into a sideshow barker.  "The ladies will soar for you, they will fly for you, and they will even crawl on their bellies like reptiles for you."  He directed his attention to the table of conventioneers and pointed his microphone at them.  His mustache lay on an even keel.  "You will see the sensuous Treasure Island gyrations of Captain Hookette in our showroom window."  He paused again still concentrating his attention on the six conventioneers then lowered his voice into a devilish hush.  "You've also experienced our Jolly Rogers Girls serving you your favorite libations."  He lifted his gold eye patch and winked.  "If you treat them nice, they may even serve you more than you bargained for."

"We want tits!" chanted the conventioneers, ice splashing into their second drinks as two more waitresses skated up to their table, a tray each with a total of twelve more glasses.

Bo took out a bos'un's pipe from his uniform breast pocket and whistled into the microphone. Arvia pushed her hands to her ears even harder. "Don't forget La Tinkerbelle's menu of delectable gourmet delights. The First Mates will serve your sumptuous, scrumptious selections directly to you from our galley, speeding on their roller blades so you can get it hot. We are talking yum-yum hot just like everything we offer for your enjoyment here at La Tinkerbelle's a Go-Go." He paused, winked with his uncovered eye and said in a deep voice, "Hot, hot, hot is what we have plenty of."

"Tits!" hollered the conventioneers, pounding the table top with the palms of their hands.

Bo blew into the pipe again getting what resembled the sound of a child blowing bubbles in a bath tub. "Now hear this you landlubbers. Don't forget to visit our world famous boutique where Leading Chief Petty Officer, Franco and First Class Harpoonist, Charles will spear your every need. And, by all means, if in need of a trim, cut or latest style, Ramon is in his salon ready to clip you. I'm Skipper Bo and for your music pleasure this evening on our maiden voyage, I present Cap'n's Kids featuring the new singing sensation, Obadiah Ledbetter and the creative tambourine accompaniments of Scullery Maid Emerine Randall."

"I want tits" shouted the pumpkin-looking conventioneer. "Where are the tits?" He raised his heavy on-the-rocks glass in a throwing position. "Show me dem chi-chi's." His hand with the glass started to move forward but was stopped in mid-throw. In a single motion the glass was removed from his hand by a smiling waitress who pushed her cleavage inches from the conventioneer's nose.

"Will these do," said the undercover cop waitress with a smile. "And while your window shopping, how about another round?" She nodded at the other conventioneers who were leering at her. Five other smiling waitresses, blouses unbuttoned but tied at the navel, skated up to the table surrounding it, Chicago Police Department shields on partial display. The waitresses picked up two empty glasses each from the conventioneers and roller skated toward the bar.

"You do have really nice ones," the pumpkin shaped conventioneer said to the first waitress, his nose trying to keep a fraction of an inch from her retreating blouse until he found himself on his hands and knees crawling after her.

"Thank you," the waitress said seductively. She patted him on the few thin hairs remaining on his head. "Enjoy the show. Your next drink is on me," she said before roller skating back to the bar, the cheeks of her rear end oozing out of her cut off shorts.

"I think I'm in love," said the conventioneer to his buddies after he crawled back to the table.

Bo finished introducing the band members and stepped down from the stage as the band began to play the theme from Love Boat with a disco beat.

"Thank you, Sam," Arvia said as she accepted the champagne cocktail just as Bo sauntered to the bar after shaking each of the conventioneer's hands.

"Well," Bo said to his sister and nephew, looking for approval. "What do you think so far?"

"What I think is that I'll no longer have my job as mayor once the word gets out that I am linked to being the owner of your brilliant idea."

"See," said a jubilant Bo, ignoring his sister's concern. "I told you that afternoon by the pool that I had a brilliant idea that would make you famous."

"And, perhaps, a jail bird," said Arvia taking a sip of champagne."

"Oh, Sis," how can you think about such nonsense with what's happening right over your new quaff from Ramon?" He pointed to the ceiling. "Take a look."

Arvia, Ben and Sam looked up to the ceiling as the band switched to their version of the, "In Crowd."  Six spotlights focused on six cages each with a scantily clad girl wearing white go-go boots and sequined G-strings with a skull and cross bones emblem.  The cages inched down in a slow teasing decent until they stopped just above the heads of the band and out of reach of the conventioneers, two of whom were standing on their chairs trying to grab the cages.

The girls in the cages gyrated, seemingly lost in the music, no expressions on their bland, painted faces, their hair not moving.  The conventioneers whistled, jumped up and down and took frustrated leaps trying to grab at the cages.  Three of them stood under a cage nearest them and started dancing, their dance steps likened to a fertility ritual for the agility challenged.  The attentive waitress's roller skated up to the table and set down a dozen more drinks while scooping up the half emptied glasses.

Bo's excitement stayed guarded.  He kept looking at the maitre d' stand.  It was vacant except for undercover Chicago police officer, Noel Jones, his assistant maitre d' and Matilda Newton's secret bodyguard.  He also noticed that his walkie-talkie was sans static and had him questioning the quality of the merchandise he had purchased from John Cinderella.

The band changed tunes and began to play, "Matilda" as Obadiah jumped up on the bandstand as if bandstand jumping were an Olympic event.  He was wearing a white Elvis jump suit splattered with sequins half missing and a pair of white boots, the heels worn down so far Aladdin could wear them.  Bo had bought the suit and shoes at John's Junk Store.  John Cinderella had bought them from a secondhand costume shop that was going out of business.  The jump suit's crotch had been ripped out and sewn together with a coarse royal blue thread, but Bo knew a bargain when he saw one.

Obadiah smiled, the cavernous cap from his missing teeth

sucking in air causing his freckles to vibrate.  He offered his hand to a pear shaped Emerine Randall, her blond, lacquered hair, created by Ramon, piled up like a real beehive.  Ramon had placed two live bees encased in a tiny gauze covered cage at the top of her hair.  She was, as usual, crammed into a white sequined sheath dress.  Obadiah, with Emerine at his side, took the microphone and began doing an impersonation of Harry Belafonte with a good old boy southern accent.  As if on key, blinding beams from two more spotlights illuminated two girls arcing across the ceiling.  Their bodies were covered in black leotards and sparkling silver glitter.  Thigh high black vinyl boots stopped at the area of their crotches.  The heels of their boots sported a pair of miniature red, white and blue wings sparkling in the spotlights.

Peter and Pan were attached to the same hoist holding the Go-Go dancers and their cages.  One end of a cable was bolted to the hoist and the other end fastened to a special harness.  The black ceiling and background hid the cables as Peter and Pan swung high above the dance floor.  Their arcing course took them to where it appeared they could almost touch each wall.  Having no specific instructions, they improvised their choreography, forcing smiles and giving one handed waves; their other hand in a death grip on their cables.  Then, as they became more familiar with their roles and trusted being suspended from a wire, they let out shouts of glee, waved at the conventioneers with both hands and blew kisses.  They looked at one another and knew what they had to do next.  When they were both side-by-side, their hands reached down and grabbed at the tops of their too high boots.  The boots were rubbing the area around their crotches raw.  A matching pair of hands pushing down didn't go unnoticed by the conventioneers. They went crazy.

Obscene shouts erupted from the table below as the conventioneers had shed their suit coats, ripped off their ties and knotted their dress shirts in the same fashion as the waitstaff and the bartenders. Their ties were now bandanas.

Just as another volley of, "Tits!" came from the conventioneers a third spotlight ignited with a loud, static pop, the noise so loud it drowned out Obadiah who had Matilda taking all of his money and running off to Venezuela.

Unbeknownst to Ben, Arvia and Sam, it was Matilda Newton who streaked across the ceiling speeding between Peter and Pan. A father and a boyfriend never recognized her.

Matilda, after her audition, had accepted the offer Ben's uncle had given her with a secret phone call she made from the library office when her mother was at lunch. She never told a soul, not even Ben.

"I want to be a star," she had whispered into the phone to Bo. "Do you still want me?"

Bo almost swallowed his phone along with the bos'un's pipe he was practicing in his office; the pipe a gift from John Cinderella. "Be here Friday night," he had said to Matilda his mustache sticking straight out like two porcupine quills. "Curtain goes up at eight."

That Friday before school let out she had asked her mother if she could go to a slumber party after the football game. Her mother gave her permission to attend the party but nixed the slumber part of the party. Matilda knew she had time on her side with the football game lie and calculated she could make it back to the apartment above the mortuary before her mother got suspicious. With her lie out of the way and school out, Matilda surprised herself with a new found bravery and confidence taking two buses and the El from Wilmette to get to La Tinkerbelle's. Not even her best friend, Ben, knew nor did he recognize her soaring across the ceiling.

Bo had kept his promise to Sam about being discreet, respecting his daughter and preserving her anonymity with his special mask, mainly out of fear of being pummeled by Tinker

Bell's father.

Once Obadiah had started to sing about Matilda, she followed her cue and stepped from the platform as if she were on Broadway in the play *Peter Pan*. She was a picture of grace adorned with her black cat girl mask covered in red, white and blue glitter, silver glitter covering her leotards. Her looping arc took her directly over the heads of the conventioneers and quickly between her two companions, Peter and Pan.

"Yeah, yeah, yeah!" screamed the conventioneers, one of them standing on the table trying to leap up and grab any one of the three girls arcing high above him. He jumped, lost his balance and tumbled onto two of his companions, bodies and toppled chairs sprawled on the dance floor.

Just then, Obadiah let loose with one of his hog calls, the one that had won him the Arkansas State Championship Hog Calling Contest at the state fair two years earlier. "Sueeey, Pig Sueeey! Sueeey! Ya Pig" he shouted, as Rommie turned the volume knob on their amplifier to a maximum, ear splitting high.

Bo's attention was now solidly fixed on the maitre d' stand. Not a soul stood between the stand, Police Officer Noel Jones his assistant and the entrance door. He caught a glimpse of a bored Naomi Schmitt leaning against the small protective safety door at the back of her window that was wide open.

Naomi glanced into the parking lot; arms folded across her chest and saw Juan and his attendants looking back at her, bored, their arms also folded across their chests. Bo could feel the sweat beginning to soak through his white captain's jacket.

CLICK/SNAP.

Obadiah sucked in a breath of air that made his face blow up like a beach ball during a sultry August day in his hometown of Badbreath; a tiny community located about twelve miles southwest of Fayetteville. Obadiah, his face resembling the inside of a live volcano, had his mouth open and his hands turned to fists.  From deep down at the bottom of his lungs arose a hog call to end all hog calls startling even Emerine, almost vibrating her tambourine from her hand.  Then, in a heavy southern drawl, he continued singing: "La Tinker.  La Tinker.  La Tinker, she take all me money and run Venezuela."

Ben continued looking up at the ceiling.  His uncle had outdone himself.  Then he couldn't believe what he saw.  "Matilda," he muttered, his jaw almost hitting the top of the bar where he stood.  At first he didn't recognize his girlfriend.  Several sweeping arcs later, he knew it was her as she soared overhead like a graceful Tern.  "You did it," he said in a whisper, his words filled with admiration.  The mask may have hid her identity from her father and Arvia, but Ben recognized what black spandex cloth and silver sequins couldn't conceal.  He also couldn't believe that Sam hadn't vaulted over the bar and headed to the back of the disco and the metal, spiral staircase leading to the platform where the girls were launched.  Ben was convinced that Matilda's debut performance would be her last, her being escorted down the same spiral staircase secured firmly under her father's arm as if he were carting a sack of grain.  Ben gave a nervous glance in Sam's direction and then to where his uncle was standing.  He didn't know what to do so he did nothing.

Sam wasn't the least bit interested in what was taking place above him.  He was too busy getting another round of drinks for the conventioneers.

As the show continued, so did the quest of the conventioneers trying to get what they thought their ten dollar cover charge covered.  "Tits!" they shouted as they were in the midst of building a human ladder with one standing atop the other's shoulders.  A series of teetering, wild grabs came up empty handed as a soaring Tinker Bell, Peter and Pan whizzed by.  Their human extension ladder managed to start its third wrung before a trio of prostrate bodies covered the dance floor.  The conventioneers laughed like a pack of hyenas, each series of howls punctuated with demands for: "Tits!"

* * * * *

Bo felt the static sound from the large awkward walkie-talkie strapped under his arm like an oversize toy cannon and sprinted to the maitre d' stand. He tugged at his uniform jacket, glanced at Noel, smiled and looked into the red face of John Brown dressed in a tuxedo. Juan trailed right behind the lawyer saying, "Senor, you owe twenty dollars for de valet parking." He sounded as if her were pleading. His plea continued: "Twenty dollar to keep da BMW convertible from being stolen by vandals."

"Piss off, Pedro," said John Brown, his eyes wild and his hair looking like he had put on his tux in a wind tunnel.

Juan grinned, an errant sweep of a spotlight making his two gold front teeth sparkle. Si, Senor." He turned and saw his three valet parkers standing in the doorway. He gave them a single nod and they turned and headed toward John Brown's BMW convertible.

The lawyer leaned over the counter of the maitre d' stand like a cobra ready to strike. "Who the hell do you think you are not inviting me to Arvia's charity ball, you schmoe?" the lawyer hissed.

Bo straightened his captain's hat, gave a jaunty salute and said: "I'm sorry, sir, the charity event of which you speak was last week." He smiled politely. "You're a week late and, oh, yes, it looks like your thirty dollars short." He paused. "Nice tux, though."

"Thirty dollars," screamed John Brown, trying to shove over the gold wooden stand. It didn't budge; four bolts fastening it to the concrete floor.

"Thirty dollars is correct, sir," said Bo, a professionalism in his demeanor that infuriated the lawyer even more. "That's twenty dollars for valet parking and another ten dollars for the cover charge, mate."

"Up yours," sputtered John Brown. He tried to get around the maitre d' stand, didn't see Noel Jones, misjudged his distance, tripped over Noel's extended leg and ended up on his hands and knees along side of Bo. "I'm going to sue your ass, Schmoe," he sputtered as he picked himself up off the floor. "Now point me toward the bar and that dead beat derelict, Yosemite Sam?"

Sam, his attention focused on Bo and John Brown, still hadn't noticed what was going on above him. He saw John Brown staggering toward the bar where Arvia and Ben were seated. His right hand disappeared under the bar and grasped the section of high tension electrical wire. A quick, gentle tap to the lawyer's head with his homemade sap would send the lawyer into the Land of Nod for the rest of the night.

John Brown stumbled into the front of the bar his hands shooting out as if he were blocking an opponent in his college football days. His hands hit the solid, rounded wooden elbow rest of the bar breaking his forward momentum. He blinked and blurted out: "You, kitty cat man, give me four fingers of your finest tequila." He exhaled, a stream of saliva running down his chin. "And snap to it."

"Yes, sir," said Sam, polite and professional. "Four fingers of our finest tequila." He turned and muttered, "One more finger and you'd be a complete hand job." His right hand placed the end of the sap in his back pants pocket and he picked up an on-the-rocks glass. He showed the glass to the lawyer then turned and placed it on the back bar. His left hand reached down into the stainless steel trough holding the generic well drink bottles and pulled out a brand of tequila that's only social redeeming value was for making margaritas in a bar for singles and lonely hearts. No self respecting Mexican would touch the stuff. Just before he poured the tequila, he heard John Brown's order. "Hurry your ass up, you faggot dead beat."

Sam heard a belch and John Brown's next order.

"Don't get any of those dirty cat hairs in my drink, ya hear."

Sam turned, smiled and said to John Brown: "No problem, sir. Animals of any kind on the premises would be a violation of The Chicago Board of Health."

"I don't need the hired help quoting legal statutes to me," said the lawyer, gripping the edge of the bar for support. "I'm a lawyer, remember," he said with a smirk. "And you're a bartender. Just do your job, if you're capable and pour my drink."

Sam smiled, turned around to face the back bar and picked up the glass. Then he made a noise as if he were clearing his throat. He was. The noise was followed by his spiting into the glass. Satisfied, he lifted the tequila bottle high enough so that John Brown could see the liquor being poured, and then filled the glass to the brim. He turned, smiled and set the glass in front of John Brown. "My very best tequila for you, Sir," he said, his smile growing. "Four fingers just like you ordered. He squelched his smile. "Neat," he said. "And this one's on me."

John Brown took a gulp and swallowed the tequila. Another half gulp wormed its way down his chin and neck where it was absorbed by his shirt collar. He shoved the glass in Sam's direction. "Again," he sputtered, his face showing the burning sensation ripping through his throat. He wiped his mouth with the back of his right hand. "And this one will also be on you," he slurred. "I know the owner."

"Yes sir," answered Sam, taking the glass. "Another it is."

"You know," John Brown continued, trying to be sophisticated. "Your wife was a bum lay. But, then, she was married to a bum. Once a bum always a bum," he continued, every other word a sputtered, unintelligible statement of fact. "Cats never change their spots or something like that. Know what I mean, huh? Know what I mean?"

Sam looked over his shoulder, nodded and smiled.  Then he repeated the process of filling John Brown's glass, a bigger glob of saliva preceding the cheap tequila.

John Brown turned, squinted and saw Arvia standing next to him.  "Guess you can't toss my invitation into the shit can now, can you, Miss Holier-than-thou-Frigidaire," he said, then sliding himself along the edge of the bar until he was next to her.

"No," Arvia said politely, "but I can ask you to leave, Mr. Brown."

John Brown didn't say a word, his face radiating, *try and make me.*

"Will you please leave, John." she said softly.  All eyes of the staff were focused on them.

"Who the fuck do you think you are telling me to leave," said John Brown, way too loud.  His try-and-make-me-leave look added a demeaning sneer as he held up his drink glass in mock toast to Arvia.  He gulped down the tequila, set the heavy glass down on the bar and said: "I ain't leavin' and you can go fu...."  His last word hung unfinished in mid-air as Arvia Bell, La Tinkerbelle's and his world turned totally black.  He never saw Sam's hand, the thick section of electrical cable a blur making contact with the side of his head.  He never heard Sam say: "That's no way to talk to a lady."  John Brown never felt the chill of theclub's floor.  He didn't have time.  Before the lawyer could crumble to the painted concrete, Sam indicated  to his bartenders and several of the waitresses that John Brown should be moved to another part of the disco to savor his sweet dreams.  There was a nod and three bartenders and an equal number of waitresses gently lifted the lawyer off the floor.

John Brown had no memory of his being carried and roller skated to the front seat of his BMW while the waitstaff sang, "A Closer Walk with Thee."  Juan and his valet parkers took over from the waitstaff, stuffing the lawyer into the front seat of his car, relieving him of all of his cash. Juan said to his parking crew, "Keep twenty for the parking fee, take a tip for each of you and give the rest to Senor Bo."

John Brown never felt his head come to rest on the plush leather of the passenger side seat. He never felt the polished wooden gear shift knob sticking up from the center of the BMW's console trying to penetrate his rib cage. His legs were curled up by two of the valet parkers, one doing the curling and the other slamming shut the door of the car. John Brown missed the sound of the clanging of chains and the whine of a winch as the Lincoln Park tow truck driver readied the BMW for a ride to its notorious private auto pond. The waitstaff members had used their Chicago Police Department influence on the towing company.

John Brown did remember waking up, a heavy rain beating on his car. He struggled to sit up and would have felt every bone in his body cry out if the noise coming from his head hadn't snuffed out his agony. "I'm an attorney," he said to his empty car. "And all of your asses are going to jail," he vowed. His vow continued: "And your ass, Mayor Bell, is going right along with them." He paused, his smirk returning and said: "As soon as I get a piece of it first."

* * * * *

As the attorney was being unceremoniously carried out of La Tinkerbelle's, Bo heard another blast of static from Juan indicating that another car had pulled into the lot. Bo became his sea going best as he saw his next customer walk in without giving Captain Hookette and her male member-shaped hook hand a notice. "There's a ten dollar cover charge," said Bo, a smile on his face.

"And twenty dollars for parking," yelled a frustrated Juan chasing after the customer.

"My driver dropped me off and left," said the man. "Forget

the twenty." The customer walked by Bo with a wave of his hand. "Put it on my tab," he said, a blank look on his ruddy face, an out-of-control salt and pepper mustache reaching out in all directions like a growth of wild tropical vines. His eye brows matched the mustache and his cheap ill-fitting hair piece wilder than all of it put together.

Bo watched his customer go to the far end of the bar, plop down on the last bar stool, point at Sam and say, "You, my good man, appear to resemble a master mixologist." He nodded over his shoulder at where Bo and Officer Noel Jones were standing. "Not like Popeye and Sweet Pea." He gave a flick of his wrist and ordered, "Chartreuse up," without looking at Sam. "And run a tab." The customer took a small spiral notebook from his suit coat pocket along with a gold fountain pen.

Bo gave a shrug and left Noel at the maitre d' stand to join Arvia and Ben. They were still seated at the opposite end of the bar after John Brown's unusual departure. Sam joined them after placing the new customer's drink in front of him with a polite, "Enjoy." All eyes had switched to the new customer.

"Do any of you know that guy sitting down there?" Bo asked.

Arvia and Ben didn't. Sam gave a shrug. "His face looks kind of familiar, can't place him."

Ben still didn't know what to do about Matilda. He wanted desperately to see her, to find out why and how she got to La Tinkerbelle's. He glanced at his mother and then Sam and decided that doing nothing was still in his best interest.

* * * * *

The conventioneers sat in silence, heads back, watching the cages with the go-go girls being hauled up and out of sight to the ceiling. Pumpkin Head started snoring first followed by Ichabod Crane and Black Curls. In a minute, the other three joined them. None of them saw Tinker Bell, Peter and Pan land safely on their metal launching platform, Matilda the first to land.  She bolted down the metal, spiral stairs and headed for her dressing room.  Her costume was off along with her mask and winged boots before Peter and Pan entered the tiny, shared cubicle behind the boutique and Ramon's salon.  The six Go-Go dancers followed them, each sharing their thoughts about dancing in a cage.

"Boring," said one dancer, the others behind her not hearing her one word, but Matilda, Peter and Pan did.

"I'm cross-eyed from having to look through those stupid bars all night," said another.  "I think I'll file for Worker's Compensation."

The false eye lashes of another dancer were peeled off and placed on her separate wooden pallet that she shared with the other three as a dressing table.  "Now I know how my grandmother's parakeet felt being caged up in her kitchen all those years," she said.

You're getting a paycheck, girls," said Peter, slipping out of her thigh high boots and massaging an aloe lotion between her legs. "Count your blessings."

Pan reached for the same bottle of lotion and took it from her partner. "Peter's right, girls," she added.  "We can make more money in one month here than we can teaching kindergartners for a year.  Now that ain't bad."  She took a handful of lotion from her partner and rubbed it between her thighs.

Noel Jones left his maitre d' stand and gently woke up the conventioneers. "Show's over, gentlemen," he said politely. He smiled at each of them and said.  "Our performers wanted you to know how much they appreciated your applause and hope that you'll come back again."

"They did?" asked Pumpkin Head, fumbling with his conventioneer's badge. "Was it the one with nice tits?"

"All of them," said Noel.

Bo, who overheard the conversation, walked over to where

Noel was standing, "We at La Tinkerbelle's are elated you gentlemen enjoyed the show," he said.  "Please tell your friends."  Then, ever the entrepreneur, he added.  "I understand that the girls left personal messages for you."

"They did?" asked Pumpkin Head.

"Really?" added Black Curls.

"They did and really," said Bo, nodding in the direction of the men's room.  "They told me they left each of you a personal message in there.  They said to look in each of the stalls."

"Gee," said Pumpkin Head.

"How 'bout that," said Black Curls.

Ichabod Crane didn't say a word and was in the Men's Room before the others could stand up.

* * * * *

A taxi cab waited outside the front door of La Tinkerbelle's for the conventioneers who had spent a little over an hour in the Men's Room.  The same driver they had earlier stood alongside the open back door of his cab, smiling as if an earlier confrontation had never taken place.  Juan arranged for the cab earlier after Pumpkin Head had tumbled off the table doing the Twist.

The cab driver smiled even more when he saw his six fares stagger out the door.  They were followed by Noel and Naomi Schmitt.  The cab driver smiled because Juan had given him a generous gratuity in advance.  "Consider it as a peace offering from the conventioneers," he had said.  Juan also handed him triple the fare that would take the six back downtown to the Palmer House.

As the conventioneers stumbled into the parking lot appearing as if they had lost their sense of balance, Juan convinced Ichabod Crane that his group would have to pay a small valet parking fee for retrieving the cab.  Ichabod emptied his pockets of forty dollars in quarters saying: "What the hell do I need all this change for?  The girl of my dreams who left me that video message in the men's room stall told me she wanted me.  As soon as I get home, I'm going to tell my wife, then come back here, sweep her off her feet and marry her."  He paused then said, "I think we'll honeymoon in Venezuela."

"I like St. Croix," added Pumpkin Head.  "I saw every message in my stall from start to finish."  He belched and followed his companions who had started singing, "Matilda, Matilda," as they squeezed into the cab.

Noel and Naomi Schmitt waved as the cab pulled out of the parking lot, Naomi adding exuberance to her wave with her false hook while the faint strains of:  "She take all me money and run Venezuela," faded away.

* * * * *

With the conventioneers and John Brown gone, the inside of La Tinkerbelle's now resembled a bar for only the lonely.  Sam and his bartenders washed glasses, checked their inventory and kept an eye on the lone patron at the end of the bar who sat with his head down and, for all they knew, was sleeping. Cap'n's Kids sat on the edge of the bandstand exhausted. Rommie sipped a cup of Sanka; Reggie waited for his Orange pekoe tea to cool before drinking it and Regis nursed a high ball glass of water without ice, two lemon wedges floating on top.

Peter and Pan joined the trio on the bandstand, sitting on the edge.  They were wearing black silk robes, their names embroidered across the back in sequins.  Peter's legs were spread apart and she continued to apply a liberal coating of her aloe skin cream to the area between her thighs where her harness had chaffed her raw.  She passed the bottle to Pan who did the same.

Matilda sat alone hiding in the shadows of a darkened corner in the dressing room cubicle located several strides from the club's fire exit door trying to comprehend what had just happened in her life.  She had changed out of her costume into jeans and a Glen Forest on the Watercourse High School sweatshirt with the saying, *Seniors Rule* across the chest and waited for Naomi who had promised her a ride back to Glen Forest on the Watercourse in her Peugeot. Matilda gave a series of nervous guilt-filled glances at the worn Army surplus blanket that substituted for a door to cover the entrance. "Daddy, please forgive me," she whispered in the direction of the blanket. She dreaded that her father had seen her act and that she had embarrassed him. Worse yet, she feared he would vanish from her life again. Another fear struck her. By the time she got home, her curfew would have been violated and her mother would have been sitting up waiting for an explanation, a warning speech preceding any excuse Matilda could concoct.

* * * * *

Frank and Charles scurried to the bar like two Olympic heel and toe walkers to join the others. "It was your fault we didn't sell more than we did," Frank said to Charles as they sat down next to Arvia and Ben. "Six baseball caps, half dozen tee shirts, one medium, four XL and one jumbo to that Charlie Brown great pumpkin and two three packs of designer condoms. We could have done so much better if you hadn't..."

"Me," said Charles, limp wrists flapping in spasms. "I almost had one of our Erte's sold to that man who resembled the divine bean pole of a cute scarecrow. Then you had to step in, Mister Butinski."

"You had your hand half way down the back of his trousers, you homo," said Frank, unable to hide his indignant feelings. "We were hired to run a class, sophisticated boutique and you, according to our British neighbors across the pond, were turning our beautiful emporium into a Knocking Shop."

"Poo," said Charles. "Get your mind out of the gutter you poor excuse for an Anglophile." His limp wrists hung like two soggy lasagna noodles. "I was simply giving the dear boy some support when he was leaning back to view our Erte. In case you didn't notice, he did have a teeny-weeny too much to drink."

"I noticed, you horny toad," said Frank, his indignant feelings growing. "I was ready to call 9-1-1 to get that poor fellow medical attention after you sunk your canines into his, oh, pardon the expression, ass. I should have had our entire waitstaff arrest you for solicitation. My word, I thought you were going to draw blood."

"And who's to say I didn't?" he asked with a smile.

The argument got suspended by laughter and Spanish coming from Juan and his valet parking staff as they staggered out of the Men's Room, the smell of marijuana following them. Two of the undercover waitstaff giggled as they trailed behind them; one saying to the other, "Let's go check out the kitchen and see what's to eat. I've got a severe case of the hungries."

The lone customer was still seated at the end of the bar. He was on his third Chartreuse, hunger and sleep the farthest thing from his mind as he stared at Arvia and Bo, his eyes concealed by the growth hanging down from his brows. His curious, creative mind propelled his gold pen across and down the pages of his pocket notebook. Several more strokes found him placing the cap on the gold pen, the pen and notebook finding their way into the inside pocket of his rumbled suit coat. He couldn't take his eyes off of Arvia and Bo. The more he watched them, the more he knew he had stumbled onto the biggest story of his career. This would be the Mother Lode, the Lost Dutchman, the ultimate diamond that would cause collective drooling around the De Beers' boardroom table. The Five W's of his lead paragraph rattled inside his oversized head like numbered balls in a tiny rotating cage ready to spill out and spell, BINGO. His desire to write grew. Finally, his right hand reached across the bar to the edge where a stack of napkins stood neatly aligned. Sweat drenched his forehead. Instinctively, he reached into his coat pocket and his hand emerged holding a cheap ball pointpen, teeth marks, his, covering the entire pen. "Ah, he muttered. "Come to papa my little good luck charm." He winked at the ballpoint pen and kissed the blue tip. Two tiny blue smudges appeared on his thick lips. He spread out the bar napkins in front of him and started writing again like a man possessed; all but one of his W's aligning with the stars. As each napkin got filled with writing, he muttered, "Another one bites the dust," and stuffed it in whatever pocket his hand came in contact with first. He began to shake the ballpoint pen in a frenzied up and down motion to keep it writing. With each pen shake there was another, "Come to papa." In a blur, another napkin joined the others, his coat pockets soon sprouted white. The hand with the pen wiped at his sweaty head leaving a streak of blue ink across his forehead. "Sassafras!"

✳ ✳ ✳ ✳ ✳

"I'm sorry, Berthold," said Arvia softly, putting her hand on her brother's shoulder. "Six customers wasn't much of an opening night.

"Eight," said Bo, unable to hide how dejected he felt. "That is, if you count that guy down at the end of the bar and that obnoxious John Brown." He tried to smile. "According to Juan, the attorney was relieved of the twenty dollars he owed for the valet parking. He also gave his crew a tip." He paused. "Juan turned the rest of money to me and I factored in a gratuity for the waitstaff, Go-Go girls, Tinker Bell and Peter and Pan." He smiled. "And you, Sam. Your gratuity was most generous." He continued to smile. "I didn't realize lawyers carried around so much cash on them."

"It was probably the money my wife had to give him for the screwin' she gave me," said Sam, trying not to smile at Arvia. "Then she got screwed in the end."

* * * * *

A ballpoint pen continued to shake at the end of the bar, the pile of napkins almost gone, but the lone customer's eyes stayed fixed on Arvia and Bo.

"I'm sorry, Berthold," said Arvia quietly

"Sorry," repeated Bo, as he placed his hand on his sister's. "Why should you be sorry?"

Another napkin felt the heat of the ballpoint pen.

"Because you were so optimistic about tonight," she said, her hand stroking his shoulder.

A ballpoint pen sailed toward the bandstand hitting the floor with a bounce and landing in Rommie's Sanka. "You picked a fine time to leave me, Lucille," muttered the lone person at the end of the bar as he fumbled in his pocket for another pen.

"I appreciate your concern, Sis," said Bo, turning and giving her a loving, playful chuck under the chin.

A gold cap flew off the lone customer's fountain pen and landed behind the bar.

"Don't worry, Berthold," she said, running her finger across his mustache. "I'm sure things will get better." She gave her brother's trembling hand a gentle caress as if she were stroking Heckle and Jeckle.

The last of the napkins got jammed in the man's back pocket and his spiral notebook reappeared from inside his jacket. He flipped through the pages as if on a mission.

"I'm not worried," said Bo. "Tomorrow's Saturday. Date night. Eat out night."

The customer at the end of the bar leaned so far toward Arvia and Bo that he almost fell off his stool. "Louder," he muttered under his breath. "Where are you two going on Saturday?" he asked. No one heard him. He squinted harder and asked, "What's all this night out stuff?"

"I'm sure it will be standing room only tomorrow night," Arvia said, her smile trying to put reassurance into her words. "You'll have so many people in here they'll be pressed together like sardines in a can."

"You'll be pressing him like you had him in a can of sardines," the man at the end of the bar repeated, his gold pen bouncing from spiral notebook pages to filling up more napkins with royal blue ink words. "I knew you had a reputation for being wild and crazy, but pressing your can into slippery, oily fish elevate you, Miss Miz, into the world of kinky." He slowly slid one bar stool closer toward Bo and Arvia. "Speak up, Miz. Don't be shy. When and where are you going to press him?"

"You're right like always, Sis," Bo said to her, his feeling of despair leaving him. "If we had eight customers tonight, we'll have eighty tomorrow, even eight hundred Sunday." Optimistically, he blurted out, "And Monday morning we'll take a break and count our money. Monday will be our day; our special fun day."

"Monday a fun day," repeated the customer at the end of the bar. "How perfect," he said. "A story and a headline both at the same time," he said, then signaling Sam. "Another," he said holding up his glass. "And could you get the top of my pen? It's on the floor back there."

Sam gave a nod.

* * * * *

Tomorrow came and went, the night twice as good as Friday as far as numbers. Seven ladies with a limited budget on a bachelorette party reluctantly paid the cover charge and nursed their two drinks. They each bought a t-shirt in the boutique. Two bought baseball caps. Charles ignored the women, but Frank convinced two of the ladies to buy designer condoms to spice up their love lives and a third bought two packages of AAA batteries to go along with the custom Pleasure Provider she had removed from the top of the neatly stacked pink boxes of Providers.  When Charles got the chance after the lady customers left, he stood toe-to-toe with Frank and said, "You transsexual bitch."  Then he turned and left in a snit going out to the parking lot in search of one of Juan's parking attendants, Jesus to smoke a joint.

Four students from Columbia College were also a part of the Saturday night crowd.  They were doing research for an assignment in entertainment history and were excited about having the chance to experience a part of an earlier generation's life style; their parent's generation.  They didn't even need a second beer to start pointing, poking fun and ridiculing the Go-Go dancers in their cages, one student corking his beer bottle with his thumb, shaking the bottle violently and then releasing his thumb.  Sam ended their history lesson along with three waitstaff employees, badges exposed, clamping handcuffs on to four individual wrists.  They were escorted from La Tinkerbelle's threatening to sue and one shouting out.  "Now I know where all the Go-Go's went!"  There was a harsh laugh. Then another shouted, "Gone with all those stupid flowers you old farts used to sing about!"  The final outcry came from the smallest of the four, a pudgy junior girl majoring in directing. She screamed from the safety of their VW bus:  "Go-Go's suck! This place sucks!  All old people suck!"  She and the others didn't notice they were minus their wallets, each wallet containing their phony ID, dorm admit pass, meal tickets and what little money they had.

"What's with this suck?" asked Charles, standing behind the waitstaff and Sam.  Before Sam could reply, and just as the grey-black exhaust fumes from the VW bus had dissipated into the night, the same patron from the night before walked in and said to Bo who was about to ask him for the cover charge, "Put it on my tab."  Bo looked at Sam who gave a single nod and walked back behind the bar.  Chartreuse was ordered and a gold fountain pen found the left hand of Isadore Izzy Inman, a small spiral note book appeared in his right.

Had Sam's memory been better the night before he would have recognized Izzy Inman as one of Chicago's leading gossip columnists writing *Izzy's It's* for the Daily Examiner.  Izzy qualified to take early Social Security, but his insatiable appetite for power brushed off retirement like the dust and airborne dirt from his cheap toupee that congregated on his shoulders.  He ruled Chicago; his *Izzy's It's* column more popular than Ann Landers or the late Irv Kupcinet's and the maker or breaker of the climbers and the clawers.  His stubby frame looked like he could have blocked for Quintin Bell and John Scats Brown.  His ill-fitting hair piece resembled a flattened raccoon with tire tracks running lengthwise over its body.  His eye brows and mustache looked like parts of the same road kill.  Appearances be damned.  Izzy could sense a headline grabbing story before the actors or the action made it happen.  This was his second trip to what he referred to as a garish getaway and hallucinogenic hideout for the famous and their foibles.  Patience was his forte and his patience was about to pay off.  His gold pen throbbed and his nose, when sensing a story, started to bleed.

* * * * *

Arvia fretted about her brother and the apparent failure of his business venture.  She knew it would fail; she just didn't have the heart to tell him.  All day she worried as she went through her late husband's collection of memorabilia, tossing almost everything into a garbage bag more suited for lawn clippings and the droppings from Schickle and Gruber.  She was alone in Dogwood, but not alone.  It may have been the start of a Saturday night, but Arvia Bell had a full calendar of events, not including exterminating the residue of Quintin Bell from her memory.  One item on her agenda was penciled in with a single, two letter word: Bo. That's when she decided to drive into the city to see him. She knew he spent the end of opening day glued to his maitre d' stand anticipating the crowds that never came. Sam had called her with his concerns.

"Miss Arvia, your brother looks like he's in shock," Sam had told her. "He's ignored my suggestions to get some sleep. He just stands there waiting for the customers to come in. It's sad, Miss Arvia. The doors are locked and the staff left hours ago. He doesn't seem to hear me. Just stares; doesn't even snap that old lighter of his."

Arvia had listened to Sam explain how he stayed with Bo, not having the heart to tell the beleaguered entrepreneur that ninety percent of all new businesses fail within the first year. In Bo's case, failure always seemed to come within the first day. Sam told her that he finally got Bo to follow him to the office in back. He had spread out a large sheet of heavy plastic on the floor and then covered it with several months worth of Sunday Chicago Tribune's, Daily Examiners and a collection of *The Reader*, the free weekly Chicago paper chock full of entertainment ads along with personal pleas, requests and, in some cases, direct orders for relationships between and among the genders. Bo, exhausted and fighting failure yet again, followed Sam's request: "Lie down and get some shut eye."

Bo, like an obedient child, curled up on the newspapers and was snoring in less than a minute. His hat sat perched on his head, the gold buttons of his captain's jacket still buttoned to the neck while visions of George Washington, Alexander Hamilton and Abraham Lincoln danced through his head. He was oblivious to *The Readers* ads lining his bed with requests from m/f, m/m and f/f pleas for a relationship. The ads beckoned to him, almost guaranteeing, never ending happiness from b/d/f, bi, cuddly, cute and disease free. He slept, dreaming and cuddled up with his presidential pictures.

* * * * *

While his mother was dealing with her psychological house cleaning and fumigating, Ben was trying to make sense out of what the weekend and its unexpected downpour of surprises and shocks had caused him.  He was the only one who had recognized Matilda as Tinker Bell.  "I knew you were going to do it, but I didn't know it would be so soon," he said to his computer on the desk in his room, a game of spider solitaire going nowhere.  "I should have known.  She was so quiet in the library.  I can't believe that she took the buses and the El to La Tinkerbelle's last night by herself, and that Naomi Schmitt gave her a ride home."

* * * * *

Ben wasn't alone in disbelieving what had happened at La Tinkerbelle's over the weekend.  Peter and Pan sat in the living room of their basement apartment on Lincoln Avenue in Old Town counting and recounting their money from the first weekend of work for Bo Pepperwall.

"He didn't lie," said the cute Italian  Davia Countie to her friend and roommate, Cubbie Cubbertson, her big, brown owl eyes aglow.

"He could have at least told us that those cheap, thigh-high pirate boots would rub our crotches raw," said Cubbie.  She looked like she had no eyes at all; her light blue ones no bigger than BB's fired from an air rifle.  They giggled like their kindergarten students as they both sat on matching, burgundy colored bean bag chairs sandwiched in between two end tables made of cement blocks stacked four high.

"He could've also told us that those creepy, old men were trying to pull us down from the ceiling," said Davia, her full lips sporting a moist smile.  "What do think the rabbi would have thought if he knew?"

Bo Pepperwall would have become our sole means of paying

the rent," answered Cubbie, still giggling. "Anyway, Pepperwall told us what we'd make and we made it."

The two kindergarten teachers from the El Al Shalom Temple Elementary School that Bo had hired as his Peter and Pan didn't know if they'd be back to work. "We've got more students than Pepperwall had customers," Davia said to Cubbie after they had seen the number of customers that had come into La Tinkerbelle's on their debut Friday and Saturday. They did know they had made more money in those two days than they did teaching for an entire semester. Cynthia Cubbie Cubbertson and Davia Roberta Countie were friends of Naomi Schmitt. They had just been hired again as teachers after being laid off from a well-paying suburban school district because they lacked seniority. The two friends jumped at the chance to moonlight. Behind in their rent and student loan payments and tired of eating Wheaties and water three times a day, they almost stampeded Bo Pepperwall to get to his job interview. They agreed to everything Bo wanted. So did Matilda. Well, almost; none of the three wanted leotards with no crotch.

The day Ben took Matilda to see the finished La Tinkerbelle's, they were met in the parking lot by Juan who knew of Bo's offer for her to become Tinker Bell. He also was aware of her fear, if she took the job, of being discovered by both her mother and father. With his assistance and that of his crew of valet parkers, she was shown, along with Cubbie and Davia how to enter the club through a rear fire escape door. Ben had known about the door having discovered it during some adventurous exploring in the early days of the foundry being transformed into a discotheque. The valet parkers showed the three girls how to open the door even though there were no outside handles. "Eeet's eeeze," said Jesus, one of the parkers. His left knee pressed against a spot near the edge of the door while the fingers of his right hand slid into a small seam of the rusted metal. "Just like uno, duos, tres." He gave a grunt and the door popped open. "You try now, Senorita."

* * * * *

One man's bust had been another man's bonanza. Izzy Inman felt he had struck gold; he was sitting on the motherlode of all journalistic stories. He had no idea that Bo Pepperwall's dream was about to vanish and didn't know who Bo Pepperwall was and didn't care. He had waited patiently, his right thumb and forefinger toying with his glass of Chartreuse, his spiral notebook open, the gold fountain pen lying on a diagonal across it. He didn't care if it was the witching hour on a Saturday night and he was sitting at an empty bar. He relished it. There would be no glad-hander types and the curious interrupting him. "Patience," he said quietly. "Patience is a virtue. Practice it if you can. It is always found in women; seldom in a man." He paused, smiled and muttered. "But, it's always found in the Izzy Man."

* * * * *

Arvia's concern for her brother shoved aside her disdain for her late husband. She had grown weary of purging her late husband's belongings into the trash, and she decided to drive into the city to see Bo.

The moment Arvia entered La Tinkerbelle's, Izzy sprang into action, his body sliding so fast over the bar stools that he knocked several of them over as if he were a giant bowling ball. Ten stools later he was within easy hearing distance of where his mystery lady was seated. She would be a mystery no more when his Monday column hit the streets. Neither would the identity if the man sitting next to his mystery lady. This time he would hear every word. On Monday morning, all of Chicagoland would be privy to what he felt was the greatest secret since Liz and Richard first set the bed sheets blazing several decades back. Izzy Inman didn't pride himself as being king of the gossip columnists by divulging tabloid trash. Izzy's word was gospel.  Izzy wrote the truth, the whole truth and nothing but the truth and his readers worshiped every word.

He saw the man in the crumpled, white, sea captain's suit sit down next to the woman at the end of the bar.  She had been talking to the bartender who he thought he recognized.  Only one woman in the world looked like his target, the woman wearing her hair in a style created by the famous European hair designer, now a Chicago transplant, Ramon.  "That's her," he muttered to himself.  He sipped half of his Chartreuse.  "And that's him," he said, the rest of the Chartreuse disappearing.  "Nice try with the sailor suit, Barnacle Bill," he continued to mutter.  "But I know a television preacher cheating on his wife when I see one, you hypocritical weasel."  He fumbled with the cap of his gold fountain pen, forgot it wasn't a ballpoint and gave it a shake.  He shook his head as he watched the ink stain create a unique blot on his white shirt.  Ink stains didn't concern him, not with eavesdropping on who he had dubbed, among other things, The Clepto Cutie and the TV Tear Jerker.  "What in the hell are they up to?"

* * * * *

Monday morning found a forlorn Berthold Bo Pepperwall sitting in his tiny cubicle of an office near the fire exit door counting and recounting the receipts from his first three days in business.  He counted the number of customers over and over again; seven on Friday, double on Saturday and four on Sunday.  The four customers on Sunday evening were hockey fans from Calgary who got lost trying to get back to the O'Hare Hilton after attending a Blackhawk's game at the United Center.  "Is this Hawkeye's?" one of them had asked Juan when they drove up in their rental car.

Juan had lifted his eyepatch, winked and said: "Aye, Mate. How did yee know it was a hawk took me bloody eye?"  His eyepatch flapped back before the four men noticed.

The Calgary hockey fans didn't have the cover charge and Bo, not one to let potential customers walk away, gave them complimentary admission.  They bought two rounds of drinks, yelled obscenities at the Go-Go dancers in their cages, sang several raucous choruses of, *Oh Canada* and left before Obadiah could let out one hog call and Tinker Bell, Peter and Pan could make a single arc.  La Tinkerbelle's turned into a tomb, even Izzy Inman wasn't there.  He was, however, at his Gold Coast apartment beating out his story on his computer keyboard.

* * * * *

It was Monday morning and all Bo knew was that his spine felt like it ran in more directions than an Elkhart Lake, Wisconsin road race.  "Bills, bills, and more bills," said Bo to the walls of his tiny office.  What happened? Where did it all go wrong?  It was the ideal Sunday.  So what if no one showed up for out lavish brunch buffet.  The Bears and the Blackhawks were in town.  Heck, and they both won."

CLICK/SNAP!

"La Tinkerbelle's should've been hosting the world's biggest Sunday night sport's party in this city's history."

CLICK/SNAP!

"What happened?"  He placed his cigarette lighter on the pile of papers that sat atop his makeshift desk of stacked wooden pallets.  "I get several Calgary hockey fans that have more lint in their pockets than I do.  Geez, I even gave them complimentary admissions.  Never again," he vowed as he stared at his cigarette lighter and fought back his tears.  His mind felt empty as if his creative brain had gone on hiatus.  "Why?" he sniffled, his hands turning into fists.  "What went wrong?" he asked, his sniffles punctuated by a frustrated repressed sob.  "I was doing all the right things; had all the right people working for me.  My sister was going to be famous, she was going to be rich.  I was going to be rich."  His sniffles shifted gears and became sobs. He was choking and gagging on his tears. "What happened, Malcolm?" he asked the vision of his hero. I didn't cheat. I didn't lie. I really didn't." Gagging and choking increased. His fists uncurled; his hands and arms hung limp. He ignored the vision of Quintin Bell's killer laughing at him, calling him Bo the Schmoe and saying, "Go, go, going, going gone." Bo sucked in air sounding like a giant vacuum cleaner. He folded his hands in prayer, an action he hadn't taken since he made his First Communion. Just then he heard Sam's voice.

"Ah, excuse me Boss," said Sam, his head the only part of him visible from the door. "Did you see today's paper?"

"I think I slept on it."

"Today's paper," Sam repeated. "I think you slept on the Sunday funny pages from a week ago."

"Sunday, Monday, so what," said Bo, barely looking at his friend. "I'm sorry, Sam, but what about today?"

Sam walked slowly into the cramped office and put Monday's edition of the Daily Examiner on Bo's desk then placed his index finger directly on the head and shoulders picture of Izzy Inman.

"What should I be looking at?"

"I think you should read it, Boss," said Sam, his index finger smudging Izzy Inman's face. "And then when you finish, I think you'd better come and take a look at what's going on outside your office."

Bo began to read where Sam's finger pointed. "The Clepto Cutie and the TV Tear Jerker?" he asked, looking at Sam, not understanding. "Marketing Maven of Smut, the Skirt Chasing Cleric, the Mullah Miz, and the Randy Reverend all here in La Tinkerbelle's?" He stared at Sam not believing. "Where was I?" He continued to read bits and pieces of the article out loud. *Amorous encounter in front of the bandstand; Sources tell us there's a knot to be tied. Could be this early p.m. or sooner provided the Randy*

*Rev. can keep his Talon from zipping down; if you know what I mean? Get it?*

Bo looked bewildered. "What's this guy talking about, Sam? Zipping Talons?" Bo continued reading the article out loud. *At our 'Toddlin' Town's trendy new cabaret, La Tinkerbelle's, the reincarnation of the discotheque, the new fun place to schmooze, snicker and get smashed. Could be one of the great lunch hours Chicago has ever seen. I'll wager hotter than the great fire. Then, again, what do I know? I'm only Izzy Inman and It's my word.*

All that stuff doesn't make sense to me either, Boss," said Sam. But I do remember the guy who sat at the end of the bar on Friday and Saturday nights." His finger pointed at the smudged picture in the upper left corner of the column. "He looked familiar, but I couldn't place him until now."

"That was him?" asked Bo, glancing back and forth between the newspaper and Sam. "A celebrity was here?"

Sam nodded.

"I don't remember collecting the cover charge from him," said Bo, a concern in his voice that only showed when dollars were discussed.

"You put it on his tab."

CLICK/SNAP.

"Now I really think you'd better get out of this office and see what's going on," said Sam, as he turned and started back toward the bar. "I ain't ever seen anything like it."

"Ah, okay," said Bo getting up from the rickety metal folding chair, several new layers of Duct Tape covering the old layers of electrician's tape. He followed Sam and froze in place when he got to the entrance of the bar area. He couldn't believe what he saw.

CLICK/SNAP! CLICK/SNAP! CLICK/SNAP!

The only lines of people Bo ever remembered seeing were those lined up for free bread and soup in an old movie about the Great Depression that he saw when he was in high school.

His only other experience with standing in line was waiting for a free taste sample of a new food product in a super market. He blinked; and the knuckles of both hands dug into his eyes. When his focus returned, his jaw appeared as if the muscles had atrophied. He saw every bar stool filled. People were standing three deep behind the seated patrons. Every chair around every table circling the perimeter of the dance floor had a body and at least three or four more behind each person seated. He saw that Sam had his bartenders and some of the waitstaff set up more tables on the dance floor. He blinked as several of the waitstaff roller skated back and forth with additional chairs; bumping into patrons as they tried to squeeze through the crowd. Numb, he muscled his way into the mass of humanity randomly stopping and asking: "Did you pay your cover charge?" The people he asked looked at him like he walked off a spaceship.

"My God" Bo yelled to Sam. "It's not even lunch time yet." CLICK/SNAP.

Sam didn't hear him, couldn't hear him with all of the noise coming from the crowd. He was his professional, neighborhood saloon-keeper-self, returning behind the bar to pour drinks without a spill or a splash. His hands and arms were a blur as he shouted out instructions to his additional bartenders-- Rommie, Reggie, Regis, Obadiah and Emerine--who he had pressed into service to mix drinks. He had temporarily suspended his rule about no women behind the bar. The horde of screaming customers, their money clutched in waving fists, called for adjustments and Sam realized this was not a time for rigid behavior. He nodded his head at Bo indicating that he should join him behind the bar. Bo got on his hands and knees. He crawled between three patrons before squeezing in between more legs that turned out to be those of a female patron wearing a skirt. He felt cold liquid spill on his neck and back but kept crawling.

"Sam, we've got to call the rest of the staff back," he said, as he grabbed a bar towel and wiped off the back of his neck.

"They're all here, Boss," said Sam with a smile.  A couple of them have their collars handcuffed and sitting in their unmarked cars.  Juan and his boys are keeping an eye on them when they're not parking cars two blocks from here out on the street.  The poor guys are running ragged."

"Oh God!" said Bo feeling flustered.  "Did they get the twenty dollar parking fees?"  He blinked, caught his breath and stammered:  "We need Peter and Pan."

"They're on their way," said Sam, his cool efficiency staying cool as he talked to Bo without missing a drink order.  "They've got substitutes covering their kindergarten classes.  Don't worry."

"Are Charles and Frank here?" he asked, as he stood on his tiptoes trying to get a view of the boutique that had been blocked by a swarm of customers.

"Here they come now," said Sam, as he noticed the tops of two heads bobbing up and down through the crowd as if they were a pair of jumping jacks; patrons jumping and turning as the two passed by.

Bo yelled to Sam, "Did you call Tinker Bell?"

"Who," Sam asked?

"I'll call her," said Bo, fearing that Sam may have changed his mind about allowing his daughter to be a star.  "And oh, yeah, Arvia," he sputtered.  "I've got to call her."  He blinked and gouged at his eyes again.  "Oh God!" he said again when he noticed that a line of people four abreast had stretched from the front entrance across the street to the entrance of the housing project.  "Ten dollars each," he said, calculating.  "Twenty a car," he said aloud, but no one heard him.  "Why didn't Juan use his walkie-talkie?"

CLICK/SNAP.

"Arvia will never believe this," he said to Sam who didn't hear him.  "Peter Pan won't ever believe this," he continued unable to move; unable to feel; his blood pressure pounding. "Go, go, going, going gone," he stated remembering the grinning vision. "You'll be going, going gone," he said to the killer of his brother-in-law. I'll make sure of it." He paused. "Ayway, I promised my buddy, Malcolm Forbes I would. And, I will." He paused, his eyes scanning the crowd; each person in the mob wearing a dollar sign across their chest. "Whenever I get the chance. Whenever I get all of this money counted."

CLICK/SNAP!

## Title:  The Jacket

- Author: Richard Baran
- Publisher: TotalRecall Publications, Inc.
- HARD COVER ISBN:  9781590955659
- PAPERBACK, ISBN:  9781590955666
- EBOOK, Nook, Kindle, ISBN:  9781590955673
- Number of pages: 352
- Publication Date:  2013

Tidge Mackiewicz, new patriarch of his family, received several orders from his dying father, Kid Scream.  One order stated that Tidge should quit believing in Santa Claus and stop acting like every day was Christmas.  Tidge should also abandon his belief that the Luftwaffe shot down Santa Claus on Christmas Eve in 1944 and Santa survived.

### Title:  The Dutchman's Gift

- Author: Richard Baran
- Publisher: TotalRecall Publications, Inc.
- PAPERBACK, ISBN:  9781590952979
- EBOOK, Nook, Kindle, ISBN:  9781590952986
- Number of pages: 128
- Publication Date:  2015

Riley "Rocky" Stone, a twelve year old boy on a family vacation in Arizona, finds what he believes is an Apache arrowhead while hiking with his grandfather and family in Arizona's Superstition Mountains.  When Riley returns to his home in Chicago after the vacation, he closely examines his arrowhead.  He discovers that one side has etchings of three circles—two small and one large.  His grandfather had explained to him that the Native Americans communicated with crude drawings using circles and stick figures; the circles representing stages of life; a figure drawn upside down meant death.  When Riley rotates his arrowhead where the two smaller circles sit atop the larger circle, he sees death replaced by the image of Mickey Mouse.

**Title:  Where Have All the Go-Go's Gone**
**Book One**

- Author: Richard Baran
- Publisher: TotalRecall Publications, Inc.
- Hard Cover ISBN:
- Paperback, ISBN:  9781590952979
- Ebook, Nook, Kindle, ISBN:  9781590952986
- Number of pages: 283
- Publication Date:  2015

Bo Pepperwall's intelligence dwarfed Mensa's parameters.  He was perceived as strange thereby resulting in his being ridiculed by many, shunned by most and being called Bo the Schmoe by all.  Then he faced a dilemma.  He had to choose between money (which he never had) and morals ( which he also lacked).  Should he weasel a part of his recently widowed sister's inheritance for a business venture or should he turn in the killer of her husband, his despicable brother-in-law?  He chooses both.  Bo opens La Tinkerbelle's a Go-Go, a 1960's retro discotheque in an abandoned factory building in a Chicago slum using a theme from the legend of Peter Pan. Surrounding himself with bizarre employees (each having a unique vision of reality) who put fun into dysfunctional, his dream nearly goes bust.  Then a Chicago gossip columnist prints a story that has customers lined up and Bo collides with  his dilemma.  The collision buries him in money and public adulation.  Success, however, can't cover his moral guilt in the surprise ending to Book One of this screwball murder mystery farce that is more farce than mystery.

**Title:  When Will They Ever Learn?**
**Book Two**

- Author: Richard Baran
- Publisher: TotalRecall Publications, Inc.
- Hard Cover ISBN:  9781590955659
- Paperback, ISBN:  9781590952979
- Ebook, Nook, Kindle, ISBN:  9781590952986
- Number of pages: 350
- Publication Date:  2015

Bo Pepperwall is a card carrying member of Mensa, dreamer, conniver and ridiculed lifelong loser.  He has witnessed the murder of his despicable brother-in-law, the mayor of Glen Forest on the Watercourse, a prestigious Chicago North Shore community.  While wrestling with this moral guilt, he opens *La Tinkerbelle's a Go-Go*, a 1960's retro discotheque located in a Chicago slum and uses a theme from the legend of Peter Pan that includes a scantily clad Tinker Bell. Bo, however, remains a loser and his garish disco faces bankruptcy until an article by a Chicago gossip columnist turns it into a bonanza. That same day, Tinker Bell's outraged mother accidentally sets fire to La Tinkerbelle's and destroys the booming business.  Bo and his employees—along with two black cats named Heckle and Jeckle—end up in court charged with violations of the Mann Act; contributing to the delinquency of minors; ignoring EPA laws; multiple business violations; cruelty to animals and presenting lewd and indecent performances.  Bo turns in the killer and the court finds him innocent of the criminal charges in the ending to Book Two of this zany murder mystery comedy.